SELECT PRAISE FOR KELLY RIMMER

Before I Let You Go

"Ripped from the headlines and from the heart, *Before I Let You Go* is an unforgettable novel that will amaze and startle you with its impact and insight."

—Patti Callahan Henry, *New York Times* bestselling author of *The Secret Book of Flora Lea*

"Kelly Rimmer's shimmering and poignant new novel broadens our current national conversation about seeking to combat the deadly yet curable disease of addiction while being ultimately a story of relationships."

—*Library Journal*, Editor's Pick

Truths I Never Told You

"For fans who appreciate emotionally wrenching reads such as those by Sarah Jio or Kristin Hannah."

—*Library Journal*

"Illuminating . . . engrossing [and] harrowing . . . Rimmer's suspenseful narrative will enthrall and move readers."

—*Publishers Weekly*, starred review

"Everything Kelly Rimmer writes turns to gold."

—*SheReads*

The Things We Cannot Say

"Fans of *The Nightingale* and *Lilac Girls* will adore *The Things We Cannot Say*."

—Pam Jenoff, *New York Times* bestselling author

"An intense story of survival, hardship, and heartbreak, *The Things We Cannot Say* is sure to evoke emotion in even the most cynical reader."

—*New York Journal of Books*

"I thought that *Before I Let You Go* was one of the best novels I had ever read . . . [but] if you only have time to read one book this year *The Things We Cannot Say* should be that book."

—*Fresh Fiction*

The German Wife

"Skillfully researched and powerfully written . . . Kelly Rimmer always delivers a poignant story—this book is no exception."

—Madeline Martin, *New York Times* bestselling author

"Once again, Kelly Rimmer has turned my emotions upside down. With every book of hers I read, I become a more thoughtful and empathetic person, but *The German Wife* is, without a doubt, the jewel in her crown."

—Sally Hepworth, *New York Times* bestselling author

THE STORY KEEPER

ALSO BY KELLY RIMMER

The Paris Agent

The German Wife

The Warsaw Orphan

Truths I Never Told You

The Things We Cannot Say

Before I Let You Go

THE STORY KEEPER

A Novel

KELLY RIMMER

MIRA

MIRA™

ISBN-13: 978-1-525-80511-0
ISBN-13: 978-1-525-83166-9 (Hardcover Edition)

The Story Keeper

MIRA
22 Adelaide St. West, 41st Floor
Toronto, Ontario M5H 4E3, Canada
MIRABooks.com

HarperCollins Publishers
Macken House, 39/40 Mayor Street Upper,
Dublin 1, D01 C9W8, Ireland
www.HarperCollins.com

Printed in U.S.A

26 27 28 29 30 LBC 5 4 3 2 1

THE STORY KEEPER

CHAPTER 1

Fiona

NEW SOUTH WALES, AUSTRALIA
MAY 2010

My uncle Tad always said that books have a certain pattern to them—a rhythm in common regardless of genre. Every story has a beginning, a middle and an end, and around those things, you have certain changes in the momentum that readers recognize: rising and falling action, climaxes, black moments. Sometimes you sense an inflection point coming—a certain buildup that you recognize subconsciously, even if you might not be able to explain why. Tad said that life is like that too, and I've never felt the wisdom of that statement more than this year.

It's the palms I spot first as I near Wurimbirra, and the sight of those waving fronds in the distance has my shoulders relaxing, releasing tension I've been carrying for far too long. I thought I'd be excited to arrive back here today, but as I steer my car through the concrete gate posts and onto the circular drive, the feeling that washes over me is a lot more like relief. I haven't lived here for more than thirty years, but for some reason, this is still the place that springs to my mind whenever I hear the word *home*.

I park right outside the front doors and stare up at the facade of the mansion. Built in 1886, Wurimbirra was designed in a Victorian Filigree style—eight enormous bedrooms upstairs and five living spaces downstairs including a grand ballroom. The brick walls are stuccoed, lined to imitate stonework, painted in a once-bright beige that has faded to a weary grey, stained in places by red-brown dust. Verandas surround both stories, the top bounded by friezes and columns and brackets and balustrades. Like much of the interior of the house, that cast iron detail was once a crimson red, but it's now blistered and patchy. The remaining paint has become rusty and browned—close to the color of dried blood.

The windows are filthy. There are thick nets of spiderwebs in the gaps between surfaces all around the front facade. Knowing this house as I do, that immediately tells me there's a bad foliage webbing spider infestation. Those little grey-brown spiders aren't any danger to humans, but Uncle Tad always told me they do attract redbacks—one of the world's most venomous spiders—and huntsmen, which don't do humans much harm but they are big and hairy and the mere thought of them makes me shiver in disgust. I make a mental note to call around right away to find an exterminator.

I'd call a gardener too, but I can tell immediately that the existing gardens are beyond saving, at least here at the front of the property. Each bed was once a curated mosaic of flowers and carefully shaped shrubs. What's left after ten years of drought and neglect in the wake of Tad's death is a collection of sticks poking up from a thick cluster of weeds.

The icy wind seems to slice right through my coat as I slip from my car, the heavy key ring my cousin Jon gave me last night in my hand. He was originally supposed to come with me today, partly because this is a big moment for me and he's not just my cousin; he's also my best friend. But there are also practical considerations ahead that involve him too. The house is still full of his dad's stuff, for a start, and Jon sold me the contents along with the property. We both understood all along that he'd walk through it one last time around settlement to help himself to anything he wished to take. That's why I was so surprised when he arrived unannounced to break the news he wasn't joining me today after all.

"I wanted to come with you for moral support and I'm sorry to dump the cleaning on you but to be honest, Fi, I wasn't going to be much help with what little time I have and I really don't want anything from the house," he told me. "Maybe see if your mum can help sort through Dad's papers, but as for everything else, just throw out anything you don't want to keep. My deadline moved up and I have a ton of work left to do—it can't be helped." Jon is a novelist just as Uncle Tad was, and, also like Tad, Jon always puts his work first. I do get it, even if, deep down, I'm disappointed that he's not here.

I tell myself there's something fitting about me being on my own today anyway. I'm standing on my own two feet, facing the future as a single woman for the first time in twenty-five years. This is a moment of true independence. It calls for courage and self-reliance, not sulking because my cousin has a life of his own to tend to.

I wonder what Uncle Tad would say if he could see me as I make my way up the concrete stairs, across the veranda to open those double front doors with his key for the first time. I suspect he'd be pleased to see the house lived in again, but mostly nervous, worried that I might change the place as I restore it.

"I'll protect it, Tad," I murmur aloud as I lift the weathered brass key towards the lock. "I'll look after your home, I promise. No one loves this place more than I do."

It's possible that my whole life has been leading to this moment. I dreamed of restoring Wurimbirra even before my degrees and my decades-long career in conservation architecture—in fact, it was this very building that inspired me to go into that field.

In the past I've designed restorations where structures were entirely gutted but for the facade, projects where complex extensions were added or layouts entirely re-imagined. This will not be one of those projects. I haven't figured out the detail but I already know the end goal: I want to strip back the veneer of neglect and time to highlight the original character of this remarkable home.

As I push the door open, the hinges protest with a long, low screech that sounds so ominous it almost startles me. If Mum was here, she'd think that deeply unnerving sound was an auditory bad omen. It's a very good thing that Mum *isn't* here, and not just because of the creepy-sounding door—but she's a problem for another day, and the door hinges can be fixed simply with a burst of lubricant spray. I'll pick some up in town later when I'm gathering whatever else I need to make this place livable in the short term.

I draw in a deep breath as I step inside, a huge smile on my face as I look around. There's an enormous, triple-width staircase directly facing the door, leading to a grandfather clock at the landing on the second floor that has, as far as I can tell, been in that same position since it was gifted to the original owners in 1887. The parlour is off to the left of the foyer, the formal dining room to the right, and a long, dark hallway runs horizontally, right behind the stairs. Above me is an enormous chandelier—potentially stunning under a century of dust, but also useless, given it hasn't worked since the '70s.

And that brings me to the central problem with this house—the lack of maintenance, not just since Tad died in 1999, but for decades before it. My uncle was a brilliant man and he was proud of the grandiose scale of Wurimbirra. Life had been very good to him and he had plenty of money. For some reason I never could understand, he seemed to have no interest in maintaining the house the way he should have, outside of the gardens, which were his pride and joy. He would spend hours out there every week, plucking by hand every sprout out of place, trimming the hedges the instant errant growth appeared, bringing in gardeners at the drop of a hat if his schedule or the scale of the one-acre block meant he couldn't keep on top of it alone.

It was utterly confounding that when it came to the house itself, if I so much as suggested he get the shingles on the roof replaced or install some air conditioning units, he always reacted as if I was threatening to bulldoze the place. I suppose I should be grateful that he did at least repaint the interior of the house in 1957, so there's no lead paint inside. The "new" paint is in terrible shape but at least it isn't a health hazard.

I drop the keys onto one of the two matching hall tables flanking the staircase and wince at the cloud of dust they dislodge into the air. Jon did warn me last night that I'd likely find the house in need of a good clean.

"It's been a long time since I went inside," he said. "I'm sorry."

"You have nothing to be sorry for," I said. "Your dad's death was such a shock, it only makes sense—"

"That's not what I'm sorry about," he said grimly. Jon's imagination is vastly more vivid than mine, and even as a kid, the eccentricities of his father's stately home were fuel for all sorts of nightmares. I've seen that haunted, tortured look in my cousin's eyes before. "Please, *please* take care out there. You're capable and brilliant and you know what you're doing. But you've got rose-colored glasses on when it comes to that house and . . ."

"It's not haunted, Jon," I said. If my tone was shorter than I intended it was probably because I was disappointed he wouldn't be joining me for the trip out to the house after all.

"The logical part of my brain knows you're right," he said, but then gave me a sad smile. "But Dad always said that where there's smoke, there's fire. And Fi, you have to admit there's a lot of smoke in the stories people tell about Wurimbirra."

"Tad *would* say that," I laughed. "He was the one operating the smoke machine!"

Uncle Tad was a storyteller by nature as well as profession and he loved to tell elaborate stories about the "ghosts" he supposedly shared Wurimbirra with. So many ghosts. Not a menacing one among the crowd of them, at least in the stories Tad told me. I was possibly the first child in history to grow up believing she lived in a haunted house and thrilled about the excitement of it. I used to hope and pray I'd see one of Tad's ghosts. Only as I grew older did I learn that there were other stories that circulate around this region—about the mansion's dark past, about spirits lingering on the land because of unfathomable injustice and unresolved pain. There's a terrible truth behind all of that—a few years before this house was built, something unthinkable did happen right on the other side of the low concrete wall that bounds the existing property. Even so, I don't believe in ghosts, and that's mostly because I lived right here for sixteen years and in all of that time, I never felt anything but safe and loved.

I walk into the parlour first. It's dark in here, the space illuminated only by scattered light through a series of alarming vertical tears along the bottoms of the velvet curtains. It takes me only a moment or two to wonder about those tears, because the air is so heavy with dust I can taste it with every breath, but there's another scent, a faded hint of musk and decay. Growing up in the country, this is a smell I know all too well. Rats and mice have thrived in this house over the years.

This realization has me walking quickly across to tug the curtains open, then unlocking all six sash windows. I push the lower panes up to let fresh air in, and as light floods in I sweep my gaze over the space, sighing happily as I pick out the very best details. I love the pressed-tin ceilings throughout this house, and here's the second of six chandeliers—smaller than the one in the foyer, functional the last time I used it, but no less dusty. The wall above the dark brown picture rail is a soft shade of cream, but below this is that same familiar crimson which echoes through most of the rest of the house. The only room with a marked difference in color theme is Uncle Tad's office, where the lower half of the walls is painted a stunning forest green.

The parlour is startlingly dramatic, made homey by familiar possessions. Hundreds of books, mostly mine and Mum's, are still stacked across the four tall built-in bookshelves. Mum was widowed before I was born, back in California, where she and Uncle Tad grew up. He brought her here to his new home to recover from the shock, and she never went back—instead, we lived here until she married Alan in 1976. We couldn't help but become voracious readers living with Tad, and Alan's place is tiny compared to Wurimbirra, so when we moved we left most of our collection behind.

Antique furniture is scattered around the room—a circular table and matching wooden chairs, and armchairs, comfortable and otherwise, some beside small coffee tables, some placed strategically near the enormous fireplace. I remember what these chairs used to look like: an array of deep red to match the walls, some green and navy and beige to contrast, some patterned with floral motifs. I run my finger over the top of a worn upholstered armchair and wince at the stain on my fingertip. The furniture is all brown now because like just about everything else, it's coated in dust.

I'd hoped that Jon would have thrown some covers over the upholstered furniture at least, especially given how bad the weather has been for the whole time the house was empty. Like most homes of its era, this one is far from airtight—the wooden window frames have shrunk in places and are worn just about everywhere, and the ornate vents, originally designed to maximize ventilation, now funnel dust and pests right into each room. The Millennium Drought started in 2001 and dragged on through ten agonizing years—it's only broken in the past few months. Rolling dust storms would have choked this house in dust for days on end at times over the years it was empty.

It's all fixable. If the upholstery is stained, it can be replaced—the bones of the furniture will still be good. And if the rest of the house is this dusty it's going to be a pain to clean, but this enormous old house is *always* going to be a pain to clean, and I expected the first few months would be particularly challenging. I'll relish the scrubbing and sweeping and when it gets too much, I'll bring in a cleaning crew.

I leave the parlour to walk through the hallway, across to push open the double ballroom doors. The curtains in here are in much better shape than those in the parlour, but they've been left open so I can see the sweeping expanse of the backyard all the way up to the small private cemetery in the back corner. The earliest occupants of the house, and some of their near descendants, were laid to rest there around the turn of the last century.

What was once an extensive formal garden is now utter chaos—a jumbled mix of dead and overgrown trees and vines and shrubs and weeds. It's in even worse shape than the gardens out front. In time, I'll find a way to restore beauty to the gardens, but for now, it's almost a relief that Tad isn't here to see what has become of his beloved oasis.

The ballroom is mostly empty, except for the ever-present dust over the floors and the once-gleaming grand piano in the corner. There used to be armchairs in here too but we cleared them out to squeeze in 180 plastic chairs for Tad's wake. The rented chairs went with the caterers at the end of the day, and it seems that Jon never set the room right afterwards.

I find the missing armchairs shoved into the formal dining room, around the twenty-four-seat table, which is lined with florist boxes and vases just as it was the day of the wake. Back then, the table was awash with white-and-cream floral arrangements—sent by Tad's many fans and publishing colleagues from around the globe, celebrating his long life and illustrious career. Over the years, the boxes have decayed, and the vases are stained with dried brown scum around the bottom, the last remains of the decayed flower stems and wire sticking out of the florist's foam. I pick up a card that's fallen from one of the largest vases onto the table. Tad's first ever agent, Elsie Rins, died the week before he did, so his other agent, her daughter Rita, was unable to make the funeral.

> Dear Jon, Ginny and family,
>
> What a man, and what a loss to the world. I wish so much I could have made it to be with you today to celebrate our brilliant Tad's life.
>
> All my deepest love and sympathies,
>
> Rita and the team at Rins Literary

My eyes prick with tears as I read Rita's beautiful words about my uncle. The wake was a celebration of a man adored and revered all around the world, and a reflection on a life well lived. My cousin might think he doesn't want any keepsakes from this house, but he might not remember cards like this one.

I knew Jon had a tough relationship with Wurimbirra. Maybe over the years I underestimated just how tough it really was, especially after his dad died here, because I'm beginning to suspect he hasn't set foot in this building since the day of the wake. No wonder he dodged the question whenever I asked him about the house. Until a few years ago, Aunt Daph lived just down the road and Jon and his wife, Ilona, visited her a few times a year. I always assumed they were checking in on Wurimbirra at the same time.

I'd probably have realized otherwise except that I haven't been in this area much either. Mum still lives nearby, but something in our relationship changed when Tad died. He was like a magnetic force, dragging the whole family together a few times a year, and once he was gone . . . it just became so much harder. Mum and Alan came to Waverly and spent Christmas with me and my then-husband and our daughters for a few years after Tad's death. But it's a long trip, and it was always hard for them to leave the farm for more than a day or two, especially over bushfire season. She'd sometimes suggest we come out to the farm instead, but it was always a half-hearted request. Mum would say she didn't want to put us out. She'd say she understood we probably couldn't make it. And the truth was, most of the time, it was easier to just lean into that. To say sorry, it was too much, and we'd catch up with her soon. She came down to the city for my girls' high school graduations, and again for my fiftieth birthday party, but I think it's been five or six years since we managed Christmas together.

My phone rings in my pocket and I almost jump out of my skin at the unexpected sound. I didn't even have a mobile phone when I was last here in 2000—I was refusing to give in to what I was convinced would be a passing trend. I recall that other guests' phones had absolutely no service here that day and I had hoped the coverage improved in the decade since. But Australia's inland mobile coverage is still spotty at best, so it's a relief that my phone will work while I wait for a land line to be reconnected.

"Hi, Caitlin," I greet my eldest daughter. "Guess where I am?"

"You're there already? What time did you leave?" she asks, surprised.

"The electricians are coming to check the wiring at 2:00 p.m. so I had to make an early start." Besides, I hardly slept a wink.

"Mum—I think I messed up," Caitlin says suddenly. "Grandma called me this morning."

"She did?" I say, heart sinking. "Why?"

"She knows I don't have any lectures on Wednesday mornings so she often calls me for tech advice," Caitlin muttered. My mother has absolutely no clue about technology. I'm pretty sure she still does the bookkeeping for Alan's farm in physical ledger books. She worked as Tad's business manager and assistant for decades, but she had only just started to learn email when he died in 1999, and that was the end of that. "I think it's an excuse to talk to me, to be honest. A few weeks ago she was thinking about getting 'an internet.' Today she wanted to talk about whether or not you really can put radios onto 'aisle pods.' But . . ."

"Tell me you didn't mention—"

"Well, Mum, funnily enough it didn't occur to me for even a second that you wouldn't have mentioned you'd *bought* her brother's house and were moving five minutes down the road from her farm!" Caitlin cries. "I explained iPods to her and offered to help her pick one next time she's in the city, or I said, 'Maybe Mum can take you shopping in Forbes now that she's going to be so close.' Imagine my surprise when she had no idea what I was talking about!"

"It's all happened so fast," I say weakly.

"Seriously, Mum."

"It did! Jon only agreed to sell me the place three weeks ago and I'm already here!"

"You couldn't find time to call her in the last twenty-one days? Seriously?"

"Maybe I've been avoiding it a little too," I mutter.

"I don't understand. She must get lonely all the way out there with Alan and their farm workers. Surely she'll be thrilled to have you so much closer." I wince, and Caitlin hesitates before she adds, "Once she gets over the shock, I guess."

"When did you speak to her?"

"I got off the phone about five minutes ago—"

And just then, I hear the roar of an engine on the road out front.

"She's here, Catie. I'll have to go."

"I'm really sorry."

"Don't feel bad, honey. It's my fault for not telling her sooner. Have a good day."

We swap our *I love you*s and end the call, just in time for me to hear a car door slam, followed by pounding against the front door. I sigh as I walk to pull the front doors open, then wince as the hinge gives that long, ominous *creak*. Mum winces too, but she doesn't comment.

"What have you done, Fiona?" Mum whispers fiercely. "What have you *done*?"

Virginia Winslow is famously calm and reserved. I don't think I've ever seen her angry—maybe I even assumed she was incapable of the emotion—but right now, her small hands are curled into fists by her side. Her cheeks are flushed, her eyes narrowed.

She's standing a few steps back from the door in the middle of the wide veranda, dressed in her usual chinos with a busily patterned button-down. Her only concession to the cold wind is a knitted navy vest. Mum's thick hair has been a steely silver for as long as I can remember, cut into the same short style. She's eighty years old but she's always looked much younger than her age. She brushes off compliments on how "well" she's aging, crediting good genes and her daily use of Oil of Olay. I've attempted to follow the same regime but I'm not sure it's been anywhere near as effective for me. I never knew my father; in fact I've never even seen a photo of the man, but I assume I inherited my rather ordinary skin from him.

"Come in," I say carefully, and I step back from the door to hold it open, making room for her. A pained, fearful twist passes across Mum's face as she glances into the foyer. All at once I am reminded that we held Uncle Tad's wake here in the ballroom because it was the logical place to do so, but my mother tried everything to insist on a different venue, to the point that Jon had to put his foot down about the matter. As much as Mum loathes this house, Tad loved it, and there was no more fitting venue to celebrate his life.

But even at the time I understood where Mum was coming from. It was Mum who found Tad the morning after he died, and she found him right here in his bed. Plus, she didn't exactly love Wurimbirra even before she discovered her brother's body here. Even when I was a child, Mum jumped at every creaking floorboard, and shuddered every time a window rattled in the wind.

And then to arrive one ordinary New Year's Day to find her brother had died in his sleep overnight . . . I can't imagine how that moment has haunted her.

Her shoulders slump, and she takes a step backwards, towards the stairs.

"Tad treated you like his own daughter," she says, shaking her head. "He showered you with love and generosity and care. After everything he did for you, he asked *one* thing from you and Jon, and you kids can't even honor that."

"Mum, Jon couldn't ignore this place forever. He had legal obligations—"

"You think you know this house," she interrupts me, nostrils flaring again. "You've been so sure that you had already figured out everything there is to know about it. Well, now you're going to be here all alone, and maybe you'll finally understand."

She turns to leave, and goosebumps break out all over my skin as a shiver runs down my spine. I take a step out the door towards her as I blurt,

"Understand *what*, Mum?"

She glances back at me and gives a heavy sigh. Her gaze is hollow.

"History doesn't always stay in the past, Fiona. I hope to God you know what you're doing."

CHAPTER 2

Fiona

There's no time to collect my thoughts because just as Mum's truck disappears through the gates, the electrician's van turns onto the driveway and parks behind my car. Two men climb out. The first is an older man, and he stands scratching his head as he peers up at the house. The other is a teenager who's probably an apprentice and who might just be the older man's son.

"Hey!" the younger man gasps. "This is that haunted house, isn't it?"

The older man glares at him and mutters something under his breath before he turns to look at the house again. His frown suddenly deepens, and I know he's read the stained glass lettering over the door that spells out *Wurimbirra*.

"You just told me the address, Mrs Winslow. You forgot to mention the property name," he says, frowning.

"Does it matter?"

"Oh, it matters, all right," the younger man mutters. "I've heard the stories about this place—"

"They *are* just stories," I assure them as I hasten down the concrete steps to stand closer. "I grew up here. It's a big old house, sure, but about the scariest thing you'll find in there are cobwebs and maybe some mice and I bet you've seen plenty of those over the years . . ."

The men exchange a glance, then the older one turns to me and shakes his head.

"I'm really sorry, Mrs—"

"Call me Fiona," I correct him automatically. I never took Lucas's name, and that's been a blessing this year, so I'm not about to let this man get away with calling me *Mrs* anything. "Please. The house has been empty for ten years and I'm moving here from Sydney. I can't get the power reconnected until you've checked the wiring and I can't exactly live out here without it. *Please.*"

"Fine. I'll take a look," he finally sighs. "But if I see anything, or hear anything, even . . . *sense* anything in there with us—we're out of there."

I lead them upstairs to the bathroom near Tad's bedroom—that's where the hatch into the ceiling cavity is—and I tell them they'll find the wiring box on the western exterior of the house near the kitchen. After I've left them to get to work, I walk back down the hallway. This would be a dark space with the wood paneling on the walls but for the beautiful stained glass windows at either end, bathing the hallway in green-and-red-and-gold light. At this end of the top story, the rooms were all Tad's—his own room, his guest room, the bedroom he used for storage, Jon's old bedroom. *That* room was rarely used even when Jon was a kid. Tad and Daphne divorced when Jon was very young. She moved to a house in town, and Jon lived with her until he left for university.

It's not that Jon and Uncle Tad weren't close. Jon spent every weekend with Uncle Tad, from Friday afternoon until after dinner Sunday. To my great frustration, he almost always went home to his own bed to sleep. If we were caught up in some particularly exciting game, I'd have a sleepover with him at his house, but it had to be a *very* special occasion for him to agree to sleep at Tad's, and even then, he would never use this bedroom. Instead, he'd insist on sleeping on a mattress on the floor of my room in case he had a nightmare—which he frequently did. When we were quite young, I'd often wake to find some frightening dream had sent him climbing into bed with me. Poor Jon was always so ashamed, as if seeking comfort and company were cowardly.

I pause in the doorway to Tad's room. Someone must have cleaned up in here after the ambulance took his body away. There's no way Tad wouldn't have left empty mugs and plates all over the place. Under a layer of dust, the bed is neatly made.

Tad probably wrote in his study until he got tired that night, then climbed into bed to read. He died on New Year's Eve and he was here alone, but he wouldn't have been sad about that. Uncle Tad liked his own company and he loved being here. The only ending more fitting for him would have been if he died slumped over his keyboard, midway through a sentence.

I reach the landing above the stairs, and the first of two doors leading into the mammoth library which served as Tad's office. This was his workspace, but it was also his favorite place in the world. There are built-in mahogany bookshelves encasing the windows and door frames to make the most of every inch. Tad crammed books onto every shelf, both his own novels and those written by others. He was passionate about literature and read widely—genre fiction, classics, literary fiction, non-fiction. Heck, he's even got a whole section dedicated to atlases and from memory, I know there are a few baskets of comics in here somewhere.

He used to tell me that being surrounded by books made him a better writer, as if he could absorb the brilliance from the pages others wrote, simply by close proximity to them. The success of his career might just be proof that theory was correct. Tad wrote sixteen novels during his forty-five years in this house. Tens of millions of copies of his books sold around the globe and he won just about every major literary prize in the world across his career. This house is remarkable in part because of the key role it played in the creative life of one of the most adored literary voices of a generation.

Tad's library/office is every bit as long as the mammoth ballroom below it. The couple who built this home, Charles and Flora Fowler, were avid readers, and it showed. Even in a home with a literal ballroom, this library was the focus of luxury and expense.

There are rugs scattered over the wide floorboards—covered in dust so that their patterns are now unidentifiable, but I know they are all a dreadfully out of context mid-century style, geometric shapes and repeated patterns of swirling narrow lines, somewhat lost in a room with original 1880s windows and floors, and a twenty-foot, pressed-tin ceiling. Tad told me once that one of the first things Mum did when she moved here from their hometown in California was to drag him out to buy the very first rugs they saw. The echo in this cavernous space had never bothered him, but it almost drove her crazy.

On the eastern side of the room sits a stretched oval writing table with small drawers down the rounded sides. There are yellowed sheets of paper and a fountain pen resting on a desk blotter right where Tad left them—the mug Jon made him in grade 8 still on his desk, as if Tad might return to finish his coffee any second. If I close my eyes, I can still see my uncle there, his lip caught between his teeth, his shaggy eyebrows drawn, concentrating fiercely as he slipped into a world of his own creation.

I take my phone from my pocket and dial Jon as an impulse rises in me to share my nostalgia. He answers on the first ring.

"You will *never* guess who just rang me," he says.

"Hmm. Whoever could it have been?" I wince. "How bad was it on a scale of one to ten?"

"Ten being much worse than I expected and one being much better? On that scale I'm going to say it was . . . oh . . . maybe a few hundred billion. No one guilts like your mother. *No one.* She could take down armies with passive aggression."

I wince again at the heaviness in his tone.

"Sorry, Jon. I really should have told her sooner. I just wasn't sure how she'd react and I guess . . . with everything else going on . . ." Maybe I just wasn't ready to be disappointed, because on some level I was holding on to a foolish hope that Mum would at least be happy to have me living so close to her again.

"It didn't matter when she found out," Jon says. "Ginny was always going to try to manipulate me into changing my mind. She just kept talking about the terms of the will but . . . even that is . . ." He breaks off, then sighs. "Well, even that is complicated."

"I didn't get much in the way of guilt. Just a whole lot of vague threats. I think they were supposed to be hints that ghosts are going to torture me or something," I mutter. Jon is silent for so long I say, "Hello? Are you still there?"

"Fi, there are things I should have told you in person before you left the city," he says suddenly. "That's why I really went to your house last night. I had to drop the keys off, yes, but I also . . . I wanted . . . I *needed* to tell you some things, and the truth is I lost my nerve when I got there."

I wipe my forearm across one of Tad's hideously uncomfortable chesterfield lounges and push the dust onto the rug, then sit gingerly. There are dusty books scattered all over the coffee table, most propped open and face down, because Uncle Tad always had a heap of books on the go at once. It hurts my heart to see five more coffee cups and a small stack of plates here. Tad was a grown-up Hansel and Gretel—he left a trail of mess everywhere he went in case he got lost and needed to find his way home.

"You can tell me anything, Jon," I say gently. The gravity in his tone *seems* dire, but knowing my cousin, this could be about something as simple as his guilt over helping himself to the last cupcake at my birthday in January, so I'm not unnerved.

"We grew up in an unusual family, right?" he says softly. "Most people I know aren't close with their cousins like you and I are."

"We only had each other." Jon and I are both only children and we grew up with three parents between us who were the best of friends—Mum is as close to Aunt Daph as she is to anyone. Mum and Tad were the best of friends. Tad and Daph had the most amicable divorce in history and remained one another's fiercest champion right up until he died. Three and a half years' age difference between me and Jon meant nothing under those conditions. We all lived in one another's pockets. "You're more like my brother than a cousin."

"To this day I still tell you pretty much everything, and I know it's the same for you."

"I know this, Jon," I say, frowning. "But why—"

"Something happened right before Dad died." There's a decade worth of pressure behind that sentence. The words fly from Jon's mouth as if a dam has broken. "You and I were supposed to see one another for Ilona's birthday. That party we planned for the fourth of January, remember? I was going to tell you then. But then Dad died over New Year's and . . . I don't know. I was overwhelmed. Heartbroken. I didn't know how to explain."

"What happened?"

"I was out in Forbes, staying with Mum," he says. Aunt Daphne lives in a retirement community near Jon and Ilona in

North Sydney these days, but until a few years ago, she lived in the house she bought in Forbes after the divorce. "She was hosting a New Year's party that year. She'd invited Dad like she always did, and he declined—"

"Like he always did," I finish for him, sighing fondly. "He hated parties."

"I know. So it was wall-to-wall perms and blue rinses—you know how it was with her students and friends." Aunt Daphne is a former high school art teacher who ran adult classes from a large studio she built at the back of her house. Over the years, she built an incredible community among her students, who were mostly older women. "I think Mum was probably the youngest person there except us. Ilona was in her element talking about Rodgers and Hammerstein and the kids were hiding in Mum's studio watching a movie so I snuck out of the party and drove over to see Dad. We'd all had lunch that day and he seemed a bit off. Preoccupied, I guess you'd say." Jon exhales slowly. "I let myself in and could hear them shouting from the lobby."

"Who was there . . . er . . . *here*?"

"Your mum and my dad were having a bang-up argument. I've never heard anything like it."

"Mum doesn't shout," I protest, and I'm almost laughing at the incredulity of such a statement. Even when she was here half an hour ago, she barely raised her voice above a whisper. And although Tad was physically imposing, towering over most people, he was also softly spoken and by nature, calm and steady.

"I could hardly believe my ears at first."

"What were they squabbling about?"

"Dad wanted you to have something. He said you deserved it. Aunt Ginny vehemently disagreed. That was about all I could make out before your mum stormed out of Dad's office, slamming the door behind her. She looked so shocked when she saw me. Ashamed."

"Jon, you don't think . . ."

"What else could it be? He had to be talking about Wurimbirra. But you have to understand that this was an *ugly* fight, Fi. Your mum spoke to Dad with so much venom. I didn't know she was capable of it. It sounded like she was ready to murder him with her bare hands."

"I can't believe you didn't tell me about this." I'm instantly annoyed. It seemed to go without saying that as Tad's only child, Jon would inherit the house—but even Mum was baffled by the additional request we discovered when we read the will. Tad asked that, if he predeceased Mum, Jon should hold on to Wurimbirra in its present form until the end of *her* life.

No restoration work, no improvements, no sale to another party until Virginia Winslow has also passed.

Uncle Tad's lawyer made it clear that although Tad had every right to ask this of Jon, he couldn't legally demand it. This request—this baffling, nonsense request—was never enforceable. That doesn't mean I haven't felt some guilt ignoring it. As desperately as I wanted to get my hands on Wurimbirra and even though I know to my core that me taking over this place is best for all of us, I *have* hated going against Uncle Tad's wishes. If I hadn't been so desperate to find something—anything—to focus on after my life imploded earlier this year, I'd never have even entertained this move.

"I tried to get Dad to talk about the argument but he said it was between him and Ginny and I needed to let them sort it out," Jon says. "It was obvious that he was upset so I let it drop . . . I just assumed there'd be time for them to smooth it over, you know? But then . . ."

"He died that night," I gasp, suddenly joining the dots. But then Jon's words come back to me: *It sounded like she was ready to murder him with her bare hands.* "Wait! You don't think Mum—"

"No! No, I don't," he hastens to assure me, but then he swallows heavily and my heart plummets into my stomach. "I don't think that *now.* It's just . . . the timing, you know? I mean, I had to wonder at first . . ."

A sudden memory comes to me, of me and Lucas and Jon and Ilona and Aunt Daphne at Mum and Alan's farmhouse in those tender days after Tad's death. Mum and Jon barely spoke to one another. It was odd enough that I noticed it even then, but while Tad's death hit us all hard, Mum and Jon were even closer to him than I was, so I figured they were in shock.

"They said an autopsy was optional because of his age but I just had to know," Jon admits, his voice just above a whisper. I feel instantly sick. Jon must have truly been suspicious to go as far as this.

"*That's* why the funeral was delayed?" At the time, Jon told us that we had to wait a few weeks to bury Tad. And the funeral was a significant affair, with publishing folk from all over the world traveling to attend. The delay stretched out the acute phase of our grief and left us stranded in a heartbroken limbo for weeks, but it made enough sense that I didn't question it at the time.

"Yeah, this was a big part of it. I got the preliminary results the day before the funeral. It was entirely conclusive—Dad had a massive cerebral aneurysm. There's no way his death was suspicious. Maybe the stress of the argument hastened things, but I could never blame your mum for that. His time was up, that's all."

I release a giddy sigh of relief. She drives me crazy but there isn't a sinister bone in my mother's body.

"Why didn't you tell me this earlier?"

"I couldn't tell you, Fi. Not while I waited for those autopsy results. What would I have even said? It all happened so fast. The autopsy came back. Then we had the funeral. The next day, we read the will and the lawyer told us about those stipulations about not renovating or selling. After what I overheard, I suspected Dad was about to change that, but the lawyers said he hadn't contacted them, so I couldn't be sure."

"But why would Mum be so determined to *stop* him from giving me this house?" I ask uncertainly.

"I don't know. But what else could they have been talking about?" We sit on the phone in silence for a few moments, each of us pondering that. Eventually, Jon sighs. "This is part of why I was so paralyzed over the past ten years. I hate that house and you love it and Dad *knew* all of that and he burdened me with it anyway. So was I supposed to obey the instructions in the will, or trust my interpretation of a thirty-second argument and assume he had seen sense and was about to change it? The only person who knew the absolute truth was your mum. I did ask her a few times, but she always shut me down. You know how she is when it comes to difficult subjects—she'd have walked through fire to avoid that conversation. So I sat on that place for *ten freaking years*. It was weighing so heavily on my mind and you seemed so sure this was what you needed for this next part of your life. I just couldn't say no. But . . . my God. In some ways . . . I already wish I had."

"Jon, I *need* this."

"You know I had nightmares as a kid in that house."

"Your parents were divorcing at the time. Everything was chaotic and your dad happened to live in a big spooky house. It's only natural that you had some bad dreams."

"Fi. I don't think they were dreams."

"Don't be silly—"

"I was lying in bed and a man was hovering over me. He was whispering something. I can't remember what he said but his very presence was menacing. I just remember the terror and screaming but no one came to help. It felt like I was alone with him, and then *all* alone, forever." My cousin is not playing around. There's no mistaking the fear in his voice. "This is one of my earliest memories and it's a huge part of why I never could feel safe there. You want to know the truth, Fi? I walked out the door five minutes after you left the day of the wake and I haven't been back there since, not even once. That house has haunted me forever and now I've passed it on to you."

"It was just a dream . . ." I try to protest, but something about this conversation feels different to Jon's habitual histrionics. The stale air in Tad's office has been cool since I stepped into the room, just like the rest of the house, but as I sit on the sofa, the temperature seems to plummet, until I'm shivering and the hair on the back of my neck starts to rise.

"Even the worst nightmare couldn't be this vivid after fifty-odd years," Jon says heavily. "I can't explain it, but Fiona, you need to be careful."

"Look, I'll grant you that in its current state, it does feel like some kind of Halloween-themed haunted house," I admit, but my voice is rough. I stop and clear my throat, then try to force a lightness into my tone as I promise, "Once I've cleaned the place up and finished the restoration, this place won't even feel spooky!" I picture my mother at the front door, shaking with frustration that I've taken on this house and dropping hints about its dark past lingering, and I shiver again. This is *so* silly. I got exactly what I wanted—exactly what I know I need for the next chapter of my life! Why am I letting my family unnerve me?

"I better go, Fi. Just . . . you know I love you, right?"

"Of course," I whisper, and I'm suddenly misty-eyed. I know Jon loves me and he knows I love him, but I think the last time we *said* the words was after Tad's wake. We aren't that kind of family, ordinarily. "And I love you too."

"I know you don't like asking for help—"

"I ask for help when I need it."

"Right," he says wryly. "You do know I've *met* you, right? Just . . . don't be a stranger, okay? Keep me posted and let me know you're okay?"

"Absolutely."

After I hang up, I sink back onto the dusty sofa and look around the room.

I still love this room and I love the house more than ever, but I grudgingly admit that sitting here alone, in the cool light of this icy afternoon, that maybe there's a kernel of truth to my mother's accusations about my rose-colored glasses.

I wander through every room and it's the same story everywhere I look—ever more dust, sometimes with alarming claw marks across it, sometimes tracks, as if some creatures have walked the same path so many times they've worn the dust away. Silvery rodent droppings and cobwebs are everywhere, but in the pantry, they are mixed with the spoils from old boxes of oats and flour and God only knows what else that mess used to be.

It's not the end of the world. I'll eventually replace lots of the cabinetry anyway, and I can't see any recent droppings, so I'm hopeful that whatever was here is now gone.

Some rooms, like Tad's bathroom, look just as they probably did when he died—cluttered, a little chaotic. There's a cardboard toilet paper tube on the dispenser on the wall, but there's a half-used roll sitting on the floor beside the sink. That kind of detail makes it feel as if the house has been frozen in time.

Wurimbirra is still every bit as beautiful and grand as it is in my memories, but unlike my beloved uncle, I'm a tidy person and I'm keen to start getting this place in order. As soon as I run out of rooms to survey, I head out to the water main, which is buried beneath a tangle of weeds and grass at the front of the block. Most houses out here rely on rain water but the town supply line happens to run straight past Wurimbirra so we've long enjoyed the luxury of treated water. I wince at the spiders around the cement lid on the main and gingerly pry it open to turn the tap back on. I've been nervous about this, just like the power. Over ten years anything could have happened to the plumbing; pipes could have burst or been damaged.

But when I walk back inside to run the taps in the kitchen and the laundry, brown water sputters for a while as the pipes flush, but the water soon runs clear and the pressure is good. I run every tap in the house for a while to clean them out. I'll get myself a filter for the kitchen tap because most of this plumbing is very old—but for now, it seems water access won't be a problem I have to deal with.

The kitchen runs the entire western edge of the house—a long, narrow space incorporating an informal dining room, and just off that area, a tiny door that leads to what was once my favorite place in this whole house.

I can't remember how old I was when I went through my obsession with *The Lion, the Witch and the Wardrobe*. I was certainly young—maybe five or six. I would sit with Tad in the parlour while he read me "just one more chapter," as Mum nagged at us to stop so I could go to bed. In my mind's eye that house in the English countryside looked just like Wurimbirra, and by the time we finished the book, I was convinced there was a magical land hidden somewhere in our house too. I checked every single closet just about every day for a while in case the portal had appeared overnight. It was driving Mum and Tad batty that I kept making a mess in the bedrooms, then inevitably crying in disappointment yet again.

One day I came home from school and Uncle Tad was waiting at the door, a battery-operated lantern in his hand.

"You're not going to believe this," he said, wide-eyed. "I found the magical portal."

I ran behind him through the house into the kitchen to find that little door was open for the very first time. Up until that moment all I'd known about the door was that it was strictly off-limits to me and Jon. Now I could see that the door itself was a full foot thick, with a steeped edge and a matching steeped edge on the inner wall. Later I'd learn that tiny room had to seal precisely, and that heavy door and the walls around it were all stuffed with compressed sawdust for insulation. It was a built-in ice chest—groundbreaking technology when the house was built in 1886.

All I knew that day though was that Uncle Tad had discovered a tiny room with shelves on one side and a floor covered with brightly colored cushions.

"See," he whispered conspiratorially. "Children have used this very portal to escape to other worlds in the years gone by."

"How does it work?" I whispered back.

"See that door up there?"

He helped me inside, then lifted me up by the hips and I saw that at the top of the room was a tiny external door leading to the outside of the house beside the laundry. And now that he'd shown it to me, I could remember seeing it on the outside of the house—a metal door with a silver handle, beside a long-broken contraption with a pulley wheel at the top.

"What's that for?"

"It's for the fairies, obviously. It's where they drop their magic off to make this room special. Now, Fiona, you must understand that they are fast, so you probably won't spot them, but the fairy magic in the air in here will help you move into other worlds."

"Really?"

"Really. If you sit here long enough, you'll understand, but you have to be very patient and—Oh! What's this?"

I had already clambered down onto the pillows and immediately noticed the baskets on the lower shelves. As I pulled one out, a little jar of hard lollies came into view, and so did several dozen books.

"What if I get locked in here?" I asked him, feeling suddenly unsure as I looked at the heavy door.

"Let me show you something," he said, and then we shuffled around, and I climbed out and Uncle Tad climbed in, and then I climbed back in, but this time to curl up on his lap. We pulled the door shut and suddenly we were in that tiny, dark space, illuminated only by the lantern. "Now. Push the door." I pushed it gently with my foot and it swung open easily; the hinges didn't so much as squeak. "Don't worry, love. There's no latch now and I greased the hinges so it's very easy to open and close. You are perfectly safe in here—in fact, if that magic works the way I think it will, it'll be the safest place you ever go."

For years, that cabinet was my absolute favorite place to sit and read. I think I still went in occasionally in my early teens. I had friends over to play all the time, but the secret portal was off-limits to them. Only Jon knew about it and I did let him look in there sometimes, but I never let him share it—he had other games he played with his dad that I wasn't a part of, and it only seemed fair that I got to keep this one to myself.

I don't remember when the cushions were moved or thrown out but I do remember that the pile of books in that room constantly changed, with a brand-new book appearing as soon as I finished one, and even if I gorged myself on those hard lollies, the next day the jar would be refilled. The fairy door never did open while I was in there, but I was convinced that there was magic dust in the air because when I read a book in that room I really could disappear into it—experiencing every story as if it were my own.

I know now that the chest was designed such that a delivery man could place fresh blocks of ice right into the room to keep the food chilled, without bothering the lady of the house by coming inside. There was even a drainage system built in to channel the water outside as the ice melted. By the '60s, when I was a child, fridges were easy to come by and the feature was redundant. But this was what my uncle did—he took the ordinary, and he turned it into pure magic.

Maybe that's what I've come home to find.

There's a ten-seat farmhouse table in the kitchen, a mammoth, bulky thing as old as the house. There's a small cardboard box seated on top that's instantly familiar but I can't quite remember why. I blow the dust off the top and discover it's from a publisher in the UK. The postmark says November 1999.

A memory stirs. It was the day of the wake, and the guests had gone. Jon and Ilona were finishing up inside but we had said goodbye and I was headed back to Mum's to sleep for the night. I stepped out onto the front veranda and there was a box there—some hapless courier had just dumped it by the door during the day. I took it inside and sat it on this table. It never occurred to me that Jon wouldn't come back to sort the contents of the house later.

I sigh as I slice the decade-old box open with one of Tad's kitchen knives. Inside there's a folded letter, and twelve copies of a novel.

> Dear Mr Winslow,
>
> Please find enclosed twelve copies of *The Midnight Estate* by Charity Wilkie.
>
> With all best wishes,
>
> Spencer Kallaide and Michaelson Books, London

I pick a book up and stare down at the front cover. The image is dark and moody—a shadowy oil painting of a beautiful young woman, donning a masquerade mask as she stares into an ornate-framed mirror. The description on the back is almost as vague as the cover.

> Silas thought he was going home to say goodbye. To be forgiven.
> Marie thought the stranger in the cafe would pass through her life. To be forgotten.
> Fate, in all of her mysterious wisdom, had other plans.

It was not uncommon for Tad to buy bulk-lots of the books he especially loved. Countless times after I left home I was surprised by a parcel from him and inside would be a book—sometimes without explanation, sometimes with a long letter in his barely decipherable scrawl, telling me all of the things he loved about the story and how I *"absolutely must read it right away!"* Often Mum and Daphne would be gifted the same book and he'd send one to Jon and he'd drop one off to Roberta at the town library and Marilyn, the woman who runs the Forbes cafe bookstore, Turn the Page. I always read the books he sent and I'd try so hard to read the way he did—pondering deeper meanings, dissecting the story, parsing every line for brilliance. And as soon as I finished, I'd call him and we'd talk on the phone for hours. I like to think I have a reasonable intellect but it didn't matter how hard I tried, Tad always found insights I missed.

I'm not surprised to find that he'd ordered twelve copies of a book from the UK before he died, and I am more than a little excited to see what it was he was going to share with us all. I set the books on a chair and walk out to grab the cleaning supplies from my car so I can wipe down the table. As I'm wiping, my gaze keeps drifting back to the box, and I am very tempted to start reading right away. But no! I want to at least make a dent in this room—I have to be disciplined, to work before I relax. I rinse the cloth and move to the countertops. This is messy, frustrating work, because every time I wipe something down and move on, the *next* surface I wipe sends dust flying into the air, and it inevitably settles back over whatever I just cleaned. Soon enough I'm sneezing and my eyes are watering and it feels a whole lot like the book is *calling* to me, so I finally give in. The job is too big and I'm wasting effort and time starting it with the tools I have on hand today.

I take a seat beside the only-slightly-less-dusty farmhouse table and reach to pick up a copy of *The Midnight Estate.*

After all, what better tribute could I make to my uncle than do exactly what he would have—sit with the chaos and the mess, and lose myself in a book?

THE MIDNIGHT ESTATE

BY CHARITY WILKIE

When Silas first told his sister, Maeve, that he was moving abroad, she reacted with such fury and distress that for a split second, he entertained the thought that he should just abandon his fiancée and stay in California after all.

"You told me you were going on another research trip."

"Yes, it was for research originally, but—"

"You said you'd be gone for three months, then you were gone for six. And now you've finally come home, only to tell us you're leaving forever?"

"It's just that I met Christine right after I arrived and . . ." Silas wasn't sure how to explain what happened next. It was a miracle of the highest order—a meeting of minds, the spark of a chemical reaction, one soul split in two long before time, disparate halves suddenly reconnecting. Even in a year of shocking developments, he wasn't at all sure anyone was ready for him to start making such flowery pronouncements, so instead, he cleared his throat then mumbled, "The rest is history."

Silas had delivered the news to his mother the night before. Linda had been shocked and sad but was also dignified and supportive. This was the exact reaction he'd expected, so he had no reason to prepare for an altogether different response from his sister.

He was, belatedly, realizing he'd made a dreadful mistake in blindsiding Maeve. He might have written or sent a telegram. He might even have booked a call and told her over the telephone—it was a complicated and expensive process to phone someone internationally in 1955 but Silas had to make such calls for his work from time to time so he did know how to do it.

He just figured it would be kinder—more mature—to face his family while he delivered the news. He even thought they might sense the monumental changes that had taken place in him while he was overseas. That they might understand if they could see him.

"You'd get it if you met her," Silas said, but what he wanted to say was *if you saw us together*. He was a completely different person when he was with Christine. Someone smarter and braver and kinder and infinitely more likable, someone more like Maeve herself He desperately wanted his sister to meet this version of him, and that's why in his letters over those past few months, he'd worked so hard to convince her that she should visit him. He sensed she was warming up to the idea. She'd even arranged her passport. "I'll buy you and Mom a ticket to fly over for the wedding and you can—"

"No."

"But in your last letter you said that you wanted to see the—"

"Even if I wanted to take a vacation there one day, things have changed now that I know you're abandoning me and Mom forever."

He hadn't considered it to be abandonment, but Silas did intend to forge a new life for himself with Christine, and Christine happened to live in another country. He just had to make Maeve understand why that was the right decision for him. It still felt strange to say the words, even though he'd said them to Christine dozens of times.

"I love her, and she loves me. We need to be together."

Romantic love was not something Silas had ever anticipated experiencing. He had long believed he simply wasn't capable of feeling it, or indeed, any other massively heightened emotion. It wasn't that he was oblivious to such things, just that something about his nature made him more suited to observing other people than engaging with them.

Maeve, on the other hand, was a woman who adored being in all kinds of relationships—family, romantic, friendship, professional. She bounced from one exciting activity to another, all the while experiencing a never-ending roller coaster of emotions, swinging between extremes both high and low. Over the years, Silas had seen his sister weeping with joy over music she admired, or a date that had gone well, or even one startling evening, the particularly excellent roast dinner their mother had prepared.

"We're all here together and Silas is doing so well with his work and we just got that big donation to the church soup kitchen so we can help more people and these potatoes are so delicious and I'm just so happy!" she'd sniffed as her mascara ran down her cheeks and her chest heaved with sobs.

Other days, she was so bereft over some slight, real or imagined, she'd fail to drag herself out of bed. She seemed to feel every emotion at the maximum intensity, but this was especially true for rejection. Perhaps that was her greatest challenge, but Silas felt it was more than offset by the enormity of her empathy. Maeve was generous to a fault and seemed to think nothing at all of giving from her own pocket, even beyond what she could afford. That was just the nature of his beautiful little sister—she was immense in heart and in spirit.

But Silas had never experienced wild, chaotic emotions before. Even when life was hectic, his inner life remained steady and calm. Truth be told, he wasn't exactly sure how to handle wild swings of the heart.

That's probably why he was woefully unprepared when he met a spirited young woman with a bouncy black ponytail, sitting beneath a tree in the park, reading a book. He would never have introduced himself, but fortunately for Silas, Christine was every bit as outgoing as he was reticent. She asked what book he was reading and he showed her it was *The Old Man and the Sea*, a book he'd read so many times, he knew some passages by heart. She was just a few pages into her first reading of *Rebecca* and she wasn't sure what to make of it.

When Silas first opened his mouth to comment, he initially intended to simply tell her to stick with her novel, that she'd come to love the twisted brilliance of du Maurier's genius if she gave the story some time. But Christine had inadvertently stumbled on the only way to make Silas chatty: conversation centered upon books. He would never be quite sure how it happened, but the next thing Silas knew, several weeks had flown by and the two were spending every minute of every day together.

When the time came for him to leave Australia to return home to the United States, he just couldn't see how he would survive if he were to separate from Christine for good. The inclination to uproot his entire life to be with this woman was so uncharacteristic that Silas wondered at times if he wasn't in love at all, but rather, having some kind of breakdown. That seemed a much more likely eventuality than falling in love.

Either way, sitting there with Maeve in their humble childhood living room, his skin itched to return to Australia. To Christine. And he would.

"You're being so selfish," Maeve said, her eyes shiny with tears. "You always have been, Silas, but this is bad—even for you. We are all Mom has in the whole world. After everything she's been through, and everything she's done for us, how could you move so far away from her?"

He tried hard to convince Maeve of the necessity of the move over the following weeks, but she simply would not budge. Their family was everything to her, and she was furious with Silas for "breaking it up."

"Maeve will come round eventually," his mother assured him. "She's going to miss you, that's all. And she never stays angry for very long, does she? Just give her some space for now."

He took his mother's advice and left with Maeve still furious at him. He assumed they'd reconcile over letters at some point once she cooled down. He was wealthy now—properly wealthy, beyond their wildest childhood dreams. Silas could easily afford for Maeve and even their mother to visit him and Christine as often as they felt inclined to do so.

His mom flew out for the wedding. Linda had never been on an airplane before so that exhausting journey was quite a shock to her system. Still, she made the trip, but she made it alone. The expensive ticket Silas purchased for his sister went unused.

"I don't understand it either, Silas," Linda admitted.

"She just flatly refused to come. But try not to think about it, my love. This is your moment with Christine." Then she rested her hand over his and glanced towards Christine, who was busy making refreshments in the expansive kitchen of the home Silas had purchased for his bride. Linda's eyes swam with tears, but her lips were curved in a smile as she glanced back to her son. "I never thought I'd see you this happy. You have to live your own life, son, and it's plain as day that your life is here with her."

After the wedding, Linda stayed a month with Silas and Christine. Just as Silas had secretly hoped, his new wife and his mother got along like a house on fire.

"I'll talk to Maeve again," Linda said tearfully as they parted at the airport. "Who knows? Maybe you'll get a letter from her asking if she can visit herself."

But Maeve ignored the wedding photos Linda took home with her. She ignored each of the letters Silas sent over the four long years that followed—each one more effusive than the last, begging her to reply and keep in touch. She even ignored the photo Silas sent after the birth of his beloved son, Ernest.

In fact, the very first contact Silas had with Maeve in the years after he left was via a telegram that came late in 1960.

> *Mother sick with influenza* STOP
> *Doctor says may not survive* STOP

Silas immediately began to plan a trip home.

It was a startling thing to find himself standing outside of the home he had grown up in. Of course he remembered his childhood, but his memories had taken on an oddly gilded sheen that reality just didn't match. He'd thought of his upbringing as somewhat normal, perhaps defined more by his father's absence than any material lack . . . but after five years' absence, everything looked different.

Had his childhood home always been so small? Why had he never realized that they lived in a terrible house on the worst block? As a child, he'd never questioned the need to share a bedroom with Maeve. They were siblings and best friends; why would they want any other arrangement?

When he first became successful, Maeve gently nudged Silas towards repaying some of their mother's kindness. She suggested he might help Linda repaint the house or buy a new sofa—something she'd been saving to do for years. That he needed a prompt to even think of such a thing shamed Silas deeply. His mother had single-handedly kept the family together after his father walked out just before Maeve's birth. Instead of some paint or a new sofa, he purchased her a brand-new apartment, just one bus stop from the grocer and the butcher, and he made sure she had a monthly stipend so she no longer had to work as a typist for the principal of his old high school.

Linda had lived in that home ever since, but that's not where Silas directed the taxi driver when he left the airport. Instead, he went straight to his childhood family home, the place where Maeve still lived. She had been pleasantly surprised when Silas bought their mother her new place, but insisted on staying behind. She said that into her twenties, she wanted independence more than she wanted to live one stop from the grocer. For a little while she had various friends live with her, but as each of these married and left, Maeve ended up living alone.

Now, home after so many years, Silas stood on Maeve's

covered stoop, procrastinating. He was anxious to reconcile with his sister and desperate to learn of his mother's condition. Silas already knew that regardless of what had transpired since Maeve's telegram, he'd spend their entire first conversation groveling. He was still stung and confused by how she reacted when he moved away, but none of that mattered now—he was going to beg her forgiveness anyway, especially for leaving her all alone to deal with Linda's sickness without help. And since receiving her message, Silas had moved as quickly as he could, but the logistical gymnastics it took to schedule all of the connecting flights from his new home to his old had slowed him down. Seven days had passed since the telegram arrived.

He always imagined that he would rush home in a crisis, but when the crisis finally came, the tyranny of distance easily defeated his good intentions. Silas held his breath and rang the doorbell, but there was no movement inside, not even after he rang it a second and then a third time.

"Are you looking for someone, young man?" Mrs Ristevra called from next door. Silas should have known she would be keeping a watchful eye over his family home. Mrs Ristevra was always the first to unearth, and to share, neighborhood gossip. "Silas? Is that you?"

"Yes, Mrs Ristevra," he said. His throat was suddenly dry. "Is . . . my mother . . . ?"

"Oh, dear boy," the older woman said, stricken. "I'm so sorry. She passed, son. Six days ago, I think. She was buried on Tuesday."

Silas nodded slowly. He had prepared himself for that as much as he knew how to. Linda had been an extraordinary parent, and a ray of sunshine just like Maeve—good and kind and vivacious and fun, despite the challenges her marriage to Silas's father had presented. She'd taken such delight in the photographs of Ernest over those past few years. They'd exchanged letters frequently, and he called her on her birthday and at Christmas. Linda had continued to lobby Maeve to let bygones be bygones and to make a trip to see Silas and his new family.

But now, Ernest would never meet his grandma, and his grandma would never meet Ernest, with his cheeky grin and his brilliant, vibrant imagination. For a moment, this seemed like the worst thing in the world, until Mrs Ristevra cleared her throat and added, "Silas dear, you should know . . . Maeve is also sick. Last I heard, she was in the hospital."

On the other side of town, Marie was going about her morning ritual. She had carefully set her hair and taken great pains to get her make-up just so. She was wearing her favorite yellow blouse, one with sweet little pearl buttons along the front, and a flared green skirt adorned with big red flowers and a blue trim. She made sure to wash up the breakfast dishes and vacuum, and by the time the telephone rang, she was waiting by the little table in the hall, ready to answer it on the first ring.

"Hello, love," her husband, Rupert, greeted her. "How has your morning been?"

"Uneventful," she told him. "And yours?"

The call took no more than a minute or two but the second Marie replaced the handset, she slipped her handbag over her shoulder, double-checked that she had her keys and her daily allowance, then opened the front door. Outside, it was a cloudless day and the air was perfectly still. It was always a relief to leave the house on cooler days. Unless she really rushed, she wouldn't sweat her make-up off and there was no wind to ruin her careful hairstyle.

"Good morning, Mrs Knightly," the postman said as she passed him by the corner of the street.

She returned the greeting with a demure "How are you, Mr Nolan?" She was greeted by name at the butcher too, and then at the grocer, and even by people on the street she recognized but couldn't quite place. Everyone knew Rupert's wife because everyone knew Rupert in one capacity or another. Still, even though Marie understood herself to be something of a minor local celebrity, she didn't have time to stand around and chat. When Jim Hawthorne tried to strike up a conversation, she pointed vaguely at her wristwatch, mumbled apologies and kept right on walking. When Nancy Middleton asked her how her day was going, Marie told a white lie about sleeping in and "running dreadfully late" before rushing off.

When her crocheted grocery bag was laden with dinner supplies, Marie finally paused just long enough to check the time: 11:05 a.m.

She was fifteen minutes ahead of schedule, just as she'd hoped to be, and that meant she had time to call past the diner for a coffee. Much to her disappointment, her brother, Irving, had recently started working there. She had wanted him to go to college, but his grades slipped terribly after the accident. Irving was once the top of his class but in the end, he didn't even stick with school long enough to get his diploma.

Marie's father used to say that all work was dignified work, but she couldn't help but wonder how Derek Underwood would feel seeing his son hand-washing dishes in the kitchen of a diner at eleven o'clock on a Tuesday morning when he might have been studying science or law or medicine at college. Marie mostly worried for Irving's future because she knew how hard it was to make a living working in the diner. How would he support a family when the time came? He could barely support himself on the wages he was earning.

But her brother wasn't even seventeen years old. Surely he was years away from considering such things and by then, he might turn it all around. Somehow. And Irving wasn't just smart; he was also kind and good. Marie tried to reassure herself—a kid like Irving was going to be just fine no matter what happened, because he deserved to be fine.

"Coffee, Mrs Knightly? We have that blueberry pie again, the one you enjoyed so much last week?" Helen the waitress called as she bustled past with her notepad, making a beeline towards a table of customers awaiting service.

"Thank you," Marie replied as she took a seat in one of the vinyl booths along the front of the diner. "I'd appreciate that, I'm famished." But she glanced at her watch again and saw that it was already 11:08 a.m. She had to be on her way within twelve minutes and the diner was busy—there was every chance that pie would take too long to arrive. "Actually, Helen, just the coffee. I'm watching my waistline, you know how it is. And I'm in a bit of a hurry, would you mind . . . ?"

Marie was mainly at the diner to check in on her brother anyway, and besides, Rupert really didn't like her eating sweets.

Helen poured the coffee as Marie watched Irving through the serving window, and gradually felt herself calm. There had been so much to worry about since their parents died and it didn't seem to matter how hard she tried to make things right; everything felt broken, as if a flaw in the very structure of the world had been exposed.

But as long as Irving was okay, she could cope. That's why she tried to stop at the diner most days, even though Irving never really seemed to want to talk to her much now, and even though it was very difficult to find the time. Marie felt a low level of anxiety at every moment of every day. In fact, sometimes it seemed the only break she had from the worry was the time she spent in that diner. The reprieve was always ever so brief.

By 11:17 a.m., she was growing antsy again. Technically she could afford to linger a few more minutes, and she'd intended to do just that when she first sat down, but now it occurred to her that staying would mean she'd have to rush as she walked home and was it really so cool out there that she wouldn't sweat? She couldn't risk leaving herself short on time and she *would* be short on time if she had to fix her hair or her make-up before lunch. Her black coffee was still far too hot for her to finish, so she decided to leave it and use the extra time for the walk.

Just as she pushed the cup away, she saw movement out of the corner of her eye. She startled guiltily as if she was committing some kind of crime in leaving the coffee half-drunk, but when she looked up, it was just Carmen—the cafe's owner. Irving's boss.

"Mrs Knightly," Carmen said, easing herself down into the booth beside Marie, inadvertently trapping her in place. "Do you have a moment to talk about your brother?"

"I'm afraid I don't," Marie said, gathering her things. Her thoughts raced wildly, bouncing this way and that in her mind, and her mouth had gone dry.

She was going to be late and Rupert was going to be so

disappointed in her. He might even realize that she'd been visiting the cafe not "every now and again," as she'd assured him last time he asked, but almost every day. And what was this little interruption about, anyway? Maybe Irving wasn't fine after all. Marie really needed to hear Carmen out but she couldn't be late—not after what happened last time . . .

"It won't even take a minute," Carmen said softly. "It's just . . . Honey, you know he's a good worker. Smart. Loyal. He's here early, he only leaves when the work is done and every last bit of the work at that."

"So what's the problem?"

"You know I can't offer him any more than this dead-end job and we all know he's too smart for it. That boy should have been valedictorian, Marie! But I'd swear to you, if it was just that, I'd hold my tongue and enjoy the unfair blessing, since I'm the one who benefits the most, you know? And maybe he is the kind of kid who'd learn to be content with a small life like the one we can offer him here. Mind you, I don't think he is, but maybe I'm wrong about that."

"Carmen—"

"There's so much more at stake than just his clever mind going to waste. You get that, right?" Marie held herself stiffly. She did know exactly what Carmen was referring to, but she could never give that away. "Now, I don't know how to say this delicately so I'm just going to blurt it out. I like the kid—I truly do. That's why this is troubling me so much. He's spending more and more time with . . . less savory people." Carmen paused to clear her throat. "Troublemakers. If you know what I mean." Marie raised her chin stubbornly and prayed harder than she'd prayed in her life that her eyes wouldn't fill with tears until she was safely home. "I know this is complicated, given your . . . situation . . . and I do feel bad about that. I mean, I feel we all let you down too, but at the time we didn't realize—"

Marie looked at her watch: 11:21 a.m.

She shot to her feet and Carmen startled but stood automatically too. After a pause, she looked closely at Marie, then shuffled out of the booth.

"I'm sorry," Marie said breathlessly. She gathered her groceries, heart pounding in her ears. She couldn't so much as bring herself to look at Carmen as she stumbled away from the table, but she did drop her voice to a whisper to say, "It is what it is. I can't do anything about how it all turned out. And I have to go—I have a—I have—I'll miss—"

"Coffee's on the house today, Mrs Knightly," Carmen said, gaze softening. "We'll pick this conversation up again some other time."

But as Marie all but sprinted along Main Street, her feet aching as she raced for home, she knew she wouldn't pick up that conversation with Carmen another day.

If anything, she'd go out of her way to avoid resuming that chat, even though it would keep her awake at night for the foreseeable future.

Marie had already cooked a fresh meal for Rupert that morning—Swedish meatballs, a recipe from that cookbook he bought her for Christmas. She pulled two pots from the cupboard and set them on the stove—one for the noodles, one for the meatballs in their oddly pale gravy. It would have been easier to throw it all together but Rupert wouldn't have liked that—the resulting mixture would have looked like leftovers, and the whole point of fresh meals for lunch and dinner was that he didn't like leftovers.

She twisted the knobs to start the gas, but she didn't hit the igniter button. This was a habit she'd formed over those past few months and Marie just didn't know what to make of it—worse still, she couldn't seem to stop herself from doing it. It was a ridiculously dangerous ritual, but it was also a type of mental vacation—brief seconds of fantasy, a hint of relief and escape. She had thought it all through, right to the end. She would let the gas run and she would shut the kitchen window and the doors and she would sit down on the vinyl floor with that photo of her with Irving and her parents at her high school graduation and—

But Marie didn't have time for this fantasy. Not today. Maybe not any day. She kept promising herself she would stop but then every time she touched the damned stove the gas called to her like a siren's song.

Cursing her own weakness, Marie flung open the windows and waved her hand over the stove and she turned on the exhaust fan and she tried so hard not to cry because tears would only mess up her make-up. When she was certain the gas was gone, she hit the igniter as she turned each burner on again. She tossed a knob of butter in with the noodles and she knew it really needed to be stirred to stop it sticking but she didn't have time—she'd just have to chance it over a low flame.

Marie ran through the house towards the bathroom, her heels clattering against the linoleum floor. Her heart sank when she saw herself in the mirror. Her light brown hair was fine and frizzy, but she set it every night and held the style in place with a generous burst of hairspray in the morning. It usually worked, but today she had rushed away from Carmen and she was frazzled and flustered, and now she had a halo of sticky, stiff frizz all around her face. Her hands shook as she tried to push it down.

Marie liked to look her best for Rupert. Or Rupert liked her to look her best. She was increasingly confused about where the line was between her own desires and his. That, in itself, was confusing.

Marie had been the kind of child who knew where she was going in life from a very young age. Her mother used to say, "This one knows her own mind." Her grandmother used to tell people, "Marie is an old soul." But lately, the headstrong, determined child Marie had once been seemed like an old friend Adult Marie had lost touch with. She struggled to make sense of this. What exactly was the pivot point? The months around her parents' accident felt blurry, as if a thick pane of frosted glass stood between her and her own memories.

All that she knew for sure was that she came out the end of all of that with Rupert by her side. He was her knight in shining armor. He had saved her, and he was still saving her, because she could do just about nothing right without his help.

Marie did the best she could with her appearance and then rushed back through the house, but as she neared the kitchen, she could smell the noodles were burning and just then, she heard the crunch of tires on the gravel drive. She looked at the clock on the wall—red frame, white face, bold against the lime-and-forest-green wallpaper: 11:59 a.m.

Her heart started to race.

Marie tipped the noodles onto the plate but in her haste she burned her wrist on the side of the stainless steel pot. It immediately began to throb but there was no time to cool it with water or to rub butter on it, as her mother always said she should do with a burn. Instead, she picked the top layer of ruined noodles from Rupert's plate and smoothed down what was left, then reached for the meatballs and gravy but—

Oh God no.

In her haste to fix herself up for lunch, she'd put the noodles on too high and the meatballs on too low. She dipped her finger into the gravy and hesitated. It was warm. Maybe she'd get lucky and he wouldn't complain.

She tipped it all onto Rupert's plate, stopped at the fridge for her salad and hurried through to the dining room. Thank God she always set the table before she left the house.

By the time Rupert came into the dining room, she was standing beside the table, a radiant smile on her face. He had collected the mail on his way in, so she waited patiently while he flicked through the envelopes, then dropped the little stack onto the credenza.

"Darling," he greeted Marie at last, brushing his lips against her cheek for a kiss, but then he paused, his face close to hers. Marie found her chest felt so tight, she couldn't so much as breathe. "You don't seem well put together today."

He whispered the words, his tone heavy with something she might have heard as deep concern except that— No, it was deep concern. Of course it was. Rupert loved her. Everyone said he lived and breathed for her.

"I was just . . . Silly me," she said breathlessly, trying to give a careless little laugh on the words, as if that would make her seem coy. "I was daydreaming and I burned myself a little bit. That's all. That's all it was."

She lifted her wrist to show him the burn, because even though she knew he would be furious that she hurt herself, she couldn't think of any other way to explain why she was so flustered. He took her wrist in his hand and peered down at the bubble forming on her skin.

"You really must take more care," he said softly. "I couldn't bear it if anything happened to you."

He used the forefinger of his other hand to gently stroke around the angry burn. Marie couldn't take her eyes off his face—his lips thin, his gaze tight with frustration and disappointment. Finally, he released her and walked around her chair to his meal. As he sat, she sat too, but she waited until he'd sliced a meatball in half with his fork and raised some to his mouth before she took her first bite of her salad. In their first few months of marriage, Rupert taught her that there was a natural order to things and that a wife should never begin eating before her husband does. It was about respect, and authority.

"This is cold," Rupert said suddenly.

Marie looked at the plate.

"I—I could—"

"You know how busy I am, Marie. You know how important my job is."

"I do! I just—"

"I need my food hot and ready when I walk in that door. Do you understand that?"

"I do. I'm sorry, Rupert."

He reached across the table and flipped the edge of her plate. Marie knew better than to try to catch it. The plate went flying, shattering on the floor beside her chair, a mess of lettuce and tomato and porcelain and cucumber.

Rupert went back to his cold meatballs. Unhurried, he ate every bite, then he wordlessly rose and went to use the bathroom. Marie sat ramrod straight, her eyes dry, gazing unseeing towards Rupert's place. When he returned and saw her staring, he swiped his finger over a smear of leftover gravy and he brought it to her mouth.

"Open," he said. She did as instructed, and he wiped the gravy inside her lip. "You see? Tasteless. Cold. You can do better. And that kitchen needs your attention." He caught her chin between his thumb and his forefinger and stared down into her eyes. Marie swallowed and forced herself to smile, and Rupert's gaze softened. He touched her cheek gently. "We'll speak at 2:30 p.m. Follow me out."

He liked her to kiss him goodbye when he slipped into his police car. He liked her to stand on the drive to wave at him as he reversed and then drove away. Often, they would see neighbors during this little farewell routine. Mr Peterson next door, an elderly widower with a fluffy white dog named Percy, would just happen to be checking his mail at the time and he'd stop to tell Rupert what a lucky man he was, or to tell Marie how blessed she was to have such a good husband. Wendy Baker across the road was often returning from the library or the park with her toddlers, and she'd look at Marie and Rupert's beautiful home and give a wistful sigh. Ethel Knox was sometimes in her garden and she'd give a knowing wink when she saw Rupert bend to kiss Marie's cheek.

None of the neighbors were on their lawns today, but Marie waved until Rupert's car was out of sight anyway. Then she walked inside to carefully pick up the shards of plate and salad from the floor of the dining room, and put the whole lot into the bin. She cleaned the kitchen until every surface was sparkling and then she answered the phone on the first ring when Rupert called at 2:30 p.m.

"Hello, love," he greeted her. "How has your afternoon been?"

"Uneventful," she told him. "And yours?"

When she finished the call, she went through to their bathroom. She took a scalding-hot shower as if the heat could wash away the shame and the fear and the powerlessness, but she did not let herself cry. Not for long, anyway, because Rupert didn't like to see her eyes red or puffy.

Then she dressed as if she was starting the day again and went to prepare her dinner.

If Marie could write a letter to that feisty, fierce version of herself that she had been as a child, it would only say one thing.

I'm sorry, little Marie. I just don't know where I went wrong.

Rupert had the very same job as Marie's father, and yet growing up Marie had lived in a simple home and there had only ever been enough money for them to get by, sometimes only just. That's exactly why, as soon as Marie and Irving were old enough to be left with the lovely young teen who lived down the block, Marie's mother had gone back to work, taking as many shifts at the nursing home as she could manage. Even then there had only been one car—the same 1945 Ford her parents had owned for more than ten years. The same car they were in together, driving home from their respective shifts, when the accident happened, three weeks after Marie's high school graduation, half a summer before she was due to start college.

She'd been aware of Rupert for a while by then but he was just another of her father's subordinates—hired on the recommendation of a chief of police at a city station. She saw him from afar at Christmas parties and on the rare occasions she called into the station to see her dad.

After the accident, there was a revolving door of police officers checking in on her and Irving. At the time Marie was reeling, not just from her parents' deaths, but also from the discovery that her father—her beloved, seemingly perfect dad—had a secret gambling habit. There was no money, two immense mortgages, and Marie had no idea how she was going to keep Irving fed and clothed and in school long enough to graduate.

Marie had always found numbers came easy to her and she had won a college scholarship, intending to major in math. But in the fog of grief and shock, not even the math made sense. The covered plates the officers' wives sent were useful but didn't really solve the main problem: even if Marie got a job, she'd never manage the mortgages on her own.

Rupert came by once with sympathy flowers and then after that, he seemed to be there every second day. He had endless time to talk things through with Marie and so much advice. He helped her deal with the bank. Helped her talk to Irving's school because her brother, who had always been the brightest kid in his year, was suddenly struggling academically and getting into all sorts of trouble in the schoolyard. Rupert even helped Marie tell the college that she wouldn't be utilizing that scholarship after all.

At first, Marie didn't have a single romantic inclination towards him. Of course he was handsome and suave and kind, but he was also fifteen years older than she was and at a whole other stage of life. But he was suddenly there with all of the answers and gifts and flowers and then it was expensive dinners and trips to the cinema and compliments—so many compliments. He loved her soft hair and the way she looked in that dress and how smart she was and how well she cared for Irving and wasn't she going to make an amazing mother one day? He loved her curves and her sense of style and how kind she was and how she knew how to talk to just about anyone. Just when she needed a boost in confidence the most, Rupert was right there, ready to give it to her.

"You're mine now," he said, smiling at her softly as he took her hand in his. "I will never let you go."

Marie took a job doing bookwork for a mechanic and Rupert insisted on loaning her the money to cover what she couldn't manage in the first month, and then it was two. When she asked how on earth he could afford all of this, he smiled and told her his family had money.

Just three months after her parents died, Rupert took Marie out to dinner in the nicest restaurant in the town and he gave her the biggest bunch of flowers she'd ever seen and he showed her a heavy silver ring with nine sparkling diamonds clustered in the shape of a daisy.

"It just makes the most sense. You can quit that terrible job—it's making you so miserable. Let me look after you," he urged her. The bookkeeping job wasn't exactly her life's dream but she had been enjoying it. Hadn't she? Why was Rupert so sure she hated it? Sensing her hesitation, he came up with the best argument of all—the one that sealed the deal and convinced her to say yes. "Irving needs a father figure, Marie. He will come live with us until he finishes school and I'll help him get his life back on track."

They eloped just two weeks after Rupert proposed and honeymooned in Tijuana, which felt like a dream to Marie. But as news of the marriage spread upon their return home, she found the people she had known her whole life didn't react at all as she expected them to. Everyone she told—from the men at the station who knew both Rupert and her father, to her boss at the mechanic's when she quit her job, and even the principal at the high school—reacted the same way. They got a look of frozen shock on their faces, like they wanted so desperately to say something but just couldn't form the words.

She put it together slowly. Through whispers she overheard here and there and a little bit of deduction, she eventually came to the conclusion that Rupert was running some secondary operation outside of his work at the station. He worked much longer hours than her father ever had. He had much more money than her father ever had. And sometimes, Rupert would come home hours late from his shift, with bruised knuckles and spatters of blood on his clothing. The phone was always ringing at all hours of the day and night. The shrill burst of sound would wake her but Rupert would leap out of bed and run down the hall to answer from the second phone in his study, not the one in the hall outside their bedroom. If she crept out to follow him and stood at the door, she'd hear the hum of his voice down low.

"Rupert," she asked one night, ready to hear some perfectly logical and legal explanation for all of this. "Those calls you take. And the extra hours you do sometimes—"

"Sweetheart," he said gently. "We have our roles in this marriage. Your role is to run the house. To cook the meals. To clean. When the time comes, to raise our children. My role is to bring home the money to enable us to live in such a beautiful home. To ensure we can have not one but two nice cars." He owned a Dodge Royal when she met him, but he'd recently purchased her an AMC Rambler station wagon of her very own. "How I do that is not your concern."

As much as Marie was confused by all of this, she wasn't at all sure what to do about it. Her inclination was to keep her eyes peeled. To try to figure it all out over time. There would inevitably be some innocent explanation and she'd feel foolish and embarrassed for doubting Rupert. After all, he was her white knight in shining armor, and everything else was perfect. She and Irving had moved into Rupert's beautiful home and Irving did indeed start to turn things around at school.

And Marie knew her brother adored Rupert. He told her so, and often.

"I want a house just like this one day," he said.

"You live here already, silly."

"No, I want my own house like this. A beautiful wife. Loads of money. Rupert is the kind of guy who makes things happen and I want to be like that too."

The adoration in her brother's eyes when he spoke about her new husband eased the last of Marie's discontent, and for a while, she successfully ignored her concerns about Rupert's "business."

The first shift came when Irving started to pull away from Marie. Even in those troubled early months after the accident he still talked to her about his grief and his anger and his fear for the future, but now he seemed to be going out of his way to avoid her. When she tried to check in about his homework or his laundry or where he was going on a Friday night, he'd clam up, or lash out.

"You're my sister," he'd snap. "Not my mother. Leave me alone."

Rupert told her it would pass and so Marie tried to be patient, but then one ordinary afternoon Irving came home from school and pushed himself up to sit on her clean countertop. She waved a tea towel at him in warning, but he ignored her.

"Now, sis, don't overreact," he began carefully. "I dropped out today."

"What?" She genuinely thought she'd misheard him, but it only got worse.

"I know I'm in your way here and it's better for me to stand on my own two feet."

Marie tried her best to change his mind. Even Rupert said he'd tried to talk to him about it, but Irving would not listen. He moved out two weeks after that, into a dingy apartment he shared with several young men, and he started work at the diner.

CHAPTER 3

Fiona

"There's good news, and bad news," the older electrician declares, startling me out of my reverie as I sit reading at the farmhouse table. "The good news is, I didn't see any ghosts."

"That *is* good news," I say wryly as I shut the book and set it on the table. They've been at it for under an hour and he told me it would take all day, so I look at him warily and ask, "Is the rest all bad news?"

"I was kidding about the bad news. This whole house was rewired fairly recently, maybe ten or fifteen years ago. Looks like they even put a new hot water system in at the same time too, which will save you a heap of hassle. So, you can reconnect the power safely whenever you please."

"Wait—no," I say, looking at him blankly. There's no way Tad would have undertaken such a big project—not without a whole lot of grumbling and complaining and trying to figure out a way to avoid it. If he had rewired the house and replaced that hot water unit, I'd know about it, because he would have called me for advice.

"Come see," the electrician says and shrugs. I follow him out the front door and realize the apprentice is already sitting in the car, studiously avoiding my gaze as we pass. The older guy notices and mutters, "My kid has heard a few too many stories about this place. He's glad we'll be out of here quickly."

At the circuit box, I'm distracted first by the spiderwebs, and then the spiders, which are everywhere. I take a step back automatically, suppressing a shudder. The electrician remains undaunted. He lifts the cover and points inside, and I gasp in surprise to see a neatly organized collection of modern safety switches. Not an old-style fuse in sight.

"What the . . . ?" I mutter, blinking in disbelief.

"This model of safety switch they've used here? They came out when I was an apprentice myself, and that was fifteen years ago, so the wiring can't be any older than that. But the hot water system is a model we were installing around the time I qualified, so putting it all together, I reckon that places this work at about twelve years old. And it does make sense they'd rewire the whole place because it looks a whole lot like the house almost burned down at one point," the electrician says, and he crouches, pointing towards the bottom corner of the new circuit box. I crouch too and wince, first at several large redback spiders, then again at the sight of smoke damage and bubbled paint behind them. "Given the age of the house, it was probably lousy with that old-style Indian Vulcanized Rubber wiring. The rubber decays over time until it just crumbles into dust. I still see it in old houses like this sometimes—" he winks at me and points to the charring on the brickwork again "—usually because I get called in to rewire after they almost burn down."

"But . . ." I was so certain that the house would have its original wiring, I didn't even think to check the circuit box myself. I'm no electrician, but even I would have recognized the new tech in there.

"Run a heap of water through that hot water system. It

looks okay, but if it's been sitting unused for ten years, you'll want to flush it well. And you might still run into trouble with it, there's no guarantees. Probably just expect to replace it at some point in the next few years even if it does work now."

"Right," I say. "Thanks."

"Best of luck to you with this place—I reckon you might need it."

After he leaves, I slip my phone from my pocket to text Jon.

> Did you know there was a fire here at some point?!

Before Dad bought the house? he replies.

> No, sometime recently. Probably a few years before he died?

Not that I know of, he writes.

I bend gingerly, trying to avoid the spiders as I extend my phone to take a photo of the charred paint beneath the new switch box. A few seconds after I send it, Jon calls. I explain about the age of the safety switches, and then we sit on the line in stunned silence for a while, trying to make sense of it all.

"Why wouldn't Dad tell us about this?" Jon finally asks.

"I have no idea."

"You know what he was like. He was so stubborn about maintenance on that place."

"He most likely had no choice in this case," I say. If anything, Tad was probably lucky the fire started down here against the brick, and not against the flammable wood in the ceiling, or in one of the internal walls. The whole place would have gone up like a tinderbox. I shiver at the thought.

"Your mum would know the whole story," Jon says.

He's right—she probably does. Mum didn't just run the business side of Tad's career; she basically ran his whole life.

"Well, I'm not asking her today," I mutter.

Wurimbirra stands a few kilometres from the outskirts of Forbes, a small town towards the center of New South Wales. It's a quaint place with less than eight thousand residents, a town built around a picturesque lake which wreaks havoc and splits the township into three islands during semiregular floods. This is a region of sheep and wheat farms, of kangaroos and brush-tail possums, of river red gum and yellow box trees. Phoenix palms introduced to the region dot the landscape, including across the front of Wurimbirra's yard. It's a species somehow now synonymous with Forbes, despite being native to the Canary Islands, some eighteen thousand kilometres away.

I've booked a hotel by the lake for the next three weeks, assuming it would take at least that long to get the wiring sorted. When I check in, I tell them there's been a change of plans, and if I can get the power connected to Wurimbirra over the next few days, I'll be able to cancel most of the booking.

I still can't believe my luck. The modern wiring feels very much like a good omen.

It's too late for lunch but too early for dinner, so I help myself to some junk food from a vending machine on my way to the room, but I promise myself I'll start eating better once I'm settled in Wurimbirra. I'm neck deep in menopause and I've stress-eaten my way to a whole new shape over the past few months.

The year started out with so much promise. Until late February, I lived with my youngest daughter, Mia, and my husband, Lucas, in a remodeled California bungalow in Waverly, in Sydney's east, not far from the famous Bondi Beach. I was the principal architect of the award-winning architectural heritage firm I co-founded with Lucas and our best friend, Keira. Our eighty-odd employees worked out of three offices: one in Melbourne and one in Adelaide, and the largest in Edgecliff, just a ten-minute drive from our home. I thought I'd be spending this year fully engrossed in challenging projects and I wasn't dismayed about that at all because I had always loved my job.

Mia fled the nest in February, to live on campus at the University of Sydney, where she had been accepted into a competitive medicine program. Caitlin was already living in an apartment just off campus there—she followed in my footsteps when she graduated high school a few years ago, taking on an architecture degree.

The day after we finished moving Mia into her dorm, Lucas sat me down and told me that he and Keira had fallen in love. My marriage ended in a single conversation, and it quickly became obvious that my best friend and my husband had already put plans in place to force me out of our business too. They'd already had lawyers draft a proposal to buy me out with a financial settlement that was, at least, generous—even if it came complete with a non-compete clause that means I can't work in heritage architecture for at least five years.

Marriage and career gone in an instant. Just as my youngest child left home.

Keira and Lucas wanted to tell our staff and clients that I was leaving because of "health issues." I wanted to tell them I was "forced out of my own business because my husband and best friend were having an affair right under my nose like the slimy rodents they apparently are." Our lawyers managed to find a compromise at "Fiona has left W&J Heritage to pursue exciting new opportunities."

I stopped coloring my hair right after Lucas moved into Keira's house, at first because I was too depressed to get myself out of bed and to the salon, and then because it just felt like it was time. I grew out a few months' worth of my now-natural grey, then last week, I went in and had my hairdresser cut the long bob I'd worn for decades into a pixie cut. I'm not sure if this bold new look I'm sporting is because I'm feeling free and brave at this stage of my separation, or if it's a clear sign that I'm halfway to some kind of mental breakdown.

After I've showered to get the dust out of my hair, I dress in fresh clothes and I sit on the bed with my notepad and pen to figure out a list of tasks I need to complete over what's left of the afternoon. Just the thought of those spiders around the switch box has me fumbling for my phone to schedule the pest controller first. I don't love the idea of chemicals or killing the things, but I have to be practical here—I'm deathly afraid of spiders and I'm going to be out there alone.

There are only a few options here in town, so I call the first result on Google, and a friendly-sounding man takes the call. He seems keen to help, especially after I explain the situation, and tells me he can come tomorrow to take a look. Then I give him the address.

"That's not . . ." He pauses. "That's not that haunted place, is it?"

"It's not haunted."

"Everyone knows there's something not right about that house. I heard that famous author that lived out there died of fright."

"That's my uncle you're talking about, and he died of an aneurysm after living happily and safely in that house for over forty years."

"Oh," the exterminator says, then there's an awkward pause, and he clears his throat. "It's just I heard . . . you know . . . that there had been trouble out there."

"Yes, I know what people say," I sigh. "But the house is perfectly safe, except for a heap of spiders. Please can you help?"

Eventually he agrees to come out to spray the exterior of

the house first thing tomorrow. I tick off the first item on my to-do list, then call to arrange delivery of some firewood, a necessity because the house only has fireplaces for heating. I'm fortunate to find a local vendor who can deliver a load of wood sometime over the next few days—and that just leaves the most important task—the electricity reconnection.

At first the power company tells me they'll need two to three business days to reconnect, but the customer service representative is surprisingly sympathetic when I explain the dust situation and how desperately I need an operational vacuum cleaner. She puts in a rush order for me and tells me it'll be done tomorrow.

The last items on my to-do list are to order the delivery of an extra-large dumpster, and then I drive to the rent-all place, and book a few industrial air filters and a commercial vacuum for the next few weeks. The clerk does pause for a moment when I give him the address, but tells me his driver will meet me at Wurimbirra tomorrow morning.

It's really happening. This time tomorrow, I'll be home for good. The very thought of that makes me so happy, even if my smile fades a little when I think back to that call with my cousin, and that confrontation with my mother on the front steps this afternoon.

CHAPTER 4

Fiona

I wake slowly to the sounds of the birds in the trees outside of my hotel window. For just a brief moment as I hover between sleep and consciousness, the warbling of magpies and the screeching of cockatoos and the laughter of the kookaburras makes me homesick for Wurimbirra, but then I remember: today is the day I move in.

The thought leaves me restless with a combination of anxiety and excitement and I am soon crawling out of my skin—it's not quite dawn, but I just can't wait another minute to start moving. I pack what little I removed from my suitcase, check out in anticipation of the electricity reconnection today and hit the road.

The sun is rising over the wide main street, casting the old buildings in a red-gold glow. Like the birdsong with the dawn, there are some things I have always associated with home, and the unique streetscape of Forbes is one of them. Until last year there was a three-story pub on this street which had been here since the 1860s—150 years of history, dating back to the days when that pub was a stagecoach rest stop and tunnels were built between it and a nearby bank after a spate of bushranger attacks. A freak fire took the pub down last year, and I'm still not used to the empty space. Everything else is much as I remember it. Change is, usually, reassuringly slow out here.

I turn down a side street and park beside a small group of people waiting on the footpath. They're in an orderly line that leads to the cafe nestled within Turn the Page. Some customers are chatting quietly, some looking down at their phones. I don't recognize any of the faces as I join the line at the back and wait my turn, but I wonder if that will be different this time next year.

I'm expecting to see the owner of the store, Marilyn Owens, working at the coffee machine. As I get closer I see there's a younger woman working this morning. She's probably in her late twenties or early thirties, with long, wavy red hair and a delicate stud in her nose.

"Oh hi, Fiona!" she says, giving me a surprised smile when I reach the front of the line. "I heard you're moving back to Wurimbirra." She does look vaguely familiar, but when I glance at her name tag, the name Aurelia does not ring a single bell.

"I am," I say, unsurprised that this complete stranger knows who I am and what my business is. This is just how it goes in a small place like Forbes. If you dig deep enough, you'll find that everyone has some link to just about everyone else, and I have one obvious, important connection to this very store—I worked here for a few years in the '70s, before I moved away for university. Tad was determined to pay for my education, just as he has done and is still doing for my girls, courtesy of the trust fund he set up for them. But Mum was adamant I should learn how to balance study and work, and how to successfully manage a budget. When I was fifteen, she told me I had to get a job.

"I know plenty of people who want babysitters," she suggested, and I heard that as a menacing threat, so that afternoon

I rode my bike to the bookstore and begged Marilyn Owens for work. This was long before the store expanded to include a cafe, and most of the time I was shelving or stickering books, but I loved every minute I spent working here.

Maybe Marilyn has mentioned me to Aurelia or maybe she's the daughter of someone I grew up with or maybe she knows my mother. Maybe she's a complete stranger who heard through the grapevine that Taddeus Winslow's niece was going to brave the ghosts and try to restore the house. It doesn't really matter how she recognizes me or what she knows of my story. Out here in the country, people notice things. It's not always idle gossip—there's a collective wisdom shared in small towns, a web of observation and concern that strengthens a community so that no one is truly alone and no one gets left behind.

Sometimes I wonder if this was why Uncle Tad went to such lengths to make sure people in this town thought he had a whole army of spirits living with him in Wurimbirra. Without some way to keep the community at arm's length, they'd have marched right into his sanctuary. My uncle loved people—but he loved them best when he could observe them on his own terms, often from afar. I understand that better right now than I did when I was a kid. I want privacy and space at the moment, but I know there are plenty of people in this town who will want to embrace me, especially once they hear why I'm back. I'm still in touch with some school friends, and I haven't even told them I'm coming home because I know the minute they find out, they'll suffocate me with well-intentioned efforts to help.

"Tell Marilyn I said hi," I say to Aurelia when I collect my coffee a few minutes later.

"She works the afternoon shift now because we run a lot of evening book clubs." Aurelia smiles. "Call past one day—I know she'll be glad to see you."

"I will," I promise, and I walk slowly back to my car, sipping the coffee, the sun on my skin and a smile on my face. I'm at the grocery store when it opens at 7:00 a.m., and I fill a trolley with still more cleaning products and a few dozen energy efficient light bulbs and enough shelf-stable food to keep me going until I have the fridge set up.

Soon I'm driving again. I pass Victoria Park, and smile at the sight of the immense old town hall, the library, the beautiful old courthouse. I take the bridge over the lake, and just a few minutes later I am through town and turning down Flint Street, where Jon and Aunt Daph used to live, and then I'm onto Reymond Street and over the Iron Bridge. Uncle Tad used to drive me to school sometimes and every time we crossed this bridge, he had a different tale to tell about the trolls who lived beneath it. Like the ghosts he invented in Wurimbirra, those bridge trolls were friendly and silly and often hilarious.

The sheer relief I feel to be back on these familiar streets, passing these landmarks I know as well as I know myself, is almost indescribable. There's something about the place you grow up. It imprints on you. Gets into your bones.

I've spent a lot of time feeling lost this year. So much time distracting myself whenever I thought of Lucas and Keira and all of the unexpected changes they forced upon my life, because it hurt too much to think it through and to face the way they hurt me.

Maybe now that I'm home, I can process all of that properly, feel the full force of my anger and frustration, and maybe eventually lay it to bed.

There's an empty dumpster just beside the driveway at Wurimbirra by the time I arrive, and the pest controller is already busy spraying the spiders. He gives me a wave from beneath his protective gear and I wave back, then let myself inside. The first thing I notice in the entryway is that the lamps are on, which means the power is already connected. The water from the hot tap is lukewarm, which means the unit is working, and by tonight I'll be able to take a shower.

The rental equipment arrives next. The young delivery driver is jumpy as he looks at the house and is exceedingly unconvincing when he tells me it's "company policy" that he can't carry the equipment inside, but he does place the three air filters and the vacuum right at the front door, so I let him get away with it.

The next few hours pass in a blur of whirring air filters and the hum of the commercial vacuum. I'm replacing the most essential light globes with the energy efficient variety, and making hurried trips outside to dump the obvious rubbish into the bin, then making just as many trips to the laundry to refresh the mop water. But by the time the movers' truck pulls in the driveway, the pest controller is done, I've cleaned out most of my old bedroom and have scrubbed a great big patch of the floor in the ballroom.

The house is every bit as dusty as it seemed to be yesterday. I'm realizing I will probably need to bring in some help to tackle the cleaning at some point, but for now, I'll break the job up into the most essential tasks, and the frenetic energy feels *good*.

By 5:00 p.m., the crew of three movers has unloaded the whole truck—most of it into that semiclean part of the ballroom, where boxes are stacked high beside furniture I'm not entirely sure I need given I have all of Tad's, but that I loved too much to leave for Lucas. The movers have shifted Tad's ancient fridge, washing machine and my old bed frame and mattress into the dumpster, and they've installed the modern replacements I've brought with me from Waverly. While they worked, I've unpacked the first few boxes of my clothes into my old chest of drawers and wardrobe in my bedroom.

I'm now standing on the front veranda, watching as the movers stow their trolleys and packing blankets back into the truck. An unfamiliar white truck pulls in the drive, headlights on, as the sun is low on the horizon and it's starting to get dark. The truck parks behind the movers and I squint, trying to identify the tall man who steps out. He offers a friendly wave as he approaches me and my stomach drops as I recognize him. It couldn't be—

But no, it *is*.

That's Jakób Krzyżanowski, or as he was more commonly known back in high school, Jack K, because Forbes in the 1960s and '70s wasn't exactly the kind of place where people made the effort to learn how to pronounce unfamiliar names.

Jack grew up on one of the two three-hundred-acre farms which adjoin this property. His family's land was originally part of Wurimbirra's parcel—Charles Fowler subdivided it into three plots as he grew older, carving off this one-acre block for himself, and giving his two eldest sons three hundred acres each. Jack's childhood home is at the western edge of their property, so it's not exactly close, but just within bicycling distance for us as kids.

We were great friends up until about year eight, when I looked across at him one ordinary Saturday morning as we were watching the television at his place, and my heart started to race and I thought I was going to throw up. It took me an embarrassingly long time to realize that I was not, in fact, suffering from some sudden-onset allergy to Jack's presence, but that I was instead suffering from something much worse—my very first crush. It was a wild, unpredictable thing, leaving me just about struck mute at times which made no sense at all because Jack and I had been friends since preschool.

I hated that crush. I hated how out of control it made me feel, how foolish I was certain it made me look. I convinced myself that I could outrun the infatuation—all I had to do was refuse to acknowledge it even to myself. There was no avoiding Jack—not altogether. Our senior cohort at Forbes High School was a grand total of fourteen kids, so there was no hiding from him there, and even after Mum married Alan and we moved out of Wurimbirra, my new house was only closer to Jack's because Alan's farm adjoins Jack's on the other edge.

Even so, I managed to put some distance between us during high school and in time, things did get easier to manage. I've bumped into him over the years, and I loosely know the trajectory of his life. Graduated from his veterinary science degree with honors, went on to some kind of specialist postgrad study—maybe it was something to do with cows?—married another vet, moved somewhere remote. His parents still run their farm as far as I know. That's probably why he's in town.

Jack is closer now and his eyes widen as he finally recognizes me.

"Fiona Winslow? What the—"

"Hi," I say, giving an awkward little wave. I pull my hand down and jam it into my pocket.

"I saw the moving truck as I was driving past and wanted to check in on the place—I thought Jon might have sold it at last!"

"He did," I say wryly, and then I shrug. "To me."

"Well, isn't this something?" he says, laughing softly. He's close enough now that he opens his arms and we briefly hug. I have never understood how Jack can smell so good, especially in his line of work. Shouldn't he smell like cows or sweat or dog food or something? He never seems to and it's quite unfair. I take a surreptitious sniff of his neck and feel a flush on my cheeks.

"Are you home visiting your folks?" I ask him as we part.

"It's a little more permanent than that. Dad's not well."

"I'm sorry to hear that," I say, then I cringe. "Not sorry that you're home, just that your dad is sick."

It's always been like this with Jack since that stupid crush. I am an intelligent, reasonable woman. I can converse with just about anyone. The second I open my mouth around this man, all of that disappears. There's something about his presence that short-circuits my brain, even now.

"I knew what you meant," he says, then he looks up at the house behind me and a soft smile covers his face. "Look at us, neighbors again after all these years. We'll have to catch up properly. Maybe you and Lucas could come over for dinner sometime."

"Oh . . ." This time my cringe is more of a full-body contraction. "Ah, no. It's just me now. We . . . ah . . . yeah. We're divorcing."

I have told *some* people. Just not many, and fewer in person. It's still so raw and I am so embarrassed at how it all unfolded—how didn't I see what was happening between them? Keira was my best friend. I had often thought of her as a platonic soulmate—she was the yin to my yang, at work and at home. And Lucas and I had been together for almost twenty-five years. How could they *do* this to me?

"Shit. Sorry, Fi," Jack says softly. "Divorce is rough. I know from experience."

"You and Winnie—"

I hadn't heard this news. Then again, I haven't exactly been visiting Forbes much so I'm probably behind on lots of gossip.

"Winnie stayed up in the Pilbara when I moved home two years ago. It was rough, but it was also time for us to go our separate ways, you know? Is this recent for you?"

"Very," I say, but the word comes out rough, and to my

horror, I could almost cry. Why *now*? I will not go to water in front of this man; I simply won't. I force the tears down through sheer force of will and even manage something like a smile. "But I'm fine. Honestly."

"And you're going to be here all alone?" he says, eyebrows high. I frown at his tone, and he hastily adds, "It makes sense, of course, being a brilliant architect as you are and this house being in need of some specialist love. I just meant— Here." He reaches into his pocket and withdraws his phone, then hands it to me. "Call yourself so we can save one another's numbers. I know you're plenty capable, but I'm right next door if you need help reaching a high shelf or something."

"That's kind of you," I say as I type my number in, let it ring, then hang up. "But I'm sure I'll be fine."

"So, still not the type to ask for help, huh?" Jack saves my number then gives me a breathtaking smile. "It's great to see you, Fi. And if you need anything—help around the house, or just to talk—*please* do reach out. I get how tough it is, I really do."

Jack has always been like this—he's just so easy to like. No wonder he's been addling my brain since my first flush of puberty hormones hit. It didn't help that when *his* first flush of puberty hormones hit, that scrawny kid with deep brown eyes too big for his face and frizzy, dirty-blond hair skipped the awkward in-between phases and seemed to become a man overnight.

We were both born in 1960 so I know he'll be turning fifty in a few months. His hair has faded over the years and there's some grey in it, and it's scattered through the neat beard he wears too. Just like his smooth adolescent transition, he's only become more dignified as he enters middle age. I reach up and self-consciously touch my own hair and wish I were wearing something more glamorous than exceedingly dusty active wear.

"Thanks, Jack," I say. "Tell your parents I said hi."

"Shall do." He pulls me in for another hug, this time a little tighter. The temptation to completely melt into him has me flushing again, and I'm more than a little relieved when he releases me, waves goodbye and turns back to his car.

It's an unexpected complication that Jack is home, but it won't be too difficult to avoid him. I'm here to lick my wounds and to heal in private. The very last thing I need is to find myself bumping into someone who has been scrambling my brain for almost forty years.

The house seems so still after Jack and the movers leave at the same time. It suddenly feels so real—that I'm here, alone, and that this is my home again, and I have to sort all of this dusty chaos into order somehow. The immensity of the challenge is overwhelming. Thinking about it is like flicking an elastic band on my wrist—a flash of discomfort to distract myself from thinking about the truly painful things in my life.

Now that my belongings have arrived, I find the box of linen to make up my bed so it's ready for tonight. I set up an electric oil heater in my room and turn it on high. There's not much I can do about the chill in the air throughout the rest of the house until the firewood arrives, so I pull on an extra sweater. At least the room will be toasty by the time I go to bed.

On my way back downstairs I stop to wind the grandfather clock, smiling to myself as the second hand immediately begins to tick. The hourly chimes were part of the soundtrack to my childhood—maybe I'll notice them when I'm trying to sleep tonight, but they'll quickly fade into the background just as they did when I was a kid. I head back to the kitchen and pause long enough to raid the groceries I picked up this morning, which I've stashed in the old ice chest to keep them safe from potential rodents. I succumb to the temptation of potato chips, but promise myself this will be the *very* last time I eat like a teenager. I have a fridge now, so tomorrow I'll stock it with lean protein. Green things. Grown-up food.

I look around the long kitchen, cast in shades of yellow from the new bulbs in the dusty pendant lights, and a smile breaks over my face, despite the mess. I'll replace the glass in those long windows—maybe the same style, if I can get them double glazed. I'll redesign the cabinets. Maybe add an era-appropriate rug under the farmhouse table, and some stronger lighting, and a fresh paint job.

In time, it's going to be amazing. For now, I need to tackle the mess in that disaster of a pantry, so I roll up my sleeves and get to work.

As the last light of the day fades, the house seems to come alive. It's noisy in old houses—wood that expands during the day contracts during the night, so there are cracks and pops and mystery sounds as the cold night air settles. It's charming at first but it doesn't take long before I'm startling a little at the louder cracks, and straining to make sense of the quieter sounds. It doesn't help that the house is bitterly cold, and I don't even have a radio or television to turn on to distract me. I spent sixteen years here and I don't remember being aware of those noises before, but the house must have always been noisy like this. I've just forgotten. That's all.

I take a breath and calmly acknowledge that this is going to feel very odd until I get used to the house again. The only way out is through, as Tad would have said. I just have to ride out the first few days.

I try to distract myself with the cleaning. There's a cast iron wood stove and oven in the corner of the kitchen, surrounded by a brick mantel, plus the cream Wedgewood electric stove and double oven Uncle Tad installed in the '50s. They are oddly beautiful, each representing an era in the life of this old house.

They are also disgustingly dirty, especially the Wedgewood, so I focus on scrubbing every square inch of it. Next I clear some countertops and set up my espresso machine and kettle, then I move on to cleaning out one of Uncle Tad's cupboards. Lots of the glassware I find can be thrown away, but I rinse some of the nicer pieces in scalding-hot water and leave them lined up on tea-towels along the cleaned countertops to dry overnight.

By 10:00 p.m., I am so exhausted I can barely keep my eyes open.

"That's enough for today," I murmur to myself, and for some reason, the sound of my own voice echoing back through that big old kitchen reminds me that *this is my life now.*

Lucas and I won't ever do that big European trip we always talked about, but never found the time to plan. I'll never walk back into my beautiful office in Edgecliff, or chair the all-hands staff meeting, or even ride the excitement of a potential new project after a client kick-off meeting. Maybe I'll never work like that again—if I have to stay in this retirement for five years, do I really want to start again at fifty-five, especially if I don't need the money?

And now that my beautiful daughters are off finding their feet in the world, I'll never wake on a Saturday morning to the TV on just a little too loud in the living room, to a kitchen already trashed with half-eaten bowls of Froot Loops and coffees made with far too much sugar.

That era of my life is over and done. And *this* is what my life is going to look like—me all alone in this big old house, with only the dust to keep me company and framework creaking and crackling the soundtrack to my lonely nights.

The sheer weight of all this change settles on me, until I feel like it might crush me into still more dust on this kitchen floor. I don't fight the tears, because I have been promising myself for months that I could cry once I was back to Wurimbirra.

I turn off the lights downstairs and make my way up the staircase to my bedroom, quietly sobbing as I go. When I push the door open I expect the room to be warm and cozy, for it to greet me like the warm hug I so desperately need.

My bedroom is no warmer than the rest of the house.

I walk across to check the little oil heater, cathartic tears once again on hold, and am baffled to see the switch is off.

I turned it on, didn't I?

I'm quite sure I did.

It is such a silly thing to feel unnerved about, but I'm sure I can remember turning that heater on and now it's off and the house is creaking and I'm all alone out here and the reason I'm all alone is because Lucas and Keira betrayed me and why did it have to be with each other? If he'd had an affair with anyone else I'd still have my best friend, and if *she* had fallen in love with anyone else it wouldn't have been a problem at all. And yet they had to choose one another and that means they didn't just betray me; I lost them both, and in some ways, *they* were my world. And although my mum is two minutes' drive down the road now, emotionally she may as well be on the moon and what am I even *doing* here?

I turn the heater on. I clean my teeth in the dusty bathroom sink, then slip into bed. I'm too wound up to sleep, too cold to brave the shower in that icy bathroom, too on edge to even cry.

After lying awake for a while, listening as the grandfather clock chimes 11:00 p.m., then midnight, I walk back downstairs, turning on every light as I go. I pick up the copy of *The Midnight Estate*, take it back to bed and curl up to read, hoping a distraction will put my mind at ease.

Maybe Uncle Tad read this book and saw a message or some wisdom or a parable he knew I'd one day need, and maybe if I immerse myself in the story, I'll find a glimmer of comfort to stretch across into my real life.

THE MIDNIGHT ESTATE

BY CHARITY WILKIE

Silas had Mrs Ristevra call him a cab and he went straight to the hospital. When he arrived he was quickly ushered from the reception area towards the intensive care ward, and with every step, his feet felt heavier.

"Is she very unwell?" he asked a nurse, who avoided his gaze and told him that the doctor would be with him shortly. He was briefly alone in a brightly lit room with an oddly domestic air—the scent of coffee in the air from the pot, the hum of a refrigerator, plush lounges with colorful cushions. Silas was too wound up to sit so he stood beside the coffeepot, shifting his weight from one foot to the other. He was exhausted so the coffee called to him, but he knew caffeine would only make his anxiety worse.

Dr Lomas entered the room, closing the door behind him. He had been the family's doctor since Silas was a baby.

"Good to see you, son," he said quietly, and he reached to shake Silas's hand. "Can I get you coffee? Maybe juice or water—I could have someone get you something to eat?"

The gentle, sympathetic tone the doctor employed only made Silas panic more. He shoved his hands into his pockets but then his trousers felt too tight and so he pulled them out and wrapped them over his chest. It was suddenly hard to breathe, so he dropped his hands to his side.

Dr Lomas motioned for him to take a seat, but Silas shook his head.

"Please," he said, voice strangled. "Please just tell me Maeve is okay."

"We wanted to telegram you, Silas. No one could figure out where to reach you."

"Maeve knew," Silas croaked.

"That wasn't much help to us when she was unconscious," the doctor said, not unkindly. "She is very unwell, son. In a coma, in fact."

"A coma? From influenza?" Silas was baffled. What kind of monstrous strain of the flu had taken out his mother and his sister? The doctor's expression softened.

"Your mother passed from the influenza, yes. But Maeve . . ."

For one terrifying moment, Silas thought the doctor was going to tell him that Maeve had harmed herself. That Silas's absence and the immense stress of everything that had happened with their mother had left her so mentally fragile that she just couldn't cope. It hit him at once—the grief, the exhaustion, the wild year he was living through.

He was trying not to think about it, but the truth was, even his relationship with Christine had been rocky of late. She was unhappy and he knew she was unhappy and he knew it was his fault and yet he could not figure out how to fix it. He had broken his family to follow Christine, only to break his family with Christine too.

Silas sank down onto the sofa and dropped his head into his hands. The doctor sat quietly opposite him.

"It was the diabetes, Silas," Dr Lomas said, and Silas was surprised by this, but also relieved. He didn't know much about diabetes except that it was treatable. Maeve would adjust in time, and of course, he could stay a while and help her get used to the insulin injections.

"Right," Silas said. "It's not great news, obviously, but she's tough, and I'll help her adjust. Can I see her?"

"Wait— No," the doctor said, frowning. "Surely you knew? She was diagnosed five years ago."

All of a sudden, Silas saw that last conversation he'd had with Maeve through a very different lens. He'd been away for six months and he'd come back home to find his sister so drawn. So desperate to convince him to stay.

He had put all of this down to Maeve's personality. But now, looking back through time, he felt so stupid. Maeve was bright and emotional and vivacious, but she wasn't needy. If anything, she was a woman who perpetually gave too much. She had begged him to stay not because she resented him for living his own life but because she was dealing with a health crisis, and she was scared to face it alone. He briefly wondered why Linda hadn't told him, but then other memories rose in his mind. Linda had been every bit as baffled over Maeve's refusal to travel as Silas himself had been. Silas was immediately sure of it: Maeve never told their mother. If she had, Linda would have told Silas right away.

"Maeve was unwell with the influenza when I saw her at your mother's funeral," Dr Lomas explained gently. "I sent her home to rest but it can be very difficult to manage insulin during times of extreme stress and particularly when unwell. There is no way of knowing exactly what happened to her—only that one of Maeve's friends became concerned that she was not answering the phone and went around check on her. Thank God she did because Maeve had gone into a hypoglycemic coma."

"She didn't take enough insulin?"

"She took too much. Most likely she miscalculated her dose and because she was so unwell, she didn't recognize the signs of her sugar dropping too low. Her body—her brain—was starved of the glucose it needed to function."

"And now she is . . ."

"That's right, she's in a coma, son. I'm so sorry."

"Can't you just give her more sugar, or more insulin, or—"

"If we'd caught her right away, yes, glucose would have solved the problem. But we don't know how long she was there before she was found. It's possible—maybe even likely—that she has suffered some degree of brain damage. We won't know until she wakes up." Lomas paused, then added very gently, "If she wakes up."

Dr Lomas walked Silas down the hall and left him alone in the room with his sister. Maeve looked like she was asleep, lying flat on her back with her arms straight down beside her torso, on top of the stiff, starchy hospital blankets. Silas sat beside her and took her cold hand in his and he started to cry.

"Why didn't you tell me?"

But he already suspected the answer to that question. She had given him plenty of clues that something was wrong—he had just been so caught up in that first flush of love for Christine that he missed them.

Silas sat down and wrote Christine a letter.

> I know you're not happy and this is an awful time for me to be away. And I am so sorry I can't say when I'll be home, but Maeve is unwell and she needs me right now. Please know that I love you and Ernest more than anything. I will be back with you as soon as I can and we can still fix things. I know we can.

When he left, Silas had promised Christine he would only be gone a week or two. His wife was kind and loving and supportive, but she she had been trying to force him to talk through their issues for some time by then. Just a few days before the telegram came from Maeve, Christine had moved out of their home.

Of course he'd heard her whenever she said "we need to talk," but his work consumed him, always, and so at first he simply did not notice the intensity of her tone, and even once he did, his natural inclination was to hide from it. One of the things that most surprised him about married life was the way that parts of Christine's psyche forever remained a mystery to him—moods that seemed to come and go without warning, motivations and desires he could never quite unpack. He'd imagined that once a person met their soulmate, it would all be easy from there. Books about people falling in love often ended at the wedding day—everything that happened from there was simply an epilogue, so how difficult or important could the detail be?

Very important, as it turned out.

When Christine announced she was leaving, he'd assumed she meant she was leaving to go shopping or to spend time with a friend. When he finally realized how serious the situation was, that she was leaving with their son to live with her mother, he panicked and they quarreled and Ernest cried and then Christine said they needed "time apart to cool down."

Silas spent two days working like a maniac, taking breaks only to try to convince himself that Christine was about to waltz through the door any second now. Then the telegram arrived from Maeve, and what was already a bad situation became so much worse.

Silas knew he should have booked an international call to explain the delay to Christine the minute he realized he'd be in America longer than they anticipated, but he still did not quite understand what was broken in their marriage and he had not yet figured out how to fix it. And he had the sense that the second he heard her lovely, soft voice, he would dissolve into a fit of humiliating tears.

The letter would have to suffice for now. At least until he got Maeve back on her feet.

He posted the letter and then settled in, ready to do what it took to get his sister back to full health. He visited the home he'd purchased for his mother but everything about that space spoke of a grief he had not yet even begun to process, and he left within a few minutes. His mother would understand. He would grieve her properly when Maeve was back on her feet.

So he went to stay at his old childhood home. Maeve had such a knack for decorating—the house looked so beautiful, inside and out. He admired the new gardens she'd planted and the lamps she'd placed in each room and the little knick-knacks she'd arranged on just about every surface. He did his best to water her plentiful indoor plants. He cleaned out her fridge, and he answered the phone calls from her friends.

So many phone calls from so many friends.

Maeve always collected friends and Silas soon discovered she had amassed an exhausting number of them. The hospital limited ICU visiting hours for anyone outside of immediate family to a narrow window between 1:00 and 2:00 p.m., and only ever one guest at a time. It was not uncommon for there to be people waiting in the hall to see Maeve, like she was hosting a celebrity meet and greet.

Silas heard all kinds of stories about his sister's life sitting in that hallway. Most were about the people she helped or encouraged or inspired.

"Hardly anyone knew about the diabetes," one of her city hall colleagues told him softly. "She told *me*, but only after my son was diagnosed and I was so worried for him—she wanted me to know he was going to be okay, you know? Your sister is so very proud, Silas. She can't bear to have people pity her—always sees herself as the helper, never the one who needs help. That's why she never told Linda, God rest her soul."

It turned out that Maeve volunteered at her church every minute she got and she was on just about every charity committee in their town. Everyone told him they were praying for her. Silas was not a praying man, but he was glad someone was on the job, just in case.

He did not feel comfortable sleeping in her room. The sheets and the blanket were all twisted, the drapes drawn. There were used cloth handkerchiefs strewn all over the place and bottles of aspirin and half-drunk cups of water on the bedstand and an insulin syringe, just lying right there, out in the open. Was *that* the syringe that made her sick?

He tried to tidy the room a little, but it was just too much, so he shut the door, almost writhing with self-loathing. He should have *been* there for her. Maeve should never have been alone to deal with their mother's death and funeral, especially not when she was unwell herself.

She had converted the other bedroom—the one they used to share—into something of a library, and so Silas slept on the sofa, which was far too soft and too short, but it didn't matter much for the first few nights. He was so shocked and tired he dropped right into unconsciousness the minute he lay flat. And after that, he considered his permanently aching back a kind of penance.

He was at the hospital when the doors opened to visitors at eight and he stayed until they closed again twelve hours later. He sat by her bed and held her hand. He took a cloth and washed her face and hands, hoping the sensation of rough fabric and cold water against her skin would act like the alarm clock that roused him from sleep before sunrise each morning. He brought books from her home library and read to her until his voice was hoarse and his hands ached from holding a book in position for so many hours.

But seven days passed, and Maeve's eyelids didn't so much as flutter. There was no change in her condition at all.

"We may have to start to face facts—" Dr Lomas said, but Silas, who was as mild-mannered as a man could be, snapped at him.

"The facts are that Maeve is unwell and that she needs more time. They are the only relevant facts."

Dr Lomas looked at him closely.

"It's your plan to stay, then."

"For the foreseeable future, yes. Until she's back on her feet."

He missed Christine and Ernest so much he ached with the force of it. And Maeve had no shortage of friends breezing through her hospital room every day, but they weren't family. Silas would not let her down again.

"And you'll be here every minute you can until then," Dr Lomas surmised.

"Exactly."

The doctor's expression grew stern.

"Then you had better start making some smarter choices, Silas. You've been here a week and all the nurses have seen you eat in that time is some pudding you took from Mr Williams's tray."

In Silas's defense, Mr Williams, the palliative care patient in the bed opposite Maeve's, had insisted.

"I need to be here when she wakes up."

Something flickered on Dr Lomas's face, and then his expression softened.

"Then you'll want to avoid collapsing with exhaustion or starvation, won't you? You won't be much help to her if you end up a patient yourself. Go visit Carmen at the diner. Her husband, Rodrigo, makes the world's best pancakes and it would be a real shame if you didn't try them at least once."

Silas paused. He was doing a very basic form of math—contemplating the energy it would take to argue with Dr Lomas, comparing it to the energy it would take to obey him.

After a moment, he rose to his feet and told the doctor he would be back in an hour.

Dr Lomas was not wrong about those pancakes. Either they were the fluffiest, sweetest pancakes on earth, or Silas was just famished after a week of existing on the scant staples Maeve kept in her pantry, because that first day he demolished one serving, then right away ordered a second.

After that, Silas took the doctor's advice and adopted a new routine. He was still at the door to Maeve's ward at 8:00 a.m. He still read to her, pausing only to turn away to give her privacy when the nurses came to attend to her care. Around 10:30 a.m., he would close his book and slide it under his arm, he would kiss his sister on her forehead and then he'd walk to the diner. He stayed just long enough for a few cups of coffee and a plate of those truly fantastic pancakes.

Although Silas stared at books all day long when he was reading at his sister's bedside, it was only when he left her side that his mind relaxed enough to absorb what he was reading. Books had been his solace and his comfort for so long that he didn't know how to sit and wait without one in his lap, without his eyes skimming over words, without the comforting sensation of the spine cracking as he pulled it open for the first time, the feel of soft paper beneath his fingers as he turned the page.

When he was at his sister's bedside, it was as though the stress and the worry were so complete that his mind was full, and the words just went right from his eyes to his mouth. And Maeve didn't seem to be reacting to a single thing he did, so maybe she wasn't hearing him anyway. But Silas kept on reading anyway because even when the words blew right past him, the very act was still a comfort to him. Stories were, and maybe always had been, the only way he knew to exist in the world.

Silas had visited that very same diner as a teen, although it changed hands while he was overseas. What he'd always known as Tom's was now called Carmen's, and truth be told, the decor was a little worse for wear. Maybe it always had been, but eating out was such a treat for him and Maeve back in the day, he would likely never have noticed.

The checkerboard tiles were scuffed and faded to dirty grey. Sputnik lamps stretched across the long ceiling, but many of the bulbs needed replacing, and what remained could have done with a decent dusting. The vinyl of the turquoise booths and matching chairs along the bar was cracked in places, exposing the fabric webbing beneath.

As he ate his pancakes, Silas liked to imagine that the place had once been a cutting-edge example of 1930s accessible American glamour, but dozens or hundreds of patrons passing through that space every day over the ensuing decades had taken a toll. Maybe every single customer had left a little mark on the place, and in doing so, had left a piece of themselves behind.

It had been at least fifteen years since he visited that diner and even then, he was a rare patron, but after a few days of repeat visits, he quickly became a regular and Carmen and Helen knew without asking to put in his pancake order. Best of all, once he opened whatever book he was reading, they left him alone unless he waved them over.

One morning, he was sitting in his booth reading when a young woman took a seat in the next booth. She looked vaguely familiar to Silas, but even after a minute or two, he just couldn't place her. Her eyes scanned the cafe and then settled on a young man, visible through the serving window as he worked in the kitchen. Just then, she glanced across and looked directly at Silas, and her eyes widened with recognition and surprise.

"Oh, hello."

"Hello," he said, then he paused. "I'm sorry, I know I know you but . . ."

"I used to live down the street from you. Maeve babysat me and my brother, Irving, while my mom worked at the nursing home."

"Aha!" he said, nodding, but then he looked across to the young man in the kitchen and frowned. The boy was tall and portly, with severe acne on his face and greasy red-brown hair. "I didn't recognize your brother, I'm sorry." Silas could summon only a vague and distant memory of a charming, precocious little boy who found all sorts of ways to extend his bedtime when Maeve babysat.

"He's changed a lot recently," she said, and there was something in her tone Silas couldn't quite identify. Heaviness. Sadness. Regret. Confusion. He tried the words on, but nothing quite captured it. Silas did this sometimes—narrating his own world, as if he were writing his life down for a book. "Our parents died in a car accident a few years back. It's been rough on him."

"I'm so sorry to hear that," Silas said. "Your father was . . . ?"

"Derek Underwood. He was a police officer. My mother was Gwen."

That's right. When Linda had been anxious after a spate of local break-ins, Derek came over on his own time and checked the locks on her windows and doors.

"I never met your mother, but I remember your father was a very kind man."

"He was," she said, and that's when Silas recognized the younger woman's tone. It *was* heavy, that particular kind of exhaustion that came along with grief. "I'm Marie, by the way."

"Nice to see you again, Marie." Not that he'd ever really met her; he was at least a decade older than she was. He had vague memories of Marie and Irving playing on the street, and when their mom and dad were both working late shifts, Maeve would stay late. On those nights, it was Silas's job to walk down the block to accompany her home. Linda never wanted her teenage daughter walking the streets alone at night.

"How is Maeve these days?" Marie asked.

"She's unwell, I'm afraid," he said, sighing. "I live abroad now. I'm home because she's in the hospital."

"I'm sorry to hear that . . ."

But then Helen came to take her order and Marie asked for a coffee, and then Irving swung by and the siblings had a very brief conversation, just a few monosyllabic responses bandied back and forth. Carmen came out from the kitchen, wiping her hands on her apron, and Marie looked at her watch and stood.

"I'm running late," she said to Carmen. "I'm sorry. Helen was getting me a coffee but I can't—"

"It's fine, sweetheart," Carmen said, tone resigned. "I know how it is. Let's talk another day."

After that, Silas saw Marie at the diner almost every day. She was always impeccably dressed, with her hair set and her face made-up, in pretty skirts in bright colors, and soft cardigans even when the weather was far too warm for her to require one. She sat in the same place most days, and because he too was a creature of habit, they often ended up at their own booths side by side but facing one another.

"Nice weather we are having," he would say, not particularly keen to strike up an extended conversation but also unwilling to be rude.

"There's nothing like the sunshine at this time of year," she would reply, or perhaps, "I heard there's rain on the way—I hope so, the gardens could do with a drink."

She always ordered the same thing—coffee, and she drank it the same way Silas did—black, no creamer or sugar. In Marie's case, she never finished the entire cup because she never stayed very long. Occasionally, her brother would come to her table and speak with her: "How are you?" "Great. And you?" "I'm fine." Silas was fascinated by this—how the siblings seemed to see one another almost every day, but there was some sense of distance between them anyway.

He thought about this a lot. When he and Maeve lived nearby one another they couldn't have been closer. Silas quietly decided that the sibling relationship was uniquely strong—after all, who else knows you from birth?—but also uniquely vulnerable. Someone who has known you from birth could be forgiven for thinking they know you better than anyone else, but maybe they know the old you—the childish version of you. Maybe it's just not possible to keep up with the changes in a person as they reach adulthood, not without real, sustained effort.

As for Maeve, her condition was unchanged even though she had now been in a coma for several weeks. Every new update from staff seemed more pessimistic than the last, which had confused Silas at first because nothing seemed to be changing, but he was gradually coming to understand that the longer Maeve's coma progressed like this, the lower the chances of her waking and regaining her previous quality of life truly were.

But all that Silas could do was to wait and to hope. He didn't dare think about what he would do if she never woke up.

She *simply* had to come back to him.

How else could he reconcile with her? And how could he possibly live the rest of his life without her forgiveness for not being there when she needed him most?

There was a lot about her life that made little sense to Marie, but the way she and Irving had grown apart baffled her most.

"It's your own fault, Marie," Rupert told her the night Irving left, when Marie could not stop crying. "Irving was miserable here with you nagging him all the time. God, the only reason he didn't leave months ago was that I talked him out of it. You know how hard I tried to convince him to stay."

Rupert had told her all about his efforts to change Irving's mind, as unsuccessful as they had been, but this was the first time she heard that *she* was the reason Irving moved out. It was true that after their parents died, her relationship with Irving had changed. It had to—overnight, she became his guardian, as well as his sister.

But nagging? She honestly thought they were getting on better than ever. Irving had seemed *happy* until recently.

"But he wanted to go to college," she whispered miserably. "Dad thought he might become a doctor one day."

Rupert squeezed her hand.

"It'll do us good to be alone. I need you all to myself."

Rupert had always been so pleasant—so smooth. She'd known right after their honeymoon that he had secrets, that he was perhaps not quite the man she'd assumed him to be. But gradually, over their first few months in that great big house all alone together, an entirely new version of her husband emerged.

He'd loved her curves, but now she was *too* curvy, and he didn't like the way that her breasts strained her blouse, and he didn't think it was feminine for a woman to eat so much, and he wanted her to stick to salads—to slim down, so she looked good for him. Didn't she understand that when she left the house she represented *him*? He couldn't have a fat pig for a wife; he simply couldn't tolerate it. And he'd loved her sense of style, but now he overruled her preferences in her clothing, and he wanted her to cover as much skin as she could, but to still look pretty—she had to look pretty. Even on the days when she was to stay at home for one reason or another, if she so much as took her uncomfortable shoes off inside the house, he was disgusted by her "slovenliness" when he came home for his lunch.

Marie slowly, ever so slowly, began to adapt to the reality that Rupert's preferences, his desires, his moods, had to take priority over even her comfort. Once, Rupert had loved how friendly Marie was, but now she was too flirtatious, and he started to reveal a jealous streak she'd never seen in him before. He'd always been attentive, but now he called throughout the day, wanting to make sure she was home. And it was never a problem for her to speak with her friends, until the day it was.

She deduced, eventually, that Rupert had "friends" at the telephone exchange who kept tabs on who she called and even what she said. After that, Marie started avoiding making calls on the telephone, but she didn't need to avoid answering them, because her friends soon stopped calling. By the time their first wedding anniversary rolled around, Marie was disoriented. Rupert had become her sole source of information, the cornerstone by which she formed all thoughts and opinions, even about herself.

The rages were rare at first, and always more confusing than frightening. Rupert would come home from work in a foul mood and he would rant at her for hours, talking in circles that only disoriented Marie further. They were arguments with no resolution, because no matter how she apologized, she only seemed to draw further attention to her flaws. She would find herself clinging to him, begging him for his favor, terrified at the thought of displeasing him so much that he cast her aside. Marie had learned by then that she couldn't survive without him. She simply couldn't. Someone useless like her needed a husband with a strong hand, like Rupert.

If she didn't meet his expectations—and she so *rarely* did—he had a series of tools he employed to correct her. He was the master of the silent treatment, utterly freezing her out the minute she stepped out of line. He always said he hated to withhold her "privileges," like food and the car keys and that one awful time, when she was vacuuming when he called and she took too long to answer, he made her sleep on the floor of their bathroom that night, a space so small she couldn't even lie flat.

"This hurts me more than it hurts you," he said gently, stroking her hair back from her face as she lay on the cold tiles and wept. "But it's for your own good. You simply have to learn, Marie. You have so much to learn."

After a while, he didn't have to speak the chastisements and the insults aloud. Marie could hear them circling through her head all the time, even when he wasn't there, because the voice she heard speaking them was now her own.

Her marriage had become a particularly toxic form of quicksand and the more she struggled, the deeper Rupert pulled her in.

CHAPTER 5

Fiona

I'm feeling brighter with the dawn of a new day. Uncle Tad always said a good book could fix just about anything, and reading *The Midnight Estate* last night certainly did help me wind down until I could sleep. Now, it's time to get back into something of a healthier routine, so I rummage through the boxes in the ballroom until I find some active wear and my running shoes, and then I hit the road.

Tad always started each day with a walk around sunrise, and I used to do the same, back before everything went to hell. I'm running a little late on that schedule by the time I get going today, but I walk for about half an hour, almost as far as Jack's house, before I turn back to Wurimbirra. The cold morning air burns my lungs and throat and I'm *so* out of shape that every incline has me panting in an undignified fashion, but the only way I'm going to fix that is to get started, so it feels good to have made a step in the right direction.

My good mood lasts exactly as long as it takes me to walk back through the house to the kitchen. My footsteps stop as I walk through that door, because there's glass everywhere. Last night when I went to bed I left a neat line of Uncle Tad's glassware drying along the countertop, and now more than half of those glasses are on the floor, most shattered.

I'm so stunned that for a moment, all I can do is to stand and stare, as if I can will that baffling mess away. And then I do the next logical thing, which is to try to explain it away.

Freak wind?

But the windows and doors are shut, so that doesn't explain it.

Did I knock the glasses somehow when I came down to get the book and did I somehow just not notice the noise?

I was tired and a little off, but I wasn't in a coma, so no.

And then in a heartbeat, my mind goes to more alarming places.

Could someone have broken in here last night?

But my handbag is right there on the table. What kind of robber breaks in, walks past a handbag, smashes five glasses, then leaves, closing the door behind them?

Could it be pests inside the house?

I have seen plenty of rodent scat, but it was all old—faded and silver. Plus there's not a single dropping on the bench this morning, and if it were rodents, they would absolutely have left poo in their wake. Could it be possums? Australian possums are nocturnal and they do sometimes find their way into homes . . . but no. They leave even more droppings behind than rats do.

Suddenly I am freezing. Was it this cold in here a minute ago? I try to tell myself it's just because I've come inside from my walk and my body temperature is dropping now, but does that explain why my teeth are chattering and I'm starting to shake?

I'm not a coward, and I do not believe in ghosts.

I spin on my heels and walk briskly through the house, up the stairs to my room, pulling the door shut behind me. I rest my back against the door and close my eyes, drawing in some deep, calming breaths.

There's an explanation for all of this; I know there is.

I just have to stay calm while I figure out what it is.

After a few minutes pretending to read emails on my phone, I'm tempted to call Jon. For any other stressful situation, he would be the perfect person to call, but in this case I just can't do it, because if I do, he will either tell me to leave, or tell me the story about his nightmare again. Neither response will help.

I decide I have to keep busy to distract myself, and I can't exactly avoid the kitchen forever, so I march back downstairs. I find an old mixing bowl in the cupboard and I pick up the largest shards of glass. I find the dustpan and broom and I sweep up the rest, then I vacuum, for good measure. I throw all of that broken glass outside into the dumpster.

I make a trip into the supermarket—*definitely* not because I'm afraid of the house and looking for an excuse to go out, but because I need milk and coffee beans and food that doesn't come out of plastic packets. I take my time walking up and down the aisles, filling the trolley until I can't fit another thing in it, but once I've loaded it all into my car the obvious next thing is to go home and unpack it all. That's when I decide I should go past Turn the Page to get a takeaway coffee. I'm not disappointed at all to see there's no line at this slightly later hour, and definitely not disappointed that Aurelia whips up that coffee in absolutely no time.

"How's the house?" she asks me cheerfully.

"Oh, just fantastic," I say, and if she notices my slightly strangled tone, she's too polite to ask about it.

I almost convince myself to go sit by the lake to drink the coffee but then I give myself a firm mental scolding and drive back out to the mansion.

As I unpack the groceries I tell myself it's absurd for me to be unnerved. Sooner or later I'll figure out what happened to those glasses and in the meantime I have so much to do. The best thing I can do is keep moving, and the space that needs the most urgent attention is right here in this very kitchen. I'll sort through every single cupboard and drawer. Throw out what I don't want. Clean the rest. And then I can start to unpack my own kitchen bits and pieces, to start making this place feel like home.

For a few hours I work away clearing out cupboards, ferrying most of Uncle Tad's old cookware out to the bin. He wasn't much of a cook, but he also did not like to throw things away, so there are mismatched plates and bowls and pots and pans going back decades in this room. When I reach a bank of drawers near the sink, I find the top full of cutlery, but the bottom three drawers are full of random bits of paper. Uncle Tad was such a pack rat! I decide I'll dump the whole lot—after all, ten years after his death, what could possibly need to be kept? But then I turn the very top page over and I see it's an invoice for thousands of dollars' worth of electrical work, and beneath that, a letter from the same electrician, with a cheque stapled in the top corner.

The invoice is dated June 1999—six months before Tad's death. The contractor came across from Orange—a regional city about ninety minutes' drive away. And the letter from the contractor is dated August 1999.

Dear Mr Winslow,

You have accidentally double-paid invoice 1742a—both times by cheque, one sent in July and one sent last week.

As we already banked the first, please find the second attached.

I look at the cheque and frown. It's in Tad's own handwriting. For just about any other adult this would be unremarkable. It's such a basic necessity of life, to pay your own bills, to organize your own home repairs. But Mum always paid Tad's bills, all of them—both business and personal. He was just so disorganized, equally likely to forget to do something as he was to forget he'd already done it, and do it twice.

The only possible reason I can think that he would have organized this himself was if he were hiding the work from Mum, and that makes no damned sense at all. It was Tad who hated to spend money on the house—Tad who never wanted anything to change. Mum so hated Wurimbirra that she surely wouldn't have cared if he had bulldozed the place.

But if he were hiding the repair from Mum, that probably explains why he didn't call to tell me about the fire, or to ask me for advice. Mum and I were much closer when he was alive.

I sigh and set the invoice and the cheque aside, wondering if I'll ever know the story. But my interest has been piqued now, so I start to sort through the rest of the paperwork. Most of the scraps probably meant something only to Tad—they say random things like "Chapter 5, remove that awful sentence and character Eliza is too flat" and "P talk W re S." There are old TV guides—not that he ever watched much TV, just the odd film *very* occasionally, and only when he was between books. There are town council newsletters and Chinese restaurant menus and a brochure about a holiday resort on the Great Barrier Reef, not that he ever took holidays either. The rest are clippings from newspapers, almost all from the *Forbes Advocate*, the local newspaper, about subjects as diverse as the price of wheat, the opening of the cafe in the bookstore, about the time the town flooded and politicians from all over came to promise relief funds.

Classic Uncle Tad. He would often have little newspaper clippings to show me when I came to visit. He'd ask me if I'd seen this or heard of that, and whether I was well aware of the issue or clueless about it, he'd wander up to his office or his bedroom or a drawer down here, to fetch the article he'd clipped to remind him to talk to me about it. I know he did the same with Jon and Ilona, with Mum and Alan, even with Lucas sometimes.

The whole house is probably full of random tidbits like this. I can't wait to see what else I'll find—I only wish I knew *why* he'd saved these things, and who he wanted to talk to about them.

When I reach the very bottom of the bottom drawer, I find another newspaper clipping tucked at the very back. I almost miss it because it's stuck in a little crack between the base of the old drawer and the side, and when I tug at it, the corner tears off.

This one is much older than the others. It's a small yellow square, print faded, the paper a little curled. It's been cut close to the text and there's no date or publication name, just a small article on the front, and half an ad for Brylcream on the back.

BODY IDENTIFIED AS THAT OF MISSING WIFE

Police have used dental records to identify historic remains found at the bottom of a steep cliff in the Salt Point State Park. The remains belonged to a Mrs Gertie Lentfer. Mrs Lentfer was first reported missing by her husband Julian in 1956.

Julian Lentfer has also been missing, along with his second wife, Jennifer, since 1960. Police would like to speak to Julian Lentfer in connection to the suspected murders of both women.

I set the newspaper clipping down on the table and sink back into my chair, pressing my hands to my cheeks. What a dark, awful piece of news, and what a random thing for Tad to have kept.

Perhaps it was inspiration for one of his books? He did love to tackle the difficult subjects. His breakout, award-winning debut novel, *The Humans of Tern Creek,* was about a family dealing with what we would now call generational trauma, but what Uncle Tad called "the family mind curse" when it was published in 1949. His last novel, published to astounding commercial success and acclaim in 1998, was *Walk with Me*—a tale about an aging man desperate to connect with a distant son he doesn't understand. I remember when it was published how people would ask Jon if it was autobiographical, and Jon would laugh and laugh and tell them his dad was his best friend. In between those books were twenty others, and I've read them all, so I know none matched this newspaper clipping. Maybe I'll find a half-finished manuscript somewhere in his office when I get around to sorting through it.

When I was seventeen, over the course of a single summer just after I left Wurimbirra to move with Mum into Alan's farmhouse, I read everything Tad had written. An artist is not the same as their art, and every story existed separately to my uncle, but I saw glimmers of him in his work. He had woven pieces of himself through the pages, through scenes and themes so powerful I could scarcely believe I shared DNA with that man. After that, I begged him for early copies of his upcoming books, and he would always give me pages the same time he sent them off in the post to Elsie and Rita.

God, I loved my uncle. I loved his brilliant mind and his expansive, generous heart. If I find words that he wrote but never shared with me as I am cleaning out this house, I will consider myself the luckiest woman on earth.

As the sun sets on my first full day at Wurimbirra, I stop and look around the kitchen, then nod in satisfaction. It feels good that I've made *some* progress. Like the rest of the house, the kitchen is an oversized space and it won't be spotless anytime soon, but the main surfaces are no longer covered in a thick layer of dust, and at least I have some of the cupboards and drawers cleaned out. I even managed to unpack the first box of my things into a clean cupboard, and I fired up the Wedgewood stove and cooked myself a proper grown-up meal—a steak and oodles of vegetables. It was hardly gourmet, but it was the beginning of an apology to my body for surviving on sugar, caffeine and wine for the past three months.

I make sure there is not a single thing left on the kitchen countertops before I leave the room. I still have no idea what caused that mess last night, but I'm not risking a repeat. I take a bucket full of cleaning supplies and the mop upstairs, stopping to wind the grandfather clock, then I walk along the hall to the bathroom I once shared with Mum.

The bathrooms in this house are simple, four in total, all identical—black-and-white-checkered tiles, a claw foot bath with a shower head, a small vanity and sink and an old-style pull-chain toilet with the cistern mounted to the wall. There's one of these bathrooms at either end of the hallway upstairs, carved off a corner of Tad's guest room and Mum's guest room, another just off the hallway near the kitchen, and one beside the ballroom. These were all added to the house in the 1920s. The original occupants made do with an outhouse and jugs and washbasins for bathing, because indoor plumbing was not yet ubiquitous when this house was built.

I reach up to gingerly tug at the plastic shower curtain hanging from the ring around the bath, and the punch holes around the hooks give way, as if I've put my full weight on it. I throw it out into the hallway before I drag the vacuum into the room to run it over the tiles, then I mop the tiles several times, until the ones I know to be white are finally white again.

The vanity was once a beautiful thing—with carved, ornate doors to hide the plumbing, and a marble countertop with a basin built into it. Like the claw foot bath, the basin is stained with rust and mineral build-up, and the brass tap is awfully tarnished. All fixable, except maybe the wood. It's in terrible shape—faded and water damaged, warped in some places, even cracked horizontally along the top of the doors. There's a good chance that the water damage is mostly my fault. I had no clue about how fragile old wood like this is when I lived in this house. I'm certain I was less careful than I should have been when I was washing my face or cleaning my teeth as a teenager. I wipe the top and sides, wipe the empty interior, then crouch to wipe the dust from the carved detail around the base.

As I move my cloth along the base, the strangest feeling comes over me. It's like my gaze is involuntarily pulled back towards the gap between the vanity and the wall. The sensation is unnerving and strange, and I'm starting to wonder if I'm unwell when I think I spot something stuck back there.

But no, surely not. Even if something *were* there, I couldn't see it; it's so dark behind the unit. There's surely just a whole lot of dust and—shudder—some very old hair back there, probably mine. I'm about to move on, to crawl around to wipe the other side of the vanity, but then I stop again. I don't even know *why*.

I take the small brush from the dustpan and I swipe it at the gap. Some of the dust shifts, and now I'm sure something is in that space that should not be there. I can't reach it and the bristles on the brush aren't firm enough to move it, so I reach up and snatch my toothpaste from the vanity. I use the pointy end to push at the thing until it pops out, flicking forward and hitting the tiles with a metallic chime.

I pick it up and dust it off, and to my absolute shock, it's a ring—small and filthy and old, but also quite heavy. I stand

and hold it under the tap until the water runs clean, and what is left under the dust is a silver ring, set with what looks like diamonds. There's one large diamond in the center, and eight smaller diamonds around it, set into the shape of a daisy.

Now why on earth does that ring a bell?

A thought strikes me and I march down the hall to my bedroom and pick up *The Midnight Estate.* It only takes me a minute or two to find the reference:

> Just three months after her parents died, Rupert took Marie out to dinner in the nicest restaurant in the district and he gave her the biggest bunch of flowers she'd ever seen and he showed her a heavy silver ring, with nine sparkling diamonds clustered in the shape of a daisy.

"What the hell?" I say, as I stare between the book and the ring. This has to be some kind of joke. Or maybe a coincidence? Yes, that's it. There are surely many rings fashioned into this shape every year, and one just happened to find its way behind that vanity at some point over the past 120 years, and—

But I have cleaned that bathroom myself dozens of times over the years, maybe more. It was always my job to clean that room, since I was always the one to mess it.

For the second time today I find myself scrambling to find logic. Maybe there's an innocent explanation here. I don't know who the author of this book is—the name Charity Wilkie doesn't ring any bells—but I *do* know that Uncle Tad had writer friends visit from time to time. It stands to reason that after Mum and I moved out, he might even have put them up at this end of the house to sleep.

Maybe Charity Wilkie stayed in this house, and she dropped her ring, and I'm hyper-aware tonight because I'm still getting used to being here. In the cold light of day, I'm sure I'll see that this is all perfectly innocent. Maybe the books were a gift from Wilkie to Tad to thank him for his hospitality, rather than gifts for the rest of us *from* Tad.

Or maybe there's something more going on here.

One thing is for sure, though: my interest in this book has intensified. I sit the ring on my bedside table, change into my pajamas and climb into bed to read.

THE MIDNIGHT ESTATE

BY CHARITY WILKIE

Weeks flew by Silas in a monotonous blur. There had been no change in his sister's condition—not so much as the flutter of an eyelid.

Occasionally, Dr. Lomas tried to talk to Silas about her prognosis.

"Son, the problem is that the longer this goes on, the less likely—"

"She just needs more time," Silas would interrupt, as if hearing the odds of recovery would make them even longer.

His daily pancake breakfast was the one bright spot in an otherwise grey routine, marking another day gone in the same way the sunrise did in normal times. The dreary environs of the hospital were heavy and dull, depressing in every way. By contrast, the diner was a place of rich turquoise vinyl and shiny chrome light fittings and warm sunshine through the window. The pop of the honey on his pancake. The warm, rich brown of his coffee. The soft, pretty colors of Marie's outfits, the peach of the lipstick she wore.

She came by most days. If the booth beside Silas was empty she would sit there, facing him. Some days, she would look at Silas and her face would transform into a breathtaking smile. Often they made perfectly brief small talk and then sat quietly, together but apart.

"What are you reading today?" she'd ask. He was reading through whatever he laid his hands upon in his sister's library, glad even for the books he didn't particularly enjoy, just because they represented a link to Maeve. The longest conversation Silas and Marie had during those weeks was about *Brave New World Revisited*, which he was reading for the first time.

"I've read *Brave New World* five or six times," he told her. "I keep rereading it over the years and it just seems truer and truer. Huxley is a genius, obviously—I mean it captures so much of the modern age, and he wrote it almost thirty years ago! This new analysis of advancements and developments since the original publication is fascinating—" The startled expression she wore at this outburst was one Silas was well familiar with. He considered himself to be a quiet, somewhat dull man but felt he came alive when someone asked him about books. "Tell me you've read it. *Brave New World*, I mean." Marie shook her head, and Silas winced. "Well, we can't have that. I'm sure Maeve has a copy in her library—if I can find it, I'll bring it with me and you can borrow it."

"Thank you," she said, and she offered him a quiet smile. "You're very passionate about books, aren't you?"

"Books are everything," he said. "Whatever you need in life—escape, wisdom, knowledge, power, pick up the right book and it will all be there. Humans have created a lot of useful technology but the ability to share stories, between friends around a fireplace or neighbors across a backyard fence, or even across great distance and languages . . . why, that's the *making* of us." He paused, then sighed wistfully as he looked back down to his book. "At least, it could be."

Marie never stayed more than about five minutes, but some days, that was more than enough for her to brighten

Silas's day. She was a warm, gentle touch point during an especially lonely and difficult period in his life.

That made it all the more confusing on the days when Marie would rush into the diner just as she always did, but she'd barely make eye contact with Silas. Her gaze would flick this way and that, as if she was waiting for someone to leap out to frighten her. On those days, she usually ordered her coffee, watched her brother through the kitchen window for a few moments and then left whether she had a chance to speak with him or not—whether her coffee had arrived or not. Silas just could not pick the pattern to it. There was something bafflingly familiar about Marie's unease on those days, although for the life of him Silas couldn't figure out where he'd seen it before.

It eventually occurred to him that his mother's apartment would need to be cleaned out so it could be sold. What a terrible waste, to have a beautiful home like that sitting empty. He sat at Maeve's bedside and explained to her that he would still be by every morning, but during the afternoon he would be at Linda's apartment, sorting through her things. He told his sister not to worry, that by the time she woke up, everything would be sorted and anything precious would be back at their childhood home waiting for her.

When Silas stepped inside his mother's apartment this time, it hit him all at once. Grief delayed is grief multiplied, and he thought for a few moments that the brutal sharpness of it would crush him. He sat on the floor in her foyer and he didn't even try to hold back the sobs. Silas had so adored his mother, and now that she was gone, he found himself deeply conflicted about the choices he'd made in his life. Did he do the wrong thing in moving to the other side of the world, even if it was for love?

His fortunes had changed so unexpectedly as he reached his late teens. Silas won a scholarship to college but dropped out before the start of his sophomore year, when a great big cheque arrived in the mail and the world unexpectedly became his oyster. Instead of classes and tutorials and textbooks, he studied and learned by watching people going about their lives in Malaysia and Canada and Bolivia. He drank warm beer in London and ate baguettes and cheese in France and he walked parts of the Appalachian Trail and he watched the sunset over lakes and beaches and rivers in Yugoslavia and Spain and in New Zealand.

He always came home to Linda and Maeve, stopping for weeks or months between his adventures. But once he locked eyes with Christine, that was the end of that too. Should he now regret the choices he'd made, the time he'd spent away? Should he mourn for the days and weeks and months and years he could have spent with his family when he was adventuring then settling down elsewhere?

When the torrent of emotions settled, Silas looked around his mother's home and finally accepted that there was a chance that he was the last left standing in his family of origin. His mother and sister might really be gone.

And added to that, there really was a chance that he'd already broken his marriage beyond repair.

Eventually, he started packing and cleaning, with a burst of energy that left him almost manic. The thought of being alone was so terrifying his instincts screamed to keep busy to avoid facing the reality of it.

As he packed up his mother's life, it was only natural that Silas might return to the oldest parts of his memory, moments he generally refused to visit. Images and scents and feelings came to him in bursts and intrusive, irrepressible explosions, as though the simple act of packing up Linda's clothes for the charity shop was enough to force the screening of a film in his mind.

He was five years old and hiding in her closet, too terrified to even breathe. When his lungs felt as though they would burst, he'd finally inhale—catching a deep, reassuring burst of her scent among her dresses and coats. Outside of that closet, his father raged, throwing anything he could get his hand on, chasing Linda from room to room, reminding her that he was so much bigger than she was, so much stronger. That he could take from her anything he chose to take, even her life if he wanted to.

Silas shook the memory off. He promised himself that he had suppressed it once before and he could do so again. But the next morning he was drinking coffee at Maeve's square kitchen table when he remembered a different table—the circular table the family had used in his earliest years. It was marked with age and stains. Silas remembered hiding beneath it, arms wrapped around his knees, trying not to make a sound as his father held his mother over the kitchen sink, a knife against the soft skin of her throat. Young Silas kept closing his eyes but he couldn't keep them closed so he saw it all. Cruel, spiteful words flew from his father's mouth and spittle right along with it, right into Linda's eyes and onto her cheeks. Frank had been so wild with rage that although Silas had been hiding less than three feet away, he had been blind to his son's presence.

But Linda wasn't blind. As Silas peeked around the table leg she had pleaded with him with her eyes. *Stay quiet, stay still. It'll all be over soon.*

No. Silas shook himself from the memory, but as he left Maeve's house and walked towards her car, he recalled the very last time he saw his father. Frank didn't leave the family in shame or guilt, not pushed away as punishment for terrorizing Linda and Silas for five long years. The man abandoned his family for the worst kind of cliché: Linda was pregnant but so was Frank's girlfriend, and Frank had made his choice.

The last Silas heard of his father, he was living in Ohio with his new family. Knowing Linda, knowing the strength of her integrity and her kind heart, Silas was certain his mother would have sent word to Frank that he had a daughter. The one good thing that man had done for his family was to never return to rejoin it, not even to meet Maeve.

Try as he might, Silas couldn't stop these memories from circling through his mind over the weeks as he packed up his mother's home. And on the morning the truck from Goodwill picked up the last of her furniture, Silas took himself to Carmen's for pancakes to celebrate.

Marie was there, and it was one of those days when she was so skittish. She gave Silas a fleeting, hesitant smile, then went right back to watching Irving through the window into the kitchen, and then after just a few sips of her coffee, she hurried out the door, like some invisible ghost was on her heels.

That's when Silas finally joined the threads in his mind, and in an instant he knew why Marie's expression looked familiar.

His mother had worn that look often.

This was the tortured, hunted gaze of a woman who feared for her life.

"Do you have a minute to sit with me?" Silas asked Carmen a few days later.

"Sure, honey," she said, giving him a wide smile that faded only a little as she sat opposite him.

"Do you know my sister used to babysit Marie and Irving when they were little? We lived on the same street."

"That's nice," Carmen said, but Silas could read in her gaze that she was confused about why he was telling her this. He didn't know either—he just felt an instinct to establish a longstanding relationship with Marie and her family before he leaped into probing questions about her life.

"Listen, about Marie . . ." he said hesitantly. He finally found Maeve's copy of *Brave New World* but it was still in his backpack where he'd placed it four days earlier. Marie hadn't been at the diner, which meant he hadn't had the opportunity to give it to her.

Carmen winced.

"Oh, honey, no. She's married. And—"

"No, no. So am I," Silas said quickly, holding up his left hand to reveal his wedding band. "It's not like that. I just can see that she's . . ."

"She's scared, huh?" Carmen said softly. Silas nodded. "Her husband is a cop, like her daddy was. But her daddy was one of the good ones, and her husband is not. He has a bit of a scheme going around here—likes to collect money from business owners to keep them safe."

Silas looked at her in surprise.

"Is it really so dangerous around here these days?"

"It is when *he's* here," Carmen muttered. "This is a nice town and people look out for one another. Rupert is a thug, plain and simple. But he got a promotion after Derek died and he basically runs this part of town—who do you even complain to when it's the deputy police chief harassing you? The chief himself? Maybe, except that he *must* know, maybe he's even in on it. I pay Rupert his money each month and stay out of his business but . . ." She shrugged sadly and looked towards the kitchen. Silas followed her gaze and saw Irving at the sink, chatting happily to Rodrigo as he washed dishes. "I worry for those two. Irving was the smartest kid in his grade. He's a charmer, you know? The kind of kid who can talk to anyone. He should be at college now, not chopping vegetables for us and spending his nights hanging around with Rupert and his band of degenerates."

"Irving is involved in this protection racket?"

"The silly kid has been hanging around his brother-in-law outside of work. Play-acting as one of his goons, I'm assuming. Didn't you see his bruised cheek last week?"

Silas hadn't noticed—then again, Irving tended to look unkempt at the best of times, and Silas only saw him from afar.

"Sad, isn't it? Such a waste. I tried to talk to Marie, but you've probably seen how she avoids me now. And I'm guessing Rupert rules her life with an iron fist, so she's maybe pushing things enough just calling in to see her brother on her morning chores. That poor kid has found her way into enough trouble, I don't want to get her into more by forcing the issue." Carmen placed her hands flat on the table, then pushed herself into a standing position. She dropped her voice as she added, "But listen, this is not your problem, and it's not mine either. Sometimes you have to let people figure it out for themselves, you know?"

Silas thanked her for her time and he took her advice. After all, he barely knew Marie—her sad situation was truly not his problem.

But Marie didn't come to the cafe the next day, or the day after that. Silas started to wonder. During the very worst years, the years Frank made every living moment of Linda's life hell, how many bystanders had noticed that haunted look in her eyes and decided it was a private matter between a husband and a wife and therefore not their problem?

"Hello, Rupert." Marie's teeth were chattering. She pressed the telephone handset into her jaw to steady herself and flashed a forceful smile at Mr Peterson, her next-door neighbor, who stood beside her. "I'm so sorry to interrupt you at work. I tried to call earlier—"

"I don't sit around and wait for you to call, sweetheart. We can't both laze around all day. I work hard to afford the fancy home you enjoy."

He sounded annoyed already, and Marie turned away from Mr Peterson's watchful gaze and briefly closed her eyes.

"I accidentally locked myself out of the house," she said, voice low. She was always so careful to ensure she had everything she needed when she pulled that front door closed, but this week, everything felt *different*. She was out of sorts and that meant she was out of routine and out of habit.

There was heavy cloud above that day and she had been rushing, trying to get her errands done before the rain hit. She got halfway down the block before she realized her handbag wasn't over her shoulder where it should have been. That meant she didn't have her daily allowance to pay for what she needed from the butcher and the grocer and she didn't have keys to get back inside to get it.

Marie spent the next hour trying to break into the house so she could avoid asking Rupert for help, but every door and window was sealed shut. And her plan had been to just wait for him to come home for lunch but it was raining now, absolutely bucketing down. She'd been sheltering under the little awning over the back door but when Rupert called at 10:30 a.m. that day he'd told her he wouldn't be home for lunch and so her choices had been to stay outside in the rain until he came home that evening or to swallow her pride and call him.

"You can't even close up a house properly, can you? *Useless.*"

Oh, Rupert sounded furious. Marie tasted bile in her mouth.

"Yes, I know," she whispered, and she glanced back at Mr Peterson, who still stood watching her with an innocent smile on his face. Outside, the rain was pelting down and the wind was picking up now too.

"And now you want me to rescue you, don't you? Poor Marie. Always needing rescuing. It's pathetic."

"I'm sorry."

"I'm not saving you. Not this time." Oh, he was in a mood, all right. Of all the days for her to make such a stupid mistake! "Where are you?"

"Mr Peterson kindly invited me in to use his phone."

"You're inside his house?" There was an accusation in his tone. Marie looked again at Mr Peterson, a long-retired teacher, probably more than forty years her senior. He was still smiling that sweet, reassuring smile, his gaze just a little unfocused, as it often was. Mr Peterson was a sweet man who was possibly in the early stages of dementia. He was the last person on earth Rupert should feel threatened by.

"Y-yes."

"Thank Peterson and tell him I'll be home soon. And then go *outside* and wait for me in the backyard."

"It's raining q-quite heavily here—"

"Stand in the middle of the backyard. Right beside the clothesline. Wait for me but make sure no one sees you."

"B-but . . ."

"Are you questioning me?"

She wouldn't, and nor would she disobey him. Marie thanked Rupert and hung up the phone. She turned to Mr Peterson.

"Thanks so much."

"Coming home to let you back in, eh?" Mr Peterson said, his eyes crinkling as he smiled. "He's one of the good ones, isn't he?"

"Oh, he is," she said, forcing another smile. "Thank you."

There were a million ways Marie could have responded to Rupert's request. She could have told Mr Peterson what Rupert had said. Begged him for help. She could have walked out of his house into the street and she could have kept on walking even though she had no place to go. She could simply have gone to sit under the awning at the back of her house, to wait in a relatively dry spot.

She did none of those things. Instead, Marie walked into her own backyard, and just as she'd been told to do, she waited for Rupert by the clothesline, as the rain poured on and on. It was the only way she'd get back inside her house. It was the only way to minimize his wrath and win back his affection.

It wasn't as though Marie just accepted her lot without a fight in the beginning. She had thought about leaving, especially in the days after Irving moved out, when she first began to have the sense that Rupert had wooed her with the promise of a loving, supportive marriage that he had never intended to provide. Marie supposed that most people hid some small parts of themselves during courtship but Rupert had presented a front that was entirely false. If that wasn't reason to leave a man, what was?

The question was initially one of logistics. It was a fine thing to think she'd just leave; where would she even go? To Irving's crowded apartment, one he shared with three other young men? She had been in regular contact with a several friends when she and Rupert first started dating, but that had all changed. Even when Marie walked about the town doing her daily errands, she was *alone*, too scared to chance extended conversations or to build real friendships.

Confidence is an armour, a brittle shell that grows around a person to protect and shield the softest part of them. Even the strongest armour gives way under enough pressure, erodes after enough attacks. And Rupert had spent two years chipping away at the strength of Marie's armour.

She did make one half-hearted attempt to leave some months after Irving moved out. By then, Marie was doubting herself—if she couldn't even figure out a way to get out, to find happiness again, maybe Rupert was right to question her intelligence. Even so, some voice within her cried out that if *this* was what early marriage looked and felt like, things would only get worse, and she simply had to try.

She'd managed to save very little out of her daily allowance, but it was still something, tucked away in the back of the closet. That morning, she waited until Rupert left for work and then she took the little wad of notes and she slipped it into the side pocket of her handbag. She left without so much as packing a suitcase.

When Marie reached the end of her street, instead of turning left towards the shops, she turned right, towards the residential areas farther out. She walked six blocks, smiling at passersby, waving to the postman. Eventually, she turned onto the quiet avenue where her school friend Donna now lived. They'd been close, right up until Rupert decided that *no one* could be close to Marie except him.

But Donna was a good person. Marie felt hopeful that she'd have some idea how Marie could get out of that house. She walked up to the front door, her steps light, a smile still pinned on her face. Her stomach was churning and she felt light-headed with fear but the smile didn't slip, even as she knocked on the door.

"Be right with you!" she heard Donna call from the recesses of the quaint little cottage she and her husband, Ryan, lived in. Then at last, the door opened and a heavily pregnant Donna appeared. As she recognized Marie, her face blanched.

"Hi," Marie said, suddenly a little breathless, and now that she was there it occurred to her that she didn't know what to say. Best to ask to come inside. To sit down, maybe over a cup of coffee, and explain her predicament. And until then, Marie would keep it light and casual. "How are you, Donna? I was just in the neighborhood—"

Donna pushed open the screen door and grabbed Marie's elbow. She looked this way and that, checking the street for cars, then dragged her inside.

"You shouldn't be here," Donna said as soon as the door closed behind them.

"I—" Marie was mortified to find her throat was suddenly dry. "I was just wondering if we could talk, that's all."

"No, that's not a good idea."

"But . . ." Marie cleared her throat. The shame and humiliation of the mess she was in washed over her. Her face flushed hot and her knees felt weak. "Please, Donna. I just don't know where else to go."

Donna hesitated, but then she groaned softly. "I can't get involved," she said. "I'm really sorry, Marie, but I just can't."

"But . . ."

"Rupert pulled me over, Marie, in his police car. He told me it was best to give you space for now, that you're not coping well—having mental problems. He said that even Irving couldn't deal with it anymore so moved out on his own."

"But that's not—"

"Of course it's not true." Donna sighed impatiently. "Honey, I wanted to check in on you right away but Ryan was spooked. We've heard things . . ."

"About me?"

"About Rupert. Surely you must know . . . ? Ryan's boss said he's mixed up in some awful business—nothing more than a bully and a thug . . ."

Hot tears prickled behind Marie's eyes but she blinked them away. She hated to be so desperate and powerless and in need of rescue yet again. *Useless.* Pathetic, just like Rupert always said.

"I need to get out," Marie said unevenly. "Could I borrow a little money, maybe? Just enough for a bus fare . . ."

"Marie," Donna whispered gently. "You need to go home." She touched her hands to her swollen stomach. "I have a family to think of, honey. I just can't get involved."

Marie went home. She told herself she'd think of something else—some other way out. She washed her face, fixed her hair. She put the little nest egg back in her closet and she told herself she'd just keep skimming and saving.

She made Rupert a pot roast and she ate her salad.

A few weeks went by after that and Marie kept trying to find some thread of hope to grasp on to, but it was like she was reaching for a lifeline that kept slipping out of reach. And then one morning she woke to Rupert sitting at the edge of the bed beside her. He held a small wad of cash in his hand.

"I was married before, you know," he said quietly. Marie was still half-asleep. She sat up, touched a hand to the rollers in her hair, rubbed her eyes.

"Did you say you were—"

"She left," he said, as if she hadn't spoken. "Ran away." He folded up the money and he pushed it into his breast pocket and then patted it. His expression was mild, as if he were talking about the weather. "And do you know, it didn't matter where she went. I was always going to find her."

He bent to kiss Marie's forehead, then stood. He reached down to stroke her cheek with the back of his forefinger and then he dragged the finger down to run it horizontally across her neck. Marie stared up at him, frozen.

"You're mine, Marie," he said softly. "You know that, don't you? You know I'll never let you go?"

He'd told her that time and time again since they were married. In the beginning, that phrase brought relief. She had felt so alone and overwhelmed after her parents' accident, now she had her dream husband, and a beautiful home, and a golden future that she could confidently know she would always share with him.

But now, she heard that same phrase, and she understood that he meant it as a threat.

She nodded mutely.

"Do you know where my first wife is now?"

Marie just stared at him, until he cupped her shoulder in his palm, then tightened—not hard enough to bruise, just a warning shot. She hastily shook her head.

"Neither does her family, Marie. And they'll never know because they'll never find her. I made sure of that."

A bolt of shock went through her. Rupert released her and walked to her dressing table. He bent until he could see himself in the mirror, then straightened his tie.

"Have a great morning, darling," he said. "Remember, I'll speak to you at ten thirty."

And after that, Marie finally understood there was already a noose around her neck, and it was likely that one day, she would stumble across the line of one of those unspoken rules and that would be how her story would end.

In the absence of any way to help herself, in the absence of any active help from others, all Marie could hope for was a miracle—that some door would open up somehow that would enable her to escape.

But five days before she locked her keys in the house, Marie went to button up her blouse and realized that she had gained some weight. How on earth that could have happened with the scant little she ate baffled her at first—until she suddenly realized that she had not had her period for some time.

And after that, she tumbled into a fog of depression and panic.

She had no idea if Rupert really had been married

before. She wouldn't put it past him to tell her a story like that just to scare her, given he seemed to delight in keeping her in a perpetual state of terror and loneliness.

She knew one thing for sure though. If the thought of Marie walking out on him riled Rupert up enough for him to hint at murder, he would only become more incensed if she were ever to try to leave once his child was involved.

Now when she reached for a shred of hope, she realized there was simply nothing there. No way out. No chance of rescue.

She would live in Rupert's house and raise his child until Rupert decided otherwise, but it was clear that she would never leave alive.

Silas pulled Maeve's car onto the concrete drive beside the largest house in Summer Hill Street. It was a modern home of tidy red bricks with a long flat roof and large windows just about everywhere. He checked the address he'd scrawled from the phone book one last time. Yes, this was it—this was the house of the only family in town with Marie's surname.

It sure did look flashy for a police officer, even for the deputy chief of the station, but then again, Silas understood that Marie's husband was enjoying the fruits of two labors, so he supposed it made some sense.

Silas popped open an umbrella against the pouring rain as he slid from the car. He ran towards the front door but something caught his eye over the gate. He took two steps in that direction instead, until he could see into the backyard.

Marie was standing in the center of the long, narrow yard. She was drenched through, her arms wrapped around her waist, crying softly as she stared down at her waterlogged shoes. She hadn't noticed him yet, and Silas hesitated.

What was she doing out there in that horrendous weather? Was she having some kind of episode? He wasn't equipped to help a near stranger with something so serious. He wouldn't even know where to begin.

But he'd tracked down her house not so much to drop off the book and then leave, as he'd been telling himself all morning he would do, but to check on her. And now that he knew she was very much *not* okay, he couldn't just walk away. As Silas opened the gate, Marie looked up and he saw a bolt of terror in her eyes. She held up her hands and waved him back.

"I just wanted—" he started to shout, but her eyes grew frantic and she pressed a trembling finger over her lip. Silas cursed under his breath, then jogged through the backyard to hold the umbrella over her head.

"What on earth are you doing out here?" he asked her. Her eyes were red-raw, her nose not much better. She looked up at him with desperation and genuine fear in her gaze, sobbing so hard her breathing was labored. "Marie, tell me how can I help."

"You have to leave before he gets home," she choked. "He'll kill me, Silas. You have to go."

A shiver went down Silas's spine. *He'll kill me.* It wasn't hyperbole—he could see in Marie's eyes that she believed this was a real possibility. As he stared down at the woman in that driving rain, his vision began to blur, and for just a moment his eyes betrayed him. Marie faded until he saw his mother in her place. Silas saw countless bystanders turning away and deciding *this is not my problem.* Even that one time a neighbor did call the police on Frank, that was their response: *This is a private matter between a husband and his wife.*

"Please go," Marie begged. "Please. He could be home any minute."

"At least take the umbrella," Silas said, and then he looked around and saw a shelter at the back door. "Or go stand under the awning—"

"*I can't.* Please. Please just go."

Silas hesitated again, but she pushed his arm, and he could feel how icy her skin was even through his shirt. He sighed and tried to hand her the umbrella but she wouldn't take it.

"We'll talk at the diner?" he said. She gave a helpless shrug.

Silas let himself out the gate and went back to Maeve's car. As he was struggling to put down the umbrella, he saw an elderly man stepping out onto the front doorstop of the house next door.

"Eh, thought you were Rupert," the man said. Silas frowned and squinted at him.

"Mr Peterson?" One of his old science teachers, who also happened to be one of his mother's very best work friends from her time in the administration block at the high school.

"Silas? Well, I'll be damned. Come over here, son!"

Silas hesitated, glancing between his car and the backyard. From his vantage point Mr Peterson couldn't possibly have seen Marie standing out there, freezing half to death in the rain. But Silas wondered—if the old man lived next door to Rupert and Marie, perhaps he'd overheard some things. Perhaps he could shed some light on how Silas could help.

So Silas jogged to the doorstep and crowded under the awning to shake Mr Peterson's hand.

"You missed a beautiful service, son," Mr Peterson said sadly. "Linda was too damned young. Life is just not fair. Your mother was a remarkable woman."

"Thank you, sir. I know."

"What on earth are you doing here? I have to say, young Marie and Rupert don't get many visitors."

"I just had a book to drop off to her."

"I assume she got inside?"

Silas hesitated, unsure if he should lie. But Mr Peterson didn't wait for a response.

"Silly thing left her keys inside, had to use my phone to call Rupert to come let her in."

"Is she okay, Mr Peterson?" Silas blurted.

"Your mother?" Mr Peterson suddenly looked confused, and Silas felt a pang. The man had to be close to ninety years old; perhaps his faculties were starting to go.

"Marie. Is Marie okay?"

"Oh, yes. Linda used to boast about you all the time, son. I know all about your beautiful wife and that son of yours. You live in Australia, don't you?"

"Mr Peterson—"

"In that small town way out in the middle of nowhere with the kangaroos. And how could I forget, it has the same name as the magazine!"

"*Marie*, Mr Peterson. Is she okay there with Rupert? Do you . . . notice anything?"

"Very quiet couple," Mr Peterson said, and then he smiled to himself. "Yes, a lovely couple."

"Please, sir. Could you keep an eye on her? I just have

a feeling . . ." Silas's throat worked, but the words just wouldn't come.

"She's got herself a terrific young husband there, Silas," Mr Peterson said quietly, his gaze a little cloudy. "Don't you worry about our Marie. I mean—look at that house. Have you ever seen anything as grand as all that? She's doing fine. Just fine."

CHAPTER 6

Fiona

I set down *The Midnight Estate* on my lap and stare at it in disbelief.

> *You live in Australia, don't you? . . . In that small town way out in the middle of nowhere with the kangaroos. And how could I forget, it has the same name as the magazine!*

It's Forbes—it has to be. What other town would meet those criteria? I fumble on the bedside table and pick up the ring, staring at the daisy-shaped diamonds, and then I flip all the way back to the description in the earlier chapter and confirm again that it matches.

There is unquestionably a connection between this book and my uncle. I reach for my phone to check the time. It's only 10:30 p.m., and my cousin is a night owl. Before I start texting him, a creaking noise sounds somewhere out in the hall and a full-body shiver runs right through me.

I'm not going to tell Jon that I'm jumping at shadows—I don't want to worry him, especially since he's already got himself tied up in knots about that nightmare.

Instead, I ask, Have you heard of an author named Charity Wilkie? Perhaps one of Tad's friends?

He replies right away, Never heard of her. I assume you've googled her?

Jon's idea is a good one, so I swipe out of the messages to my browser. I quickly discover there is no Wikipedia page for Charity Wilkie, and she doesn't have a website. There are no news articles or even links to online bookstores where someone might buy a new copy of this book—it isn't even available in any digital format. All I can find online is a handful of old listings for the book at secondhand stores and a few references to library catalogues. All based in the UK.

I don't know much about publishing other than what I learned from Jon and Uncle Tad, but I know enough to deduce that this book was not exactly a best-seller. Maybe it went out of print quickly after it was released in early 2000. My phone hums with a new text from Jon.

Why do you ask?

My thumbs hover over the screen as I think about how to respond. There's nothing particularly alarming or exciting here; it's just a ring I—somehow—found under a vanity that also appears in a book that probably references Forbes. And do I tell Jon his dad bought twelve copies and might have wanted us all to read the book? Jon would be very excited about the possibility of one last gift from Tad, just as I am. He'd be parsing every line looking for hidden meaning. Just as, I suppose, I am.

I'll tell him, of course, but I will wait until I finish it. It's not like he can start reading right away anyway—I'll have to post his copy down to him. Maybe this is just a story Tad enjoyed and wanted to share, or maybe there's some message in this novel that he specifically wanted us to see. If there is, I'll want to prepare Jon before he dives in.

Started reading a book I found here at the house. I was just curious if they knew one another.

Jon replies, If Charity Wilkie was one of his author friends, you'll find letters somewhere.

Uncle Tad took great pride in ignoring the phone most of the time, especially before caller ID. In his later years he did get a little better—he'd answer family, at least, and calls from his Elsie and Rita *most* of the time. He preferred to write to just about everyone else.

Do you think he would have kept all those letters?

Definitely—your mum made sure of it. They're probably in his storeroom. Knowing Ginny, you'll find a box labeled "letters from author friends" and it will be in perfect alphabetical order by surname.

Mum has flaws, but disorganization is not one of them. I've barely looked in the storeroom since I came home, but tomorrow I'll take a peek.

I put the phone back onto the nightstand and turn off the light. I'm thinking about poor Marie and Silas but growing sleepy, far too sleepy to dive back into the book.

As I drift off, I hear a sound from somewhere in the house and this time I'm sure it's the sound of something falling. Not glass, something . . . lighter. And not in the kitchen, someplace closer. Maybe the parlour, or the formal dining room.

A flush of frustration suddenly comes over me. This is absurd. There has to be a simple explanation for all of this.

I flick the lamp back on and walk briskly to the door of my bedroom, but as I stick my head out into the hallway, my bravado disappears and in a heartbeat I'm spiraling into lonely paranoia.

I'm alone in this enormous house and something is moving things when I'm not in the room, and how did I spot that ring tonight, and did I really forget to turn the heater on last night?

"Hello?" I call, timid. There's another sound from downstairs. Not a voice, but a *skittering*—plastic rolling over hardwood floors, then movement—not footsteps, just *something is moving in this house.* I look around for a weapon but the only thing I can think of is the wand off the vacuum cleaner, and that's still in my bathroom. I walk briskly along the hall. My hands shake as I break the thing down to free it. I tell myself I'm shaking from the cold but I'm not; I'm scared—I'm properly scared, and I have to walk downstairs on my own to figure this out.

I tug the hallway light on then make my way down the stairs, wishing that chandelier were functional so I didn't have to walk into the foyer in the semi-dark. I keep moving, and march straight to the parlour, tugging the light on as I step into the room.

And I see the source of the noise immediately: I left a bucket sitting on the circular coffee table—a clean, dry cloth inside, ready for tomorrow.

The bucket is now on the floor on the other side of the room. The cloth is metres away—a distance that makes no sense, even if a freak draught did knock the bucket off the table. I briefly convince myself it's rats or possums and while I'm not excited about the possibility, it does give me a moment of relief—until I realize that there's still not a single fresh dropping in this house.

Toilet-trained rats or possums?

I give out an uneasy laugh, shaking my head as I look around, then I laugh again as I recall the ghost stories Tad used to tell me.

There were vague spectres who didn't have names and others who did—Clarence the farmer died doing some work on a paddock next door and now roamed the halls looking for his wife, Nancy, desperate to confess that he did not like the blue hat she wore to church, unable to face eternity having lied to her every week for most of their marriage. And Mitchell, a cheeky child ghost who would leap out at Uncle Tad sometimes and laugh when he startled. There was Bethany, a floating woman in long nightgowns who would sometimes appear when he was writing but only to offer criticisms for his sloppy grammar, and Doris, who was once a housekeeper and was distinctly unimpressed with how messy Tad was. One night, when he was up working late, a whole family of ghosts appeared sitting on the chesterfield lounges in his study, having a full-blown conversation about how boring it was living with an author and how they wished Tad did something more exciting for work.

He never mentioned ghosts knocking over buckets and glasses, but it's just the kind of silly mischief he would have come up with.

As a kid, I always assumed Tad was telling the same stories to people in town, and that's why everyone got that startled look on their face when they first learned where I lived. In that long stretch of summer between high school and university I buried myself in the town's historical society archives and researched Wurimbirra. It always struck me as odd that this house, surrounded by farms of hundreds of acres, sits on precisely one acre, so I was curious about that but also, I wanted to learn everything I could about Charles and Flora Fowler.

I thought I'd find a quaint tale about a wealthy couple who were more interested in reading than farming. Instead, I discovered a story of racism and mass murder, and a family torn apart by shame. It's no wonder most of Forbes thinks this place is haunted—great-great-great-grandparents probably warned their children of the dark past of this house, and over the generations, the detail just got lost. Uncle Tad bought the house in the fifties, he heard whispers about a haunting and he put his own spin on it, making the story a fun one to try to put Jon and me at ease, but he had no idea where the myth originated.

By the time I learned the truth I was old enough to have concluded that ghosts do not exist and I've dealt with plenty of upsetting history in my career and never once felt the echoes of it lingered into the present day in any supernatural way.

That was before things started moving of their own accord right in my own house.

History doesn't always stay in the past, Fiona. I hope to God you know what you're doing.

Mum's words circle through my mind as I walk through the ground floor, checking every room. It's freezing and my teeth are chattering and I'm clinging to that vacuum cleaner like it could actually help me protect myself if I did run into something nefarious.

I check every single room. Every window and door is closed. I don't see anything out of place, other than the bucket and the cloth.

The house is still, just as it has been for ten years, and it's empty, just as it should be, except for me. It defies all sense of reason or logic, yet somehow, I know that something else now calls Wurimbirra home.

I manage to make it out of bed at sunrise the next morning, but not because I'm well-rested enough to wake easily. I heard the grandfather clock chime every single hour last night, until I promised myself I wouldn't wind it again today, so it falls dormant again and stops chiming the change of hours. I used to sleep right through the chimes the first time I lived in this house—in fact, I barely even noticed them during the day, but that was when I felt entirely at ease here. Things have certainly changed.

As the sky began to brighten outside, I was staring at the

ceiling, thinking about the bucket and the glasses and the ring and the book and the history of this land and how it all might hang together.

I'm feeling sluggish and exhausted, but I pull on my active wear and promise myself I'll be glad once I'm in a routine again and this walk becomes a habit. It's a relief to step out the front door of the house into the cold morning air, with the pink-gold of the dawn before me.

And half an hour later I'm walking back through those double doors, a little sweaty beneath my hoody, even though my fingers and my ears are freezing, and I do feel clearer. Brighter.

After a shower and some coffee, I'm ready to tackle the day. I go straight to Tad's storage room because that's where I might find answers to my questions about the book, and that is a lot more fun to think about than whatever moved the bucket last night.

The storeroom is in the western wing of the first floor, right next to Tad's bedroom, right opposite Jon's. It's just a bedroom—the same size as the other seven, but it's laid out differently. There are heavy wooden shelves lining the walls, so it feels more like an archive room at a library than a bedroom. And Jon was right—every single box is labeled in Mum's careful script, denoting the contents and the date. There are boxes of tax paperwork and boxes of contracts and boxes of reader letters. Good grief, *so many reader letters*, at least one box for every year from 1960, and then a little cluster of boxes that just say Pre-1960. I open one of the pre-1960 boxes first and there's utter chaos inside—just papers stuffed into it in no apparent order. Some are crinkled, as if they'd been crumpled into a ball then straightened out.

A glimpse into Uncle Tad's working life before Mum arrived, I guess. I open the 1960 box next, and this is clearly Mum's work. There's dozens or maybe hundreds of clusters of handwritten and typed pages in here, each carefully paper-clipped in the top left-hand corner. The first is dated January 1960.

> Dear Mr Winslow,
>
> I read your remarkable book *Forgotten* last week for a college class on creative writing. My professor said this book would change our lives and I was skeptical at the time but I felt like you had looked into my family and captured us . . .

The writer goes on with effusive praise for several pages, and then there's a faded carbon copy of a typed reply from Tad.

> Dear Annaleigh,
>
> Thank you so much for taking the time to write me about *Forgotten.* When I first had the idea for this book in 1953, I had just returned home after a long stint away and I was so overjoyed to be home with my family again.

And then he goes on for a whole page, answering some of her questions, giving her advice about her creative writing course and her college career. My eyes mist over as I read the letter—it's such a generous exchange. But as I flick through the other boxes, it occurs to me that there are thousands of letters like it here. What am I supposed to do with all of this? I decide to text Jon.

> I am in the storeroom looking for letters from Charity Wilkie. Do you understand how much paperwork is in here? I just found all of Tad's fan mail over the years and it looks like he's kept copies of all of his replies too.

Yeah, Jon texts back. I knew there was a lot there. We've been approached by a few libraries and museums over the years interested in setting up a collection in his honor. Ginny has the details.

I look around the room and sigh. I was hoping I'd quickly find letters between Tad and Charity Wilkie that would shed some light on the book, but it's not going to be that simple. I'll figure out the rest of the house in time, but now that I've seen what's here, this room feels too important for me to sort through myself. And of course there's been interest in a Taddeus Winslow collection over the years—now that I think about it, that only makes good sense.

I'm not the person to figure out how to make that happen, but I do know who is, and she lives just down the road. Fortunately for me, she managed every aspect of Tad's professional and personal life, so she probably also knows exactly who Charity Wilkie is.

"Hello, love!" my stepfather, Alan, bellows, waving with surprised delight as I step from my car at the farm he shares with Mum. It's fair to say she caught me off guard in 1976 when she told me they were getting married. I knew they were acquaintances, but everyone along this road and in this district knew Alan. Mum didn't even tell me they were dating until they were setting the date for the wedding.

She's always been the kind of woman who holds her cards close to her chest. Even back then, that was frustrating and sometimes baffling to me. I'd often talk to Tad about it and he'd listen calmly and empathize, then tell me I absolutely had to be patient with her. It was one of the only areas of my life where he didn't give me any useful advice, but I still knew it meant everything to him that Mum and I cared for one another. He always acted as mediator when things between us were rocky and when too much time had passed between calls or visits; he always seemed to find some vitally important reason for us to all get together.

I've always wanted to understand Mum but she holds more of herself back than she ever reveals. It must have been different with Tad, because it's only since he died that her reluctance to open herself up has become a giant, insurmountable barrier between us.

"Hi, Alan," I say, and he approaches me to kiss me on the cheek.

"It's so good to have you back in town, love. I've been meaning to come down and say hello but we've been sowing the mid-season wheat, you know how it is. Are you settling in okay? I hope you won't be lonely in that great big house all alone."

I bet I'm going to hear those words dozens of times over the next few months as people realize I've moved back into Wurimbirra. Alan means well, and he's always been kind to me, so I just smile and shrug.

"It's going to be a lot of work but I'm sure it will be worth it in the end. Is Mum home?"

"Yes, cooking up some scones for the boys, I think." Alan has a few farmhands employed here—two or three at a time, usually. There's a cluster of worker's cottages and a large work shed a few hundred metres away from the house he shares with Mum. Their roles on this farm divide sharply along traditional gender lines. Hers is to feed the menfolk and keep the books. He handles the labor, the machinery, the crops and the livestock.

Alan leaves me to drive his farm truck up to the big shed to "the boys," and I let myself into the house, calling out so I don't startle Mum.

"Is that you, Fiona?" she calls back. "I'm in the kitchen."

I follow the sound of her voice through the house. The scent of baked goods hangs heavily in the air, and the digital timer on the oven is counting down six minutes. Mum is wearing an apron over her chinos and collared shirt—today, it's patterned with tiny polka dots in purple and blue. She looks at me warily, then asks, "Would you like a coffee?"

It's clear she's still adjusting to the news that I've moved home—her lips are thin, her nostrils flared, her shoulders locked tight. It's probably just habit and good manners pressing her to invite me to stay for a drink, but actually, coffee does sound good right now after the rotten night's sleep.

"Yes, please," I say, and I pull out a stool to sit at their breakfast bar. "I'm sorry I didn't tell you."

"I'm not sure I want to talk about that right now."

I hear the words she doesn't speak at the end of that sentence—*or ever.* Even once she forgives me, she still won't want to talk about it, because it will be tense and awkward and Virginia Edendale does not handle such things well at all.

I let silence descend as she makes two coffees, both black and strong, because we take ours the same. She comes to sit beside me at the breakfast bar, sliding the coffee across as I murmur thanks.

"How have you been?" I ask her hesitantly. She flicks me a glance.

"Fine. Everything here is fine. And you and Lucas . . . it's all unwound now?"

I called Jon right after Lucas left that day in February. I couldn't stop crying, and my cousin dropped everything to come and sit with me, while I told the story ten times, trying to get it to make sense in my head. Later that day, once I'd calmed myself down a little and Jon had gone home, I found myself missing Tad so much I couldn't bear it. He'd have fixed this for me—not my marriage, of course, but he'd have had advice and words of comfort that would have soothed the ache of pain and rejection and humiliation. With Tad gone, I had an overwhelming instinct to call Mum. If I'd been less distressed, that might have surprised me.

She and I sat in near-silence for most of that call. I'd been crying all day and my voice was so hoarse it hurt to speak. Mum was apparently so shocked she couldn't think of a single thing to say except *I'm sorry.* But she called me every Sunday night for the first few weeks after he left. They were brief phone calls—*Are you okay? Yes. Of course you are, you're very strong*—but at the time I was exhausted from dealing with the fallout and breaking the news to people and I actually appreciated how simple those calls from my mother were.

"They bought me out of the business," I tell her now. "We have to live apart for a year to finalize the divorce but we've already agreed on a financial settlement. He's moved in with her already, so we're selling the house at Waverly."

Mum nods, then blows on her coffee before she takes a sip. "You had no inkling . . . ?"

"Not a hint of suspicion."

Lucas didn't even seem anxious the morning he ended our marriage. It was an ordinary Monday, after an emotional Sunday afternoon moving Mia into her dorm room, then a somber Sunday night spent watching a movie. He got up early and went to the gym just as he always did, and when he came home, I was sitting at our dining room table eating my oats and reading email on my laptop. He sat opposite me with a cup of green tea and I asked him what his day looked like. He told me he was planning his team's performance reviews, and then he said he had something to tell me. I thought it was something about work so I barely looked up until he raised his voice.

"See, Fiona? You barely even know when I'm in the same

room as you! A man needs to be needed and Keira needs me!"

Mum sighs suddenly, and for a second I think it is a sigh of disappointment in me. How could I be so blind as to miss what was happening right under my nose, so clueless as to not wonder *why* they'd grown so close? It's a question I've asked myself a million times over the past few months. Keira was widowed in late 2004, and in the wake of her husband Rob's death, Lucas and I agreed we'd do everything we could to support her and her sons. For me, that meant carrying more than my share of the workload at our firm. For Lucas, it meant acting as stand-in father to her young twins whenever the need arose. At what point did that innocent, altruistic act become something more, and why didn't I see it? I might never know.

But I realize I've misunderstood Mum's frustration when her lips thin further and she shakes her head in disgust.

"You deserved better than that. Especially from *them*. I'm . . ." She clears her throat. "I really am very sorry this happened to you."

I stare down into my coffee and blink until the tears that prick my eyes are gone. I'm left feeling guilty that I doubted even for a second that Mum would take my side in this, especially given the circumstances. In my defense, even that small display of regret and sympathy from my mother is about as close to vulnerable as she'll ever allow herself to be with me.

"Thanks," I eventually croak. "It's been a rough year."

"The girls seem to be adjusting well, at least."

"They have their own lives now. In some ways I'm grateful for the timing."

Mum makes a sound of agreement, then we fall into silence again.

She was a tough but fair parent for all of my childhood—firm and consistent to Uncle Tad's soft and unpredictable, cool and aloof to his intense and warm, at least when it came to me. She's not demonstrative and she rarely says the words, but I do know my mother loves me. It's one of the few things I'm sure of when it comes to Virginia Edendale. She doesn't like to make a fuss, so I rarely know if she's displeased or thrilled by something. With the exception of tech support from her granddaughters, which we all recognize is actually just an excuse to call them, she refuses to ask for help, so I've never seen her sad or low or stuck. She's shy with strangers, shy sometimes even with friends. She's much more likely to mutter under her breath or make some passive-aggressive comment than she is to stand up for herself.

Virginia Edendale is not the kind of woman to shatter glass ceilings or burn her bra. She's most comfortable at home, and, I suspect, most comfortable home alone. She's a deeply anxious person, although she'd never admit it. It's like she's been on high alert, afraid to let her guard down even for every second, for my whole life, even when it comes to me. Maybe especially when it comes to me, and I have no idea why.

I wish I understood my mother. I wish she'd let me *know* her.

"It's not too late," she says hesitantly. I look at her, startled. Did I say that aloud? Or does she mean—

"Not too late for me and *Lucas*?" I blurt, horrified by the suggestion. Even when he left our house that day in February, I knew there was no going back. "Oh, I assure you it is."

Mum's lips thin. "Wurimbirra, Fiona. It's not too late for you to back out. To tell Jon you've changed your mind. He'll understand."

"What on earth gives you the impression that I've *changed my mind*?"

"Haven't you?"

Images flash through my mind—glass shattered on the kitchen floor, a bucket that moved itself across the parlour, me stalking the hallways carrying the barrel of a vacuum cleaner in lieu of a weapon, me lying wide awake staring at the roof listening to sounds through the house that I can't make sense of.

I shake my head fiercely anyway.

"No!"

"Then why are you here?"

"I came to see *you*, Mum," I say. She gives me a look and I suddenly feel like a silly teenager again, caught out on a lie . . . then doubling down on it despite the fact that she already knows there's an ulterior reason for this visit. "I did!"

"Hmm."

"The house is full of Tad's things. The storeroom alone is . . ." I break off, wincing, as a flush steels up my cheeks. "And Jon said there's been interest from libraries and museums about a collection?"

"Yes, we've fielded several inquiries over the past ten years from institutions looking for donations for an exhibit about Tad's life."

"Well, I just—" I clear my throat. "I was hoping you might help me sort through all of that. That's all. I don't know how to make any of that happen but I think we should." Mum calmly sips her coffee, then rests the cup carefully on the breakfast bar. I suddenly have a vision of her in the house with me, working to figure out what from that mammoth collection of paperwork is worth donating to a museum. It wouldn't fix the noises at night or the fact that I'm feeling unnerved about the house, but at least I wouldn't be alone, all day every day, for the foreseeable future, which sounded perfect just a week ago but is now starting to feel like a bit of a nightmare. "Maybe just a few hours a day, Mum. It won't take us long—"

"I can't."

"But—"

"I have not set foot in that house since the day of your uncle's wake and even then it was . . . uncomfortable."

"I know," I say softly. "I can imagine what it was like to find—"

"But you can't imagine, Fiona. You weren't there."

"So tell me about it."

Mum looks at me, startled, as if I've asked for something else ridiculous—first help with the paperwork, and now *this.*

"I don't want to talk about it," she snaps.

I don't want to upset her. I really *do* want her help figuring out that paperwork but even more than that, she's my mother and I'd love to have a better relationship with her. It might be nice if I could call in here sometimes, to share a cup of coffee and a chat, or if we could get to the point that she'd stop by when she's driving past, just to say hi.

I moved home for Wurimbirra. But maybe, at least on some level, I also moved home for her. But if I push too hard, she'll shut this conversation down. I know that for sure, because it's what she's always done when I've asked her about the hard things.

Her childhood.

My father.

I don't remember the first time I asked Mum about him, but by the age of nine or ten, I understood the subject was off-limits. She's always reacted like this—she gets prickly and wound up, even if I'm asking for the most benign details. But Uncle Tad, lovely, patient Uncle Tad, was always happy to talk about things. Even the difficult, awful things. But for Uncle Tad, I'm not sure I'd know much at all about Aaron West.

Tad had flown home for my parents' wedding and was about to return to Australia when the accident happened. Aaron was killed instantly—the news came as such a shock that Mum collapsed. Tad delayed his return to support her but couldn't stay forever, so convinced her to come visit him here in Australia for a while.

Mum realized she was pregnant after she arrived, but in those days, it was unclear if air travel was safe for pregnant women and so she had to stay until the delivery. But by the time I was born, Mum had reached the conclusion that there was nothing back in the US for her anyway, so she stayed for good. Aaron had died so soon after the wedding, she hadn't even had the chance to change her name. She flew to Australia as Virginia Winslow, and she was only supposed to be here for a few weeks, so of course she didn't bring her marriage certificate with her.

It was very late in her pregnancy that she and Tad realized they should have had someone post the certificate over, but by then it was too late for them to do so. At that time in Australia, particularly rural Australia, it was commonplace for single mothers to have their children forcibly adopted. Mum and Tad became worried that if she told the story of my conception and her widowhood at the hospital, but didn't have paperwork to back it up, I might be taken away from her.

My birth certificate lists Mum's maiden name as Virginia West and her married name as Virginia Winslow, which was still her name on her driver's license. My father is listed as Aaron Winslow. There's even a signature beside his name, which I'm pretty sure Mum or Tad forged.

There are so many things I'd love to ask my mother about, especially now that Tad is gone and I have no one else to ask. What was it like to realize she was going to be a single mother in 1960, in a brand-new country where she only knew her brother? How did she meet Aaron, and how deeply did she love him? Did it feel like she would never get over his loss when he died? When did it start to get easier?

I can only dream that she'd let me close enough to ask things like that.

"Do you remember if Uncle Tad had an author friend named Charity Wilkie?" I say instead, changing the subject before she does.

Mum pauses as she thinks, then finally shakes her head. She gives me a wary glance, as if she can't believe I'm not going to ask her more about the house or the paperwork or the day Tad died.

"I don't think so, no. Why?"

"Just curious. I'm reading one of her books."

"He liked to correspond with other authors. You'll probably find letters in the—" She breaks off, as if she's afraid to even mention the storeroom after the conversation we just had, but then she raises her chin. "Letters to his author friends are in the boxes on the shelves at the back, near the window. There's only a handful of those boxes. Shouldn't be too hard to find letters from this author, if they exist." The oven timer sounds, and she slips off the stool and pulls on oven mitts, before she slides three trays with fat scones up onto the cooktop. She pauses with her back to me, and then says, very quietly, "Fiona, do be careful. I can tell you think I'm silly worrying about you in that house but I have good reason."

"We had sixteen happy years there, Mum," I say carefully. She glances back at me, then fusses with the scones some more.

"*You* had sixteen happy years there. Of course you did. You were caught up in Tad's fantasy world."

"You weren't happy when we lived with him?"

"He was the best man I've ever known. More generous than you can imagine. But that house—" She breaks off, then clears her throat. "Just don't change too much. Don't go . . . *Please* don't go digging around over there."

"I have no intention of making drastic changes. It'll be a restoration, not some grand renovation."

"Good. But that's not even what I meant."

"What *did* you mean?"

She shakes her head as if she's said too much, and it's maddening how she does this—like she teases me by cracking open the door just a little, then slams it shut in my face. After Tad died I tried so hard to be here for her, and I know she was heartbroken, but she never even let me see her pain.

"Mum," I say, and my frustration is building, leaving my tone shorter than I intended. "I'm not going to play games with you. If there's something about the house I should be afraid of, you're going to have to tell me what it is. Otherwise I am going to make it my home again. I'm going to change what needs to be changed and I'm going to find a way to be happy there again."

"I just don't want you to make rash decisions because things with Lucas haven't worked out," she says stiffly. "You've already gone against your uncle's dying wish—"

"But that's not even true, Mum," I exclaim. "Jon told me that he heard you—"

She swings back to face me, eyes flashing with surprising fire. "Jon doesn't *know* what he heard that day. You kids don't understand—" She squeezes her eyes closed for just a minute as she collects herself.

"Well, what did he hear, then?" I demand. "What is it we *don't understand*?"

Oh, what I wouldn't give for her to lose control. To shout at me, if that's what it takes.

"Tad expressly asked you to leave that place be until I pass too. Has it even occurred to you that maybe he didn't ask that for our benefit, but to protect you?"

I think about the bucket and the glasses and that eerie, prickling feeling I had last night.

"Protect me from what?" I ask uneasily.

She stares at me for a long moment, then she deflates, turning back to her scones, as if they require her full attention as they cool.

"Wurimbirra has secrets, Fiona," she finally says. "And I

pray to God that even if you do stay there, you never find out what they are."

The back door slams, and a soft voice calls out, heavy with a British accent. "Ginny? I was just up at the shed and Alan said you had morning tea for the boys so I thought I'd come collect it and save you going up there—Oh, hi!"

It's a young blonde woman, maybe in her early twenties. If she notices that the air in that kitchen is thick with tension, she doesn't let on. She just offers me a sweet smile and extends her hand towards me.

"Erin Davies. I'm Vince's girlfriend."

"This is Fiona," Mum says, and Erin's eyes widen.

"The famous Fiona! I heard you've moved back into Wurimbirra. On your own? Really? Aren't you *scared*? One of the girls I met at the gym told me your uncle did a talk at her high school and the stories he told them about that house—"

"Were fiction," I say even though my stomach is still churning at my mother's comment. It's habit to argue for logic when it comes to Wurimbirra, even if I'm not feeling quite so "logical" myself at the moment. "My uncle Tad was a novelist. He made things up for a living—that was his job. He made a very boring, run-down house seem spooky and mysterious because he loved the drama. That's all there is to it. But . . . sorry, who is Vince?"

"Vince and Erin are backpackers. Vince is working for us for six months. He and Erin are living in the too-small cottage," Mum tells me as she reaches into the fridge and withdraws a mixing bowl, covered in foil, and I know it will be full of cream she whipped earlier for the scones. There are three worker's cottages on the farm. We visited this farm for some reason or another when I was five and I jokingly called them "too small, too big, just right" and those nicknames have stuck. "Fiona and I are done here, Erin. I'll help you carry this up to the boys at the shed."

And like that, I'm dismissed. I slip back into my car and turn down the driveway, back out to the main road and beyond that, Wurimbirra.

THE MIDNIGHT ESTATE

BY CHARITY WILKIE

Silas stewed on Marie's situation day and night after he found her standing in the rain. He wanted to talk it through with someone—someone smarter than him, someone more compassionate. He found it all spilling out of him a few days later in a long, unbroken monologue of frustration and concern as he sat at his sister's bedside.

". . . so, that's the whole mess and I just don't know how to help her. It's not my place but I just can't help but feel that I should, you know? I think it's what you would do . . ."

Silas looked at his sister, who remained stubbornly unconscious, even as he poured his heart out to her. He reached out to brush a lock of her brown hair back from her forehead. Her skin was so cool to his touch, and over those past weeks, she'd become pale. Maeve was now a living, breathing ghost.

It felt good to speak the truth of it aloud, although he'd never have dared to do so if Mr Williams hadn't passed a few days earlier. Now Maeve was all alone in the room when the nurses were busy elsewhere, and Silas knew it was absurd, but he worried about her feeling lonely.

"She reminds me so much of Mom, Maeve," Silas whispered, reaching to take his sister's hand. He had to stop talking—the lump in his throat would choke him otherwise. "I wish you'd wake up. I really *need* you to wake up.

Everything here . . . everything back at home. It's all so broken and I don't know what to do."

He stared at her through his tears, willing for something—*anything*—just a sign that he was right to hold on to hope. A sign that she might yet come back to him. A sign that there might yet be a miracle for his sister, because he had finally realized that's what he was holding out for. She had been in that bed, completely unresponsive, for more than a month.

This was different too. She always sat in the booth next to his but was usually facing him. If she followed his instructions they'd be seated back-to-back.

Ah. He was giving her the opportunity to talk to him privately.

She'd been worried about someone spotting them chatting for a while. Some days she pushed the fear out of her mind, but other days, it would just about drive her mad, to think that someone might see her talking to Silas and report back to Rupert that she'd made a friend. A male friend.

The fallout from something like that would be catastrophic.

"Thank you," she murmured, after she took her seat. "And Silas, I'm really sorry about—"

"No," he said, voice just above a whisper. "Don't you dare apologize. Just tell me, Marie—does he hit you?"

"No," she said honestly. "No, he does not."

She could sense Silas's confusion even though she couldn't see his face. And this was what it all came down to—the brilliant twist in the way Rupert hurt her. Perhaps some might have sympathy for her if he was physically abusive, but he wasn't. Maybe he'd grabbed her wrist with a little too much force from time to time, he'd certainly squeezed her shoulder a time or two and they were intimate when he wanted, whether she wanted to or not.

Despite all of that, Rupert had never once bruised her.

She sensed that it was coming closer all the time, that direct physical violence was an inevitability. But knowing how Rupert liked to torture her, she wondered if he was playing with her even in that, leaving her existing in a heightened state of fearful anticipation.

"But you do need help," Silas said. Marie looked down at the booth's table. She rubbed her thumbnail through a ridge in the cracked vinyl.

"Yes," she whispered hoarsely. She couldn't bring herself to think much about a possible pregnancy and what it would mean, but it was at the front of her mind that the high stakes of her situation would soon be even higher. "Yes, I think I do."

"I'm not sure I understand, Marie. Can you try to explain the problem to me? If you're comfortable, of course."

Marie knew she should be careful. Sharing her situation with anyone was a dangerous proposition, and she barely knew Silas. She was just so very desperate for help, and he was the first person to invite her to explain what was going on. In doing so, he'd offered to ease the loneliness of her nightmare.

"I'm not allowed to check the mail. He checks the odometer on my car every single night. The girls at the exchange tell him if I make calls. He tells me what I can wear and who I can see. What I can eat. What time I go to bed. Sometimes I think I should be grateful that he's so attentive . . ."

"There's a difference between 'attentive' and 'controlling.'"

"He even decides who I can *talk* to. That's why I didn't dare . . ."

"That's why you always sat in the booth next to me, even though we often spoke, and it might have made more sense for you to sit *with* me."

"That's right."

"Are you scared?"

"Terrified."

"Have you tried talking to your brother?"

Irving? She hadn't dared. He'd grown much closer to Rupert than he was to her by then. And besides that, he was a kid—only seventeen years old.

"I'll help you in any way I can, if there *is* any way I can. But I'll have to go home soon, Marie. At the end of the day, and in a time like this, family is really all you've got."

It was busy in the diner that day and Irving was out clearing tables. He made his way around the diner chatting to customers, flirting gently with Helen, who was easily twice his age. Marie knew—she had seen over those months—that Irving was charming and polite, even to Carmen and Rodrigo. Their relationship had grown distant, but Irving was still kind and good. When their parents died it had been Marie desperately scrambling to care for him, but now, it might just be his turn to return the favor.

It was a risk, but there was so much at stake now, and every single choice before her involved some kind of risk.

"Okay," she breathed. "Yes, you're right. I'll try to talk to him."

"Good," Silas said quietly. "Now?"

"I can't now," she blurted, panic sending her pulse racing. No, she needed time to prepare herself—to think about what to say and how to say it.

"Tomorrow," Silas said. Marie closed her eyes and tried to steady her pulse.

"Tomorrow," she whispered back.

Marie walked into the diner the next morning just as Irving took a trolley loaded with cutlery through to the kitchen. She looked for Silas but was surprised to find him missing. Maybe he was running late.

She could have done with the morale boost of a friendly smile, but no matter. She'd been up more than half the night planning this and she couldn't afford to hesitate even for a second—if she did, she'd just turn around and go home. And so she nodded a greeting to Carmen, who was standing at the register, and then for the first time ever, she slipped through the swinging doors to follow her brother into the kitchen. She grabbed his elbow and dragged him back past Rodrigo, towards the door to the back alley behind the diner.

"Marie, I'm working right now."

"I know. Carmen will understand," Marie said. Her voice came out husky and uncertain—a far cry from the assertive, clear tone she'd intended to use. She cleared her throat and waited until they were through the doors and in the alleyway to speak again, but as soon as they stepped through the doors to the outside, the heavy smell of rank garbage hit her.

She pressed a fist to her mouth and concentrated fiercely as she tried to convince her stomach to hold on to breakfast.

"What's wrong?" Irving asked, impatient, but then he maybe read something in her face and his tone softened. "Hey—are you sick?"

The moment passed and the violent churning in her stomach eased—replaced instead by equally violent butterflies. With razorblades for wings. She pressed her shaking hands to her belly now and looked up at her brother. God, he'd changed so much in those terrible years since the accident. All she wanted to do was to drag him home to wash that greasy hair, force him to have a haircut and to iron his clothes and maybe feed him a vegetable or two.

"I need to talk to you."

"What about?" he said warily. "You've hardly wanted anything to do with me in months and now you want me to sit here while you lecture me?"

"What are you *talking* about?" she said, bewildered. "You wanted me to stop mothering you, Irving. So that's what I did."

"Whatever," he sighed impatiently. But Marie felt a pang of uncertainty now. Irving was already on the defensive. "Listen, if it's about the other work I've been doing. It's just for a while, okay? Just for some extra cash, so I can get myself set up. I was thinking of going to community—"

"What extra work?" She frowned, and Irving hesitated, then looked away.

"Nothing," he said too quickly. "Nothing. Well? What is it, then?"

She looked down at her watch and felt her pulse quicken. This was already getting off track and she didn't have long—Rupert would be home for lunch in less than an hour.

"I think I need to leave Rupert," she blurted. There, she'd said it.

Irving's eyes bulged.

"What? Why would you—"

"I j-just do."

Her voice was so small. All she had to do was to open her mouth and explain. To roar to get Irving's attention, to demand he rise to the occasion and help her.

"Does he hit you, Marie?" Irving asked cautiously. She squeezed her eyes closed. The simple way through this would be to lie. *Yes. He beats me mercilessly.*

But Irving would see right through her. He could always tell when she wasn't being honest.

"It's m-more complicated than that," she whispered. "He controls everything I do."

"So he's bossy. He's bossy with everyone and you *are* his wife, it's not unreasonable. But has he ever laid a hand on you?"

She looked away as she shook her head. Irving frowned down at her.

"Then you need to sort this out with him. Don't go dragging me into your domestic problems. He's a good husband. A brilliant provider—hell, look at that fancy house you have! That car! He works damned hard to give you that lifestyle—so what if he's raised his voice at you or something? He's got to blow off steam somewhere, for God's sakes."

She started to cry then, big, heaving sobs that echoed around the alleyway and left Irving alarmed, and more than a little annoyed.

"Sis, stop it!" He took two steps away from her, and she knew he was frustrated and embarrassed by the display of emotion. "See, this is what he always says. It's like this with women, isn't it? You don't get what you want so you turn the tears on to manipulate us. You have to stop being so hysterical."

"Don't tell him," Marie blurted. "I didn't mean it. We just had a fight and I was upset. I shouldn't have—"

"Go home and work it out with Rupert! Like an adult, Marie, okay?" Irving muttered irritably. He left her there in the alleyway, pulling the door to the diner shut behind him.

The call from Dr Lomas had come as Silas was about to go for his walk. The morning nurse found that Maeve had slipped away in the night, easing silently from the limbo of the coma into whatever lay beyond.

When Silas arrived at the hospital, he found her on the same bed in the same room, and yet it was obvious to him now that whatever it was that had made Maeve the person he knew and loved, that part of her was gone.

He sat beside her bed and he took her hand in his and he looked at his sister's beautiful face and felt like the grief would split him in two. Perhaps he'd known for some time that this moment was coming but it still felt so wrong, so unfair. It wasn't supposed to be like this. He just needed two minutes—just long enough to say *I'm sorry I wasn't here when you needed me* and just long enough for her to smile that beautiful smile and to say *That's okay, Silas, I forgive you.*

He'd have given it all back just for that moment. Every surprising cent he'd earned. Every amazing adventure he'd had, except, perhaps, the wildest adventure of all—marrying Christine, having his son.

That's what he had to focus on now. It was awful and it was hard but this odd period back home was coming to an end.

Silas kissed her gently on the forehead before he left the hospital room for the last time. He would bury her right beside their mother. He'd pack up Maeve's home, list both properties. He'd tie up all the loose ends so he didn't have to return because God only knew there was nothing for him in California now.

And then at last, he could leave, to travel to his new home, back to his son and to Christine. He'd been gone for weeks, and he had tried so hard not to think about the reality of what he'd left behind—not the happy family he pictured when he thought of them, but a mess so large he didn't know where to start to untangle it.

Marie was on edge for days after she spoke to Irving. Would he tell Rupert, or would he keep her secret? She wanted to trust that Irving would be loyal to her—after all, they were family.

And when the first day passed without incident and then a second and a third, she started to relax. Silas hadn't been at the diner, but other than that, things seemed normal, and she told herself that there was every chance Maeve had woken up and he was spending time with her.

It was four days after she spoke to Irving in the alley that she heard the front door slam. She was mopping the hallway at the time and hadn't even started dinner yet. She put the mop back into the bucket and called out uncertainly, "Rupert? You're home early—"

He grabbed her wrist and he pushed her up against the wall. Rupert's face was red and he was panting as if he'd sprinted home. A wild, unrestrained violence danced in his eyes.

"I told you what would happen if you left me, Marie. Did you really think he wouldn't tell me? You're as pathetic as each other—he's a simpering puppy chasing after me for scraps and you're a disloyal bitch—"

Later, as she held a bag of frozen peas to her blackening eye, Marie wondered bitterly if Irving would be willing to help now, or if he'd try to tell her that Rupert was such a brilliant provider he was entitled to use his fists on her every now and again to blow off some steam.

CHAPTER 7

Fiona

I'm lying in my bed and there's a man hovering over me. He doesn't have a face, but he does have a knife, and it's close to my neck. He's speaking, and I can't make out the words, but I *know* he's threatening me—telling me to stay quiet.

I scream and cry until I run out of breath and then I'm suffocating but no one comes and I'm alone with him and time seems to be stretching and stretching and *how long have I been stuck here like this*—

I sit up with a shout and my surroundings snap back to reality in an instant. I'm alone in my room—of course I'm alone, but the fear feels like a physical sensation, like a hot current of terror running through my blood, into my legs and my arms and my stomach. I am drenched in sweat and shaking. Outside my window, the sky is brightening with the dawn of a new day. I can't stay in this house another second.

I pull my walking clothes on and run down the stairs and out the front door, gasping at the cold morning air as I step onto the veranda. I'm trying to talk myself down as I walk, telling myself that Jon's nightmare simply got into my head and Tad's stories around town are haunting me.

And the stern self-talk works—to a degree. Ten minutes

into my walk my heart rate has come down a little and I feel like my mind is clearing, like the fog of the fright is passing.

A car pulls out from Jack's family farm's driveway up ahead, engine roaring quietly, headlights on. I haven't seen cars out here my last two mornings—this is a quiet road most of the time. It slows down as the driver sees me, and my heart sinks when I realize it's Jack.

Oh my God. I'm a mess. I reach up and touch my hair, only to find it is sticking out at all manner of angles—frizzy and matted from the tossing and turning as I slept. There's nothing I can do about it now, but my face heats anyway as he pulls to a stop beside me.

"Hey, Fi," he greets me. "Nice morning for a walk."

I decide not to tell him I am not walking so much as sprinting away from my haunted house.

"You're up early, too," I say.

"I'm doing some farm visits over at Condobolin today so have to get an early start. But I was actually going to call you today—wanted to invite you to reader's group tonight at Turn the Page."

I wince at that. "I'm not much of a fan of book clubs, Jack."

A group of school mums started a book club when Mia was in grade 2 and I went a few times, but the meetings were an odd mix of gossip and pretentious literary criticism and it just wasn't for me. I went to another once, comprised primarily of my team from W&J Heritage, but most members of that group never got around to reading the actual book and in time it just dissolved.

"This isn't a *book club*, Fi," Jack scolds me gently. "It's a reader's group."

"Aren't they the same thing?"

"Not even close."

"But I won't have read the book . . . !"

"It's not like that. Just bring something to read—anything you want. I'll pick you up at 6:40 p.m.?" I hesitate again, but he flashes me a half smile. "It's not like it's out of my way. This thing at the bookstore is really relaxed, I promise. You'll love it."

What I'll love is not being all alone with my thoughts for a night, rattling around in that house with too much time to think and work myself up into such a state that even a nightmare feels like a haunting, and so although I'm not exactly in a sociable mood, I agree to go.

"Hi, Fi," Jack greets me that evening as I walk down the front stairs towards his truck. I offer a smile and slip into the passenger's seat.

"How was Condobolin?" I ask him.

"I had to retrieve semen from a bunch of Angus bulls today. Just another day in the life of a vet," he chuckles. "Were you architecting here today?"

"I don't know what you picture when you say 'architecting,' but I'm going to be at the drowning-in-dust stage of the project for a while yet," I mutter. I spent most of the day trying to dust the ballroom and didn't even make a dent. Those massive living areas might just be the death of me. "Tell me about this book club—"

"Reader's group."

"Reader's group."

"It's the kind of thing better experienced first-hand," he tells me. He takes his eyes off the road just for a second to glance over at me and smile. "I remember how it felt in those first few months after Winnie and I split. I didn't much want to see or talk to anyone, but after a while, I figured out that too much of my own company wasn't great either. You might see some familiar faces here tonight but there's not much time for chatting the way Marilyn runs this group. And if you hate it, you never have to come back."

"It's kind of you to invite me."

"You've always been deeply unpleasant company, but what can I say? It was the neighborly thing to do," he says solemnly, and I laugh and playfully nudge him, like we're twelve years old again.

The farther we get from Wurimbirra, the more relaxed I feel.

Maybe this was a good idea after all.

There's at least twenty people at Turn the Page and even at first glance, I recognize maybe a third of them—including, to my surprise and dismay, Alan and my mother. But before I can even digest that, Marilyn the bookseller runs through the crowd to greet me and Jack at the door.

"Jack! Welcome, you know the drill." He playfully salutes her and wanders into the store, but Marilyn grabs me by my upper arms and plants a kiss on my cheek. "Thank the Lord you're back, Fiona, because this town is not the same without you. I think we've missed you every day these past—what—thirty years?"

"I've visited you plenty of times, Marilyn," I protest, laughing.

"It's not nearly the same as having you back here for good," she says. I'm not sure if that statement is overly generous or completely misguided. I wasn't exactly a local celebrity, other than my association with my uncle and much cooler cousin. But I love everything about Marilyn Owens—from her elegant sense of style to the white-blonde hair she now wears in a sharp bob. I remember a hint of Muelhens 4711 in the air of the bookstore when I was a teenager working here, and that same scent lingers as she hugs me.

Marilyn opened the store just as I started high school in the early '70s. In the beginning, this was a dark, narrow space—with haphazard, mismatched shelving and a category system that could best be described as "loose." By the time I started working for her in '75, Marilyn had found her feet. The space was still small and a little dark, but she knew exactly how to categorize and display books in a way that locals responded to. Once I moved away, the store continued to evolve. For a while, it felt like every time I came home, Marilyn had made some dramatic improvement—first, she replaced the narrow plate glass windows with beautiful heritage-style wooden frames, lending the store an air of elegance and drawing in more natural light. Then the mismatched shelving disappeared, replaced by expensive custom shelves in a rich cedar. By the time my children were born, Marilyn had taken over the lease of the shop next door, and when my girls were approaching high school, she was operating a simple coffee shop there—ahead of her time for Australian bookstores, which were much slower to embrace the coffee-and-browse trend than their North American equivalents.

"Jack invited me, but I'm still not sure what a reader's club is," I admit to her sheepishly, and Marilyn throws back her head and laughs.

"Darling girl, you are about to find out. I think you'll love it but if it's not your cup of tea, that's just fine. You could always come back tomorrow night—that's our crime club. We alternate between true crime and genre crime, and every now and again we mix it up with something exotic like Nordic noir. On Tuesday night, we have our literary club—that one's popular with my most fancy-pants customers. Basically, they won't read anything that hasn't won multiple literary awards, unless it's poetry, of course, which only needs to win a single award. On Saturday mornings, we have a primary school club, and Saturday afternoon I'm thinking of starting a graphic novel club for the high schoolers, but truth be told modern teenagers scare me so I've been putting that one off. All of those clubs run pretty much year-round, except for breaks for Christmas and Easter—Oh, and I cancel all of them in January. Obviously."

January: Australia's dead zone. It's so hot here in January, about the only thing that operates on a normal schedule is the public swimming pool.

"You run all of those book clubs every week?"

"No, every second week. Do you know what I do on the off week?"

"Tell me."

"I bloody sleep, Fiona," she laughs. "All of this socializing is exhausting!"

I do a quick headcount. There are twenty-one people in the room with us, some sitting alone already reading quietly, like Mum and Alan, who don't seem to have noticed my arrival—they're seated at a small table with their books already open in front of them. Others sit in groups, chatting. There are about a dozen upholstered bucket chairs around the room, spread across both the coffee shop side and the bookstore—plus a handful of beanbags and a few plastic chairs too. Mr Bretts, my old maths teacher, is sitting contentedly in the wheelchair he has used since he was involved in a terrible car accident when I was in grade 7. He's got a beer resting in a holder attached to his armrest, and he's engrossed in what appears to be some kind of werewolf romance novel.

Jack has taken a seat beside our mutual friend Stefanie Blaxland, who gives me a pointed look, and I know exactly why. She's wondering why I haven't let her know I'm back in town. Stef and I have been friends since preschool so I know she'll forgive me. Eventually.

Beside her is Patience Hutchkins, who might have gone to university but instead opted to remain behind to train with her father to become a mechanic. I'm embarrassed now at how I reacted to that decision. At the time, I was convinced that there was nothing for "smart kids like us" in a place like Forbes—that it was sad, maybe even a little pathetic, that she didn't have the courage to move to the city like me and Stef and Jon and Jack. I know I told her so too. But Patience has always lived up to her name and she never held my high-and-mighty attitude against me. She gives me a happy wave as soon as she catches my eye, and indicates that I should come sit in the chair currently occupied by Stef's feet.

"Excuse me," I say to Marilyn, and I make my way across the room and join the group.

"Look what the cat dragged in," Stef says pertly. "Do you know how I heard you've moved back, Fiona Winslow? I was buying a bacon-and-egg roll yesterday for breakfast and this kid in front was telling his mates that he did an electrical job at Wurimbirra for some crazy lady who's going to live there all by herself. Oh, and by the way, *he saw three actual ghosts* while he was there and *it is as haunted as everyone says.* I thought to myself—there's only one person on earth Jon would sell that house to, and she better be letting me know she's back in town soon or I am going to be *pissed.*"

"Sorry, Stef," I sigh. "I'm a rubbish friend, and it's been a rubbish year."

She reaches across to squeeze my forearm gently.

"I'm playing, honey. I get it. But what happened, Fi?"

I sent a group text to a bunch of friends back in March just to tell them Lucas and I had split, but I didn't say much more. Stef being Stef, she called me immediately, but I couldn't talk about it yet without weeping, so I declined the call and texted her that I'd call her when I was feeling up to it. I never did, but it wasn't because I don't love her. It's just that this whole disaster has felt so embarrassing, like I've walked out into a crowd of people with my skirt tucked into my undies, toilet paper stuck on my heel and lipstick on my teeth.

But something feels different now. Three sets of eyes look to me waiting expectantly, and I know that no matter what answer I give them, they'll support me.

"Lucas and Keira had an affair and pushed me out of our business," I say. There's a collective gasp—and then a collective scowl.

"Fiona," Stef says, nostrils flaring. "I am so sorry. That's . . ."

"I'm going to be fine," I tell her hastily, because she looks a bit like she's about to get in her car and drive to Edgecliff to tear them limb from limb. "The truth is the betrayal hurts more than the loss." And then all of a sudden I am flooded with memories of the years I spent with Lucas. I got my degrees and started my firm and then when I hit my mid-twenties, the next thing on my life to-do list was marriage and babies, and Lucas was right there, working alongside me. Keira and I brought him on as our business manager and quickly made him an executive partner.

He was a good friend. We had plenty of things in common. We wanted the same kind of life. If anything, I felt like he loved me more than I loved him. I thought that was a good thing. It made me feel safe.

For two and a half decades, we had a perfectly functional partnership. I told myself that the fading of our sex life was natural and normal as I approached menopause, as he approached middle age. But a stone-cold-dead sex life is one thing—how long had it been since we showed affection or tenderness to one another? Months. Years? Maybe once upon a time we'd been going through the motions but even that had faded until we weren't even pretending anymore.

Lucas never gave me butterflies, not even in the very beginning. He was a sensible, practical choice of spouse. But he wasn't the love of my life. If anything, my *work* has been that—maybe my kids.

When I think of everything I've lost this year, I'm saddest about my career. I'm sad for the girls that their family has changed forever. And I'm sad that the two people I trusted most in the world betrayed me.

I'm not sure *losing my husband* is even in the top ten things I'm upset about, and that's telling.

"I'm not excusing what he did. Not one bit. But I can see now that my marriage was over for a very long time," I admit. "It's still . . . You know. It's all a lot. But I'm not grieving *Lucas*, if that makes any sense."

"Good riddance to bad rubbish," Patience announces.

"Well, honey, when you're ready to get blackout drunk and curse that bastard to hell, you know where to find us," Stef says.

And Jack . . . he just gives me a very sad smile, and a gentle nod.

"Thank you," I croak, and I don't know why their easy acceptance makes me emotional, but it does. I moved all the way out here to be alone—to process and recover in private. I didn't expect I'd feel relieved to be around familiar faces again, especially so soon.

Marilyn stands on a chair and raises a glass of water and a spoon high into the air. She taps the glass to gain the attention of the group.

"Welcome, everyone, to the Tuesday night reader's club," she says. "We have a new member tonight—welcome home, Fiona Winslow." There's a smattering of applause and a few cheers. My cheeks heat and I sink in my chair as I give a self-conscious wave. "And since Fiona doesn't know the rules, I'll take this opportunity to remind you all of how this works. It is officially

7:00 p.m. and so we will commence our forty five minutes of quiet reading. Hopefully you came ready with a book to read, but as always, if you forgot to bring one you can take one from the basket of free titles on my counter or you can purchase anything from the shelf but you *must not speak.* That means, do *not* whisper to the person beside you. Do not comment on what you are reading. Do not, for the love of all that is good and holy, take your mobile phone out of your pocket, and if one of those rotten things *rings* in the next forty five minutes, I will personally see to its destruction." A wave of nervous laughter rolls through the room. I suspect this is not an idle threat.

"At 7:45 p.m. you may resume quiet chitchat with the people seated around you, but only if they are willing. Some people come to this club at seven o'clock every Tuesday and sit in complete silence until I kick them out at nine. Other people talk at a blistering pace from the minute they walk through the door up until I announce that the silent window has commenced—Stefanie Blaxland, you *know* I am talking about you." Another wave of laughter, only this time I'm in on the joke. "Some people will engage in riveting literary analysis of their books when the silent window has finished. Other people will leave this room without speaking a single word. That is the magic of this reader's club, friends. We get to experience the wonders of reading in community, without any of the performative nonsense that goes along with some other kinds of book clubs. We get to experience the wonders of reading in community even at those times when our enthusiasm for socializing is low, and God knows we all have days like that, don't we?" There's a ripple of agreement around the room. Marilyn lifts the glass again. "And our silent window will commence . . ." She taps the glass once, and mouths the word *now.*

I want to turn to Jack and tell him how surprised I am by this, and to thank him for inviting me, because if I was ever going to enjoy book club, it would be one just like this. I don't have the energy to engage in much conversation right now, but after these past few days, I *have* been lonely and caught up in my own mind.

I quickly discover that there is something truly magical about cracking open a book and immersing myself right into the story, surrounded by people who expect nothing from me, because they too are lost in their own fictional worlds.

THE MIDNIGHT ESTATE

BY CHARITY WILKIE

The next few weeks were some of the worst Silas could remember—a hideous combination of necessary practicality and a crushing, unrelenting grief. He had delayed processing the loss of his mother while he dealt with Maeve's illness, but there was no way to avoid it now. Maeve was gone, and Linda was gone, and every connection he had to his old life had been severed.

The kindly undertaker helped him plan the funeral but there was no one but Silas to work through Maeve's Filofax, calling friends and acquaintances he'd met and others he'd never heard of. He hated phone calls at the best of times—phone calls to strangers even more so—and this meant three excruciating days of calls, one after the other, with breaks only for food and sleep and bouts of weeping.

By the day of the service, Silas felt he was just about out of tears. He watched, dry-eyed but heartbroken, as Maeve's casket was lowered into the grave. Linda's grave was right behind him, so fresh that the dirt on top was still mounded and had not yet settled flat. He looked at a sea of grieving people—several hundred had attended the church service, and most had followed to the grave site. So many faces from that crowd of strangers were vaguely familiar to him now because they had been passing through her hospital over those weeks, sharing stories about her kindness and her light and her love.

Silas felt sure of very little by then but he was certain that when he passed, there would be no such outpouring of mass grief. He didn't consider himself to be kind or good or selfless, not like Maeve. He was just a man who seemed to attract good fortune, who had shared the spoils of his good luck only minimally. He had bought his mother a house and supported her for years, but even at *that* he didn't think to help her out until Maeve told him he should. He had showered Christine with expensive gifts and even an enormous home when they were married, but that was only to impress her . . . only to soothe the ache of the chip on his shoulder left over after the experiences of his own childhood.

What would his legacy be? Was it enough that people might remember his work one day?

After the funeral, his mind turned to loose ends. Almost everything from Maeve's house would go into the very same charity shop truck that had taken away his mother's furniture just a week or two earlier. He kept just a handful of things . . . Maeve's glasses—the black cat-eye frames that she had worn for so many years—the simple string of pearls Linda gave her when she turned twenty-one. He also took the very last photo he ever had taken with his mother and sister—a shot of the three of them together, standing outside of the house the day before he flew out of the United States for the very first time in 1949. Silas had used some of his newly found wealth to hire a photographer to come take the photo and to print and frame it as a gift for Linda. Maeve was beaming in the photo, but she was also clinging to his arm. Linda was standing tall and proud and happy. There were other photos—but none were so clear, and none captured such a perfect moment of hope and optimism and love. He couldn't take them all, and this was his favorite, so this was all he took.

In the end, every material possession left over after Maeve's and Linda's lives fit into one small box.

An agent toured both properties and decreed that there were jobs to be done before Maeve's house could be listed—repainting, new floors. But the lawyer who was handling both her estate and Linda's had offered to help coordinate things if Silas could just line up the contractors before he left. So Silas did that too. He called ahead and spoke to a car lot near the airport. He would drive Maeve's car to San Francisco and sell it there before he flew out.

Just about every little thing was sorted. He went to the travel agent to book the next ticket home, then he went to sit between his mother's and his sister's graves.

"I don't think I'll come back," he said. He drew his knees up to his chest and closed his eyes. "You two were my whole life here. I hope you'll understand if I don't visit but I'll miss you and I will love you forever, no matter where I am on this earth."

He sat there for a while, until his backside was numb and the cold from the earth had seeped up through his clothes to chill his body. He stared at those miserable graves, side by side and so very sad and so lonely—not even a headstone in place yet. He'd agonized over the wording for each stone before he ordered them, but it would take some time for them to be crafted. The lawyer had promised to send a photo once it was done.

Silas pressed a soft kiss to his fingers, then touched his hand to the earth on each grave.

"Goodbye," he whispered, and his voice cracked. "Goodbye, Mom. Goodbye, Maeve. I love you." He took two steps, then turned back and looked at the dirt one last time. "I'm sorry. I'm *so* sorry."

If the story of Silas's relationship with his mother and sister were in a novel, there probably would be closure—some satisfying conclusion to the dangling thread of his estrangement from Maeve. He'd have arrived just a little quicker, in time for one last conversation, or in packing up her house he'd have found a letter from her telling him he was forgiven.

But this was real life and it rarely works so neatly. Instead, Silas had to walk away from their graves unredeemed, unforgiven. The guilt would not be lifted. Instead, it would become part of who he was, and it would influence every single step he took from that day forward.

Marie had weighed heavily on Silas's mind over the week he spent packing up Maeve's life. Every now and again thoughts of her, concerns for her, would burst through the fog of his grief and capture his full attention. On those days he'd think seriously about checking in on her, but there was much to do, and he could not afford distractions.

Besides, Silas was confident that he'd given Marie excellent advice. Her situation was dreadful but she had a brother right there in town who was best placed to help her. He half expected he'd arrive at the cafe and Irving would quietly approach him, clap him on the shoulder and thank Silas for bringing the situation to his attention.

"She got out," fictional Irving would say confidentially. "I put her on a bus to some place far away and she's settling there. I'll go in a few weeks' time to support her. All thanks to you."

Ten days after he encouraged Marie to ask her brother for help, Silas walked back into the cafe and took his usual booth. He peered into the kitchen and made eye contact with Irving, who went right back to chopping vegetables, and to Silas's great disappointment, did not immediately come out with a reassuring story about Marie's well-being. Instead, Helen approached his table. She didn't know his name or where he was from or even why he was there, but she knew immediately what he wanted.

"Coffee and pancakes?"

"Yes. Please."

It was about the right time and if Marie was indeed still in town, Silas expected he'd see her any minute. While he waited, he opened the novel he had in his bag, and enjoyed a few minutes of quiet reading. The pancakes came and he made light work of them with no sign of Marie. It was now well past the time she'd usually breeze through, and her schedule ran like clockwork ordinarily. When Carmen brought the cheque, he cleared his throat.

"Was Marie early today?"

Carmen winced. "No, she hasn't been in for a while. Not sure what happened there. I did ask Irving but . . ." She hesitated, a worried look in her eyes. "Honestly, I can't get involved. I wish I could—but I can't."

Silas started driving back to the hotel, drumming his fingers on the steering wheel. He hardly knew Marie and she certainly hadn't reacted well to his last, unannounced visit to her house. Besides, surely if she needed help her own brother would come to her aid.

And Silas just wanted to go home. To Christine and to Ernest, to figure out the mess he'd left behind there and to be a better husband and father. A better person, just like Maeve had been.

It was that thought which undid him.

Maeve would never have walked away from someone in

a dire situation like Marie, not without checking that she really was okay. That's why Maeve's funeral was packed with hundreds of mourners. That's why everyone who spoke of her got that soft, sad tone in their voice. Because she was good and kind and proud and all of the things Silas wanted so badly to be.

He drove down Marie's street and checked—only one car in the drive, that same Rambler that had been there last time he visited. He didn't park behind it, not this time. Instead, he drove a little ways along the street and parked outside of a stranger's house, then he walked back. He checked this way and that, making sure no one was watching, and when he was as confident as he could reasonably be, he let himself into the backyard and knocked on the back door.

There was no answer at first, and Silas was more than a little relieved. He decided he'd knock one last time, and if she didn't answer, he'd take that as a sign that she'd left Rupert and was probably halfway to somewhere better by now.

But at the second knock, he saw movement inside, and there was Marie—or at least, just the top of her face, because she was half-hiding behind a wall as she tried to figure out who was there. He waved, and expected she'd give a relieved smile and come to the door, but she shook her head mutely instead. When Silas raised his hand to knock on the glass again, she held up her hand.

"You have to leave," she said urgently, her words sounding muffled through the glass.

"I just wanted to check on you," he said. But then a thought struck him and he winced before asking, "Is he here?"

She shook her head again, then sighed and walked to the door. She pulled it open just a crack and now that she was closer Silas saw it. The faint outline of a fading bruise around her left eye, a healing split in her lower lip.

He'd experienced many emotions since he came back home, but the surge of pure fury that shot through him was almost as big as the grief and the worry and the sadness. His vision went hazy and for the briefest second he had another moment of confusion, just as he'd had when he saw Marie standing in the rain. She faded altogether and all he could see was his mother, with her bruises and her trauma that everyone else ignored and that Silas could not fix.

"Did you talk to—"

"I did," she murmured, then raised one wry finger to point to her face. "That's why . . ."

"*Irving* did this?"

"Irving told Rupert I wanted to leave him."

"Ah."

"This isn't your problem," Marie said stiffly. "*I* am not your problem. I . . ." Perhaps she'd been about to lie, to tell him she had a plan, another option. Instead, her eyes filled with tears and she leaned her forehead against the door. "How is your sister?"

"She passed away. That's why I've been . . . I'm . . . It's all wrapped up. I'll drive to San Francisco tomorrow. I fly home soon."

A large part of the success of Silas's career was his ability to link ideas and concepts in ways other people just could not, but an idea came to him in that moment, a solution so wild—so creative—that he would never really believe it had come from within his own mind. Perhaps, from the other side of whatever lay beyond this life, Maeve had grown tired of watching him flounder to help this poor girl and shouted just loud enough for him to hear her.

He looked at Marie properly, assessing her features. Her eyes were brown, but not a dark brown, so in the right light, a person might even call them hazel, as Maeve's had been. And Marie's hair was closer to blonde than it was to brown, but women changed hair color all the time.

Maeve's passport had never been used. He'd found it in her top drawer, beside her bed, dated five years earlier—about the time they'd been writing to one another discussing her coming for a visit, about the time of her diabetes diagnosis. He'd almost tossed it in the trash, but at the last second, he put it in the box of documents to take back to Australia. The dreamer in him liked the idea of some part of her taking the trip, even if it was only her passport. He'd even taken her glasses—the very same frames she was wearing in her passport photo, and the pearls too . . .

"How tall are you?"

Marie narrowed her eyes at him.

"I'm five-four," she said. Confusion had distracted her from her tears and she was looking at him with something bordering on suspicion and hurt. "Why would you ask me that?"

So, she was a little shorter than Maeve, and certainly much thinner, but with heels and perhaps some layered clothing . . .

The biggest issue was their ages. Marie was nineteen or twenty at best. Maeve had just turned thirty. But maybe with some make-up . . . maybe different clothing . . .

"Do you want to leave him?"

Marie froze.

"I *can't*," she choked. "He'll find me. He'll *kill* me. I know he will. Besides, there's no opportunity—I'm not even allowed to run my errands without him now. I can't leave."

"He's not all-powerful. There are places you can go—"

"He told me he hid his first wife's body so well that no one has ever found it," Marie whispered tearfully. *"I cannot leave."*

Silas sucked in a sharp breath. He had no way to know if what Marie said was even true—someone who would physically injure his wife was certainly not above lying to keep her in line. But he did take just a moment to sanity check his idea. There was a real possibility this man was a murderer. Did Silas really want to get involved?

It wasn't even a question in the end. This young woman was in desperate need and he was apparently the only person in the world willing and able to help her.

"Will you trust me, Marie? I have a plan, and I promise you I will do everything in my power to get you to safety and to keep you safe, but you have to trust me. And we have to go right now."

Her first instinct was to say no, to close the door, to rush back to the kitchen and start preparing Rupert's lunch, because he was due home in less than an hour. It was too risky. Too terrifying. Better the devil she knew than having the devil somewhere behind her, invisible, chasing her down until he found her and then—

It was that thought that gave her pause because Marie had long concluded that even if she stayed, her days were numbered. She would live out the next few years of her life according to Rupert's needs and his schedule. She would have a baby if she was indeed pregnant, and Rupert would control the baby too.

But given the way the noose around her neck had grown ever tighter over that year, Marie knew that it was inevitable that his control would escalate. Already he decided what she ate and who she spoke to and what she wore and how she did her hair. And now he'd physically hurt her too, and she couldn't even pretend that would be the last time.

She had the definite sense that Rupert was some kind of monster who craved blood and violence, but he had learned to restrain himself to achieve the things that he wanted to achieve. Like making lots of money. Like running the town with an iron fist.

She felt those fading marks on her face were some kind of foreshadowing of a future where staying inside to wait for bruises to fade was a regular occurrence. When she closed her eyes, she could imagine her child, a little boy or girl dressed in a sweater Marie herself had knitted, hair freshly combed and the cheeks rosy and shiny with tears, hiding under their bed to escape the violence their father was meting out to their mother for some real or perceived offence. Marie could so easily imagine that child pressing its hands hard over its ears, trying to block out the cries of pain from the bedroom next door. She could imagine that child growing up conditioned to think that it was okay to take whatever they wanted from other people or learning to forget their own needs in the service of keeping others happy.

And ultimately, she could imagine that child growing up

without a mother when one day, Rupert lost his restraint entirely.

The only way to give this child a fighting chance was to leave.

"Yes," she said, her voice firmer than it had been maybe in a whole year. "Please help me, Silas. Please."

CHAPTER 8

Fiona

I've just reached the end of my chapter when Marilyn rings the glass-of-water bell to signal the end of silent reading time. I reluctantly look up from the book. That's a tough spot to leave Silas and Marie—I am dying to know his plan to help her, and if she's going to make it out alive.

"So, what are you all reading?" Stefanie asks, something like a millisecond after Marilyn has clinked the glass, as if she couldn't wait another moment without speaking. She holds her book up to show us *The Man Who Mistook His Wife for a Hat and Other Clinical Tales* by Oliver Sacks.

"Isn't that technically work for you?" Jack asks her. She's a doctor now and works at the hospital.

"You might be surprised to learn there's not a lot of cross-over between pop neuroscience and emergency medicine," she chuckles. She peers at Jack's book and he lifts it so we can all see the cover.

"*Beowulf*?" she gasps. "Didn't we read that in grade 7?"

"I hated every word of it then, and I might just hate every word of it now," he laughs. "I saw it on the shelf in my bed-room and wondered if I could appreciate it more as an adult."

"I'm reading sci-fi," Patience offers, showing us the front of her copy of *Galileo's Dream* by Kim Stanley Robinson.

"You're always reading sci-fi," Stef says.

"It's the best genre, that's why. What's that book, Fi?"

I hold up *The Midnight Estate* and everyone looks at that striking cover. Marilyn has wandered over and she peers down at it too.

"What you think so far?" she asks me.

"It's intriguing and I think it's going to be a little heart-breaking," I say carefully. "Have you read it?"

She shakes her head.

"I don't think I've ever seen it. I'm quite certain I would have remembered that cover!" She takes the book from my hands and opens it near the front. "Ah. This is a UK edition, published in 1999. How did you get your hands on it?"

"I found it at the house. Is the author familiar to you?"

She shakes her head again.

"No, love. Do you think she was one of your uncle's author pals?"

"I did wonder," I admit. "I can't find any information about her online."

I look up to see that Mum and Alan are chatting quietly together. Mum points to something on the page of Alan's book, and he laughs softly and nods.

All of a sudden, I remember my mother coming into my bedroom at Wurimbirra to announce the news that she and Alan were engaged. I was neck deep in my first infatuation with Jack at the time. I had regular daydreams about him—a whole catalogue of fantasies I used to play through my mind when I was bored. In my favorite, we were sitting in the school playground eating our lunch and he suddenly reached over and held my hand. And in my daydreams, where I was confident and bold, I let him.

But in reality, I was terrified of how out of control my crush seemed to be. Love and relationships and sex and all that went along with it seemed a little bit like skydiving to me. I was certain it was a thrill, but the fun couldn't possibly outweigh the risks.

Even so, when my mother sat me down and told me that she was going to marry Alan Edendale and we would be moving up the road to his farm, I couldn't make sense of what she was saying. Stef and I sat up late into the night trying to figure it out. Her parents had been married since they were in high school and were demonstratively affectionate. With Mum and Alan there had been no handholding or hugging, no pecks on the cheek.

"You have to ask her what she's thinking," Stef told me. Mum was talking about changing both of our lives, and I felt I owed it to myself, and in some way to her, to be sure this was what she really wanted.

"Are you in love with Alan?" I asked her. Mum seemed very tired in that moment, as if the mere question had exhausted her.

"People talk about love as if it's a binary thing—in love, not in love. It is nothing so certain as that and you'll understand that when you're a bit older. People make all sorts of foolish choices because they think they're 'in love.' When that flutter of hormones fades away—and trust me, it *always* does—what happens then? They wake up one morning and look over and on the bed next to them is a person they don't even like, maybe a person they hate, or even fear! What Alan and I have between us is so much better than infatuation. He needs a wife who can organize the farm's office so he can run the sheep and tend the crops, and if I marry Alan, I secure a suitable life companion. We have hobbies in common and we enjoy one another's company. So am I love with Alan?" Her gaze softened. "It's the wrong question, Fiona. Am I looking forward to a life with him? That's what you should be asking me, and if you did, I'd tell you the answer is yes."

And here we all are, thirty-four years later. They are still married and seem happy enough. But it suddenly occurs to me that Ginny Edendale may be a woman who is cautious and cynical not because it's her nature, but because once upon a time, she learned to be wary of love. What if those lessons she tried to pass on to me were lessons she learned first-hand? What if she was once wild and free in her love for someone . . . for my father, perhaps? And what if his death so broke her heart that she refused to leave herself open to hurt like that again, and even made her scared to allow *me* to follow the whims of my heart?

I only wish we had the kind of relationship where I could ask her about these things, because whether I knew it at the time or not, her thoughts on the matter have had a huge impact on the choices I have made in my life.

"Excuse me," I say quietly, and I pick up my things and make my way over to the table where Mum and Alan are seated. She looks at me warily as I join them, but Alan greets me with a great big smile and a booming greeting. I sit my book on the table, and as I sit, I see two messages on my phone.

The first from Mia:

> Love you Mum! Really hope you're settling in and happy. Can't wait to see what you do with that house! Sorry I haven't called, end of semester exams are coming up and I've joined the soccer team and the debate club and I went to a protest last week so it's been hectic.

And one from Jon:

> Just checking in. You okay?

I'll reply to both later, so I turn the phone over so it's face down and I'm not distracted.

"What did you think of reader's group, Fiona, love?" Alan asks me.

"It's such a great idea." I smile. I glance at their books. To my surprise, Mum is reading a historical romance. Alan's choice is a little more predictable—it's a book on sheep husbandry.

"And what's this?" Mum asks, picking up *The Midnight Estate*. She frowns as she stares at the cover. "This is that author you were asking about."

"Yes. I still haven't found any letters between her and Uncle Tad yet, but . . ." I'm not sure how much to say. In the end, I go with "I do suspect they were friends."

Mum opens the book and frowns. She begins to flick through it, reading just for a moment or two on what seem to be random pages. All of a sudden she snaps the book closed and thrusts it back at me.

"It looks like rubbish," she says, and I'm surprised, because like Tad, Mum is usually far from a book snob. She's always been the kind to see value in any kind of words on a page, but her voice is low and sharp . . . and almost . . . strained? "Surely there are better choices than that for you to find in Tad's library. It might even be a nice opportunity for you to read through his backlist since you're living *in his house*."

I ignore the dig about the house, but it's not actually a bad idea to read back through his works again. Later. After I finish this book.

"How's the cleaning going, love?" Alan asks me. "I bet that house was a bit dusty after these last few years."

"You're not wrong, Alan," I sigh. "It's a big job."

"Erin needs work," Mum says abruptly.

"Erin . . . ?"

"You met her yesterday, Fiona. Our farmhand's girlfriend."

Mum nods to herself, pleased with this idea. "I'll send her over tomorrow. She can help you clean and you can pay her cash."

"I don't really need—" I start to protest.

But Mum cuts me off with a firm "You were asking me for help and I can't but Erin can. This will do her some good. And you too."

"Right," I sigh, because apparently this is happening. "Thanks, Mum."

I'm not sure what I expected when I went to join Mum and Alan because while the circumstances change—the words we speak, whether we're on the phone or in a bookstore or her house—the end result is always the same. I want Mum to embrace me, but she always holds me at arm's length.

Reader's group winds down, and people start to drift out. Stef and I find ourselves standing in a quiet corner of the store alone.

"I really am sorry I didn't let you know I was back," I say.

"All is forgiven, Fi. I wasn't really upset. You know that I'm here when you're ready and I'm happy to give you space if that's what you prefer." She pulls me close for a hug, and I squeeze her tightly as we embrace.

"Thanks," I say. "God, this year has been so *shit.* I can't even begin to tell you."

"If you start to feel lonely out there in that house, you call me, okay? It's one thing to lock yourself away to mourn but it's another if you start to feel really flat. Promise me you'll reach out if that happens."

"Yes, Dr Stef," I say softly, and I hug her again. "You're the best, you know that?"

"And don't think I'm not going to ask questions about you and Jack," she adds with a grin as we part.

"He just picked me up, that's all. There's nothing to tell."

"Come on, Fi," she laughs. "I don't know how smooth you think you were as a teenager, but it was obvious you had a massive crush on him. And the reverse was true too! And now, the fates have delivered him back into your hands, right when you need a fling the most."

"Stef!" I exclaim, then I mutter defensively, "Firstly, I didn't have a crush on him and he certainly *didn't* have a crush on me." I don't think she's right about Jack, but she's definitely right about me and I have no idea why I'm lying about it. It's not like there's any shame in having a crush, especially as a teenager. "Secondly, my marriage just ended. I'm hardly in a position to—I can't even think about—I just don't—"

I look up just in time to see Jack approaching us. Stef laughs softly and adjusts her handbag on her shoulder.

"Let's catch up soon," she says, before she hugs me goodbye and makes her way to the door.

"She hasn't changed one bit, has she?" Jack smiles as he comes to stand beside me.

"Still the same old Stef," I agree lightly.

This private little corner was perfect for a quick apology to Stef, but it feels way too intimate now that Jack is here. There's a moment of silence and it must feel a little awkward to Jack too, because suddenly he says, "Imagine trying to tell seventeen-year-old Jack and Fiona that they'd both wind up back here at fifty."

I flick a glance towards Patience, who is happily browsing the sci-fi section.

"Seventeen-year-old Fiona would never have believed you," I tell Jack. "Even if you did convince her she'd immediately get to work on a plan to prevent such a tragedy befalling her."

"Seventeen-year-old Jack probably wouldn't have heard me anyway. He was too busy swimming laps in the pool, ignoring a nagging pain in his shoulder," he says dryly. Jack was the star of our school swimming team, and I know he was in discussions with a scout from the Australian Institute of Sport in our final year of school when he started having trouble with his shoulder. I remember thinking it was inevitable he'd swim for the national team, maybe that he even had a chance of Olympic gold. But he tried to swim through the pain and did permanent damage—even after surgery, his swimming career was over.

"Do you regret the way your life panned out?" I ask.

"Well, I can't change anything, so regret would be a waste of energy." He shrugs. "It's too easy to look back and pick out things that "went wrong." To chastise ourselves for mistakes we made along the way to now. But isn't the person we are at fifty the culmination of everything that happened in the first part of our lives—the good, the bad, the downright ugly? I reckon I've pretty much made peace with that now, especially in these past few years."

"Will you stay in Forbes?"

"Yeah, I think I will," he says. "I told you Dad was sick. Not a lot of people know this yet because his deterioration has been slow, thank goodness, but Dad has dementia. Mum is plenty capable of running the farm with our manager for now but I don't think she should have to deal with Dad's illness on her own."

"Oh, Jack, I'm sorry."

"Thanks, Fi. It's rough, and it's unfair, but that's life, isn't it? I'm glad I'm here with him now, to make the most of the good days we have with him. How about you? What will you do with Wurimbirra once you've renovated it?"

"I honestly don't know," I say, and I feel the weight of that unknown as I admit it. Since before I left Forbes the first time, I had a plan in mind—a clear path of progression to follow for my future. Undergrad, postgrad, a few years' consulting, starting my own firm, then marriage and kids. *All* of that is behind me now and what's ahead?

Wurimbirra. A beautiful, slightly spooky old house I longed to return to for decades. Maybe I'm like a dog chasing a car. I got what I wanted and now I have no idea what to do with it.

"That's the problem," I admit to Jack. "I know the building has amazing potential. It could even be a boutique hotel or a function center. I can imagine the space used for all sorts of things, but there are some real challenges."

"Like the cemetery in the backyard?"

"Exactly."

"Can't you just move the graves?"

"It is possible to move historic graves," I concede. "It's done from time to time, mostly at the behest of large developers who can't make their desired use of land because of historic burial sites. I've spent a lot of time fighting against that kind of thing in my career. To justify disturbing someone's final resting place, there must be a uniquely vital reason and absolutely no alternative. It's incredibly rare—on every project I've ever worked on, we've found or created an alternative. It's so important that graves aren't disturbed—obviously for moral reasons, but also in terms of preserving history. In this case, these graves belong right here. There's a fascinating history behind Wurimbirra and the cemetery is a key part of it."

"I'd love to see the place again. To hear about some of that history. Maybe I could call in one day and you could show me around?"

I'm conscious of my heart pounding against the wall of my chest. And also conscious that this is an innocent request from someone who really is just being friendly.

And yet it's still Jack, and I'm right back in that same spot I was thirty-five years ago—affected by him, and terrified of that. Back then, I'd have refused a request like this. I'd have shut him down before he got friendly with me. I'd hear my mother's aloofness in my voice when I did so, and I'd be confused by it, but feel powerless to make any other choice.

But isn't this the upside to a future that is suddenly, unexpectedly unknown?

Maybe this time I can make my destiny my own. Leap out of the plane and trust my parachute to work. Let myself feel those butterflies instead of avoiding them.

"Of course," I say. "Anytime."

I had a great time at the reader's group and was feeling refreshed by the time Jack dropped me back to Wurimbirra. I climbed into bed with *The Midnight Estate* and was very tempted to keep reading, but after only a page of the next chapter, my eyelids were so heavy I thought I might fall asleep sitting up. I sat the book face down on my nightstand and promised myself I would have a good night's sleep at last and do some more reading in the morning.

Just as I was drifting off to sleep, I heard a thump from Uncle Tad's office, then the sound of small objects scattering across the floor. It's like the second the house goes dark, whatever is taunting me gets to work. Just like the previous night I got out of bed, intending to investigate, but I knew what I'd find if I went in there—a room now still, items inexplicably knocked from high places onto the floor. So I flopped back into bed and put a pillow over my head, determined to ignore the sounds. I tossed and turned most of the night, unsure of which noises were in my fitful dreams and which were in the house.

When I finally gave up on sleep around 5:00 a.m., I went into Tad's study and found that a cup of pens had been knocked from the desk.

I'm not sure I've had any deep sleep at all in the past two nights and it is entirely possible I am simply losing my mind.

It's windy and cold outside, and my eyes sting and water as I force myself to take my walk. It's not much warmer inside the house when I return, but at least I get a reprieve from the wind. I down a few cups of coffee, then carry a dining chair upstairs, placing it in Tad's storage room so I can sit as I work. I'm going to read through the boxes of his correspondence with his author friends today, since I'm far too tired to do anything else physical.

Mum was right—there's not as many boxes of letters from other authors . . . only eight in total. They are sorted by surname, and once again copies of the letters Tad received and carbon copies of his replies are clustered with still more paper clips. There must be thousands of paper clips in this room.

The window beside me rattles in its frame as the wind outside buffets the house, but I'm wearing enough layers that I can pretend I'm cozy there in the storage room, engrossed in Tad's correspondence. I'm interrupted briefly when the firewood truck arrives—but I stop my work long enough only to run downstairs to pay the man, and to instruct him to unload the wood around the corner, under a little shelter Tad had built in the '60s. Then I'm right back upstairs, and I spend the next few hours engrossed in the reading. I smile to myself as I read through Tad's fond exchanges with Ruth Park and Thomas Kenneally, his polite correspondence with Toni Morrison and Flannery O'Connor, his extended back-and-forths with Patrick White and Kurt Vonnegut. But my favorite letters are from the correspondence he shared with Patricia Highsmith. Tad so loved to talk about his feud with her. I'm sure I heard dozens of versions of that tale over the years, each one more dramatic than the last, so it's been a strangely nostalgic experience to read the reality of it at last. He was a fan of her work and wrote her to compliment her on *Strangers on a Train*. She had read his first two novels and apparently found them to be "derivative and trite." Their correspondence descended into a slow-motion argument over international mail but it continued for decades, and as I read, I see a hint from each of them that they were rather enjoying the sparring.

As amusing as all of this is, I can't find any mention of Charity Wilkie in the first few boxes, and eventually I start to feel a little guilty about sitting here reading letters when there's so much to do in this house. I set the stack of letters from Patricia Highsmith down, intending to do some cleaning. Maybe I'll return to this later in the day, once I've been productive.

I'm feeling jittery from too much caffeine and it feels like my soul just about leaves my body when a strong gust of air blows through the storage room, sending yellowed paper flying everywhere and forcing the door to slam closed. For a moment I'm so stunned I can't quite figure out what's happened—this window is closed, but did I leave another open elsewhere in the house? But the door slammed *closed*, and besides, the house is so damned cold I know I've shut it up as much as is possible.

The only logical explanation I can come up with is that for a split second the wind hit that leaky old frame just right and somehow . . . *somehow?* . . . forced an unusually large movement of air in the gaps around the glass.

It's absolute nonsense, but it's the best I can come up with.

I fumble to put the Highsmith letters back in order then stuff them back into the box before I scramble to the door, eager to get out of the storage room. That prickling, uneasy sensation—one I am fast coming to associate with this house—has returned, and even with all of the layers I'm wearing, I'm so cold my teeth are suddenly chattering. Maybe I'll take myself for a drive—I could go browse the bookstore for a while, or maybe I can call Jack or Stef or Patience or anyone else I can think of to see if they have time to meet me for brunch?

But the house isn't done with its unpleasant surprises today. I reach for the round doorknob and twist, expecting it to shift the bolt so I can open the door, and find the knob is entirely seized. I can't even remember seeing this door closed before, but now there's no apparent way to open it.

My palms and my back are soon burning from effort but I'm getting absolutely nowhere. I twist and I tug and I'm soon close to tears of frustration but that doorknob refuses to budge even a millimeter and that means the door is latched shut. The doorknob feels so stiff, it's like it isn't even built to open that door.

I tell myself to take a breath, and then I do. I simply need to call someone and ask them to come help.

I pat the place where my pockets should be only to realize I'm still wearing leggings from my walk, and that means my phone is probably still downstairs, on the kitchen table where I last saw it.

I have no way to mark the time, especially now that I let the grandfather clock wind down so there are no chimes upon the hour. My mind feels like it's running at a million miles, turning over and over the mystery of that gust of wind and the slammed door and the pens on the floor and this impossible feeling I have that I'm not alone in the house.

Eventually, I go back to the boxes of author correspondence. What else is there to distract myself with other than to continue reading? Every single time I finish with a page, my heart starts to race, and my thoughts right along with it, and I hasten to pick the next one up.

No one will miss me if I'm trapped in here. Jon or Mia or Caitlin will probably text me today or tomorrow, but it might be days before they get worried that I haven't replied.

I have no access to water or a food or a toilet.

This isn't how it was supposed to be.

I read a little faster, and soon I'm nearing the end of the last box of author letters. I haven't read every word—but I've at least skimmed each letter, and I've found not one letter from nor even reference to anyone named Charity Wilkie. It's confusing, because there's clearly *some* connection between Wilkie's story and this house, and the more I think about it . . . the more familiar this work seems. It's certainly not that I've read the book before—I have no idea where the story is even going. There's just *something* about Wilkie's telling of this new story that I'm certain I've encountered before.

Suddenly there's a sound outside—tires crunching over gravel, the low hum of an engine. At first I think I'm imagining it—maybe it's wishful thinking? But by the time I scramble to my feet and run to the window, a little red hatchback, an older car and not one I recognize, is parked beside the verandah. I throw the window up and am immediately met by a blast of cold wind to the face, but at least this time, that makes perfect sense.

"I'm up here!" I shout to raise my voice over the sound of the wind, and for one heart-stopping moment, I think my visitor hasn't heard me—but then she steps down from the verandah, peering up at me in confusion. It's Erin, Mum and Alan's tenant.

I'd entirely forgotten Mum was sending her around to help me clean today.

"The door blew shut and I can't get it open," I call. The wind is making my eyes water, and I hope that hides the fact I'm so relieved I'm close to *weeping*. "I'm stuck in here."

"How can I help?"

"You might need to go to Mum—see if she still has a key? Maybe Alan will come over and try to force the door . . . Maybe a crowbar? Or maybe the lock just needs some lubricant spray . . . I just don't know but—" She's already taking steps towards the car and my heart starts to race at the thought of her driving away. "Actually, I could have left the front door unlocked . . . Could you try that before you go?"

I can't remember locking it after my walk and I am so tired today, anything is possible. Besides, when I lived here the first time, we hardly ever locked the house up—people out here leave their homes unlocked all the time, and there's at least a chance I've slipped right back into that habit. Erin waves to indicate she understands then she runs back beneath the verandah. I hear her faint shout of victory and then the front door slams closed behind her.

I slump with relief, leaning heavily against the window frame until it sags ominously beneath my weight. Upon closer inspection this wood is badly worn, even worse than the other windows in this house. That still doesn't explain the strange events of this morning.

There are footsteps in the hallway and then the door swings open. Erin is standing there, one hand on the door handle, a baffled look on her face.

"How did you do that?" I gasp, rushing towards her. She releases the handle just as I reach for it and I am horrified to find the doorknob turns easily from the outside, the bolt sliding in and out with each movement. "It must just have been the inside that was seized . . ." I say, but when I swing the door to reach for the other side of the door handle, I find it turns just as easily from that direction.

Erin steps out of my way as I make my way into the hallway then pull the door closed. Once again, it takes no effort at all to twist the doorknob and open the door.

"Maybe when I opened it from the outside, it loosened something inside the mechanism," Erin says kindly, but there's a wary, suspicious look on her face, and I don't blame her. I'm racking my mind now—replaying my memory of the morning's happenings. Maybe the door slamming startled me so much my palm was sweaty and I wasn't quite gripping the door?

Or maybe I imagined the whole thing.

Erin suggests we go downstairs for a "nice, soothing cup of tea." She uses the kind of tone a nurse would use with a disturbed patient, and I don't blame her. I'm rattled as all hell but trying to restore some dignity, so I follow her down the stairs. Erin stops at the front door and retrieves a mop and bucket and a caddy of cleaning products. She carries both through to the kitchen, then rests them by the farmhouse table.

I busy myself—putting the kettle on, taking deep breaths. Ten minutes ago I thought I might die trapped in that storage room upstairs but now I have to have a mature, calm conversation with this stranger I've only met once about how and when she might help me clean my probably haunted house. My life seems more surreal by the minute.

"You don't have to do this if you don't want to," I tell her, which is as close as I'll let myself come to warning her to run while you can.

"Oh, I really don't like to disappoint Ginny and she gave me some very explicit instructions," Erin says, and there's a slightly nervous edge to her laugh. "I'm to stay out of your way—just dust, dust, dust. Does that sound okay?" She reaches into her bucket to withdraw a small radio. I recognize it as the one Mum had in the laundry when I lived in the farmhouse with her and Alan. She used to listen to talk radio while she did the folding. "She asked me to give you this. Said this old house can be noisy especially at night and background sound might help."

It's a brilliant idea and I'm a little annoyed I didn't think of it myself. But this is typical for Mum. She clearly doesn't want me in this house, doesn't even want to talk about it, but she loves me enough to worry for me and to try to help me settle in.

"Thanks, Erin," I say, and I take the radio from her hands, resting it in the very back corner of the countertop. My mother does not like to see her belongings damaged, and if some mysterious force wants to push this radio down onto the floorboards, I'm not going to make it easy for them.

Erin and I have a brief discussion about her working arrangements. We agree on three or four hours a day, and she names a very reasonable price per hour and asks that I pay her at the end of the week. That all suits me just fine, so we shake hands on the arrangement, then I show her to the parlour, where she gets right to work.

I wander back into the kitchen and sit at the table, resting my head in my hands. Sleep deprivation really can send a person crazy—would a few rough nights be enough to tip me over the edge? I'm not even sure what to do, other than to try to keep moving, to hope for a better sleep tonight and a clearer head tomorrow.

With that, I force myself to stand, to make myself busy as a distraction.

I take Mum's little radio and pop it on a local classical station as I work on clearing off the dining room table. I take the little card from each of the vases and the rotten flower boxes, and I tuck them off to the side for Jon to keep. I ferry all of the trash outside to the dumpster, and then I'm dusting and wiping, and the hours start melting past.

It's just past 2:00 p.m. when Erin comes to find me. She's carrying a bucket in her hand, almost overflowing with filthy rags.

"I can wash those—" I say, but she pulls it away and shakes her head.

"I insist," she says lightly. "I've left my mop on the back landing to dry. I'll see you at eight tomorrow?"

"Of course. Thanks for today."

"No need to thank me," she insists, and I laugh softly. She's got a smear of dust on her nose and her blue shirt is tinged with brown.

"Of course there is. I'd still be stuck in that room if it wasn't for you! Besides, you're doing me a huge favor helping with the cleaning. Have a great night and I'll see you tomorrow."

Just as the front door closes behind her, a text message hits my phone. It's from Jack. I wipe my hands on my jeans and pick it up.

> I'm on call tonight so I've got the afternoon off and I'm headed home to help with some farm jobs. Maybe I can pop in with some afternoon tea on my way past?

I stare at that message for a long moment before I reply. I wanted a distraction, and a visit from Jack would be exponentially more distracting than cleaning this dining room.

> Of course! I'm not going anywhere so see you when it suits.

I put the phone down and exhale a shaky breath as I tell myself that he's just being friendly and this isn't a big deal.

CHAPTER 9

Fiona

I pull the door open an hour later to find Jack waiting with a tray of coffees in one hand, a brown cardboard box in the other.

"Fi," he says warmly as he leans forward to brush an innocent kiss against my cheek. "Aurelia told me you usually get a black coffee. Hope that's okay?"

"Perfect," I lie. I'm still so anxious after the events of the morning, I need more caffeine like I need a hole in my head. "Come in."

I back hastily out of the way so that he can walk into the foyer. He looks around, eyes going wide.

"I reckon it's been almost forty years since I was in this house. I forgot how imposing it is."

"Imposing?" I repeat, looking around and trying to view it through fresh eyes. "That's an interesting way to put it."

"Not in a bad way. It's just that rich crimson and the dark wood paneling and the stained glass . . . there's a feel of historical luxury here. It reminds me of beautiful old hotels I've stayed at from time to time, especially in Europe. Does it feel homey to you?"

"No place has ever felt more like home to me than this one."

Is that still true, even after this weird week? I'm not even sure anymore.

I lead Jack through to the kitchen, then retrieve some of the freshly washed plates from the pantry, along with some cutlery. Jack opens the box to reveal an assortment of slices. We talk easily for a while—catching up. I tell him about the girls' university studies and he tells me about the vet practice he's bought into in town. When we've finished eating, his gaze drifts to the door at the back of the room—the one that opens out onto a landing, and then into the backyard.

"I remember when that garden looked like something that belonged at a British castle."

"Well, my friend, it doesn't anymore," I laugh, and I push back my chair. "Want to take a look?"

We step out onto the landing together to survey it. This enormous space was once broken up into garden "rooms," discrete, enclosed pockets surrounded by formal hedges and roses. It was a wonderland for play and adventure when Jon and I were small—we had this whole make-believe game where the backyard was a house of its own. One room featured a flowing fountain—that was our kitchen. Another room had a wide, flat bed of creeping vines and flowers and a swinging chair in the middle—that was my bedroom. There were hedges and roses everywhere, among a sea of ash and archer and birch trees, dogwoods, maples and oaks. There are hardly any deciduous trees native to Australia, but in autumn, this yard was always awash with oranges and reds and yellows. In spring, the roses and the camelias burst into bloom.

That English-style garden was highly impractical in this arid climate and it took a massive amount of work for Tad and his gardeners to keep it alive and thriving. I'm not sure I blame Jon for letting it go like this. The cost to maintain the previous garden over the course of that last drought would have been obscene.

Any plant that required regular watering is long dead, and

plants that could endure the dry have survived *too* well so they've spread, meaning the structure and shape of the gardens are entirely gone. Some of the imported trees have died and are reduced to skeletal forms, empty branches stretching out as if they were reaching for help as they perished. Even so, there are trees everywhere, from sprawling oaks to palm trees and wattles, plus the inevitable gums—river red gum, yellow box, ironbark. Some are young enough that they must have seeded somehow over the last ten years, but most of those are in inconvenient spots. One is at least as tall as I am but it has sprouted right in the middle of a brick path. The wooden seat on the swinging chair has rotted through, and the fountain is crushed beneath the fallen branches of a peppercorn tree. Even the paths are looking worse for wear, uneven as the soil has moved over the years and as weeds have popped up between the pavers.

"The house restoration is going to be tough, but the bones are good," I tell Jack. "This yard is a whole other story."

"What are you going to do with it? Will you restore it the way it was?"

"No," I say, shaking my head. "I don't want to spend money and waste water trying to keep plants alive here that won't naturally thrive with this climate. And the space also needs to be reverent, because . . ." I point to the cemetery, situated just before the tall concrete wall that bounds this property and separates it from Jack's family farm and the mirrored three hundred acres on the other side. The graves are less than one hundred metres from the house, and through the chaos that is the rest of the garden, I can see that the grass around them is wildly overgrown.

"I always wondered about the cemetery."

"Do you want to brave the jungle and walk up there to have a look?"

"Sure," he says. He steps from the small platform that hangs off the back of the house, down onto the brick path, then reaches back to offer me his hand. The stairs are a little rickety but even so, I don't need help navigating them. I let him help me anyway, and while I do not hate the feel of his hand against mine, I let go the minute my feet hit the solid ground.

"People never visit to lay flowers up there?" he asks me as we start to gingerly make our way towards the back of the block, around towering weeds and downed branches and thick grass.

"No, most of the Fowler family moved away by the 1930s for one reason or another."

"The Fowler family built the house?"

"Yes, Flora and Charles."

"Well, spill the beans. What was their story?"

"I don't want to bore you," I laugh weakly. "I tend to get too excited about this subject and . . ." I feel awkward enough talking to Jack without boring him to death. Even Lucas, who worked with me at our consultancy, would sometimes visibly check out while I was rabbiting on about this project or that.

"I wouldn't have asked if I wasn't interested."

"I should warn you, when I start talking about this kind of history, most people's eyes glaze over."

"Maybe you're just better at historical architecture than you are at assessing body language. I'm sure it's fascinating."

"It *is*," I say. "But it's not a pleasant story."

"I do have some sense of that. My grandfather told me once that someone awful is buried here."

"Yes, most people in town know that much," I say. "It's even worse than that, though. In 1860, Charles Fowler traveled from England to Sydney to start a new life in the colony. Gold had just been discovered here in Forbes and people were flocking to try their luck. Within a few days of his arrival, he discovered a chunk of gold. A big one. It wasn't a nugget, rather a mass of gold encased in some quartz, but it weighed close to three hundred kilograms in total. To this day, it's still the biggest specimen of its kind found in this country."

"Wow. Talk about luck!"

"The payoff from the gold extracted from the specimen was life-changing, but Charles was determined to invest it wisely and he was equally determined to keep busy. He opened a general store here in town, on Templar Street. That went well enough for the first few years, but as I'm sure you know, the tens of thousands of people who came here looking for gold all left once the discoveries started to dwindle. Charles had fallen in love with Flora Smythe, a farmer's daughter, and exactly ten months after their wedding their first son, Trevor, was born, and the babies just kept on coming after that. By 1870, Charles and Flora had eleven children, and the general store was quieter than ever, so he decided to use some of his earnings from the gold to buy some land to start farming. He selected the original plot of land here—the six hundred acres encompassing your family's farm, the Wilkinsons' and this block—mostly because of the creek and the waterholes."

Even in the longest droughts, that creek still has a trickle of water, and the waterholes have been a reliable source of water for the original occupants of this land for tens of thousands of years.

"Charles had underestimated how difficult it would be to build his dream mansion all the way out here and the house took a lot longer to finish than he'd anticipated. It was 1886 before the family were able to move in. By then, Trevor was twenty-four years old and had just married a woman named Eileen. As a wedding gift, Charles decided to give Trevor a little under half of the land so he could earn a living to support a potential family."

"Did Trevor get my farm, or the Wilkinsons'?"

"The Wilkinsons'," I tell Jack. My throat tightens. "It was a generous gift. Your family farm is beautiful, of course, but the Wilkinsons' farm has the waterholes, and Charles thought that would make running stock on the land easier."

"Was there no cemetery in town at the time? Is that why the family are buried here?" Jack asks as he lifts the remains of a small gumtree off the path and pushes it off to the side to clear the way.

"No, the cemetery was already established in town. But Ezekiel was the youngest son and he died just after the family moved in here. He was just six years old. Diphtheria, I believe. I assume poor Flora and Charles just wanted to keep him close. They weren't breaking any rules at the time and after that . . . I guess it made sense that they'd all be laid to rest together."

We've reached the cemetery and there they are, right near the edge. Flora and Charles Fowler, resting beneath grand granite headstones carved with their names and dates of birth. Their graves both have thick concrete caps across the top, each cracked across the middle as the soil settled and shifted over the years.

"So these are all of the children?" Jack asks.

I point to a small grave, with a carved concrete angel on top. "That's Ezekiel's. The rest of the kids all survived to adulthood, beating the odds at the time before childhood immunizations."

"And . . . Trevor?" Jack says. He's frowning at the final grave. The bulk of the cemetery is an orderly, cohesive collection, each grave sporting some kind of ornate decoration, most with a little corner border around the site, some with thick concrete caps.

Trevor Fowler's grave sits a little apart from the others. There's no border. No concrete cap. The headstone is a plain concrete cross that reads Trevor Fowler 1881–1916.

"This is where the story turns dark," I sigh, and I motion

towards a concrete bench beneath a towering red gum tree. Jack and I sit.

"As soon as Trevor took possession of the land, he tried to evict and ban a group of Wiradjuri people who camped by the waterholes there from time to time. They refused to leave—and why would they? The ancestors of that very same group had been camping on that precise patch of land for tens of thousands of years."

I can tell from Jack's wince that he knows exactly where this story is going.

"Shit."

"Trevor took some strychnine from the general store and poisoned the waterhole."

"How many people did he murder?"

"It's impossible to know for sure. There were no survivors from the group. One account suggests as many as fifty or sixty people died over the course of a week."

Jack shakes his head in dismay. "I know the history of this country is littered with stories like this. But we're only talking—what—one hundred twenty years ago?"

"Give or take, yeah."

"Just a few generations ago."

"Exactly."

"I'm guessing Trevor was never charged."

"The murder of Aboriginal people was a crime under the relevant laws at the time, and it was punishable by death too, but this was rarely enforced and when it was, there was usually an uproar—many settlers more offended by the punishment of one of their own than the massacre of large groups of First Nations people. And no, there were no legal consequences for Trevor, but there were at least social consequences. Eileen left him—she moved away to live with her parents. And when Charles found out what had been happened, he and

Flora banished Trevor from the family. Charles was beloved in the region—he was even mayor of the Forbes Shire for a few years—so people took notice. By the early 1900s the entire town had shunned Trevor. He died young, at just thirty-five years old, virtually destitute and all alone on the very farm where he murdered dozens of innocent people."

"So how on earth did he come to be buried *here*?"

"A combination of grace and spite," I say wryly. "Flora felt strongly that her son had sullied the family name. This property had always been known as Fowler Estate, so that's what was on the original stained glass transom over the front door." I had seen photos of it in the archives—just a handful of black-and-white images taken during the construction of the house. "Once the full truth came out Flora was so incensed by Trevor's behavior that she insisted that they change the name of the property to Wurimbirra."

"It's a Wiradjuri word?"

"It means *to care for.* To protect, or to restore."

"It's hard to imagine this house with any other name."

"Trevor died estranged from everyone. He should have had a pauper's burial at the town cemetery, but Charles and Flora buried him here. Was that because of some sense of enduring love for a son who had grown to be a mass murderer? Or did they just get a kick out of knowing that this property would be known as Wurimbirra, and it might have driven the racist bastard crazy if he knew he'd have to rest here forever?"

"A cemetery in your backyard is one thing, but to have an evil man like that right here . . ." Jack murmurs.

"And you know how close the waterhole is," I add, pointing to the concrete wall. "No one knows for sure what Trevor did with those bodies, but there's every possibility that the remains of several generations of innocent people, all murdered in cold blood, are scattered or buried not far from here."

"Do you think that's where the rumors about this house started?" Jack asks me.

"Keep in mind everything I know about Trevor and Charles I learned from a handful of oral histories taken over the last few decades—stories people heard from their grandparents before they passed. There's not much in the archives about Trevor Fowler, which tells me this is a story our town would rather forget. And it's often the case that the detail of historical events—particularly shameful events—fades with time. People know something terrible happened, and they try to make sense of it in their own way."

"What do you do with a property like this when there's a history like *that* hidden somewhere behind it?"

"You said something last night about the person we are being the culmination of everything we've been through—the good, bad and ugly," I say. Jack nods. "It's exactly like that for historic buildings. Trevor's grave—the murder of those innocent people—that *is* a part of the story of this house. In restoring a place like this, we aim to uncover it all so that it can be known and understood by this generation and future generations. There are stories most would rather forget *all* over this country. Until we expose them, we can't confront them, and until we confront them, we can't learn from them." I'm suddenly self-conscious and I look away, feeling my face heat. "I've been rambling, I know. I'm just so passionate about this whole subject. Obviously."

"I've loved hearing you ramble," he says. "Thanks for sharing the story with me. How did you learn all of that?"

"After we graduated high school, before we moved to Sydney? I spent that whole summer at the historical society, digging through their archives," I admit. "I've *always* been obsessed with this house."

The truth of that hits me hard. Even as a kid, all I wanted to do was unearth every mystery here—to know and understand every secret buried in every nook and cranny of Wurimbirra. This is my chance to do just that, even if it means I uncover uncomfortable truths in the process. Maybe that's how I have to think about things like pens scattered across the floor and doors that slam themselves. Not something to fear or run from, but rather something to run towards, to investigate and understand.

"I don't believe in ghosts," I blurt. "But there's something going on here. Something I can't explain."

Jack gives me an alarmed look. "What on earth—"

"There's just something . . . not menacing . . . but . . ." I wince and shake my head. I don't even know how to explain what's been happening without sounding a little paranoid or maybe even deluded. "It's okay. *I'm* okay. But people have always said there's more to this house than meets the eye, and I don't think I really believed that until this week."

"As long as you're safe . . . ?"

I think about the door slamming and finding myself trapped in that room this morning—except that I wasn't trapped. Not really. The door handle turned just fine once Erin intervened. I was scared at the time but with the perspective even a few hours have given me, I can see that I was never really in danger. If enough time had passed and I couldn't open the door, I could have climbed out the window, onto the verandah, then maybe used the cast iron filigree lace to swing myself down close enough to the ground that I could jump without injuring myself. Doors that close themselves and broken glasses and random objects that move from tables to the floor are hardly menacing.

"I am okay," I say again. "I guess I just wanted someone to know. That's all."

Jack scans my face, then the tension in his expression eases.

"I'm right next door," he says. "Promise me you'll reach out if you ever need anything. Even if you're just feeling lonely."

"I will," I promise, and maybe I actually mean it.

Just after Jack leaves, there's thumping on the door again. Assuming he's left something behind, I hurry to open the door, only to find a woman in a boxy pantsuit standing there. She's scowling as she scrawls something on a clipboard. When she looks up at me, her expression is grave.

"Fiona Winslow?"

"Yes?"

"I'm Demelza Winters," she says. "From the council."

"Can I help you with something?"

"You don't have any planning approvals in place. I'm here to inspect and confirm that you're not undertaking unauthorized work to this property given it's a listed home of heritage significance."

I'm so shocked it renders me speechless. Demelza raises an eyebrow at me, as if my outrage is about her visit, not her preposterous accusation.

"I've done nothing to the house as yet," I say flatly. "I haven't even finished moving in, and I don't have planning approvals in place because I haven't planned any works as yet. Can you tell me what this is about?"

"We've had a call from a concerned member of the community. That's all I can tell you."

"That's not something—I would never—" I draw in a breath and regroup. It will do me no favors to be defensive and to get this woman offside. "Why don't you come in and we can have a chat?"

We get chatting as I lead her through the house. Demelza tells me she's relatively new to town, having worked in Melbourne until just a few months ago. We take a seat at the table in the kitchen and when I give her a quick rundown on my career and qualifications, she offers me a somewhat embarrassed smile.

"Ah," she says, glancing down her clipboard. "So that's why your name was familiar. I did a walk-through at Monteray House on an open house day last year." That's a heritage home my firm worked on in Sydney, a major project that took several years to complete. I won an international award for it.

"So I'm sure you understand, the last thing I would ever want to do is to make unauthorized changes to this property. I understand the law, the requirements, the historic significance. Maybe better than just about anyone," I say. "But I understand you need to confirm that, so let's walk through the house and—"

"No," she interrupts me. "No, the complainant had quite a specific concern regarding the cemetery."

"The *cemetery*?" I repeat, squinting at her. "Are you serious? What did they think I was doing to the cemetery?"

She clears her throat. "The call I took specifically related to the historic graves in your backyard."

"What?" I gasp, but then I remember that conversation Jack and I had at the bookstore, and I groan. There's no chance he did this, but someone else might have heard enough to become needlessly alarmed. "I had a conversation with a friend last night about those graves. Someone might have overheard parts of it and misunderstood it out of context."

"Is there any truth to it? I'm sure you know, you must not move those graves without—"

"I would never touch that cemetery," I interrupt her as I stand abruptly. "Come on. Let me show you."

And soon I'm carefully picking my way over what's left of the path to the cemetery for the second time in as many hours. Viewing the space with Demelza beside me, all I can see are things that need to be addressed—branches fallen, grass overgrown. But she's not here to judge the state of the gardens. She's here to enforce the law, and everything I am doing is entirely in line with it.

"See?" I say, waving towards the headstones. "Untouched, and that is how they will remain. The only thing I'll do up here is to mow the grass, trim the trees, fix the gardens. It's not my top priority but I will get it sorted."

"I'm really sorry to have troubled you," she says. "I'm sure you understand why I had to check."

"Of course I do." I sigh, looking back towards the house. From this angle it looks enormous—all of the stunning angles, the wrought iron features, the slate roof and the sash windows. "I'm glad you're thorough. A beautiful home like this deserves to be protected. You really can't tell me who called this in?"

She shakes her head again.

"No, I really can't. But she—ah—someone was particularly alarmed that you might be planning to move the graves. That's all I can tell you."

So it was a woman who called it in. But who could that have been? The only person I've spoken to about the cemetery is Jack.

Demelza and I walk back towards the house, and as we pass the powder room off the hallway, she hesitates.

"Do you mind if I—"

"Of course," I say, and she sets her bag and the clipboard down on a dusty hall table and disappears into the bathroom.

I know I should not look at that clipboard.

But it's right there, just a few steps away, and the temptation proves too much. I take a quick peek at the top page and I'm expecting to see an unfamiliar name, maybe the name of some distant acquaintance.

A jolt runs through me as I take in Demelza's flowery script.

9:01 a.m. Call from Virginia Edendale. Overheard new homeowner talking about moving graves from private cemetery. Mrs Edendale is very distressed. Thinks the new homeowner might already be undertaking this work and asked that we visit urgently.

I tell myself firmly that I need to have a cup of tea and calm down before I call Mum, but my body is on autopilot after Demelza leaves. The phone is in my hand before I've made the conscious choice to pick it up.

"Mum, what the hell? You called council?"

"I didn't . . ."

But she really is a very poor liar. She can't even finish that sentence. I grit my teeth.

"I'm not touching the damned cemetery."

"Well, I heard you tell Jack that you were going to move it," she hisses and there is pure poison in her tone. It's like in one simple misunderstanding I have unleashed a version of my mother I did not know existed. Mum almost sounds like a different person—someone bolder, someone direct. "This is just not okay, Fiona! Those people . . . those graves—they absolutely must *stay in place*."

"You were eavesdropping on my conversation."

"I went to look at Marilyn's crafting books and you were talking to him on the other side of the shelves! I know what I heard, and I had a moral obligation—"

"Mum. You heard me explaining to Jack that graves of historic significance should be left in place."

She hesitates, but only for a second before she says sharply, "You said graves can be moved."

"If you'd eavesdropped for a few more minutes, you would have heard me explaining my absolute hatred for developers who think they can just move graves—how that very attitude makes my blood boil! How that's exactly the kind of thing I spent my whole *career* trying to stop!" I draw in a sharp breath then pause. "Why didn't you just ask me, Mum?"

"But I thought . . ." All of the fight has gone out of her and she's back to her usual self. Softly spoken. Timid. Almost, in this instance, fearful, as if she's afraid I'm going to . . . what? Yell at her? Hold a grudge?

"I'm sorry, Fiona. This is all so very hard and I'm just trying to do the right thing. I need to go, so we'll have to speak later." It makes no damned sense, but as we end the call, my mother's voice is shaky with what I have to assume is fear. As I drop my phone down with a growl, it lights up with a text from Jon.

> You didn't reply to my text last night and I haven't heard from you for a few days. I'm worried, Fi. Are you okay? You can tell me if you aren't.

"Oh cousin," I mutter aloud. "I am very much not okay."

Jon and I text almost every day, but we call only in emergencies. I'm pretty sure this meets that criteria. He answers on the first ring.

"Fi?"

"Sorry, Jon. I'm *fine*, it's just been busy and . . . argh! Everything is so strange and Mum is acting so weird!"

"How so?" he asks me.

"She thought she overheard me talking about moving the cemetery—"

"*Moving* the graves? Good grief."

"So she called the council and reported me."

"Well, fair enough. If I thought you were about to go around disturbing two dozen graves, I'd probably call the authorities too."

"You'd *ask* me first, surely," I counter.

"Well, yes, *I* would definitely ask you. I'd say, 'Hey Fiona, are you thinking of desecrating any graves today?' and you'd say, 'Actually no, Jon, thanks for asking.' When have you ever known your mum to confront *anyone* about anything? She always does this. Her go-to moves are hints and guilt trips and when those tactics don't work, she goes to extraordinary lengths to avoid having hard conversations directly. Alan has basically been her mouthpiece for thirty years. And before that, it was my dad."

I'm silent as I ponder this. Jon is right—my mother makes snide, passive-aggressive comments, she guilt trips, sometimes she even manipulates. She does not address things head-on and she absolutely does not get angry.

That's why she sounded so different on the phone. We weren't talking around the subject and she wasn't suppressing her distress over it. She was properly pissed off and so was I and we just talked it out.

"I still don't understand. Where did she get the idea that you'd move those graves?"

"She overheard me talking to Jack last night and—"

"Whoa," Jon interrupts me. "Jack K is in town?"

"He moved back a few years ago."

"You're living *next door* to Jack again? And you've been *talking* to him? Do you still turn a fetching shade of raspberry if he glances in your direction?"

I'm turning a shade of raspberry right now as my cousin teases me. Did everyone in this town know about my crush back in the day?

"Mum completely misinterpreted what she heard," I say, trying to push on. "That's all. She heard something about the graves and she assumed the worst."

"I bet she was sitting at the farm, making herself sick with worry that you'd guess who sent the council after you."

"Probably," I sigh.

"Your mum really is a complicated woman, Fi."

"Tell me about it. By the way, I checked all of the boxes of letters from Tad's author friends this morning . . ." I'd love to tell Jon about the wind and the door handle that just would not twist, except he'd completely freak out, and I've only just started to calm down myself. "There's nothing in there from Charity Wilkie. Any other ideas how I can track her down?"

"Don't kill me for saying this but . . . ask your mum?"

"I already did that," I mutter.

"Then maybe email Rita. Her mother was the most respected agent of Tad's generation. Any author she didn't know wasn't worth knowing. I'll forward you her details."

We chat for a while as I whip myself up a plate of cheese and crackers for dinner. I pour myself a glass from the bottle of red wine—which I immediately drink, then repour. Maybe it'll help me sleep tonight. I ask how Jon's kids are going, how his book is going. He tells me his latest novel is "the worst piece of shit in the history of literature" which would be alarming if I didn't I know my cousin's process so well. Intense negativity simply means the excited rush of a new draft has passed and he's into the hard yards finishing the thing. He'll be in a better frame of mind once this draft is done and he can move on to refining it.

When Ilona calls him for dinner we say our goodbyes. Erin has done a stellar job on the parlour—even going so far as to cover a few of the armchairs with towels so I can sit on them. I ferry in a few armloads of firewood and get a roaring fire started in the hearth. Then I rest my cheese plate and glass of wine on the circular table by the fire and I walk upstairs to get my book.

I really need to relax and wind down before bed. I decide

I'm going to stop thinking about Mum now. I'm going to stop thinking about the noises in the house and things falling off tables. I'll get all toasty by the fire, and I'll eat my cheese and drink my wine and read until I'm tired.

But when I get to my room, the book is gone. It was open face down on the nightstand this morning, but now it's nowhere to be seen.

I check under the bed, behind and beneath the nightstand. It's gone. It's just *gone.*

Jack was here today, but he didn't come upstairs. He just walked through the ground floor of the house to the kitchen, through the backyard, then back out downstairs to leave via the front door. He didn't leave my sight for even a second.

And Erin was in the parlour the whole time. Maybe she did come upstairs for something when I was busy in the dining room—but why would she take a book I was so obviously reading? That doesn't make any sense either.

I have been stressed. Sleep deprived. Maybe I picked it up unthinkingly, put it down somewhere silly. That's got to be it.

Except that Mum sent Erin.

And Mum called the council.

And Mum was visibly displeased when she looked at this book last night.

No. Even Mum wouldn't go this far. She sent me that radio today, a kind gesture to help me settle in. Why would she go to such devious lengths to stop me reading a book? Calling the council was extreme, but I suppose it did make some sense if she really believed I was about to dig those graves up.

If she really thinks so little of me.

I check every single room a second time, and the book is nowhere to be found. This is nothing more than an inconvenience—another odd happening for me to overthink—

in this case, something of no consequence, because there are eleven more copies of the very same book right next door to my bedroom, sitting in Uncle Tad's office, still in the box they arrived in.

So I take one of those, and I walk back down to the parlour to my wine and my dinner, and I tell myself this is just one more thing I can't let myself think about. At least, not tonight if I want to get any sleep at all.

THE MIDNIGHT ESTATE

BY CHARITY WILKIE

A full day had passed since Marie escaped Rupert's home in a moment of pure, desperate impulse, twenty-four hours of such anxiety and terror that she felt like she was trapped in a fever dream. She was following Silas around blindly, obeying his instructions without question, constantly looking over her shoulder and leaping out of her skin every time a door slammed.

Silas had driven Marie all the way to San Francisco the minute she left Rupert, eager to get her close to the airport and far from their hometown as quickly as possible. No one in the city would recognize her—she'd only been there a few times in her entire life. He'd taken her shopping right away. She now had new shoes with a tall heel and a suitcase full of clothing she'd never have chosen in a million years. All bulky, in dark, severe colors—a much older woman's wardrobe, clothes unlike anything Marie had ever worn before. Silas took her to the salon where a stylist applied a temporary rinse to leave her hair just a few shades darker, and then he gave her the string of pearls that had belonged to his sister. The string was plenty loose, but even so, Marie felt it might choke her. She'd tried her best to match the style Maeve wore in the passport photo—bold, thick eyeliner, and darker lipstick than Marie had ever dared wear in her life.

When the embassy opened the next morning, Silas and Marie were waiting on the doorstep. He instructed her that she should remain mute and to try to look distressed, and she had no trouble at all complying with those instructions. She trembled with genuine fear as he talked his way into an emergency visa for her.

"Our mother just died and as you can see, my sister isn't coping well. I need to fly home as soon as I can but we have no other family and I can't leave her alone. Could you possibly help?"

Marie hadn't imagined that this kind, somewhat awkward man would be a convincing liar. But then she saw the barely restrained panic in his eyes and she realized that he was just doing exactly what he had promised to do—everything within his power to get her to safety.

The attendant's gaze passed over her and then he said kindly, "I'm very sorry for your loss. Let me see what I can do."

She'd never heard an accent like that before. Marie could barely understand a word the man said.

All of that was terrifying, but even so, it had nothing on her present situation, as she waited in a line at the airport. Getting the visa was one thing but using it to board a plane with someone else's passport was another altogether.

"Just hold your chin up high and be confident," Silas said, but although his advice was probably sound, he seemed every bit as terrified as Marie felt.

They were all but strangers six weeks earlier and now they were about to commit a crime together. Marie wasn't sure what exactly the crime was called but she did know that using someone else's passport was a very serious kind of fraud.

Did it count for anything that she was trying to save

her life, and a potential baby's life at that? She couldn't fool herself that a theoretical judge would be sympathetic—not if even her own brother couldn't bring himself to be sympathetic to her plight.

Whenever she thought about it like that, Marie second-guessed herself.

Had it really had it been that bad? Maybe she was being impetuous and impulsive and irresponsible, all things Rupert had accused her of being many times. Hysterical, as he and Irving would say. She couldn't do a single thing right and Rupert was going to be so disappointed in her and so angry. And now look at the mess she was in, about to board a plane with a total stranger—

No.

There was some scant trace of the headstrong child Marie used to be buried deep inside her. All she had to do was give that spirit a chance to breathe and grow and it might become strong again.

And so, she and Silas, side by side, shuffled forward a little farther, towards the immigration desk at the San Francisco International Airport.

"You definitely left your own identification papers at home, didn't you?" he whispered suddenly. "No passport or driver's license with you?"

"I didn't bring my handbag . . ."

"That's a good thing. I just didn't want you to walk up to that counter and accidentally hand over the wrong one!"

"But what will I do when we get there—"

"We'll figure that out later. Let's just get through this part first."

Marie had Maeve's passport in her sweaty hand but she kept thinking about the photograph inside and every time she did, she felt she might throw up. About the only thing

Marie and Maeve had in common was the first letter of their first names.

Maeve was older. Curvier. Taller. Beautiful in a very specific way—even in that slightly faded black-and-white photo, her eyes sparkled behind the frames of her glasses. Marie was wearing those very same glasses now, and that was the other reason she felt so ill. Maeve had been terribly shortsighted, but Marie had perfect vision, so wearing the other woman's prescription meant the whole world was a distorted, bloated blur.

And oh *God*. They were at the front of the line.

"Good day for flying," Silas said, greeting the attendant, who sat on a stool at a high counter. He opened Silas's passport and skimmed it, then checked the attached paperwork which confirmed Silas was an Australian permanent resident. Silas silently reached to take the paperwork from Marie's hand and passed it over the counter for her. His hands weren't much steadier than hers.

And this was it, she thought, the moment when their plan failed. She would be arrested and surely sent back to Rupert. Her throat filled with bile and her knees were getting weaker by the second and she looped her arm through Silas's just to hold herself up and then—

"Have a nice flight," the attendant said as he slid the second passport and visa and her plane ticket back across the bench. Silas handed Marie the paperwork then excused himself to use the bathroom before they went to the gate to wait for the plane. Marie took herself to the ladies' room and was violently, relentlessly sick. When her stomach was empty, she left the cubicle and stared at herself in the mirror. Blood vessels in her eyes had burst from the exertion.

When she left the restroom to find Silas at the gate, Marie couldn't quite be sure, but she thought she could smell bile on his breath too.

He had warned her that the flight was long and arduous but she hadn't quite understood what he meant: thirty hours in the air, with four long stops to refuel along the way.

That meant four landings with descents that left Marie convinced the plane was about to collide violently with the ground. Each time, she found herself panting and dizzy, gripping Silas's hand as if he were her lifeline. And four take-offs—sheer terror for Marie as the plane accelerated, and by the time the moment of lift-off came, she'd be whimpering through panicked sobs.

Even when they were high in the air, the incessant cigarette smoke in the enclosed space left her feeling ill, gasping for breath. She fantasized about opening the door to the airplane and sucking in the cool, clean outside air, and when she shared this with Silas, he gave her an alarmed look and spent twenty minutes explaining cabin pressurization.

Marie tried to eat a few times but her stomach just wouldn't have a bar of it. Throughout the entire trip she held nothing down but water. The glamorous hostesses kept up a steady supply of sick bags.

Silas tried to distract her by talking to her about his family. He told her about his wife, Christine, and his son, Ernest, and how much he missed them and couldn't wait to see them. He told her about Maeve—stories about his sister's kindness that made Marie feel like it was an honor just to borrow the woman's name.

She asked him sometimes what they would do when they landed.

"I'll help you find somewhere to live," he assured her. "Don't worry, Marie. I'm not going to abandon you in a strange country without a way to survive."

"Why are you doing all of this for me?"

"Oh," he said, and then he cleared his throat and looked away. "It's what Maeve would have told me to do."

By the time the plane touched down in Sydney, Marie was so weak and exhausted she could barely hold herself up. Silas walked her right to an airport cafe then sat her gently into a chair. He fetched her an orange juice and some dry toast, which she ate in a weary, numb silence.

"Some people get terrible air sickness. But when Christine was pregnant, it was like she was airsick all the time. Do you understand what I'm asking?" Silas said carefully.

Marie looked away, blinking exhausted tears away from her eyes.

"I haven't seen a doctor but yes, I think . . ."

She couldn't say the word—it simply would not leave her mouth. It had been too noisy and too crowded on the plane for a deeply private conversation, but once the adrenalin of that experience at San Francisco airport had faded and Marie was in the air, it had finally occurred to her that she was on her way to the other side of a globe with no plan, no resources, and entirely at the mercy of a man she didn't know from Adam. She was half expecting him to throw his hands up in despair and walk away from her at the news that she was probably pregnant, one further complication to deal with. He'd said he would help her find somewhere to live and a way to survive, but he'd already done so much.

Silas only reached across to squeeze her forearm gently.

"One last hurdle to jump before we're through the airport," he said, sounding almost as tired as she felt. "Should we get this over and done with?"

As they approached the final immigration desk, Marie felt a sense of doom settle over her. The make-up was long gone—that thick eyeliner had run down her cheeks as she vomited, and she had wiped the residue off with toilet tissue in the airplane's tiny bathroom. She was holding Maeve's glasses as they moved down the line, but she couldn't bear the thought of putting them back on her face, to see the world swimming again all around her again. Not when she was feeling so weak. Not when the vague echoes of nausea still rolled through her. She'd shed layers of clothing when the air sickness started and reluctantly donned as much as she could bear just as she stepped off the plane. Still, the final layer—a neat navy jacket with a large button right at her throat, was slung over her arm. It was so hot and stuffy in that airport she could not bear to put it on.

"Please," Silas said, dropping his voice as he motioned towards the jacket. "Just for a few minutes."

Marie stifled a groan but she could see there was only a handful of people ahead of them in the line now and she knew she had no choice. She pulled the jacket on, smoothed a hand over her wildly messy hair and then forced herself to don the glasses.

Silas handed over his passport first and this time, even he seemed too tired to make small talk, particularly once the attendant began sizing up Silas—holding up his photo and comparing, as if he had reason to be suspicious.

Marie crossed her arms over her chest to hide the violent way her hands shook as she waited her turn. She began to daydream—or maybe it was an exhaustion-induced hallucination. The immigration attendant threw her right onto the same plane and told the pilot to take her back to San Francisco right away. Rupert was somehow waiting for her at the airport with handcuffs in hand and he drove her right out to the desert and—

"Miss?" the attendant said, reaching for her paperwork. Marie handed it over. He repeated the same process—holding it up, intending to compare it.

But right at that moment, Marie felt the toast and the juice threatening to make an appearance. She gave a muffled sound of panic and pressed her hand over her mouth. The attendant's eyes went wide and he fumbled beneath the desk, thrusting a wastepaper basket at her just in time.

When the waves of sickness receded, Marie looked up through bleary, stinging eyes. Silas gingerly took the wastepaper basket from her and held it towards the attendant.

"What should we . . . er . . . do with . . . ?"

"I'll call someone to clean that," the attendant said, and he shoved the passport across the desk. "Looks like you've had a rough trip so I won't . . . er . . . keep you any longer. Welcome to Australia."

Silas had originally planned to drive straight home. He did anticipate that unique exhaustion that came from such an extensive trip, but he was desperate to see Christine and Ernest, and he had taken that road from Sydney, across the Blue Mountains and the Central Western Plains, enough times by then that he knew it like the back of his hand. But when he envisioned that weary final leg of the journey, he'd never in a million years have expected to have a *pregnant* companion to deal with before he could make the drive.

The simple act of navigating the immigration line had been one of the most stressful things he had ever done, and his head was spinning as he stepped out of Sydney airport. He'd barely slept at all on the flight—he spent half the time trying to help Marie with her sickness, and the other half of the time panicking.

Silas had never broken the law before, and now, he'd committed what he assumed to be a serious crime. And even *worse* than that was the fact that he had promised Marie he would find her some place to live and a way to support herself, but his mind remained uncharacteristically blank. It was one thing to tell her he'd help, one thing even to smuggle her out of the US, but her situation was incredibly complicated.

And so was his. If it wasn't, he would simply take her home with him to Forbes.

His relationship with Christine was already in trouble, and if he surfaced after six weeks away with Marie in tow—a beautiful, much younger woman—Christine would surely think the worst of him. It should have been easy enough to protest that his relationship with Marie was innocent because it was the God's honest truth, but there was so much at stake and Silas could not afford a misunderstanding with his wife. Not on the back of the many misunderstandings that had led to her moving herself out of his home.

Silas and Marie walked in silence to his blue Volkswagen Beetle. He stacked the suitcases on the luggage rack on the roof, then placed the box of Linda and Maeve's belongings on the back seat. Marie walked to the driver's side of the car, then paused, confused.

"It's the opposite . . ." Silas said. She winced and walked around to the passenger's side.

"That would take some getting used to."

But she said it as if it was a hypothetical adjustment, not one she was absolutely going to have to make. Silas wondered if she was as confused as to what to do next as he was.

Once they were in the car, and Silas had cajoled the sluggish engine into starting, he looked over at his young companion and suddenly felt the weight of all of the decisions he had not made looming over him. There was no way he'd find her a home and a suitable job in a single afternoon, not even in a bustling, cosmopolitan city like Sydney.

"Let's stop for the night. At a motel."

Marie gave him a shocked glance, then her face fell. Fear and suspicion crept into her gaze.

"No, I didn't mean—" Silas was momentarily flustered, then suddenly fierce. "Marie. Never. Do you understand me? I didn't bring you here to take advantage of you. You are here as my guest. You are here to be free. I would never—I would—" He broke off. It was only natural that she'd be nervous and suspicious. He took a deep breath. "You're *safe* with me. You always will be. I promise you that."

Her gaze dropped to her lap. Silent, heavy tears rolled from her eyes, over the dark bags beneath them, across her pale cheeks. He sensed she was beginning to spiral.

"Where will I go? How will I keep a roof over our heads? What if he finds—"

"Marie," he interrupted her gently. She looked back at him—big brown eyes swimming in tears. He tried to flash her a reassuring smile, even though his gut had twisted itself into knots. "Let's sleep. Eat something. Things will seem easier in the fresh light of a new day."

As he waited outside of Marie's motel room the next morning, it occurred to Silas that he had made very few impulsive acts in his entire life. He was a measured man, someone who tended to proceed quite cautiously. Even through the years when he traveled the world, he always spent months researching before he booked tickets. Until the previous day, he'd never once landed in a place and not been certain of where he would sleep that night.

And this situation with Marie was exactly why: impulsive decisions had rarely led him anywhere good, and now he had a woman in his care who could only represent intense complications to his already complicated life.

When Marie's door opened, he was relieved to see her looking refreshed. She was still pale but the faint traces of her make-up, those shadows left behind after the difficult plane trip, were gone. She must have washed her hair, because the temporary color was already fading. She looked painfully young, and it struck Silas that in some ways, he had a child under his wing in Marie, rather than another adult who needed some assistance.

"How old are you?" he asked her, but as soon as the words flew out of his mouth, he realized it was an especially odd way to greet someone first thing in the morning.

"I just turned twenty," she said, raising her chin. So she was a full ten years younger than Maeve. He was glad he hadn't known the age discrepancy for sure when he smuggled Marie onto an international flight with Maeve's passport.

But that settled it. He'd come up with an idea overnight, but it was almost as crazy as the steps they'd taken together so far, and he'd spent the whole morning trying to talk himself out of it. But she was *twenty years old*, for God's sakes. He couldn't just abandon her.

"Are you feeling better today?"

"I slept well," she said. "I don't know how, considering my life is basically over."

"Let's keep in mind what's important—he'll never find you. Not here, in Australia."

"I'm not even sure he knows Australia exists," she muttered. "But where am I going to go, Silas? I can't rely on you forever."

Over breakfast, he laid out her options.

"You're twenty years old and you're pregnant. You're married, yes, but Maeve wasn't. So we don't have a wedding certificate with your new name on it." He dropped his voice. "I don't want to scare you, but something you need to keep in mind is that here in Australia, young women who find themselves pregnant often do not have a lot of choices."

"Wh-what does that mean?" she whispered. Silas noticed she was twisting the rings around the fourth finger on her left hand.

"They call them mother-and-baby homes. The women stay there for the duration of their pregnancies and I've heard that the babies are taken, sometimes right after birth. They're then adopted into other families whether the mother likes it or not."

"I don't even know if I *can* raise this baby on my own," Marie said, her eyes filling with tears. "Maybe it would be for the best if someone else cares for it."

"What will be for the best is if you have time and space to make that decision for yourself," Silas said before carefully adding, "but if we aren't very careful here, you could end up in one of those homes, Marie, and then the choice will be made for you. We can't let that happen. There's another option, but I'm just not sure . . ."

"Please. Just tell me what I should do."

"I'll take you home with me," he said, and her eyes widened.

"But won't your wife—"

"And there's something I haven't told you. Christine and I going through a rough patch. So the truth is, even if you come back to Forbes with me, she won't be there. She's been staying with her mother, a few minutes' drive away."

"Oh."

Her voice was so small that Silas was tempted to leave it at that—but through those long hours overnight, he had already realized that Marie had no real choice but to come with him, to travel across the mountains and to his country home. He had to be honest with her.

"I can't lose her, Marie. I just can't. She's my whole world. And I am worried that if I bring you home to live with me—which I am happy to do as I suspect it's the best option here—there will be unintended consequences for the both of us. We have to proceed very carefully here."

"What does that mean?"

"People will think it's improper for us to stay together because you are not my wife. My *wife* might think it's improper for you to stay with me. Unless . . ."

"Unless?"

"Christine never met Maeve," he said. "She's only ever seen a very old photo of her that I had with me when I first came here, and that was taken when we were children."

"You can't lie to your wife, Silas," she whispered. "I can't ask you to do that for me."

"I'm asking *you* to do this for *me*," he admitted heavily. "My marriage is a mess, Marie. I suspect it's a mess of my own making and I need time to figure that out. I can't risk going home to her right now and telling her that I want to fix things, but in the same breath, announcing that I happened to bring a beautiful young woman from America with me and I'm moving her into my house."

"But once you do reconcile, she'll be *so angry* . . . !"

"Once you've had your baby—"

"Once I've had the baby?" she repeated, shocked. "Silas,

you've already flown me across the world, now you're talking about supporting me for months!"

"There's no way forward for you here without me supporting you for months, except those mother-and-baby homes, and I won't let that happen to you. I didn't rescue you from the frying pan only to throw you into the fire!"

They sat in the restaurant at the hotel and talked for over an hour, but there was just no other solution to be found. And so, they piled their suitcases back onto his VW, and turned the car towards Forbes. Marie would continue to use Maeve's name for the foreseeable future, and Silas was going to have to help her convince the world that she was a widow.

CHAPTER 10

Fiona

Marie and Silas are on their way to Forbes and I am dying to keep reading, but I've hardly slept in two full nights, and by 9:00 p.m., I've nodded off a few times and the book keeps falling from my hands.

I close my bedroom door when I go up to bed. I tell myself it will shield me from the mysterious thumps and bumps in the night, but all it does is force me to strain to hear them. That doesn't help one bit, so I get up again. I turn on every light as I walk to the kitchen for a glass of water, then turn them all off again as I climb back to my room. This time, I leave my bedroom door open.

A few minutes after I turn my lamp off, I hear a thump down the hall. Somewhere up near Tad's bedroom this time, I think. The sleepiness that plagued me downstairs vanishes in an instant.

I can feel my racing pulse in my ears, and I try to calm myself by taking my mind back to happy times in this house and in this room. I remember dragging the phone along the hallway from Tad's office, the long extension cord trailing behind. I remember talking to Stef or Patience or Jon or even Jack in my younger years for hours and hours on end. I remember shouting at Mum when she lifted the other handset in the kitchen and accidentally, or intentionally, eavesdropped on my conversations. I think about birthdays and quickly realize I can't remember a single one—not because I didn't have them, but rather because they've all blended into one glorious, happy blur in my memory. What year was it when Uncle Tad bought me a TV for my room, against Mum's wishes, and even though she muttered and grumbled, she didn't have the heart to take it back? Maybe it was the year I turned nine. Jon was definitely close to thirteen. I remember that because he'd just had a growth spurt and was suddenly taller than Mum. I was jealous of that for some reason but he was jealous of my TV so it all seemed even. Was it my fifteenth or sixteenth birthday when Mum took me on that holiday to Far North Queensland? I just remember we were on a train for the whole day of my birthday, but it was worth it for two glorious weeks with an ease between the two of us, just snorkeling and hiking and eating seafood right by the beach.

All of these memories begin to soothe me, and I finally drift into a light and fragile sleep, only to awaken with the knowledge that not much time has passed at all, and something is terribly wrong in my room.

At first I'm so paralyzed by fear, even my thoughts feel frozen. *My God.* Is this like the wind blowing in a closed room, the door slamming against all logic? Or is this like my nightmare last night? Is it the faceless man with the knife? Is it—

No. It's worse even than that.

There's something on my bed. Right next to my knee.

I want to scream but no one would hear me anyway. For a few terrifying moments I lie there with the thing against my leg making that sound my ears can't quite make sense of and then I wake up just a little bit more and it hits me—

I lift my head off the pillow, just a little so I can peer down the bed. As my eyes adjust to the darkness, I see it.

Against the white of my new duvet cover is a small black lump. An exceedingly fluffy black lump that happens to be purring up a storm.

And the movement I had sensed, the thing that probably woke me up? It's another cat, and it jumps up onto a chest of drawers in the corner. It's also fluffy and black, but it has white feet and a white belly and even a white patch up along its neck and over its nose.

I drop my head back onto the pillow and feel like an absolute fool.

Of course there are stray cats in the house. Possums and rats do leave droppings in their wake and they don't push things off countertops just for fun. Cats though . . . cats are stealthy, except when they *want* to be seen. And cats, in the absence of kitty litter, would probably just do their business in the garden.

This doesn't explain everything—but it does explain a lot.

"Hello," I whisper. "Who are you?"

The cat on the nightstand moves so fast I lose sight of it before it's even out the door. The cat on the bed sits up, looks at me once, then bolts after its companion. I climb out of bed and walk carefully after them, just in time to see them dart into the first door leading into Uncle Tad's office. I hasten to pull the door closed to trap them there, but the other door is still open and they dart back into the hallway and down the stairs—a blurred flash of black-and-white fur whizzing past my legs.

I follow them down, calling softly "kitty, kitty, kitty," but they've disappeared. When I turn the light on in the kitchen, I'm not surprised to see that the glass I carelessly left on the bench when I came down earlier is shattered all over the floorboards.

But the back door is closed so how are they getting in? Surely they can't have been hiding in the house, totally unseen for all of these weeks?

A memory sparks and I groan and stomp my way through to the laundry, properly furious with myself now. I'd have remembered this earlier if my brain didn't default to buying in to all of the ghost stories around this house.

Uncle Tad adored animals but always said it would be unfair for him to adopt a pet given the hours he kept when he was writing. He said a dog would be even less forgiving of this than say, an adoring niece, who always understood he'd make the neglect up to her once the book was sent off.

But then, in '68 or '69, Uncle Tad heard about an aged Jack Russel at the Forbes pound. Little Rosey was a black, brown and white dog once upon a time, but by the time she came to live with us, she was a silver, grey and white dog. Her previous owner was an elderly woman who died suddenly but no one wanted to adopt such an old dog and by the time Tad heard about Rosey, she was hours from being put to sleep.

Mum was frustrated when Tad walked through the door with Rosey. She liked dogs well enough, but she was convinced it would dig up the garden. This amused me to no end, because Mum had no interest in gardening—she rarely even went into the backyard. Uncle Tad promised her the dog would be inside all the time except when he was there to supervise her outside, but that lasted about three days before the dog's constant whining in the night drove us all mad. It turned out that Rosey was used to having access to the outside whenever it pleased her.

Uncle Tad had a handyman come to install a dog flap on the rarely used laundry door. I had totally forgotten about it because Rosey only lived a year or two before she passed away peacefully, and the dog flap was locked and never used again.

I turn the laundry light on and bend down to push at the flap, then I open the door and peer at it from the outside. It's immediately clear that the inside lock was simply not engaged. The real trouble is that at some point over the past ten years, the fitting on the outside of the door has rusted all the way through. It can't be locked.

The cats surely must be at least partially tame because why else would they have approached me, even in my sleep? Perhaps the mischief was more a ploy for my attention than anything. Perhaps they were abandoned at some point. Maybe they're lost from a family who loves them. I picture big-eyed children crying for their beloved pets, or an elderly man who looks a lot like Uncle Tad, standing forlorn at his back door, calling their names. Perhaps a past rodent infestation had drawn them into Wurimbirra at some point, but now that the mice are gone, the poor things are going hungry and can't find their way home.

Yes, the cats simply must be caught. How else will I get them home to their anxious family?

I laugh with a delirious kind of relief as I walk back up the stairs, even though I'm so tired my whole body is aching. I blame Jon and Mum for the way I talked myself into such a spiral.

As I turn into the hallway, it occurs to me that Jack is a vet—he'll know exactly how to catch the rotten things! I pick up my phone from my nightstand and check the time. It's just past 11:00 p.m.—late to call, but if I text, he'll probably see it in the morning.

> Theoretically, how would a person catch a pair of stray cats that were wreaking havoc in her new home?

Straight away I see he's replying, so I hastily add, Sorry, Jack. It's so late! You don't have to answer now.

A little time passes then his reply appears.

> Believe it or not I'm at the clinic delivering a litter of puppies. Delighted to announce that Limo the Dachshund (because stretch, get it?) is now mother to four adorable pups and their owner is taking them home shortly. But as for this cat scenario, I have to admit, it does not sound entirely hypothetical . . . ?

Jack promises to drop some humane traps off on his way home, so I pull a hoody over my pajamas, pick up my book and walk downstairs to the parlour. The fire is almost out, so I throw a few more logs on it, then make myself up a cup of tea.

THE MIDNIGHT ESTATE

BY CHARITY WILKIE

Silas and Marie drove through suburban areas for a while, then through hours of winding mountain roads, with expansive, thick bush land and steep mountains as far as the eye could see. They emerged into open countryside, with rolling hills and a wide expanse of land peppered with eucalyptus trees.

Marie was thousands of miles away from Rupert already, but now she thought herself to be disappearing from his view, dissolving somehow into the expanse of this strange new country. Every now and again she'd glance at Silas and feel a combination of gratitude and confusion.

Every action he'd taken since he came to her door several days earlier seemed to be rooted only in kindness, but was anyone really *so* kind? Her whole life was in his hands now, and that was exactly the scenario she'd been in with Rupert just a few short years earlier. Her guard would be up and it would have to stay up. Silas had given her no reason to suspect him, but the minute she could extract herself from his care to stand on her own two feet, she would go.

In the meantime, all she could do was to sit back and enjoy the strange experience of driving through a country she'd only vaguely known existed a week earlier. Eventually, the land became very flat, and she was surrounded by seemingly endless fields of young wheat, or massive herds of sheep, roaming through waving grasses.

"Almost there," Silas said wearily as he turned off a main highway. They passed a few farmhouses, dotted here or there, and then through a set of massive wrought iron gates, hung from a high concrete fence. There were palm trees scattered around a neat front yard. And beyond all of that, the largest house Marie had ever seen.

"Where are we?" she asked uncertainly.

"Home," Silas said, and he parked the car beside one of the palm trees and gave a sigh of relief.

"You . . . you live *here*?" she said, staring up at the house in shock. Then she blurted, "I assumed you were well off because you paid for my flight but . . ."

"I've had a lot of good luck in my career," he said simply.

Silas stepped from the car and retrieved the suitcases from the roof rack. He led the way to the massive double front doors, then rested the suitcases on the ground as he fished his keys from his pocket. He used a large metal key to unlock the old doors, then pushed them open to reveal an enormously wide staircase right in the center of the foyer, with a massive chandelier right above it.

"After you," Silas said, and Marie stepped into the house and spun in a circle, almost unable to believe her eyes.

"How old is this house?"

"1880s."

"How long have you lived here?"

"A bit over five years," he told her, and then he scooped the suitcases up again.

"Why *this* house? I know all houses here aren't like this—we saw perfectly ordinary homes all the way here."

"Do you remember the house Maeve and I lived in when we were young?"

Marie nodded. It was small and simple, and more than

a little run-down. Silas gave her a self-conscious shrug. "When I was proposing to Christine, I felt like I had something to prove. You're right that most Australian houses aren't like this. It's the largest in this town and I wanted that for Christine. Maybe I wanted that for myself."

Marie shut the door behind him, and automatically followed him as he mounted the stairs. She couldn't help but notice how dirty the place was—a thin layer of dust over the floorboards, a random cobweb here or there between the lines of the balustrade. She wondered how long it had been since Christine moved out.

At the top of the stairs, Silas pointed to one door, then another.

"These both open into my office, which is also the library. And my rooms are all at the western end. We don't use the eastern end much, so you can take your pick of the rooms down here."

Marie took a hesitant step towards the eastern end of the house, but was immediately distracted by a stained glass window at the end of the hallway, almost as tall as she was, in striking shades of green and gold and red. She looked into the first bedroom, the one beside Silas's office, and saw a cast iron bedframe, with a mattress covered only by a white sheet. There were bedside tables and a lamp on one side. A large antique dresser and closet stood against the wall beside the bed.

"I know it's basic," Silas said, suddenly shifting self-consciously. "There are so many bedrooms, and we scarcely used this end so it's a little neglected. But I have linens . . . downstairs, I think, in the cupboard off the laundry. Besides, it's a roof over your head, and you'll be safe here."

Something of her hesitation must have shown on her

face and Marie was embarrassed that she might seem ungrateful.

"It'll be just fine," she said weakly. "I'm eternally grateful for your help, Silas. This is lovely."

"Come on, let me show you the rest of the house."

Some parts of the house amazed her—like the beautiful bathroom she would have all to herself in the eastern wing, with black-and-white tiles and the enormous claw foot bath. And she loved Silas's library, even if it was in a state of utter chaos.

"How do you stand the echo in here?" she asked, and he looked at her blankly.

"There's an echo?"

"And it's so . . ."

She looked around and tried to think of a diplomatic way to say *disquietingly untidy*. She counted no less than thirteen mugs around the room, plus at least as many plates, and although there were shelves just about everywhere, half of the books were on the floor or on the enormous writing table. Even those that were shelved seemed to have been shelved in no particular order.

"It's clearly a creative space."

She was fascinated by the multitude of living rooms in the downstairs area, and that massively long kitchen, with the glorious windows all along one side, and the old table right in the middle at one end.

But when she walked to the back door off the kitchen, she gasped—startled by the beautiful gardens that spread across the large backyard, but even more so by the cluster of granite headstones in the back corner.

"Do people bury their dead at home in Australia?" she asked uneasily.

"This property was originally a very large farm, and the owners wanted to be buried here. At the time, I suppose that wasn't unusual, but no, it's not the done thing now."

"Isn't it disturbing living so close to those graves?" she asked, wrapping her arms over her chest as a chill seemed to move through the room.

"There's certainly no danger in living beside a small cemetery like that. Why, the town cemetery is hundreds of times bigger and there are houses around that too! When I first moved here, people kept telling me this house was haunted. I don't believe in ghosts, but I do understand why some do. Life is so short, it makes good sense to me that people would enjoy tales about it being longer and more complex than it really is. Besides, I don't mind that people think this house is haunted because if there is one thing I quickly learned when I moved here, it is that everyone wants to know everybody else's business. So if there is a myth about me being some odd American man who lives in a house full of ghosts, and that amuses or entertains people, what's the harm in that? I never discourage the myths." He touched the side of his nose and winked at her. "They only add to my air of intrigue."

"And Christine doesn't mind that?" Marie asked hesitantly.

Silas gave her an odd look. "Why would you ask that?"

"It's all well and good for you not to believe in ghosts, but plenty of people do. Is she afraid to stay here, especially when you're not here? This house is very impressive but it's also enormous. I imagine it might feel lonely at times."

"Lonely . . ." Silas repeated, frowning.

"What I'm saying is, if people think there are ghosts here, they might be less inclined to visit. If you know what I mean."

Silas stared at her a moment too long, then he sighed and turned back to the cemetery.

"Yes," he said heavily. "Yes, I suppose you're right. I hadn't considered it like that."

As he drove Marie towards the town, Silas thought about her thoughts on the mansion. He did understand that Christine was unhappy there, and he knew that when he spun his tall tales about the ghosts that supposedly shared the space with them, that she would go very quiet, and sometimes she would snap at him to stop it.

But he liked that they rarely had visitors. He'd even rather enjoyed the way that other people in the town would speak about their home as if it was some impressive but inaccessible landmark.

Silas loved nothing more than to be at home alone, except to be at home with Christine and Ernest. He had always been almost entirely self-sufficient, and truth be told, there were times when he would close the door to his office so that he could focus on his work, fully aware that he was shutting Christine and Ernest out of his space and his attention too. If he ever thought about that, and he often didn't, he would tell himself that Christine knew what he was like and that she knew the importance of his work. She was supportive. Understanding. So it was all fine.

Except that it wasn't.

"I can't live like this, Silas," she'd wept when she told him she was leaving.

"Like *what*? I'm not even sure what that means."

"I need space."

"There's plenty of room for—"

"*Silas.* I think—no, I *know*—we will both be happier on our own."

So she took a suitcase and their son and she drove herself to her mother's house. Silas felt like his head was swimming and try as he might he couldn't make sense of what she'd said.

I need space.

They lived in a house with eight bedrooms, five enormous living spaces, plus a library. How much more space could she want?

He told himself that she would calm down and she would come home—that this was probably one of those mysterious moods she had from time to time, when her emotions made so little sense to him that it was like she was speaking a foreign language. He told himself he would stay calm and wait patiently—but in the days that followed, she returned only to collect some personal effects, some furniture, her clothing.

And he had finally started to worry that perhaps Christine was serious about this but then the telegram arrived from Maeve and before Silas knew it, he was on a plane, rushing home.

Christine was the love of his life. He was happier in her company than he had ever been with anyone, anywhere. How could he have messed things up so badly that she would leave him?

"So are you divorcing then? Can you do that here?" Marie asked him as he drove, and she sounded so young and innocent that Silas himself felt older by the second.

"Yes, there's divorce here in Australia, just as there is back home. I don't know much about it and frankly I'm still determined it won't come to that," he said heavily.

Silas was going to fix things with his wife; he just did not know how to do it. And if he tried every tool in his arsenal and failed to win her back, and Christine insisted on a divorce, he would give her whatever she wanted; he would make sure that she was happy and looked after for the rest of her days. He would learn to worship her from afar, if that's what she needed. But what would become of Ernest?

Silas did not want his son to grow up in a broken family. The very thought of that outcome made him feel sick.

Silas and Marie were soon at Christine's mother's house—a much smaller and newer brick home, with a garden full of impractical roses, evolved for a climate with vastly more rain. His mother-in-law, Meg, was constantly in the yard with a hose in dry years, just trying to keep the plants alive, but she took such delight when they flowered. There was a metal slide set up in the front yard. Outside of school hours this street was always full of children playing together, riding their bikes or playing cricket on the road, scurrying to the grass when cars came past. Meg set the slide up for the neighborhood children and Ernest was just old enough now to join in when they played on it sometimes. In the summer, and sometimes in the spring and the autumn too, Silas had seen that slide get so hot it would scald the children's bare legs.

"Now *this* feels like a normal house," he heard Marie mutter under her breath as she looked at Meg's home, and he shot her a sideways glance. He had long been aware that the closer other people came to him, the less he understood them, but this afternoon with his young visitor had been so illuminating. He felt the swell of almost brotherly affection for her, and hot on the heels of that, a wave of fury towards the husband she'd run away from. That seemed to be the thing about bad men. They gravitated to the very best women, as if they could make up for something pure lacking in themselves by taking it from their wives.

Silas and Marie walked side by side to the door. Anxiety coursed through him as he raised his hand to knock, but then there were tiny footsteps in the hall, and muffled voices. He could hear Ernest trying unsuccessfully to open the door handle, and then Christine was there. She pulled the door open and gasped in surprise. Her beautiful brown eyes flicked from Silas to his young companion, and confusion twisted across her expression.

"This is—" he started to say, steeling himself to lie.

But just then Christine gasped, "Maeve!" and she gently nudged past Ernest and threw her arms around a very startled Marie. "My *God*! I am so thrilled to meet you. The things I've heard about you over the years—I wondered if you'd ever make the trip! And look at you, you are every bit as beautiful as your brother always said."

She leaned away from Marie to stare at her, then pulled her close for another one of those smothering hugs. Silas was so jealous of that hug. He knew exactly how addicting it felt to be engulfed in his wife's arms.

"Yes, this is Maeve," he said suddenly, and he reached out to squeeze Marie's shoulder gently. "I finally convinced her to visit and she has been dying to meet you and . . ." Silas crouched, folding himself down to his son's level. Ernest had hidden behind Christine's legs as soon as he saw that Silas was with a stranger. "Aunty Maeve so desperately wanted to meet you too. So here we are."

"Well, this is just a delight," Christine said, clasping

her hands in front of her chest. "Silas, you'll want to spend some time with Ernest of course, so perhaps I can pack a bag and he can go home with you tonight. But first, both of you, come in—come in!"

Silas held the door while Marie stepped inside the house, and although he knew she didn't realize it yet, into his family.

"I hope you're comfortable enough in the mansion?" Christine asked Marie later. "It's a beautiful home but it can be awfully lonely out there."

They were seated on braided iron chairs in the shade of the gum tree in her mother Meg's backyard. Meg had greeted Marie just as warmly as Christine had, like a long-lost friend returned home, with hugs and seemingly genuine delight. Silas's wife and her mother looked so similar—with warm brown skin and wavy brown hair, casual flowing dresses and enormous wide smiles.

"Silas will be there, so I won't be lonely," Marie said. Silas and Ernest were chasing one another around the backyard. Ernest was covered in sticky jam and scone crumbs, his face red with exertion, his eyes alight with joy. Silas looked like a completely different man to the one that Marie had come to know over those past few weeks. It was as though he had suddenly come back to life.

"How many years has it been since you lived with him?" Christine asked wryly, and to Marie's great relief, she didn't wait for an answer. "You've probably forgotten how he gets when he's working. You *will* be alone. He won't mean to shut you out, but he will. I suppose it won't be so bad for you since you're only visiting. How long are you staying?"

"She hasn't decided yet," Silas called from across the yard, and Marie was both horrified and relieved to realize he was eavesdropping even from afar. How did he feel about his wife's comments about him shutting her out? "She's going to stay a few weeks and see if she likes it here. She might stay longer."

"She can answer for herself, Silas," Christine said, before she turned her gaze back to Marie. "I'm so pleased you two are friendly again. It broke his heart that you'd become estranged." Estranged? Marie's heart sank. Silas had spent the better part of a month sitting by the real Maeve's bedside and his grief had been so palpable after she passed. "He wrote me and told me you'd been sick too. Are you feeling well again?"

"Christine," Silas called, suddenly scrambling to his feet and waving towards his wife. Christine went over to him, confused, and the two had a hasty, intense conversation in the middle of the backyard—Silas's mouth close to her ear, her jaw dropping in shock. After a moment, they walked in silence back to Marie.

"I told her about your husband," Silas explained. "I know it's still a little tender and I didn't want her to accidentally say something that left you upset."

"Thank you," Marie whispered.

"How long were you married?" Christine asked gently as she took her seat again.

"Less than a week," Silas murmured. "Aaron was a policeman. It was quite a shock, wasn't it, Maeve? No one could have expected a terrible car accident like that just a few days after the wedding."

"And you were there for the wedding, Silas?" Christine asked. Marie looked from her to Silas, utterly baffled by the turn the conversation had taken.

"Yes, since I was in town and it would have been such a journey to get back . . ."

"We decided to marry then and there," Marie finished for him when he trailed off to silence. Her mouth had gone dry.

"Then the accident happened," Silas sighed. "Such a tragedy."

"I'm so *sorry*, Maeve," Christine murmured. "My God. You poor thing. Of course you've come home with Silas for a while. You'll need some time to find your feet, I imagine."

"It was very sudden. I'm still in shock, I think. But Silas has been a godsend." All of this, at least, was entirely true.

"Of course he has," Christine said, reaching across to squeeze Marie's forearm. "And I'm here to help too, I promise you. Anything you need. We'll be the best of friends soon enough."

Later, as they drove home, Silas apologized.

"We should have talked about it before we went there—got our stories straight. We're not much in the way of criminal masterminds, are we?"

It was not sitting well at all with Marie that they were lying to Christine.

"Wouldn't it be better to tell her the truth, Silas? She seems very kind. Very wise. And won't you have to tell her the truth one day anyway, especially if you reconcile?"

"I have to smooth things over with her first. I can't risk this being one more thing we have to figure out. The story about your recently deceased husband isn't perfect," he added, almost to himself. "But I think, if we stick to it, it will work."

Silas didn't mean to abandon his guest, but he'd been away from his work for almost two months. It sucked him back in like a vortex and before he knew it a week had passed with him stopping only to visit Ernest and Christine a few times. Things with Christine were strained but also tender. His wife was kind and gentle to a fault, and he knew she was treading lightly, conscious that he'd lost his mother.

Little did she know his loss was so much greater than that, and he wanted nothing more than to sit with her and tell her about those awful weeks as he waited, hoping Maeve would recover, longing for forgiveness and absolution that would never come.

But while Silas didn't regret helping Marie to escape, he had trapped himself in obligation to her as much as he had trapped her in reliance to him. And so he did the only thing he'd ever known to do when he was worried—he worked. From the minute he returned from his sunrise walk to the minute his eyes felt too heavy to continue, he sat at his desk. Every now and again, Marie would knock politely on his study door and beg him for something to do.

"Why don't you rest? The television is in the ballroom." It was a large black-and-white set he bought mostly for Christine and he wasn't actually sure how to use it, but he did know Christine watched the news on it from time to time so the thing must work. That seemed to distract Marie for a few hours, but before he knew it, she was back at the door.

"Excuse me, Silas, I'm sorry to bother you but . . ."

"What is it?" He didn't want to sound impatient, but Silas felt that every interruption set him back hours. If Marie was going to knock on his study door several times a day, they were going to have a problem.

"It only picks up one channel," she said, laughing softly. "And it's showing some sports match I've never seen before—something with a bat and a ball and not much happening, actually. I didn't want to overstep but . . . would you mind if I do some baking?"

He said yes mostly because it seemed the fastest way to move her on and then he went right back to his work. But maybe a week later it struck Silas quite suddenly that he hadn't cooked a thing in days and yet he wasn't hungry. He emerged from his study, blinking as if he'd just woken up, and realized the hallway—which even *he* had noticed was a little dusty—was gleaming. He walked down to the kitchen and found Marie sitting at the table, reading a book. Something savory and fragrant was in a casserole dish in his oven. There was not a single dirty dish to be seen in the room.

"Marie—*Maeve*," he corrected himself. It felt so awkward to say his sister's name when he spoke to Marie, but he knew if he didn't keep in the habit, he'd slip when they were at Christine's place.

"I've been thinking," she said quietly. "Why don't you call me Mae?"

"Mae?"

"Well, it's kind of close to both names. And it will mean you don't have to call me . . ." She swallowed. "I just mean it must be hard to call me by her name, that's all."

"Mae," he repeated, and then he nodded. That might actually work. "Mae, have you been cooking for me?"

She looked at him blankly.

"You didn't realize I cooked the food you've been eating the last few days? Where did you think it came from?"

Now he had a vague memory of her quietly knocking and bringing in plates of food and cups of water and mugs of coffee, of her silently slipping into his study to retrieve the dirty crockery hours later. It was hard to explain how much he lived in his work when he was writing—how difficult it was to concentrate on his real life when he was fully immersed. He was never really anywhere real in the days and weeks of an exciting new project because some part of his mind was always working.

Silas was gradually realizing this was a big part of the reason Christine had been so unhappy with him, but he couldn't bear to think about that, because it wasn't like he chose to be this way and he didn't know *how* to change. Linda used to say he was born with his head in the clouds and he only visited earth when there was no way to avoid it.

He scrubbed his hand down over his face, frustrated with himself. He was going to *have* to figure out how to put some boundaries around his work if he was going to fix his marriage.

"I get a little obsessive when I'm working," he said, scratching the back of his neck. "I'm sorry. And thank you."

"What did you do when Christine wasn't here?" she asked him. "Did you just starve?"

"I tended to work until I physically couldn't keep going then I'd stop and eat whatever was at hand."

"I want to be of help and it gives me something to do," she said, and she looked back to the book on her table. He realized with a start that it was one of his—the one he wrote during his freshman year at college, the one that earned a major deal and hit best-seller lists and won awards and changed every single aspect of his life. He couldn't stand to watch someone read his work, so he turned to walk away, but Marie called out, "Wait. I've cleaned the house. There's only so much cooking to do and besides, we're going to run out of food soon again unless we do some shopping." Silas had taken her to the grocery store a few times, but every time they ran out of food, she had to nag him to take her back for more.

"You can take the car yourself. Just go into the town."

"I can't drive on this side of the road," she said, visibly horrified. "Please. I will—sooner or later—but let me get used to it some more first. Please."

"Okay," he sighed. "Okay. I'll take you later this afternoon." He hesitated. "Should we—should you—think about finding a doctor?"

She flinched as if he'd physically threatened her, then looked back down at the book.

"Not yet," she said, her voice very small. "Please. Not yet."

Over the days that followed, they fell into something of a routine, Silas writing and Marie pottering around the house. She kept him fed and hydrated and she dragged him to the store for food and to buy rugs to dampen the echo in his office, and she reminded him to visit Christine and Ernest and while he was out, she tidied his desk.

He had two months of mail waiting for him and he'd been putting off opening it because he only wanted to write, but Marie suggested gently that she could sort it for him, and he was pleased to hand the task over. He came back from a visit to Christine to find the letters opened and organized on his desk into three piles: for his urgent attention, letters that could wait until later, letters he could probably throw out. She had dusted half of his office too, and she'd started sorting the chaotic collection of books he'd acquired over the years since he arrived in Australia, shelving them into categories.

"You seem like an organized, efficient sort," he said, staring at the piles of letters and feeling so relieved he could have hugged her.

"I suppose," Marie said awkwardly. "It's not perfect. I don't really know what some of those letters mean. And there are some bills there you really should pay. I can pay them if you want me to but . . . I guess you'd have to give me your chequebook."

He looked at her thoughtfully.

"The thing is . . . I'm not. Organized and efficient, I mean."

"Everyone has their strengths. I couldn't do your work if I had a gun to my head."

"Can you type?"

"Not well. But I could learn."

"And can you balance a chequebook?"

Her eyes lit up at this. "Oh yes," she said. "Math. Numbers. *That's* my real strength."

"Mae," he said suddenly. "Would you like a job?"

As far as Marie could tell, Silas was one of those people who possessed a single extraordinary skill—but only *one* skill. He was obviously successful in his work but completely out of his depth when it came to managing the basic functions of his own life.

She was more than pleased to help him out. It gave her something to do. A purpose to her days. And best of all, a way to repay his kindness, and to earn herself some money.

Silas helped her set up an office of her own in one of the unused bedrooms at "her" end of the first floor. He bought her a desk and a chair and pushed the bed against the far wall, and then he went out and came back with a typewriter and book from the library—*Touch Typing in Fifty Lessons*. Marie practiced until her hands ached, every day for hours and hours, until she could type fluently, and quickly too. She started taking tentative drives out on the deserted country roads around the house, with Maeve's American driver's license in her purse in case she happened upon a local police officer. Soon, she felt confident enough to drive as far as Christine and Meg's house, and not long after that, into town so she could go to the post office or the grocery store.

After that, Marie drove herself to the police station and she arranged her very own Australian's driver's license—in Maeve's name, of course—but that she didn't need to ask Silas for help with this task made her feel an oddly powerful thrill.

Christine was fast becoming a friend, and that left Marie feeling conflicted. She understood the logic behind the story Silas had come up with on her behalf, and with every passing day, her old life seemed a little further behind her. Every time the fear would rise that Rupert might find her, she'd remember that arduous journey, and the way the trip itself had shown her just how big and wide the world was. Rupert would *never* find her, not tucked away in an airy old mansion just out of Forbes, a place which felt to her as though it might as well have been another planet. She had Silas to thank for that, and so much more.

But Marie wanted to tell Christine the truth, and she probably could have, except that Silas was so concerned about the optics of their situation. He had asked her to keep this secret and he asked so little of her. The last thing she wanted to do was to cause any further conflict between Silas and his wife and so she bit her tongue and tried to focus on the good things about this unexpected new life she had.

"How's Silas?" Christine asked one afternoon. She had brought Ernest to the mansion to spend the night with Silas, and Marie invited her to stay for a cup of coffee before she went home. The two women were in the back garden, in one of the outdoor rooms, Ernest climbing the low branches of a nearby peppercorn tree. Marie loved that backyard, with all of its lush plants and trees. She could sit and watch the birds for hours and had taken to refilling the bird feeder with seed every day. "He's working, I assume?"

"Yes, he's been very busy. Working all hours of the day and night," Marie told her, and she glanced towards the tall windows of his study behind them.

"I told you it would be lonely," Christine said quietly.

Marie shook her head hastily. "Oh no, it's fine. I've been helping him as much as I can with his secretarial work and the house and truly, it's fine."

"Maybe it's different as sister and brother, but let me tell you, as his wife . . ." Christine sighed heavily. "I love him, Maeve. I always, always will. I'd even go so far as to say I'm *still* in love with him. But we are not at all well-matched."

Marie thought about that phrase for a moment. If Rupert had been different—less controlling, kinder—would they have been well-matched? She never even thought for a moment about whether their personality types were well-suited, about whether they'd build the right kind of home for each other to thrive. Rupert just strode into her life when she needed help and then her heart started to flutter when he smiled at her and the next thing she knew, they were exchanging vows.

"Silas is so focused when he works," Marie said cautiously. "But he still loves you. I know he does."

"I know that too."

Marie wanted desperately to ask what the problem was then, but she couldn't quite bring herself to say the words. She'd noticed this about herself lately, and it troubled her. She had once been so bold—so headstrong. Now, she second-guessed herself in everything, even in how she spoke up in conversations. She heard Rupert's voice in her head at the strangest moments, even in that simple conversation with Christine.

Useless. Stupid.

She so wanted Christine to like her. She didn't want to ask the wrong question and offend her, to risk damaging the fledgling relationship.

"The first few months of our marriage I told myself that as the wife of someone so talented I had to just understand that I would never come first," Christine said. "I was working at the high school back then—I was an art teacher before I had Ernest—so it wasn't like I just sat around doing nothing. Then when we realized a baby was on the way, Silas was so delighted and proud and excited and I quit my job to focus on getting ready. That's when I first noticed how lonely I was when he was writing. You'll have seen it plenty of times, I imagine. The way he thinks about nothing *but* the work. The way he can sit opposite you at dinner for half an hour eating without tasting a thing, that faraway look in his eyes, because he's with you in body but his mind is upstairs writing."

Marie had noticed that. She didn't mind, but that was at

least in part because she owed Silas such a debt of gratitude and besides, and she had things to think about too. She was happy to sit in silence.

"It got worse after Ernie was born," Christine continued. "He slept so poorly at first. Silas was also up half the night working but it didn't seem to occur to him to help with the baby. I nearly went crazy with the sleep deprivation, and meanwhile Silas was just carrying on as if nothing had changed. When he finished writing his book, he'd swoop back into my life and into Ernie's life and he'd try to make it up to us but . . . I don't want a part-time husband, Maeve, and I didn't sign up for a part-time marriage. The fact that he thinks it's a *lark* that the town thinks this house is haunted so no one wants to visit it—But the loneliness of living out here almost killed me . . . It was all just too much. I tried to talk to him about it but it was like he couldn't hear me. That's why I left. Has he told you I caught him off guard when I did?"

"He hasn't said much about it at all. Just that he loves you and he wants—"

"He wants me to come home," Christine sighed. "I know he does, and I wish I could. But do you see him changing anything at all to get me to come home, aside from visiting me at Mum's house every now and again when he takes a break from his work? I think we all know he's not capable of changing, Maeve. This is just who Silas is . . . who he will always be. I was so unhappy when I was here, and now I'm not. I'm starting to think that we'll have a better relationship if we live in different houses."

Marie looked up to the study windows again. Her throat felt tight.

"Are you sure?"

Christine hesitated.

"No. Not yet."

"Promise me you'll talk to him as soon as you are. It would be cruel to let him live in hope."

CHAPTER 11

Fiona

This book is set here, at Wurimbirra. It's all here—the yard, the cemetery, the enormous staircase, the chandelier and the double doors at the entrance. Maybe I could convince myself that was an enormous coincidence, except that I found Marie's ring upstairs in my own bathroom. And could Silas be . . . Tad? The similarities are undeniable. My uncle was a wonderful man, but he was utterly lost in his work every single time he sat down to write.

When Jack knocks at the front door I am still numbly staring at the book. I walk to the door but even as I open it, I'm struggling to string a greeting together.

"Those cats really gave you a fright, huh?" Jack says, giving me an odd look. He's carrying two wire cages and a tote bag full of supplies and he's handsome and kind and he's here for me without question or protest even at midnight.

I want to hug him, but I feel like if I do, I'll just end up sobbing into his shoulders and he'll think I've lost my mind.

"It's been a big week" is all I croak as I welcome him inside. "Can I get you anything? Tea or coffee? I don't have any beer but there's wine . . ."

"I'm good, thanks, Fi. Where should we set all of this up?"

We consider a few options. The cats have been lurking in

the kitchen and the parlour, but I've seen them in my room and the study. In the end, we go with the study—mostly because I want to get some sleep tonight and I doubt I'll sleep if I'm lying there waiting for the traps to go off at the end of my bed. I take the tote from Jack and we walk up the stairs, side by side, as I explain about the dog door and the events of the past few nights.

"Why do cats push things off furniture!" I exclaim in frustration when I finish. Jack chuckles.

"Why do cats do anything? They are a law unto themselves, I'm afraid. The behavioral science theory is that they like to chase movement so when they are bored they create it for themselves, but my personal theory is they're just arrogant little jerks."

"Not a cat person?"

"I'm an every-animal person," he tells me. "But I'm not blind to their flaws. Honestly that 'pushing' behavior is more common in young cats so it's likely you've got yourself some kittens. And given one decided to snuggle up to you once you were asleep, that tells me it's at least a little tame. They're probably both skittish and desperate for your attention."

"They've aged me ten years in doing it, but they definitely got my attention."

"I've never been in this study before," he says quietly as he crouches low on the ground, beside the coffee table between the two dusty chesterfields. I wince at the creaking sound my knees make as I bend to kneel beside him. "When we were kids this was the forbidden zone, remember?"

"Oh, I remember," I sigh. "This was his sanctuary. He had so few rules, but staying out of this space and keeping quiet when he was working were not negotiable."

Jack explains these are fox traps. We'll bait them with some smelly wet food, and when the cats step inside, their weight will activate the trigger and the door will close to lock them in.

"And then what do I do with them?" I ask.

He reaches into the tote bag and withdraws a little wand.

"I'll scan them for microchips once we catch them. If they are chipped, we'll try to get them home to their owners. I should warn you . . . I'm not optimistic about that. If they had loving owners, they likely wouldn't be all the way out here, you know?"

"And if they aren't microchipped?"

"Well, that's when it gets a little more complicated. We'll take them to the pound, but black cats are always the last to be adopted, and if these aren't entirely tame . . . All I'm saying is, we're in the brief lull between mice plagues. It was probably the *last* plague that lured these cats into your house in the first place, so you might want to think about keeping them for the next one."

My first inclination is to refuse immediately. I haven't had a pet since Uncle Tad's dog Rosey, mostly because Lucas is allergic to pet dander, but there's no reason I can't have pets now.

In fact, there are quite a few reasons two cats might do me some good. Now that I know they're here, at least.

"I'll give it some thought."

He shows me how to load the food he brought into the trap, and how to arm it. As he's working, I push the coffee table out of the way to make some more room. The floorboard beneath the rug shifts as I do, making a loud shuddering sound.

"See?" I say pointedly. "The whole house is noisy—"

But something stops me, just like that. I can't explain it—it's almost like that moment in my bathroom when I found the ring, despite there being no earthly way I should have seen it back there, or the moment in the kitchen when I just needed to sit and read the book, or the moment when a wind that couldn't possibly get through a closed window pushed a door closed and locked it.

I reach down and I press on the floorboard and I am startled to realize there's a ton of movement there.

"Floorboard not seated right? Maybe that's why he had the rug and table here," Jack says as he shuffles the traps out of the way so I can roll the rug back.

"Mum bought the rugs when she first arrived from the US. Because of the echo," I whisper, and my mind is suddenly back with *The Midnight Estate.* As I move the rug out of the way I find a floorboard with slight damage along one side. Someone jimmied it up at some point and failed to repair it properly when they put it back. It's held in place by one nail on an odd angle, and another that's in the original hole, but so loose I can easily pull it out with my finger. There are indents all around the nails from where a hammer has landed in the wrong spot.

"This is Tad's handiwork," I murmur, almost to myself. "I'd know it anywhere. Tad wielded a pen like a sword but used a hammer like a drunk toddler." Jack laughs, and he's baited and armed the second trap now, so he sits it on the floor just past the edge of the rug, then stands. I am beyond desperate for sleep, but I know the minute Jack leaves I'll be diving back into that book.

"I'm glad you messaged me," he says as we walk back down the stairs.

"You are? You like setting cat traps for old school friends at midnight, do you? That's one of your favorite hobbies?" I don't know where I find the energy to tease him but I do, and I'm rewarded when he laughs again.

"No, but I seem to recall plenty of times over our first few decades when you needed help and wouldn't let me give it to you."

"That's not true!"

"How about when you were struggling terribly with Year

Eleven English? I kept offering to help you with your essays and you were adamant you could do it on your own. Or when your chain slipped off on your bike and you couldn't get it back on? And don't even get me started about how maddening it was to watch you trying to dive at the public pool before you finally figured out how *not* to bellyflop."

"So this is progress, huh?" I say softly, as he pulls open the front door, and he flashes me that oh-so-charming smile.

"Call me in the morning if we catch anything? And I'll pop in on my way to work and scan them for you."

"Thank you, Jack."

"It's my pleasure."

I wave as he slips into the car, and then I close the door. I'd probably be dissecting our interaction right now, thinking about the glint in his eyes when he was talking about how glad he was that I reached out, or the way my stomach flipped a little when he remembered so much detail about our friendship in our younger years.

But I can't stop to think about that right now.

I run through to the laundry and find Uncle Tad's old toolbox, then I sprint back up the stairs to the study. The dodgy floorboard is still exposed, so I pry the remaining nail out of it, and gently lift it up.

I'm not entirely surprised to see a little metal tin hidden beneath it, labeled with the brand of ink Uncle Tad used to buy. He loved to take notes with a fountain pen, and he went through a lot of ink, so he bought the little bottles in bulk and they always arrived in these tins. I fish the tin out and sit it on the floor, then take a steadying breath as I open it.

Inside the tin is a thick pair of glasses with black frames shaped like cat's eyes. There's a thin strand of pearls. A men's wallet, and two passports. I lift each item out one by one.

As I remove the passports, I find a little stack of papers underneath. On the top is a small black-and-white photograph of two headstones.

MILLICENT ENID WINSLOW—1898–1959
A good and kind heart is the best of all qualities

VIRGINIA JOY WINSLOW—1930–1959
She gave her family and her community loving acts of service

Milly Winslow was my grandmother—Mum and Tad's beloved mum, and I know she died just before Mum immigrated. That's a terribly sad photograph for Tad to have kept, but the thing that's making me feel physically ill right now is the photo of the second gravestone. The one placed right above a fresh grave. The one that has my mother's name and date of birth on it, along with a date of death.

There are cold, uneasy shivers running down my spine and my uncle is not here to explain himself.

I open the wallet next. There are American dollars inside, alongside a few Australian pound notes. There's a handful of business cards—mostly faded, some so faded I can't make out the text. There's a cardboard driver's license made out to Julian Noel Lentfer, born in 1927, a resident of Porterville, California. I open the passport to see a photograph of a stern man with thick blond hair and hard, cold eyes staring right back at me.

Julian Lentfer.

I've heard that name before, but where?

The answer is right under the passport, in a small collection of newspaper clippings, with headlines just like that one I found in the kitchen a few days ago.

WIFE OF DEPUTY POLICE CHIEF STILL MISSING AFTER SEVEN DAYS.

REWARD OFFERED FOR NEWS OF MISSING PORTERVILLE WOMAN.

PORTERVILLE DEPUTY CHIEF OF POLICE DISAPPEARED JUST WEEKS AFTER HIS WIFE.

HIS WIFE WENT MISSING, THEN HE DISAPPEARED. WHERE IS THE MISSING PORTERVILLE COUPLE?

"WE TRIED SO HARD TO GET HER AWAY FROM HIM." MURDERED SANTA ROSA WOMAN'S FAMILY SPEAKS OUT.

MORE THAN HALF A MILLION AMERICANS DISAPPEAR EACH YEAR. WE DIG BACK INTO SOME OF THE MOST MYSTERIOUS MISSING PERSONS CASES OF THE PAST CENTURY.

And beneath all of that, a larger photograph. It's clearly Uncle Tad—I'd recognize that lanky frame and those shaggy eyebrows anywhere, although he can't have been more than twenty in the photo. He's standing with an older woman who is beaming with pride, and a younger woman who is clinging to his arm even as she smiles.

My hands are shaking as I open the other passport. It belongs to another resident of Porterville, a Miss Virginia Joy

Winslow, born in 1930. There's a faded black-and-white photo of her and *this is not my mother*—this is a slightly older version of the girl in the photograph with Tad.

I take the tin with me as I leave Tad's office, flicking off the lights as I go. I wander down the hall to my own room and I close the door again, but this time I know I'll leave it closed. I'm bone-tired and unsettled, but there's no way I'll be sleeping tonight.

Jon forwarded me Tad's agent's contact information, so I bring up my email app on my phone and write Rita a quick note.

> Hi Rita, you might remember me—I'm Tad Winslow's niece. I'm currently cleaning out his house and I found some books by an author named Charity Wilkie. I can't find any information about her online—can you shed any light?

I don't expect a reply from her right away as she lives in New York, so I put my phone down and pick the book up. I'm not even a page in when a reply from Rita pops up on my screen.

> Fiona, of course I remember you. I think this one is easier handled over the phone. Can I call you?

I send her my number, and she calls right away. We exchange pleasantries before she says, "Fiona, do you mind telling me why you're asking about this Wilkie business?"

"Well, I'm currently reading Charity Wilkie's book . . ."

"You *are*?" She sounds gobsmacked and that makes two of us. "How did you find it?"

"There was a box of books here in his house and I thought Tad may have intended them as gifts so I was curious."

"There were copies of *that* book in *his* house? Where on earth did they come from?"

"The publisher sent them. Spencer Kallaide and Michaelson Books," I say, reading the imprint name on the spine.

"When were they sent?"

"The parcel was postmarked November '99, but they only arrived the day of his wake."

Rita sighs heavily, but then we both fall silent, and I'm not sure what to say or how to ask what I'm starting to suspect.

This book is nothing like my uncle's books. He wrote dense literary tomes, and as much as I adored his work, it was never easy to read or to interpret. But the further into *The Midnight Estate* I get, the more familiar it feels.

This book reads like Uncle Tad's conversational voice. He's telling this story exactly as he would if we were seated together having dinner.

"Did Tad write this? Was that box of books his author copies?" I blurt.

"Why do you ask me that?"

"Just a hunch."

She falls silent, then she gives a heavy, dramatic sigh. "Darling, listen to me. I'm going to tell you the truth about this but only because he's dead and I don't believe in ghosts so he can't haunt me. Okay?"

"What's the story, Rita?"

"Tad was a beautiful man. A real gem. But he could be a difficult client sometimes. Just to start with, he didn't like answering the phone, and he lived on the other side of the world. It used to drive my mother crazy. I mean, how was she supposed to work with him if he never talked to her? Then your mother came along and God bless that woman, she made it all so much easier. Everything went through her—*everything*. A force of nature! And then can you imagine I get a call directly from Tad out of the blue at the start of 1999, telling me he's written something and he wants to find a publisher for it?"

"So he *did* write this. Charity Wilkie was just a pen name?"

"It was him. That's right. I was never really certain why he chose a woman's name, but I did assume it was another way of covering his own tracks—he was so determined that no one would ever know this was his work. I said to him—Tad you are *killing* me here. If we publish this as a Taddeus Winslow novel we'll make a fortune! He just would not listen to reason. And there was more—he didn't want Ginny to know about it. Not *ever*, he said. And he had all of these rules for where we could sell it! Not into North America. Not into Australia and New Zealand. Just the United Kingdom."

"That's why it's a London-based publisher."

"That's right. A tiny, now-defunct publisher, and they paid a pittance for it because no one else wanted it and everyone thought the author was no one. And Tad insisted the contract have no provision for author copies. What author specifically asks *not* to be sent copies of their own book? None, Fiona, and that's probably why the good people at Spencer Whoever and Whoever Books assumed it was a mistake and sent them anyway."

"Did you think it was strange?" I ask her. "The book, I mean. I assume you read it."

"Oh yes, darling. It was all very odd, not his usual cup of tea at all."

"Where do you think the idea came from?"

"Who knows with these creative types? Their minds are fascinating, sometimes terrifying places. Where did any of Tad's ideas come from? A muse, the universe, daydreams, nightmares. I am impressed you recognized it as his work though!"

I'm not going to tell her it's not the work I recognized first, but the setting.

Maybe the timing of Elsie's death was for the best, because I can't see how anyone could read this book and visit this house and not immediately start to wonder.

THE MIDNIGHT ESTATE

BY CHARITY WILKIE

Another week went by in the mansion and Marie was still trying to convince herself that she wasn't pregnant. She was no longer feeling ill all of the time, but there was a definite thickening around her waist now—not quite a bump, more of an all-round swelling. The thought of confirming pregnancy filled her with panic—she had no idea how to parent, let alone parent on her own. And besides, a baby would be half her and half Rupert and how on earth would she ever come to love it?

Every now and again Silas mentioned a trip to the doctor and she told him "soon" and they went about their business. He was working and she was doing most everything else, and some nights, Ernest came to stay.

He was a chatty, charming boy, with an imagination as expansive as his father's, and he quickly bonded to his aunty Mae, so much so that he would throw his arms around her the minute he saw her. Sometimes Ernest would ask Marie to read him his bedtime stories instead of Silas, even though she lacked Silas's ability to do the good voices and to make even a dull story sound exciting. He was forever asking her to play with him, and that meant climbing around on all fours when he was pretending to be a dog or building blanket forts in the ballroom when he wanted to play camping. He even loved to spend time at her end of the upstairs floor—it seemed a treat for him to use her bathroom, to stop to look around in her bedroom, even to draw with his crayons in the office Silas had established for her.

One night, Marie took Ernest upstairs to clean his teeth in her bathroom. As he was scrubbing, she left him just for a minute, to go into her own bedroom to find her night cream. When she returned, he was standing in front of the sink, staring guiltily at the floor.

"What happened, Ernie?" she asked gently. He looked up at her, brown eyes swimming with tears.

"I'm sorry, Aunty Mae," he said. "I'm bad."

"What did you do, sweetheart?"

"I was playing and they fell. I'm sorry."

"What fell?" she asked, bewildered, and then she looked to the sink—where her wedding ring was resting beside the open drain, and her engagement ring was nowhere to be found. She'd taken them off some days earlier because her fingers were swollen and besides—she didn't have to wear them anymore.

She moved the wedding ring away from the drain, then peered down into the dark recesses below, but she couldn't see the ring there. Maybe it was already gone, flushed away when Ernest rinsed his teeth.

She knew the ring was worth a lot of money but she felt entirely numb at the thought that it was gone. Not quite excited to be free of it, but disappointed only because she had hoped to sell it, maybe to try to give the funds to Silas even though she knew he would refuse.

"It doesn't matter, Ernie," she said. He looked at her in surprise, as if he couldn't believe he wasn't going to get scolded for what he'd done. "It was just an accident, sweetheart. Now let's get you to bed."

There was one flashpoint in her new life in the mansion

and it was something she didn't quite know how to talk to Silas about. Marie could tolerate Silas's messiness and his disorganization and even the way he could go for days at a time caught up in a story, disinterested in conversation. The only problem was that the man could sleep through a hurricane, and even this wouldn't have been a problem at all, except that Ernest would *not* sleep through a hurricane. He wouldn't sleep through a light breeze.

Several times a night he woke demanding attention—a drink of water, help visiting the toilet, or maybe he was too hot, or too cold, or too hot and *then* too cold and then too hot again, which happened one particularly frustrating evening. Marie was walking around in something of a sleep-deprived daze, and she was startled to find that if Ernest so much as whimpered in his sleep, her eyes would spring open. And by the time she thought to close her door, Ernest had figured out that he got much better results calling for her in the night than calling for his own father.

Besides, after everything Silas had done for her, how could she complain?

And so, on those nights, Marie was up as soon as Ernest cried out, and she'd get back to sleep only for him to cry out again, and then she was out of bed with Ernest when he woke for good, often before the sunrise, sometimes as early as 4:00 a.m.

She resigned herself to the fact that those nights when Ernest slept over would be rough. When he came for a visit late in her third week, she said good night to Silas and went to bed not long after the little boy did, hoping to get a few hours' sleep before the chaos erupted. She drifted off into a deep, dreamless sleep, but woke with a start some hours later.

Something was different.

Unlike other nights, Ernest was not calling for her by name, not following up his tearful "Aunty Mae!" with the details of some new need, real or imagined. This time, Ernest had woken her with a blood-curdling scream that pierced through the darkness.

She sat up in fright, blood thundering through her body. Whatever the threat was, Ernest clearly believed it to be life or death.

She told herself it was surely just a nightmare—even well-adjusted children had nightmares, didn't they? And Ernest did have such an impressive imagination. He could invent entire worlds as he played in the day; why would the nights be any different?

Marie dragged herself out of bed. Her whole body ached with fatigue, but she made her way towards the hallway. Just as she reached her door, the grandfather clock struck midnight. The bells echoed out in waves all around and through the mansion. Ernest's scream had faded into heart-breaking, heart-wrenching sobs—he was crying for her and his mother and his father, and Marie turned into the hallway, about to burst into a sprint, to run to console him.

It was a full moon that night. The windows above the front doors bathed the staircase and the hall at the top in a red-and-gold-and-green-painted light and glinted off the thousands of crystals in the chandelier. Marie thought if she were not quite so weary she might even admire the beauty of that light—but then she heard a sound out of place in a house she was already coming to think of as home.

A low voice was coming from Ernest's room. A threatening voice. She knew those rhythms and tones and even that accent all too well.

"Be quiet. Be quiet or I'll make you be quiet. I don't want to hurt you, kid, but you have to shut up!"

But it was impossible. Marie told herself her mind had to be playing tricks on her—it simply couldn't be that Rupert was there, not here in the house of a stranger, not on the other side of the world. So many times in their marriage he had felt omniscient to her, but the distance and peace of those last few weeks had convinced her—had *reminded* her—that he was not all-knowing and all-seeing after all.

But maybe she'd been right the first time.

Maybe Rupert was godlike in his control and his ability to harm her. What other explanation could there be for his presence there that night? And hadn't he warned her?

You're mine. I will never, ever let you go.

Each inhalation and exhalation came in a desperate little pant and she was feeling lightheaded with the lack of oxygen and the racing of her heart—and why were her hands and her feet tingling so? Why couldn't she think clearly?

If he caught her, he would kill her. She had no doubt at all about that. Maybe he knew about the baby—if he was powerful enough to figure out where she was hiding in a one-horse town on the other side of the planet, psychically sensing that she was carrying his child was probably a piece of cake. Maybe he'd drag her home and keep her alive until the baby was born, maybe toy with her for the last few miserable months of her life.

If he caught her, that would be the beginning of the end for her, one way or another.

If the moon had not been full that night, the hallway would have been dark enough to hide and perhaps then she could have escaped down the stairs. She could have run to Silas's car. She knew where he kept the keys, and that gave her one advantage over Rupert, who surely had no clue.

But she couldn't leave that child screaming in terror while his father snored across the hall. And besides, the moon *was* full that night. If she tried to run, Rupert would inevitably come out from Ernest's room to see her flying down the stairs.

The only place she could go was further down the eastern wing, but if he was checking room to room, he'd be upon her within minutes.

She took two careful steps towards the stairs, then pressed herself into the small shadow against the wall, tight against the grandfather clock. The clock was large and bulky and she could hide herself there—but she'd be hidden for seconds, not minutes. The instant he passed it he would see her.

Her mind was cloudy but her thoughts were racing. She tried to force herself to take deep breaths, to calm down for her baby's sake if nothing else, but her rib cage felt as locked as the rest of her body. She was a tiger, crouched and ready to strike out of pure instinct in the absence of any higher cognitive function.

There was sound in the hallway now, light but steady footsteps. There was no time to second-guess herself, not even time to be sure it really was Rupert, no time to be certain this was the right course of action. All she could do was to try to slow him down long enough to get past him, so she could run to Silas's room, to rouse the heavily sleeping gentle giant who had come into her life at just the right time and who now offered her, once again, her only chance at survival.

The figure in the hallway stepped closer to the grandfather clock, and Marie realized could push him—a poor strategy, but her only chance. She imagined that he might tumble down a handful of stairs, and by the time he had righted himself, enraged even further and ready for revenge, she could be at the other end of the house. She would grab Ernest as she ran through and she would drag him into his father's room, and then she would slam the door shut. If Silas had the key in his bedroom door, she could lock it straight away but if he didn't, his heavy dresser was right there. She could scream for his help and perhaps if she was really lucky he would wake quickly enough to help her secure the door.

It wasn't much of a plan but it was all she could come up with.

But just as the man stepped around the grandfather clock, the moonlight bounced off a metal blade in his hand and Marie knew for certain that he hadn't come to take her home.

Perhaps she couldn't have found the strength to do what had to be done only to save herself—after all, she'd been trapped in Rupert's home, unable to escape, even in a town she knew like the back of her hand, even surrounded by a community she'd been a part of her whole life. But in that moment Marie finally accepted that she really was most definitely pregnant. And with that realization came another.

If Rupert killed her, he also killed her baby, and she simply would not allow that to happen.

All of the fury and the pain and the frustration of the life she had lived with him surged. All of the humiliation of loving him and trusting him to help her only for him to trap her. All of the fear and the shame and the panic of it. It all rose to the surface and Marie ran at him with force and a strength she had no idea she was capable of.

Rupert didn't tumble down just a handful of stairs and take a few moments to collect himself before he pulled himself up and gave chase. Instead, he lost his footing altogether and fell, sideways and ungracefully, the knife sailing out of his hands. The staircase was steep and wide and he had no hope of catching onto the balustrade to steady himself. He tumbled in a violent, out-of-control somersault, head over feet to the bottom of the stairs. And perhaps at first he cried out in fury and shock, but by the time he landed, he was utterly still and silent.

From the landing at the top of the stairs Marie stared down at him, too stunned to remember that her plan had been to run to Tad's room, to not waste a single second. She found herself holding her breath, willing Rupert to show some sign of life—just the movement of a limb or the rattling of a breath, just so that she could be reassured that she had not killed him.

But he was limp, his body contorted into angles that should not have been possible. His head was twisted, facing his own shoulder. One of his arms was bent behind his back. One of his legs kinked forward just below the knee.

Marie sank into a crouch, trying to hide behind the rail at the top of the hallway, trying to shield herself from what she had done.

"Please," she said in a choked whisper, although she was not sure what she was asking for. *Please wake up so I'm not a murderer.* Or maybe, *Please don't wake up because your death is the only way I can be safe and free.*

Eventually she sank further, collapsing onto her bottom, then scrambling backwards, until her back was against the wall. She pulled her trembling knees towards her chest and wrapped her arms around them. A strange, terrible wailing began to echo through the house.

Silas had never been one to wake quickly. It had driven his various housemates crazy over the years—first his mother, who constantly had to drive him to school when he missed the bus, and Maeve, who learned to sleep with earmuffs and who, on particularly exciting days like her birthday and Christmas, would sometimes rouse him with a bucket of cold water. Christine told him once that she used to shake him through the night, frustrated by the volume of his snoring, but eventually realized that it didn't matter how much she thumped or kicked or shoved him; he would keep on snoring regardless. By the time she moved out, she was spending as many nights in the guestroom as she did in their marital bed.

He was well accustomed to the groggy feeling of having woken from a very deep sleep, completely unsure how long he'd been unconscious for. That night as he roused, it slowly occurred to him that something was not right. Silas loved his child like nothing else in this world, but he didn't have the same aggressive parental instincts that Christine and even Marie seemed to have, and it took him a few moments to realize that Ernest was crying. It took more moments still to identify the sound as a panicked howling.

Finally, belatedly, Silas pulled himself out of bed. Rubbing his weary eyes, he crossed the hallway to Ernest's bedroom. The little boy was beside himself, drawing shuddering, desperate breaths, rambling about a bad man hovering over his bed.

"There, there," Silas sighed. "It was just a dream."

"No dream, Daddy, no dream," Ernie kept sobbing. "Bad man. Scary man. He's going to hurt me."

But as the last vestiges of sleep cleared from Silas's brain, he gradually became aware that his distressed son was not the only problem in the house. There was another noise coming from the hall. Marie was weeping too.

Silas sighed as he scooped Ernest up onto his hip and went in search of her. Probably, he told himself, the trauma of that last month had finally caught up with the poor girl, perhaps she even wanted to cry in privacy, but given how upset she sounded he felt he needed to at least check in on her. Silas turned into the hallway, and saw that at the top of the stairs, she was curled up in a little ball, her slim shoulders shaking violently with the force of her tears.

"Come on now," he said gently. "Let's go back to—"

"No!" she yelled when she saw him, her frantic gaze switching between the stairs and where Silas and Ernest stood in the hall. "Don't let him see . . . *don't let him see*, Silas. *Don't.*"

Marie was breathless and panicking, and Silas, bewildered, took another step towards her. She scrambled to her feet and held both hands out towards him, palms exposed.

"*Stop*, Silas." Her breath caught on a frantic sob. "Please, you have to stop."

"What's going on?" he asked, and he was starting to wonder if she'd had some kind of breakdown. "Calm down, Marie, for goodness' sake. This isn't good for . . ." He gestured vaguely towards her stomach. He took another step towards her, and she stepped back too, bumping into the grandfather clock. She startled, spinning to see what was behind her, and then she wailed again and slid to the floor in a heap, as if her bones had suddenly disappeared, leaving her limp.

"It's just a nightmare, Marie," Silas said. "Let's go make a cup of hot milk—"

"No," she said, shaking her head as she looked back towards the stairs. She sucked in a slow, forceful breath, and when she spoke again, her voice was clear and hard. "Silas.

Put him back to bed. Lie with him until he goes back to sleep."

"But—"

"*Please*, Silas."

It occurred to Silas that she must have had some truly horrifying nightmare, and that the only way he was going to be able to calm her down was if he did exactly as she requested. He turned back towards Ernest's room, but his son began to scream, throwing his arms and legs out to block Silas from carrying him through the door, his ordinarily fluid speech reverting to a baby-like babble as he panicked.

"No, Dadda! No my room!"

Linda always used to say a full moon drove some people crazy, and given the way his son and guest were carrying on, Silas was starting to think his mother had been right.

He took Ernest back into his own room and he lay his son down on the bed. He rubbed Ernest's back and murmured words of consolation until the little boy's shuddering breaths began to ease and deepen and then finally, he was giving soft, adorable little snores.

Perhaps Silas might have fallen back to sleep himself too, except that even from his bedroom he could hear that Marie was still in the hallway sobbing.

And so finally, once Ernest was asleep, Silas crept out of bed and went to the landing above the staircase. Marie was once again on the floor, her knees drawn up to her body. He crouched in front of her and she buried her face in her arms.

"I don't know if I meant to do it," she sobbed. "What if I wanted this?"

"Hey, listen, love," Silas said, very gently. "It was just a bad dream. Let's go make that warm milk. Maybe a little whiskey to help you sleep?"

She raised her face to his very slowly. The moonlight through the stained glass windows glinted off her tear-stained face.

"You've been so kind to me," she whispered.

"Anyone would have done the same if they were able to."

"No. That is *not* true. Everyone back home knew that he was a monster and no one did a damned thing." Her voice was hoarse, tears still flowing freely from her eyes. "Most people would have walked away and left me to my fate. My own brother was willing to do that. But you . . ."

"It's really not good for the baby for you to be so upset."

That only made her cry harder, and Silas had no idea why, until she lifted one shaking arm, and she straightened her forefinger, pointing towards the stairs. He turned around, fully expecting to see the staircase as it always was, ready to reassure her that whatever she thought she had seen had simply been a dream.

The last thing in the world Silas expected to see was the shape of a man at the bottom of those stairs, so twisted that he couldn't possibly be alive.

And for a long moment, perhaps longer than he could excuse with anything other than wishful thinking, he thought he too might be asleep—that the whole moment might be a nightmare of his own. That he would wake in his bed with the world still on its axis.

"I don't know how he found us," Marie was saying, but she was speaking as if from a great distance, and he heard her voice through static in his ears. "But he went into Ernie's room first, and he had a *knife*. I pushed him and he stumbled and I thought it would just give me enough time to go to you but it all went wrong. Or maybe this is what I wanted. I don't know now. How will I ever know?"

He went into Ernie's room first.

It seemed that the one time Silas did something impulsive, inviting a stranger in desperate need to live with him, he had also allowed a violent, potentially murderous man, not only into his home but into his son's bedroom.

He turned from the mangled body at the base of the stairs, back to the young woman he had only wanted to help. For a moment he was tempted to lash out at her—had she somehow contacted Rupert, exposed her location to him? But as soon as Silas opened his mouth to fling that accusation, his conscience roared in protest.

"You pushed him down the stairs?" he asked instead.

"I just wanted to buy enough time to wake you for help. He came into the hallway and I hid behind the clock and . . ."

Silas could picture it from there. It would take nothing at all for a large man like that to gain enough momentum to injure himself very badly indeed if he tumbled down that massive staircase. And so, from almost the first moment, he believed her story.

He sank down to sit on the ground beside her, both staring down the staircase to the body at the bottom.

"What are we going to do?" she whispered after a while.

We.

Silas had done nothing wrong. If anything, he had already given Marie far too much. There was a case to be made that he should call the police and let the chips fall where they may. He had a feeling that if he said as much, she would understand. He could already hear the guilt and remorse and regret in her voice.

He'd been told time and time again over the course of his life that his imagination was a gift. There was no off switch to it though, and even in that moment of panic and fear, his mind's eye roared to life. Sitting on the floor of that hallway, he knew he was sitting with Marie, but something of his mother was there too.

What are we going to do? Linda whispered to him. Silas had hidden beneath dining tables and in closets and under his bed enough times to understand that it would have taken very little for his mother to find herself in the same, desperate situation Marie was now in.

"I'll call the police. This isn't your problem," Marie blurted. "I did this. I need to face the consequences."

Silas pondered this for just a moment. He knew some of the local police officers. He could explain to them who Marie really was, and how they wound up in this terribly confused situation. They would never believe that he had done something as altruistic as rescuing the young woman and spiriting her away to another life on the other side of the world. It was too grand, too unlikely—they'd assume an ulterior motive.

The minute he told them that he and Marie were not, in fact, siblings, the police would assume they were having an affair. And if Christine knew that Marie was not his sister, she too would no doubt assume the worst of him, especially with things as strained as they were. Hadn't he worried about that all along? It would probably be the death knell for his marriage.

"If I explain to them, they might let me go . . ." She broke off. Silas could tell that she was trying very hard to be brave. To do the right thing. But she couldn't finish that last sentence, and he understood why. The missing word was *home*, but where was her home now? Even if the police believed her, even if she was allowed to go free, what was waiting for her back in America? A brother who seemed to care little about her welfare? Her now-dead husband's nefarious business contacts?

"Do you want to go back to California?" Silas asked her.

She shook her head mutely. "No, but . . ."

"When I was a child, my father used to beat my mother," he told her. Marie's eyes widened. "Yes, he did so ferociously. He left her bruised. Broke bones. And I know that at least once, neighbors called the police. They came to the house and told my mother and father that it was a private matter and that they should sort it out between them."

"I'm very sorry that happened to her."

"And my father was an English teacher," Silas added bitterly. "Not even a police officer, who inevitably would command more loyalty and perhaps even sympathy from his own."

"What are you suggesting?"

Silas looked down the staircase. He felt no sympathy for the man who lay dead at the bottom. No sense of obligation to ensure that justice was served because in fact, to Silas, it seemed that justice had been served that night, or as close to true justice as could ever be achieved in this life.

"Do you think you can bring yourself to walk past him?"

Marie looked at Silas in alarm, then down at the body at the bottom of the stairs. She shook her head fiercely.

"I can't. I can't! Please don't make me. Please, Silas—"

Silas slid his arm around her shoulders and pulled her close for a hug. He kissed the side of her hair, then whispered, "I'll move him. I'm sorry I asked you that. I'll move him away from the stairs and *then* we will go down and sit in the kitchen." She opened her mouth to protest but it was his turn to shake his head. "We're going to need our wits about us. Every step we take from here on must be carefully planned. Calculated. Are you with me?"

If they were going to hide what she had done, they were going to need a fully fledged plan, put in place with clear minds. To whatever extent was possible he would carry the load of that for her, but she simply had to be on board or she'd undermine the whole thing. Silas was willing to take another massive risk for Marie, but the reality was that she herself was responsible for the greatest of their misdeeds to that point.

He wasn't complicit until he touched Rupert's body, but he *was* complicit in another injustice. Marie said she had no idea how Rupert had found them, but Silas had already figured it out, and it was something he should have considered much earlier—something he could have avoided if he'd just had his wits about him the day he took her from the home she shared with Rupert.

Of course Rupert would have interviewed half the town. He'd have interviewed Carmen and Rodrigo and Irving and Helen, and maybe they'd tell him Marie had been speaking to a tall man with bushy eyebrows, but none of them knew Silas's name.

But then Rupert would have interviewed his own neighbors. And Mr Peterson's memory was failing but he still remembered everything about Linda's son, even the details of the little town where he lived—the one way out in the middle of nowhere with the kangaroos and the same name as that magazine.

Silas sent Marie to the bathroom to wash her face.

"Take some time," he said gently. "Try to calm yourself down."

He descended the staircase very slowly. He walked with

his hand on the banister, and later, whenever he thought back in that moment, he would remember the smooth glide of his hand over the polished wood and the noisy *thud thud thud* of his own pulse in his ears.

When he finally reached the bottom, Silas extended his hand towards the lamp switch—but then pulled his hand back, leaving the hall in the relative darkness of the moonlit night. He didn't expect any of the farmhouses in the area would happen to be looking across the fields towards the mansion at 12:45 a.m., but he couldn't afford to risk a story circulating of the mansion lit up like a Christmas tree at suspiciously early hours.

Instead, he walked through to the kitchen and rummaged around in a drawer until he found a flashlight. When he returned to the foyer, he flicked the light over Rupert's body. Blood had coagulated in his exposed ear and his face was set in a blank mask of shock, his eyes open and unblinking, both pupils blown. Even so, Silas bent and gently touched his fingers to the other man's neck. The warmth was already draining from the body, and there was no pulse to be felt.

Silas handled the body with as much respect as he could manage, closing Rupert's unseeing eyes, straightening out his limbs as well as he could manage. In doing so, Silas discovered that the man's trouser pockets were stuffed full—his passport on the left, and his wallet on the right. In the pocket of his shirt, against his unbeating heart, was a bus ticket from Mascot to Forbes, and a box of matches marked with the name of a hotel near the Sydney airport.

Silas removed all of these items from the body and left them on the floor of the foyer. He wrapped Rupert's body in blankets from the linen press, then dragged him through the threshold into the parlour. It was shocking to Silas how little Rupert had bled—there was only a single smear of blood on the floor right where Rupert's ear had rested. Perhaps his heart stopped beating even as he fell. Silas cleaned the floor with a towel, then laid it on top of the body. He opened the front door. There was no car on the driveway, none on the road out front.

Using the flashlight to guide his way, he went into the kitchen and put a pot of milk onto the stove. He added some honey, then a little more. Marie had baked with Ernest that afternoon, testing Meg's recipe for Anzac slice—oats and golden syrup and lashings of butter. It was the kind of food he had never experienced before he came to Australia but something as common in his new home as cookies were in his old one. He opened the Tupperware container and sat it beside the mugs of hot milk at the farmhouse table in the kitchen.

Silas had no idea if he could even stomach the milk but Marie was in shock and pregnant to boot. His mother would have said that anyone under such stress needed sugar and sustenance and so that was exactly what he tried to provide Marie.

Finally, Silas walked back upstairs and rapped the back of his knuckles against her bathroom door.

"Silas?" Her voice was hoarse. Raw. "Is he gone?"

"Come downstairs when you're ready but don't turn on the lights. The moonlight is plenty, and I don't want any of the neighbors to see that we were up."

The simple request to move through the house without the lights on reminded Marie of how much trouble she was in. She wanted to believe that anyone would understand it was an accident, and that there were good reasons for her to be so afraid as to push Rupert down those stairs.

The problem was that as the shock cleared, she was finding the guilt cleared with it. That man threatened sweet little Ernest. He'd come to kill *her.* It was his life or hers and her baby's, and Rupert had taken more than enough from Marie already. She was starting to worry that in a police interview, she might not be able to display a remorse she didn't feel.

Marie felt numb, certainly. And there was fear and anxiety and confusion, but the resounding, overwhelming feeling—the one that she feared would be the one to remain when the shock was entirely gone—was relief.

It wasn't over yet. Her husband's body was a matter that absolutely needed to be dealt with, and with great urgency too. But at the same time it was over. The nightmare had ended, and a glorious new dawn had broken. Rupert would never come for her again. His hold over her was broken and her life was her own again.

Marie had saved herself. And in doing so, she had saved her baby.

With this realization Marie finally left the bathroom. Silas had already gone downstairs, and just a minute or two earlier she might've been afraid to follow him, but she was strong as she cast her eyes over the now-empty lobby. She held her head high, and even though she trembled a little she walked down that mammoth staircase, over the floorboards where her husband had fallen, down the long hall and into the kitchen. Silas sat at the farmhouse table, creamy candles melting onto their holders to illuminate the room with their gentle, flickering light. Two cups of milk sat waiting, steam rising into the night air.

She took her seat on the bench opposite Silas and she reached for the milk. She couldn't taste it but the warmth of the liquid making its way through to the stomach was comforting. Silas pushed the Anzac biscuits towards her and she shook her head.

"What are we going to do?" she asked him. "Are we going to call the police?"

"No," Silas said calmly. "No, we can't do that."

"But—"

"Marie. Think about it. We'd have to tell them everything. We *can't*." They sat in silence for a while. The candles flickered and the house shifted as the air outside cooled, and every now and again there came the echo of an owl outside, the clicking sound of possums playing in the trees. Finally, Silas said, "It's up to us. We have to lay him to rest."

His tone was heavy with solemnity, as if he were speaking about a cherished community figure who had passed peacefully after a fruitful life of service.

"I think what you're trying to say is, we need to hide his body," Marie said, and it occurred to her that she was going to be far more pragmatic than her creative-minded accomplice even now.

"The man deserves very little," Silas sighed. "But as a human being he does deserve a respectful burial." Before Marie could be too chastened by his gentle scold, Silas rubbed his eyes and added wearily, "And it just so happens we also need to hide his body."

"Do you have any idea where . . . ?"

"I don't write crime novels, or even read them, really," Silas muttered. "Which is a real shame in this instance, because perhaps if I had read that genre I might have some ideas about what to do next."

They sat like that for a while. As her senses came back to her she became gradually aware of the calmness after the chaos. It was humid that night, the spring air heavy with moisture after a week of rain.

"We need to find a place that no one will ever think to look," she whispered. "But even if we can do that, people must have seen him as he made his way here. He must've asked for directions to your house at the very least. He probably flew here on his own passport—"

"Yes," Silas said, then he cleared his throat. "Yes, it was in his pocket. And a bus ticket from a station near the airport, to Forbes."

"So the authorities will know he came here."

"There are outbound and incoming passenger records of course, but unless he told someone he was traveling here, why would they think to look for him in the list of people on a flight to Australia? Even if the police back home suspect he traveled internationally, surely they'll focus on places much closer to home."

"We only had passports because we went to Mexico on our honeymoon," she whispered. That was the first and only time she'd been on a plane until Silas came along. She felt like a fool now for not questioning the luxury of that honeymoon at the time. What small-town policeman could afford such an expense, except one who had a profitable side business? "And you said there was a bus ticket to Forbes . . . but how did he get out here?"

"There's no car out front. Taxis don't run this late out here. He either hitch-hiked, or he walked—and you know how quiet this road is at night. I don't think he hitch-hiked."

"*Could* he walk this far?"

"It's only a few miles. I'm sure it's possible."

"He might have told Irving where he was going."

"He might," Silas sighed. "Or other associates. And I imagine he's been interrogating the people in your life quite frantically since you left."

"The people in my life," she repeated numbly. Who exactly would that be? She had no real friends to speak of now.

"He and Irving are—were—very close?"

"I suspect Irving would say yes to that question but no, I don't think they really were. The hero worship went one way." That made her feel so sad for her brother, and on this came another wave of grief. Irving had hurt her very deeply but she had always assumed she'd see him again at some point. That would not be possible now.

Was he even missing her? Was he looking for her? Marie highly doubted that given the way their last conversation went.

"It all depends on Rupert's motive for coming here," Silas said suddenly. "If he intended to kill you, he wouldn't have told anyone where he was going. Nor would he have risked finding his way out here with any assistance because anyone who drove him would be a witness to confirm he was here. So we can assume, if he intended to kill you, no one will come looking for him."

"Exactly."

It all came down to that. But for the knife, they might have assumed he'd told plenty of folks back home that he knew where Marie was and he was coming to get her.

But . . . there *was* the matter of the knife. Even Rupert wouldn't have told the other officers at the station that he was traveling halfway across the globe to attack his wife for leaving him. He might have made some excuse for leaving, but he couldn't have told them the whole truth, and that meant there was an excellent chance that he hadn't told them *any* truth.

"You know best, Marie," Silas said eventually. "What does your gut say?"

She raised her gaze. Silas was exhausted, heavy bags beneath his eyes—but his eyes were still so kind, and he trusted her. *You know best, Marie.* Quite a change from the last man she'd lived with, who had spent years convincing her that she knew nothing at all.

"Rupert came to kill me," she said flatly. "No one will ever know he was here."

There was still the matter of whether any locals saw him—did he speak to anyone on the bus, or did he stop in town to ask for directions? Marie and Silas decided that they could deal with that if it arose. The biggest issue that remained was where to hide the body, and in that, they both felt similarly clueless.

"We need a place no one will disturb. I want to be certain this is over. I don't want to live worrying someone might stumble upon his body years from now and ask questions," Silas said.

For a while, they considered the endless open space that surrounded the town. There were patches of undisturbed bush land, even massively expansive nature reserves.

"It has to be accessible by car, but remote enough that no one will see the car," Marie said.

"But he's probably heavier than I am," Silas conceded. The men were about the same height, but Silas was thin, and Rupert had been strong and stocky. "I won't be able to carry him far. And then there's the matter of *how* I bury him. The rain will have softened the dirt but the bush land around here is so rocky."

Marie could scarcely believe that they were calmly sitting at the kitchen table having cups of hot milk and biscuits and discussing where to hide her husband's body. Her gaze drifted to the bank of windows along the kitchen wall. Cloud had covered the moon and it was a little darker outside. Soft rain was drizzling down the glass panes.

Silas suddenly gasped, and Marie looked back to him in surprise.

"Do you have an idea?"

"God forgive me," he whispered, as his eyes shone with the gleam of unshed tears. "I have an idea, but I'm not sure you're going to like it."

When the morning came, Marie called Christine.

"Silas and I both seem to have caught a flu," she lied. "We're both so unwell. Could you perhaps come and collect Ernie?"

"A springtime flu, how unusual!" Christine exclaimed. "You poor things. I'll be right over."

Christine was at the doorstep within ten minutes, a container of frozen chicken soup from her freezer in her hands.

"It's the best I could do at short notice," she said apologetically, passing Marie the container. Ernie came flying down the stairs and threw himself at his mother.

"There was a ghost," he announced, then he promptly burst into tears. "Mama, the ghost was in my room."

"Oh, my goodness!" Christine exclaimed, scooping her son up into her arms. She pressed him close against her and whispered, "Ernie, it was just a dream. Just a nightmare. You're okay."

"It was a rough night," Marie said, and truer words had never been spoken.

"You look terrible, sweetheart," Christine said gently.

"Put that soup out to defrost and go rest. Is Silas still asleep?"

"He got up, tried to have a cup of tea and went straight back to bed," Marie lied. "But yes, I'll do the same. Thank you, and . . ." Her voice went rough, and she tried to clear it, but failed miserably. Her eyes filled with tears. "I'm so sorry, Ernie."

"It's not your fault," Christine scolded her, and Marie forced a wobbly smile. If only she knew. Ernie had no interest in apologies anyway. He was muttering to himself, cuddling into his mother's neck, already begging her to take him home.

Once Christine was gone, Marie took the soup into the kitchen and sat it on the counter. She pulled a pair of Silas's boots over her sock-clad feet and walked to the back door.

Marie had to brace herself with every new step. She had once been so enamored with this backyard and had found it to be such a magical place of peace and natural beauty. Now she knew she would never see it the same way again—in a single night it had become a place of darkness and secrets and shame.

Every new step seemed harder than the last but she kept going until she reached the wrought iron fence at the edge of the historic cemetery. And here was Silas, covered in mud and sweat, digging like a madman, out of view of the front of the house where his wife had just been.

Neither Marie nor Silas were entirely comfortable with the plan to bury Rupert in the backyard cemetery, and over the many hours of the long, sleepless night, they had debated and desperately tried to brainstorm an alternative. Any alternative.

In the end, there seemed to be no better option. It wouldn't be rocky soil. It would never be disturbed. It wasn't too far for them to move the body. And no one would see Silas digging, not in that corner behind the tall concrete fence. It was secluded from the front yard and the road, and even from the farms around them.

They had agreed that they would dig to about four feet, hoping that the original occupant had been buried at the standard six feet. They didn't discuss what they would do if they struck a historic coffin at a shallower-than-expected depth. Marie thought that possibility was so horrific she refused to seriously entertain it.

But after four hours of work, Silas had already established a hole roughly the right shape and place and close to half of the required depth. He wiped a hand over his forehead, pushing sweat away but replacing it instantly with a further smear of mud.

"Ernie gone?"

"He is. Christine told me I look terrible."

"You do look exhausted."

"So do you. Do you need anything?"

"No. But thank you."

"I thought you might want something to eat . . ."

"I couldn't," he whispered, and he seemed to turn green at the very thought. "No, but thank you."

They had already considered the minor details. To cover their tracks, they would bury everything with the body—Rupert's wallet, his passport, even Maeve's passport because Marie had an Australian driver's license now and that would suffice for identification. The passport had the photo of Maeve on it, and if anyone ever found it, questions would be asked. She wanted to bury her wedding ring but Silas insisted she keep it, at least for now. She would need to wear it for a long while yet—for the duration of her pregnancy, maybe for years after the baby was born.

Marie would fetch the wheelbarrow from the garden shed, and Silas would use this to maneuver the body from the parlour into the cemetery. Once it was all over and Rupert was in that grave, they had agreed that they would stand together and say a prayer for him. She already felt sick at the thought, but this seemed to matter so much to Silas. He was a decent man, one who respected other people, even people undeserving of that respect.

"I'll go back inside then," she said.

Silas nodded and looked back to the earth around him.

Marie still didn't feel guilty about what had happened to Rupert, but she was starting to feel very guilty indeed at what she had done to Silas. Just three short months ago they were total strangers, and now he was up to his neck in her mess.

"Silas, I really am so very sorry that I dragged you into this."

"You have nothing to be sorry for," he told her, but he was adjusting the leather gloves he wore, preparing to dig again. "Never apologize for doing what you had to do to survive."

The clouds had cleared across the course of that day. The sun was setting in the west, burning still and so hot, even with the foliage above him, Silas felt a tinge of sunburn on his nose. But that was the least of his worries by then.

The leather gloves had protected him for a while, but he had just been digging for too long, and eventually blisters had formed all over his hands. His back ached and no matter how he stood now, he couldn't find a position where he was comfortable. His eyes burned with dust and mud and exhaustion, and tears he wanted so badly to shed, but he had the sense that Marie needed him to be strong and so he flatly refused to allow himself to cry.

She stood beside him, back ramrod straight, hands stiff beside her thighs. Marie held her chin high, but there was panic in her eyes as she looked down at the fresh dirt in front of her. This grave was simply adorned—no concrete poured over the top, or even a border of concrete as some of the others had. The simple granite headstone held little weight to it and was a lie now, or at least, it wasn't the whole truth. Rupert would never have a marker to signify his final resting place. It was Silas and Marie's firm intention that no one would ever know what had happened. They had agreed that this was a secret they would carry alone together until their final breaths.

Silas's biggest worry for the next few months was the gardeners. He'd been employing some young men to come once a week to tend the place. The risk of the gardeners noticing the disturbed soil was too great—Silas was going to have to tell them not to come for a while, not until the mounded dirt had settled flat and grass had grown back across the grave. He had not yet figured out what excuse he would give for the pause in their schedule, but if Silas knew one thing about himself it was that he would be able to make up some story on the fly. The ability to spin a tale was his biggest—perhaps only—gift.

"You buried his wallet and passport too, didn't you? And Maeve's?" Marie asked him. She was pale as a ghost and shivering violently and Silas had the sense that she was barely holding herself together. He did not want to lie to her, but over the course of the day he'd come to realize that burying Rupert's passport and wallet with his body was a terrible idea. If someone *did* discover the body at some point in the future, they'd have no way to identify it anyway—unless there were identity papers buried right there with it.

And, God help him, he could not bring himself to bury the last things he had left of his sister, the last photograph he had with her and his mother. He just couldn't.

"Sure," Silas said, because he didn't want to panic her, and he hadn't made an alternative plan for those items yet. He'd have to figure it out later, when he could string two thoughts together in his mind. For now, they had to finish what they had started and lay this man to rest. "I'll pray, if it's all the same to you," he said, very suddenly aware that he was not going to be able to withhold tears much longer. His voice was rough, with dust and dirt and exhaustion but also, the sheer trauma of the eighteen hours that had passed.

"Please."

"Dear Lord," Silas said quietly. "We commit Rupert to your eternal wisdom and compassion." The reality of what they'd done—of what he had helped to hide—hit him all of a sudden. His aching knees went weak, and he could barely manage a whisper as he finished the prayer. "We pray you will grant Rupert grace and peace. We pray you will grant *us* grace and peace. Amen."

With that, Marie turned away from the cemetery. She opened the wrought iron gate and then ran down the path towards the house, her sobs echoing all through the garden. But Silas sank on his knees into the muddy, messy dirt, and he cried right there in place, right beside the very worst thing he had ever done in his life.

A few days after the incident with Rupert, a handyman arrived at the mansion. Much to Marie's alarm Silas led him straight into the backyard. She hovered in the kitchen, peering out the window as the men talked at the bottom of the garden.

Marie had not been out the back door since they buried Rupert. She had taken to hanging the laundry around the house because she couldn't bring herself to use the clothes line in the backyard. She knew it was irrational, maybe even foolish. She kept telling herself that if she just went out there a few times, confronted the backyard, reassured herself that it represented no further harm to her, she'd be fine.

But she would get to the back door and bile would rise in her throat and her hands would shake. Marie thought she was coping reasonably well after everything that had happened, but apparently that was only the case if she didn't go near the mansion's back door, or turned out the light in her room, or if she wasn't startled—because earlier that morning, a door had slammed in the wind, and several hours later she still felt as though she'd been plugged into some electrical current, her whole body humming with anxiety.

"What is he doing here?" she whispered sickly when Silas walked back into the kitchen after speaking to the handyman. He shrugged.

"The washing line has been bothering me for a while. It will make so much more sense at the side of the house, don't you think?"

The washing line made *no* sense at all at the side of the house, but Marie rushed towards Silas and threw her arms around him anyway.

"Thank you," she choked.

"It's okay," he said, wrapping his arms around her briefly. "It's going to get easier, Mae. It promise you it will."

Marie was not the only one suffering the after-effects of what had happened. Silas seemed distracted and quieter even than usual. She suspected he was worried, as she was, about what long-term effects the fright would have had on little Ernie. They hadn't seen him since that night. Christine thought they were still down with the flu.

Mae had once considered that once she adjusted to life in that new country, maybe saved up a little money and had her baby and found her feet in this new country, she might move out of Silas's home. He had been nothing but welcoming, assuring her time and time again that she should feel free to stay as long as she wanted. But she had taken something from him even in allowing him to smuggle her out of the US. It seemed a strange thing to worry about in relation to an adult, but she did worry that something of his innocence had been lost. His own freedom was even at risk now, because if Silas's role in covering up Rupert's death ever came to light he'd surely go to jail. All because of her.

In some ways Marie thought it would be best for all of them—for Silas, for Ernest, even for Christine and for Marie herself—if she were to move on.

The problem was that monstrous secret hidden in the backyard of the mansion. Marie feared it and couldn't bring herself to go near it, and she kept waking in the night too scared to leave her bedroom in case Rupert was somehow in that hallway again. As she walked down the stairs she would sometimes see flashes of that body on the floor, as if she was both in the past and in the present, somehow all at once.

But despite all of that, she knew now that she was trapped in that mansion forever, and that thought sometimes filled her with dread because what had at first seemed like an impressive, imposing building now felt like a prison. It was so noisy—the structure creaking and cracking and settling in the night, the wind rattling the window frames even during the day. She wanted to move to a smaller house, a home where there was nowhere for evil to hide, a place where she could feel at ease again.

But she needed to keep an eye on that cemetery.

Remaining in Silas's mansion was the only way to be sure that her secrets remained buried.

"Funny thing," Christine said to Marie a few days later. As far as Christine knew, Silas and Marie had recovered from their flu, and the women had gone to buy vegetables from a street vendor, a local man who sold in-season produce out of his truck on the main street of town. "I ran into Bettina Michaels yesterday. Do you know her?"

Marie shook her head.

"Oh, you'll meet her soon enough. She's married to one of the local police officers and she's the biggest gossip in town. Said an American man came through last week, looking for his wife. For some reason, he was convinced she had taken up with Silas, of all people. He went to the station to ask where he might find them. Did he . . . er . . . did he come to the mansion to speak with you?"

Marie was so startled she dropped an onion. It rolled along the street, coming to a stop in a gutter. She gave chase, taking a few steps to grab it, giving herself a stern, forceful mental lecture as she did so. It was inevitable that Rupert had spoken to someone when he came to town—perhaps even inevitable that he would have spoken to the local police, given he was an officer of the law himself. She and Silas had prepared themselves for this as best they could, although they had not anticipated that it might be Christine who asked about him.

"We've been so sick," Marie said weakly. "Maybe Silas spoke to him while I was napping. He didn't mention it to me but if it was a misunderstanding he probably just straightened it out."

"And none of that sounds familiar to you?" Christine was watching her closely. Marie's heart was beating so hard against her chest, she wouldn't have been surprised if Christine could hear it too. She forced herself to laugh.

"We both know my brother is far from a Lothario. I struggle to imagine him having nefarious affairs at any time, but while things with you are . . . well, as they are, *never*."

"Well, I did laugh when I heard *that* part," Christine admitted, but there was something very serious in her gaze. "But the timing is just . . ." She trailed off, as if expecting Marie to finish the sentence, but Marie had no idea what to say. She just stared at Christine, trying to keep her expression neutral. "Maeve, honey, I mean, you have to admit, it is quite unusual for *another* American to find his way out here. You and Silas are the only Americans I've ever even seen in this town! It's such a coincidence that a third would pop up out here, especially just a month after your arrival and . . . well, I'm so sorry to bring this up, but right after the loss of your . . . you know. The loss of your husband."

To Marie's horror her eyes filled with tears, and she looked away from Christine, overcome.

"Oh, Maeve!" Christine whispered, reaching to squeeze her forearm. "Honey, I didn't mean to upset you or to accuse you of anything, I swear! I just know Silas, that's all. If he went home because your mother was sick and found that *you* were in trouble, say if he learned that you'd gotten yourself stuck in a bad marriage since he left . . . I just know he would do what it took to get you out. If your husband *isn't* dead but he is bad news, you can tell me and I'll help."

Christine almost had it. *Almost.* Marie wanted so badly to tell her the truth in that moment but she and Silas had made a vow that they would take their secret to the grave. Marie wiped impatiently at a tear that spilled over from her eye and Christine reached to gently touch her shoulder.

"I'll understand if it didn't go the way you two told me it did. That's all. I promise."

"My husband *is* dead," Marie whispered thickly. Something about her tone must have rung true to Christine because she suddenly pulled Marie close for a hug.

"God, honey. I'm so sorry to bring it up. I just had to ask, you understand. I didn't want you to bear it all alone if you were hiding from someone awful and he'd tracked you down here."

"That *would* be terrible," Marie said dully. "Thanks for asking, but I'm fine."

They went about their shopping and didn't speak of it again.

Airmail came from California some months later. Marie brought it to Silas's desk soon after the postman visited. She'd been opening his mail for months by then, but she must have known instinctively not to open that one. She set it on the tray on his writing table, the one she'd carefully labeled Not Urgent, and let herself out of his office.

Her belly was enormous by then. It was as though it had

suddenly popped out and become undeniable the day after he finally convinced her she must see a doctor to confirm the pregnancy. She'd finally told Christine the news, and even Ernest was overjoyed to learn that he would soon have a little cousin to play with.

Silas had a lot to worry about in those days, but Marie's situation was weighing most heavily on his mind. If the doctor's calculations were correct she was due to have that baby any day, although she'd told Christine a much later date, more in line with the supposed timeline of her hasty wedding and immediate widowhood. Marie and Silas had not discussed the plan for the baby's birth in any great detail, but Silas had promised her he would help her when the time came.

She had no wedding certificate. No husband. Some of Christine's friends worked in the local maternity ward, so Silas couldn't even pretend to be the fictional Aaron West himself. It was a dreadful dilemma and had been keeping Silas awake for weeks.

Silas was so fond of Marie and also so very worried about her. It was clear to Silas that the battle scars left over after everything Marie had been through had not yet begun to heal. She was jumpy, flying into a panic at any unexpected sound or movement, and she struggled to assert herself. That was no wonder after what she'd been through, but her determination to avoid conflict had reached almost pathological levels. Silas knew he drove her mad at times—when he was working he would forget to tidy up after himself, to attend to calls and letters that had pressing deadlines attached. He knew this irritated Marie no end and yet she would never call him out about it. He only had an inkling she was angry with him when she'd go very quiet and start stomping around the house.

Because when Marie wasn't upset with him, she was not at all quiet. In fact, he was certain he'd heard her life story six times by then, every little detail from her high school years to her relationship with Irving and the death of their parents, then her courtship with Rupert. She'd even told Silas the story of how she met *him*, and the story of her escape to Australia, and the story of the night of Rupert's death. It was as though she was trying to process every difficult thing she'd encountered in those past few years by speaking it aloud again, and again, and again. Telling him and telling herself the story as if she voiced it just *one more time* she might make sense of it. It was as though she'd suddenly been struck down with a case of conversational mania.

Most concerning of all to Silas was Marie's refusal to prepare for the baby's birth. Christine had been gathering clothes and furniture and various items she deemed essential, but Marie had politely accepted all of this and set it untouched into one of the spare bedrooms in the eastern wing. He'd tried to talk to her about this but she just kept telling him she didn't feel ready and there was plenty of time.

Silas sighed heavily and reached for the envelope from the lawyer back in California. Inside was a large cheque and a letter, advising him that both his mother's apartment and his childhood home had found buyers. The last item in the envelope was a photo of his mother's and sister's graves.

When he'd asked for a photo, Silas assumed that seeing it would give him some closure. He hadn't realized back then that someone else would be walking around using Maeve's name as her own. Not in a million years had he imagined that he'd lose his sister only to immediately adopt a replacement in her place.

“Silas,” Mae said suddenly. She’d thrown open his study door without knocking, maybe for the first time ever. He dropped the photo to his desk and he shot to his feet, startled.

“What is it?” Her face was blanched with pain and she was squeezing her hands into fists, then releasing them, over and over. “Mae?”

She suddenly gave a groan of pain and stumbled forward until she was leaning over his writing desk. Silas swore under his breath and moved to gingerly touch her back.

“How long has this been going on?” he asked her when the groaning eased and she straightened, panting for breath and pale as a ghost. She avoided his gaze. *“Marie!”*

“A few hours,” she whispered. Silas looked at her and she started to cry. “Since yesterday. Yesterday morning.”

“Yesterday *morning*?”

“It only started getting bad a few hours ago.”

Silas shoved the paperwork from the lawyer beneath his notebooks. He slid his arm around her waist and led her to the door.

“I don’t want to go the hospital,” she whimpered. “I don’t want them to take her away. I know I told you I wasn’t sure I could raise her but I *can*, Silas, *I can.* I already love her. Please don’t let them take her from me.”

“Don’t worry,” Silas muttered. “I’m going to take care of you both.”

“But I don’t understand,” Christine said a few days later. Silas was sitting with her at Meg’s kitchen table. Ernest was lying beneath the table, playing with a metal truck. “Why did the baby come so early? Is she really okay?”

“The doctors said it was just one of those things.” Silas

shrugged. He'd just returned from the hospital, where he'd visited Marie and her new daughter. "And Mae was just lucky that the baby was on the large side. She's early but she's doing fine."

Christine gave him a look then, and he knew that she had seen through their lies about the timeline of Marie's baby's conception and birth. It didn't really matter—Christine would be the last person to judge Mae for enjoying her marital bed before her wedding night. Silas could personally vouch for the fact that Christine herself had done the very same thing.

The lie he didn't want Christine to see through was the other one he'd told her—that there were complications, and the little hospital in Forbes had immediately sent Mae an hour and a half away, to the larger maternity unit in the regional city of Orange. Christine did know a few nurses at their local hospital, but the town wasn't so small that she knew *all* of them. He was hopeful she'd never learn that Marie had never actually attended the Forbes hospital at all.

"And you're sure we can't go over and meet the baby in the maternity ward?" Christine asked, for maybe the tenth time, as she was desperately keen to meet her new niece.

"Like I told you," Silas said, as patiently as he could manage. "They said no visitors yet. I've been sneaking in but only because she doesn't have anyone else here to keep an eye on her. I'll let you know when that changes."

And *that* would be when she was released to come home.

"She called the baby Cynthia, you said on the phone?"

"That's right. Cynthia Maeve."

"She gave the baby her own name as a middle name?" Christine frowned. "How unusual."

Silas felt his throat tighten, just as it had when Marie first told him what she planned to name her daughter. *I owe my life to her; it's only right.*

"It's a family name," Silas said, as lightly as he could manage.

"And what was Maeve's husband's name?"

Silas had been expecting this question. Everyone knew the husband's name was the default surname for a baby.

"It was West," Silas said. The first name that came into his head all of those months ago. "But baby Cynthia will go by our family name." Christine raised an eyebrow and Silas did his very best to avoid the question in her gaze. "It's just that Aaron died so soon after the wedding and Maeve didn't think to get the paperwork sent over in time. She had to fill in the birth certificate on the spot so this was just easier than explaining."

What Silas didn't tell her and would never tell her was that as far as the nurses and the doctors at the big hospital were concerned, Marie was not a widow but a wife, and her husband, Aaron *Winslow*, had been right there by her side, ready to sign the birth certificate on the spot. Just as he'd hoped, a nurse had very briefly glanced at "Maeve's" brand-new Australian driver's license when she first arrived, but there were no further requests for identity documentation from her, and none from him.

Silas was almost an afterthought in the whole process, just there to coo over the baby and to sign "his" name on the birth certificate. It made it all the more maddening to Silas that if he hadn't been there, the absence of a husband would have been massively problematic for Marie and baby Cynthia.

He was exhausted by the lies and frankly might never recover from the fright he got when Marie started shouting that she needed to push, a full ten minutes out from the Orange hospital, but so far, the ruse had worked. When the staff at the big hospital questioned why they'd driven an hour and a half, instead of ten minutes, Silas lied and said they'd been in the regional city visiting a friend when Maeve started having contractions.

Just then, Ernest stood and excused himself, saying he was going to play in the yard. Christine cleared her throat.

"Silas, I've been meaning to talk to you," she said quietly. "For a long while, actually. It's just that you and Mae seemed to take forever to get over that rotten flu so I put it off and then she told us she was pregnant and . . . honestly, there just hasn't been a good time."

"What is it?" He frowned. He wanted to believe she was about to tell him she was coming home, but her tone was so heavy and so strained. "Chris?"

"I think . . ." She drew in a breath. "Oh, Silas, I'm really sorry but . . ."

It wasn't as if he thought his marriage had been repaired. Silas wasn't a fool; his wife had moved out of their home and she'd been gone for six months. He knew that wasn't a great sign. But they saw each other every few days; they were still warm and friendly with one another—perhaps even more since she'd moved out than they had been that last year of their marriage.

"You're my soulmate," she said, very gently.

"And you are mine."

"But . . ."

"How can there be a *but* after that sentence?"

"I love you and I always will but we cannot be married to one another—not now, not in the future. You have a very full inner life, Silas."

"That's not a crime."

"That was a compliment, not an accusation. You are wholly self-contained in a way that very few people are. You don't need the validation of others to feel happy. You are generally unmoved when people are unkind to you. But you also experience the real world through your work."

"I don't understand what you're saying."

"I remember looking over at you as I held Ernie for the first time right after he was born and you were miles away," she said softly.

"I was thinking about you! About him!"

"You were thinking about the emotional wealth in the moment. How you might mine it for a book one day. You were *narrating* the scene for yourself. Wondering *how does this fit into my character arc?* You are never really anywhere unless you're in one of your stories."

Silas opened his mouth to protest, but he couldn't deny that she was telling some kind of truth. He was even taking mental notes on that very conversation because Christine was so articulate and passionate and beautiful even as she broke his heart. The moment was too *perfect* for real life. Silas felt right away that it deserved to be captured in a story.

"Chris, I never meant to hurt you," he said helplessly.

"I know, sweetheart. That's what's so awful about this. You're who you are and your needs are your own. I would never want to change you. But I won't live alongside you, miserable and increasingly resentful that you're only a part-time spouse to me. Not when I can live on my own and be perfectly happy."

"But Ernest . . ."

". . . will live with me most of the time. I was thinking weekends could be yours eventually. He's still spooked by that nightmare he had at your place a few months ago, but that'll pass and in time he'll sleep there Friday and Saturday nights."

"Where will you live?"

"Mum's getting older. We'll stay here and care for her."

"This house is so small, Chris."

"We'll renovate it then. We'll figure it out."

"Please tell me we'll stay friends," he choked, throat tight.

It wasn't enough but it was all he could think to ask for in that moment.

"You will be my best friend and the love of my life until I die," Christine whispered unevenly. "I'm divorcing you because I need for us to stay friends."

Silas went home after their chat. He went into his study and picked up his pen, opened his notepad, tried to lose himself in the new book he was working on. When that failed miserably, he decided that Chris didn't mean what she'd said. He would never accept this. No, he would simply work on her, woo her again. He would find a way to change her mind.

But then he walked to the window to look out over the garden. He'd kept the gardener away all through autumn and that meant Silas had been maintaining the whole yard himself. He'd been surprised to find that he loved that work—the meditative nature of it, the way his mind was free to ponder his stories while his hands were busy in the dirt. Even so, he was deeply relieved that the mound of fresh dirt over the grave was sinking into place and grass was finally beginning to grow over it. Soon, no one would be any the wiser about the contents of that grave.

But as he considered this, it suddenly struck Silas that there was a kind of man who didn't respect the wishes of a woman, who wouldn't take no for an answer, who just pursued and pursued until he wore that woman down and got what he wanted.

Christine knew what she wanted for herself and she had expressed her wishes clearly. Silas had to respect that, and he would. With that thought came the realization that he'd lost his mother and his sister and his wife all within a period of months.

Christine had been correct when she said that Silas had a full inner life. He was comfortable with his own company for the most part, not a person inclined to feel loneliness. But that day, his *aloneness* hit him like a ton of bricks. He saw a future stretching out before him where Marie would one day move on and she'd take her baby with her and Christine would divorce him and maybe even remarry. Ernest was now too afraid to even sleep overnight at the mansion, and Silas couldn't move, not even for his son. That secret in the backyard was too much of a risk—he would *have* to stay at the mansion to ensure it stayed buried.

If Silas kept going the way he had been, working round the clock even when his son came to visit, the distance between him and Ernie would grow and grow until Silas lost his son altogether.

Silas made a promise to himself that day. Every single week, even when he was engrossed in an exciting draft or a deadline was drawing near, he would spend the weekend with his son. He couldn't make Ernest love the mansion, but he could make sure Ernest knew that he was loved.

Just a few months after Cynthia was born, Marie asked Silas if she could help him out around the office again. And by then, Silas's office had fallen back into a state of pure chaos, so he was glad to agree.

He was monitoring the news back home via a complicated process that involved several US national and Californian newspapers being flown into Sydney and shipped out to him in Forbes. The various newsagents involved in this process thought nothing of an American man keeping tabs on the happenings in his home country and his home town and they were very happy to make a few extra pounds off his homesickness. But several daily papers arriving in batches once or twice a week meant he was forever running a little late with his reading and there were piles of them all over his office, secondary to the piles of books, and the piles of coffee mugs, and the piles of dirty plates.

"Have you read anything interesting in these?" Marie asked him as she ferried armfuls of discarded broadsheet and tabloid papers from his office. Silas did not want the paper to go to waste so he was setting himself up a large compost pile to use in the gardens.

He knew exactly what she was really asking—had her disappearance been in the news? Was anyone looking for Rupert? And the truth was it had and they were. The sudden disappearance of a deputy chief of police just weeks after his young wife vanished had been big news in Porterville and had even been mentioned in the national papers. But it had come to light after Rupert vanished that his first wife had also disappeared in suspicious circumstances and that afterwards, Rupert simply left Santa Rosa to start afresh with a job in Porterville—a transfer courtesy of the old boys' network. No serious questions were asked about his first wife's disappearance because the police had closed ranks around their own.

Silas didn't think that information would help Marie in any way and so he told her no, he'd found no coverage. It was not news to Marie that her husband had been murderous, and by then, she had clawed her way to a fragile new normal and he did not want to set her back at all.

But he kept reading and searching, and he had found a safe hiding place both for those clippings and for all of the things that could unravel their whole story. This was part of how he kept his vow to her.

I will do everything in my power to get you to safety and to keep you safe.

He'd almost failed to fulfill that promise once, and he wasn't going to let that happen again. If the authorities started to suspect her location or if there was any hint in those newspapers that she was suspected when it came to Rupert's disappearance, Silas would spirit her away again. Somehow.

Once upon a time Silas pretended he was Cynthia's father and he had assumed that would be the end of his faux-parental duties, but as the years rolled on, their company of four in that mansion became a unique little family. Marie did most of the mothering, except when little Cynthia got her loud voice on and decided that she wanted Ernest or Silas to do something in particular—in which case they were generally powerless to resist.

And Silas, determined to build a better relationship with his son, didn't mind having an extra set of little feet running around the park with him on Saturdays. Didn't at all mind when Cynthia would climb up onto his lap and beg him for *just one story, Uncle*, even though "one story" inevitably meant three or five or eight. He really didn't mind even one little bit when she'd give him those big, sad puppy eyes and ask him to play a game with her. Having a younger sibling around kept Ernest young too, extending his childhood in such a wonderful way. It was not uncommon at all for Silas to spend entire Saturdays playing make-believe with the children in the backyard.

"You spoil her," Marie would mutter, and Silas would roll his eyes and mutter right back, "Right. Because you're such a tough disciplinarian when it comes to Ernest." He was still pretty sure Marie spent more money decorating Ernest's bedroom the year after Cynthia's birth than she did on herself. She'd been determined to make him feel at home again in the mansion, and although she never entirely succeeded, she did manage to create a beautiful bedroom for the boy that he enjoyed. During the day, anyway.

It felt like no time had passed at all before little Cynthia was not so little and she was ready to start at school. She would be at the same school as Ernest, three grades below him. Marie dropped her off at the school gate and came home to the mansion and locked herself in her office.

"You've been crying," Silas said to her when she finally emerged.

"Don't be silly," she muttered. "Coffee?"

That night, Ernest and Christine came for dinner. The five of them sat around the farmhouse table, over steaming plates of Cynthia's favorite food—lamb chops and mashed potato. Her hair still in matching plaits on either side of her head, she held court for her little family, regaling them with tales of her first day at "big school," even as she grew so tired that just about every sentence was punctuated with a yawn.

". . . and did you know that my best friend is Josh and he lives just down the road here and we can catch a bus together to get to school?"

"Josh you just met today?" Christine asked, hiding a smile.

"That's right. And Josh has a mum but he doesn't have an uncle dad. He just has a *dad*. Isn't that funny?" she said, and the adults at the table exchanged confused glances. Cynthia gave a sad sigh and she shook her head. "Poor Josh."

"Everyone has a dad," Ernest said, and Silas saw Marie wince.

"Most people have a dad," Silas corrected.

"No, I don't *want* a dad," Cynthia said impatiently, as if they just weren't quite getting it. "I have an uncle dad and that's much better."

It took a minute for Silas to make sense of what the little girl was saying and once he did, his gaze shot to Marie. Her eyes were suspiciously shiny, but she gave him a sad smile, and then she reached for Christine's empty plate.

"Let's clear this table and have some dessert," she said, effectively distracting the children and ending the conversation. A few minutes later, Cynthia fell into an exhausted sleep, her face landing right in her plate of chocolate cake. Christine and Ernest saw themselves out while Silas carried the little girl up to her bed. Marie climbed the stairs beside him and once she'd tucked her daughter in, they paused there, staring down at her.

"She thinks you're her father," Marie murmured. "Or at least, she doesn't understand that an uncle and a father are not one and the same."

"She's just making sense of the world and of how our family fits into it."

"*Our* family," Marie repeated softly.

"We are a family now," Silas said.

He would always miss his real sister, just as he supposed that Marie probably missed her real brother, but he couldn't help but feel that fate had given back to him even as it took from him.

Silas tried not to judge other people's parenting choices—God knew he'd made enough mistakes of his own. But he worried sometimes about the way Marie pushed Cynthia. No matter how hard the little girl worked, or how good her grades were or how many awards she won, Marie could never relax. Silas had seen similar in some of Ernest's friends' parents, who seemed to view their children's achievements as a reflection of their parenting. It was different with Marie. She pushed Cynthia not out of pride but out of fear.

"She has to do well at school or she'll never get to university and then she'll never make anything of herself and young people without the ability to support themselves are *so* vulnerable," Marie said to him one day, and he frowned at her.

"I dropped out of college the minute my first advance came through, and *you* never made it at all. We've done just fine for ourselves."

"It's different for her. University will make her life easier. She *has* to learn how to study and how to stand on her own two feet. If she's educated she will be able to think for herself."

"She has to learn to dream. To imagine! These years of her life are made for *play*, not study."

Silas decided to approach the problem from another angle, taking it upon himself to make sure the rest of her life was full of magic. When he drove Cynthia to school he told her stories the whole way. He made up ghost stories about their home—not frightening tales, but stories about spirits who were fun or even funny, mischievous imps who distracted him and kept him entertained when he was working. There were fairies in the garden and shapes in the clouds and every chance he got, he had that little girl playing games of make-believe with Ernest or even on her own.

Silas respected Marie's wishes for her daughter, but he knew with absolute certainty that a child who does not learn to imagine becomes an adult who cannot dream. An adult who cannot create!

Silas would never allow that to happen. Not on his watch.

As the years stretched into decades, Silas saw the scars Marie still carried in every facet of her life. She still battled panic when a door slammed in the wind or a car backfired. She still doubted herself constantly, second-guessing just about every decision she ever made. She held people at arms' length—even Cynthia at times—as if she were afraid that letting down her guard for even a second might reveal the truth about herself and bring her whole life tumbling down around her. And Marie remained utterly terrified of that secret buried in the backyard.

From time to time Silas would talk about projects he should really get around to in the mansion—new paint, adjustments to the landscaping outside, installing air conditioning units, even repairing various things as they aged. Marie reacted every single time as if he'd threatened to walk outside and dig that body up with his bare hands.

"Mae, there's no risk to . . . *that* . . . if we change the house and yard a little," he'd say impatiently, but she would turn white as a sheet and her hands would start to shake.

"Then where does it stop, Silas?" she'd ask unevenly. "What if you try to renovate the kitchen and there's a busted pipe and the tradesmen dig it up and they end up in that corner? What if you want to put an air conditioning unit into the ballroom and they need to trench a new power line in and—"

"The switchboard is *on* the house! There is no conceivable way they'd need to dig a trench a hundred yards away to run power to an a/c unit on the other side of the building."

"But once you start messing with these things, who knows how far it goes! Who knows what *they will unearth*."

And he hated, *God* how he hated, to see her so upset, so he always dropped it just to calm her. But privately, Silas worried. Her fears around their secret were so irrational, he had the sense that she wouldn't—couldn't—ever let them go. And how would she ever cope carrying their secret alone if he happened to die first? One day, Silas called his lawyer and had his will updated, and then he sat Marie down and handed her a copy.

"What's this?" She frowned.

"I wanted you to see."

"You're only fifty, Silas. You don't need to be worrying about this."

"That sounds like something I would say in response to *you* saying something like 'It's never too early for estate planning.'"

"Ha ha. Why did you do this?"

"Read it," he murmured.

He saw her eyes running across the page, the little furrow he knew so well knit between her brows. After a few minutes she looked up at him.

"You're leaving the house to Ernest."

"Yes. He doesn't want it. We both know he'll give it to Cynthia."

"But . . ." She looked down at the page. "*No sale. No restoration*. You're making sure she doesn't come in and . . ."

"It doesn't matter what happens after we're both gone. The lawyer tells me I can't enforce this but . . ."

"The kids would respect it anyway."

"I would think so, yes."

"Will Cynthia be hurt if you leave Ernest this house? We all know he still hates the place," Marie said hesitantly.

"She and Ernest will figure it out together. I just wanted you to know that you can leave this place behind and move on with your life. It's time."

Not long after that day, Marie married a kindly farmer, and she and Cynthia moved out. Silas had promised them he'd be fine in the mansion alone—and he was, for the most part. The place had never felt so empty or so draughty or so *lonely*, but he had his work, and he was happy.

Silas had learned over the years that sometimes a piece of writing takes on a mind of its own. The author sets out to capture one moment and ends up with words which entirely mark another. He *wanted* to write about a young man rising out of poverty, but what wound up on the pages instead was the story of the greatest thing he'd ever done. He had refused to turn away when he suspected someone was in dire need of help. That act of charity had complicated just about every moment of his life from that day on, but he would never regret it, not for a second. In making a choice to do the kind thing—the inconvenient thing, the uncomfortable thing—he had *saved* someone so very worthy of saving. He had changed two wonderful lives for the better.

That was a story that demanded telling, and he was powerless to refuse.

Silas wrote in fits and starts. He wrote a page here and a dozen pages there and then he set the thing aside for two years, only to pick it up again the next time it came to mind. When he reached parts he was unsure of—what was said, what the weather was like, what someone was thinking—his imagination took flight and filled in the gaps. But the essence of it, the very core of it—that was the truest thing he ever wrote even after decades of bleeding his very soul onto pages.

Silas finished writing not long after his sixty-third birthday. In the years he had been writing it, he had also written other books, stories he won awards for and stories that conquered best-seller lists. He always knew *this* story was different. It could never be allowed to find a wide commercial market. It would never attract the praise of judges or critics. It could never have his real name on the spine.

And yet, he found he wanted very much to share it anyway. It might not have been his best writing, but it was the story of his best work. The question was: *How* to share it? Silas had wished a million or more times over the years that he could tell Ernest the truth because the boy had been tortured by that experience as a child, but he could not put the burden of the whole story upon his son—he just couldn't. Ernest and Cynthia remained blessedly, beautifully close-knit into adulthood, the kind of relationship that would long outlive their parents, and the story that would help Ernest understand his own fear would rock the very foundations of Cynthia's life.

The answer came to him early one morning, as he was walking along the roads near the mansion at sunrise. Glorious golden light washed over him and the fields around him were crisp with frost and his family were all happy and thriving in their lives and he thought to himself, *The world is a very big place.* He'd simply find some other pocket, somewhere far from Forbes and far from California, and he'd have it published there.

Maybe, just maybe, someone would one day read these words from his heart and be inspired in Maeve's honor to change their own world for the better. That was the power of the kindness he had learned from his sister. That was the power of story.

CHAPTER 12

Fiona

Three nights without proper sleep. I haven't felt this wrung out since Mia was born, back in the first few days when she cried all day and night. I haven't cried myself this much since those days. It's not post-natal hormones that have had me weeping this time. It's these words, and this story, and this puzzle that my uncle accidentally set out and that I have almost put back together.

The cats started crying at 4:00 a.m. too, not in solidarity, but in protest when they simultaneously walked into Jack's traps. I've texted him and he's coming round on his way to work. I won't be here, but I'm going to leave the door unlocked so he can let himself in to check them for microchips. For now, I've left them in the traps—although I did manage to add a little saucer of water and some more food into each one. They're skinny and cranky, and the one with the white spot on its chest hissed at me when I came close, but they're kind of cute. I've picked names for them—since they scared the wits out of me, I've decided to call them Hocus and Pocus, and I'm secretly hoping they don't have loving owners to go home to so I can keep them.

Instead of starting the morning with a long walk, I once again drank my bodyweight in coffee to try to keep my eyes open long enough to face this day. It's 8:00 a.m. now, and in my handbag, I have the metal tin I found beneath Tad's floorboards, along with two copies of *The Midnight Estate.*

I throw open Wurimbirra's front doors and shriek in fright when I see Erin standing there. In the turmoil, I'd entirely forgotten she existed, let alone was coming to clean this morning.

"Shit!" I gasp, and she gasps too, and that's when I realize she's not actually facing the door like she was about to come inside. She's standing back a little, half-turned away, as if she wasn't sure she could come any closer. "Are you okay?"

"I'm sorry," she blurts, and she covers her face with her hands. "You were so nice to me and I felt terrible about it before I even did it. I don't even understand why Ginny asked me to do it, but she was so insistent and she and Alan have been so good to me and Vince so I felt I had to, you know? But I knew right away—"

"You took my book, didn't you?" I ask her gently, and she bursts into tears. I already came to this conclusion last night. If Mum had any inkling of what *The Midnight Estate* was about, it was probably driving her quietly crazy knowing I was reading it, and it's abundantly clear she's still afraid of Wurimbirra even after all of these years. I suspect her insistence that I let Erin come help me clean was simply about getting her hands on what she thought was the only copy of Tad's secret book.

"It's so ridiculous!" Erin cries. "Why would she even ask me to do it? And why would I even agree to steal a *book*!"

"Erin," I say, and she looks at me hesitantly, as if I'm about to call the police. I smile. "It's okay. You just got sucked into some Winslow family drama, and that's hardly your fault. Are you still happy to do some cleaning for me today?"

"Really? I mean, yes, but—"

"Then come in." I step out of the doorway and wave her inside. "There's two unhappy cats stuck in some fox traps upstairs—my friend will be here to check in on them shortly, and I'll be back later."

She's still begging for my forgiveness and promising me she'll never do it again even as I leave the house a few minutes later, but I'm not angry with her. This is so much bigger than any one book.

"What are you doing here so early, love?" Alan calls as I park my car on the drive beside the farmhouse a few minutes later. He's loading his two Kelpies onto the back of his truck, ready for work with the sheep.

"I just wanted to chat with Mum."

He hesitates, dropping his voice as he says, "Go easy on her. She didn't sleep well."

That makes two of us.

I let myself into the house and find Mum sitting in her sunroom, knitting. I know Alan wasn't kidding about the rough night—she's still in her pajamas, and I don't think I've seen her in pajamas during the day since the days after Tad's funeral. She was so depressed then, I wasn't sure she'd ever recover.

She doesn't acknowledge me as I take the seat beside her, resting the tin I found under Tad's floorboards and my copy of *The Midnight Estate* on my lap. Mum looks up from her knitting, but she still doesn't look at me. Her gaze is fixed on the horizon, visible across the miles of flat paddocks that make up their property. We sit like that for a few minutes while I try to figure out where to start.

"You read it," Mum says abruptly.

"Did you?" I ask her. She shakes her head sharply and her lips thin. I'm emotional and I'm trying to be patient because I'm starting to understand that she's had such a journey in her life, but I'm so tired of this distance between us. "We can do this the hard way, Mum. We can sit here and I can ask you questions and you can shut me down and refuse to talk about it. Or you can tell me the whole story yourself and you can share yourself with me. Your real name is Jennifer, isn't it?"

Jennifer Lentfer. Virginia Winslow. And Tad always called her Ginny, and that eventually caught on, because now the whole town does. Jon appears in this book as Ernest. Aunt Daph has been written as Christine. Tad named his own semi-fictional likeness Silas.

And I, Fiona Virginia, have been written as Cynthia Maeve.

Mum doesn't speak; she just keeps staring out that window. I open the metal tin and I withdraw the engagement ring. I set it flat on the palm of my hand and I extend it towards her. Mum glances at it, then she recoils.

"Where on earth—"

"It was behind the vanity in the bathroom."

I still don't understand how I saw it, just like I don't understand how I knew to roll back that rug and check the noisy floorboard, and even why I was drawn to start reading *The Midnight Estate* almost the minute I laid eyes on it despite everything else I had to do that day. I still don't understand how the door slammed shut or why I couldn't open it, but I know for sure that I was in that storeroom until I'd read every last one of the letters Tad exchanged with his author pals, and I'd confirmed there was no correspondence with Charity Wilkie.

That's when I started to wonder if Charity Wilkie even existed at all, and maybe it was that thought that led me to the realization that there was something familiar about the way the story had been told.

That's the thing with all of this. Much of the mischief in my house this week has been two very naughty cats, but the cats don't explain all of it. I don't believe in ghosts and truth be told I'm not even sure I believe in an afterlife, but I can't help but feel like something pushed me to put all of this together.

Maybe I just want to believe that my uncle dad guided me to this story himself.

"It was your engagement ring, wasn't it? He gave it to you?"

Mum reaches out and picks the ring up, her thin fingers shaking a little as she holds it.

"I had just turned eighteen. He was thirty-three," she whispers. "My parents had just died. He seemed like a knight in shining armor. I thought he was the hero I needed in the worst hours of my life. It wasn't a case of him sweeping me off my feet so much as him busting into my life in a bulldozer and cleaning up all of the hard things for me. But that help . . . that rescue . . . it came at such a cost." Her face contorts, and she pushes the ring back towards me as she stifles a sob. "Please, Fiona. Take it and destroy it. I don't want that thing."

"Okay," I say, and I put it back into the metal tin, but then I withdraw Julian's passport and wallet. Her eyes widen.

"He told me he buried them—"

"In the book, it says he realized that if the body was found one day, the police would probably never be able to identify it, but if these were with it, they'd have an answer right away. He did hide this tin really well—in a cavity beneath a floorboard *beneath* those awful rugs you made him buy for his study."

"Oh," Mum says, and she sinks back into her chair and closes her eyes. "He was always looking out for me."

"Mum," I say, and my voice is suddenly rough. She opens her eyes and looks at me warily. "Mum, I'm so sorry you went through all of that. I'm sorry I didn't understand."

"I didn't want you to understand," she says sharply. "That's why I didn't want him to give it to you."

"Give me the house?"

"Give you the *book*!" she exclaims, waving a hand towards it.

"Tad wanted me to have it?"

"Fiona, haven't you figured it out yet? *This* was what we

fought about the day he died. He told me he was thinking about writing it all down to give it to you. He wanted you and Jon to know the whole truth and I was so furious with him because for all of those years we had agreed we would take our secrets to the grave!"

"Wait—you didn't know he'd already written it?"

"I should have known he wouldn't be able to help himself," she sighs. "He was testing me that day, wanting to see how I'd react—but of course it was already too late, the thing was already finished. When you asked me about Charity Wilkie, I had no idea *this* was *that*. I picked it up at Turn the Page and saw the dedication and had my suspicions and it took reading all of about three sentences across the thing to realize what he'd done."

"The dedication . . . ?"

I flip the book open and see the words I missed the first time: "For Jennifer. Forgive me please. I had to."

"In the book he makes it seem like he never wanted me and Jon to know. Why did he change his mind?"

"I think he always wanted Jon to know. I take it he explains what happened the night of . . . the night . . . when I . . ." She breaks off, takes a deep breath and tries again. "When Jon thought he'd had a nightmare."

"The book tells the whole story, Mum."

"The best part of the way things worked out was that you were spared the trauma of it all. You grew up in this beautiful, happy family and you didn't have to know that your f-father was a monster. But those last few years of his life, Tad worried so much about what would happen after he was gone."

"To me?"

"To us," Mum says abruptly. A familiar tension has sprung between us and I can see from the reluctance on her face that she's struggling with whatever she wants to say. I reach across impulsively and put my hand on hers. "He said that these secrets were barriers that kept us from one another," she finally continues. "That you *needed* to know so that you could understand me . . . so that you could be there for me. Which was absolutely absurd because a mother's job is to protect her child! You might be fifty years old but I never wanted you to bear the burden of the mistakes I made before you were even born."

"You were a kid who trusted an adult in a moment of desperation. That wasn't a *mistake.* You should have been safe with him," I say fiercely. Mum flinches and shakes her head. Half a century of shame is written on her face, and it just about breaks my heart. I shift to kneel beside her chair, pushing her knitting off her lap to grab her hands in mine. I'm shaking with the force of it all as I stare up at her and whisper, "I'm glad I know. It changes not one thing about how I see myself and *everything* about how I see you. You saved me and you saved yourself. You're a goddamned hero, Mum."

"Tad was the only hero here," she says, jaw stiff. The rims of her eyes are red and she's looking past my shoulder, unable to meet my gaze.

"I don't love that he took your story and wrote it down without your permission—he should have respected your agency, let you handle this the way you wanted to. And the fact that he only ran it by you after it was too late for you to stop it happening just shows he knew you'd be upset," I say, and she finally meets my gaze. There's surprise in her eyes and I know it's because I'm defending her—that I would take her side. I recognize this reaction because it's the same surprise I felt when she sent that radio with Erin.

For too long, we've assumed the worst about how we see each other. This is a chance for us to believe the best.

"I hadn't thought of it like that."

"Tad was generous to a fault. Kind to his very soul. He loved people—but he loved and even understood them best from afar. It was like he was long-sighted when he came to relationships—the closer people were to him, the less he understood them. And some part of him was always distracted by his latest story, so he was rarely fully present even with the people he lived for, even in the most important moments of his life. I loved Uncle Tad with my whole heart but the man was a mess of contradictions," I sigh softly.

Mum's tears finally spill over as she nods. She turns her forearms over and squeezes mine in return.

"Fiona, surely you know by now—the best people always are."

"But I'm not sorry at all about how this turned out because I love you and I want to be here for you. So don't tell me the things I've learned today are a burden, because they just aren't. Knowing all of this makes me feel closer to you, and that's all I've ever wanted."

"I gave you Virginia's name for your middle name," Mum says, touching my cheek gently as she brushes away a tear. "I took her identity to save our lives. It seemed fair."

"Did I really call him Uncle Dad when I was small?"

"Is that in there? Oh yes, you most certainly did."

"You should read his book one day, Mum," I say softly. "Maybe see yourself through his eyes."

"I miss him every single day."

"Me too."

"I think I'm glad you know, Fiona."

I nod tearfully, and then I rise up to pull her into my arms. She hesitates just a moment before she returns the embrace and she starts to weep against my shoulder. That's when I know that the flawed, brilliant man who was my only father figure throughout my childhood has given me the gift he knew I needed the most—my mum, warts and all.

We talk for a while—I tell her more about the book, and the way Tad went about telling their story. We both agree that we'll make sure no one else close to us reads *The Midnight Estate*—except for Jon. I'll call him this afternoon and ask him to come home for a few days, because this is all heavy and complicated enough that we need to be together while we process it.

I can see that this is all very difficult for Mum to talk about, but she's trying, and that's more than enough. We're both exhausted, and when she suggests we move to the kitchen for a coffee, I happily agree.

As she's working at the machine, I say quietly, "So, you're really only seventy, huh?"

She half smiles. "Now do you think I look my age?"

"You still look good for your age! But seriously Mum, you are way too young and far too smart to be so terrible with technology," I say, laughing softly. "You need to enroll in a course or something!"

"I didn't want to learn," she admits sheepishly. "I like having a reason to call the girls."

"You don't need a reason to call them. You don't need a reason to call any of us. We love you."

"And I . . ." She looks back at me, overcome, then back to the coffee machine. "I love you all too. So very much."

I wish Tad were here to see this. He'd look at me right now, raising those big bushy eyebrows, and he'd mouth, *Did she really just say it aloud?*

"Tell me . . ." I say cautiously. "Your brother . . ."

"What did Tad call him in the book?"

"Irving."

"His real name is Rowan—or *was* Rowan, I have no idea if he's still alive. Rowan Webster—that was my maiden name. I don't even know what happened to him. He was mixed up with Julian's business so I've always feared the worst."

"We could google him?"

"Google him?" Mum repeats, slightly alarmed. "You really think we could find him if we do? Would he know?"

"No, it doesn't work like that," I say, as I slip my phone from my pocket and set it on the table, just as a message arrives from Jack.

> Cats are microchipped but I called the previous owners and turns out they abandoned them when they moved a few months ago. Kitties are healthy, already desexed. I vaccinated and dewormed them and gave them a flea treatment. Am I taking them to the pound?

I smile as I reply: Please don't. But I've never had cats before so I'm going to need some expert advice on how to care for them.

> I knew it! The best way to help them settle in is to keep them confined to one room for a few weeks. Are you happy for me to let them out of the traps in your bedroom?

> Go for it.

"That's a lot of typing," Mum says, glancing anxiously at my phone as she slides the coffee in front of me. "Is this how much typing it usually takes to google someone? I imagined there was some spot you just put the name in."

I wince.

"Sorry, Mum. I was texting Jack about something. Give me a second."

I switch out to Google and type in, "Rowan Webster." It gives me four million results, so I add "Jennifer Lentfer" and "Porterville" to try to narrow it down.

"What is it?" Mum asks, when I gasp at the results. The first hit is for an organization called Jennifer's Voice, and I feel goosebumps break out of my skin as I click the link. It's an About Our Founder page, and there's a photograph of a balding man with faded red hair at the top. He has gentle, kind eyes.

> Rowan Webster was a teen when his sister, Jennifer, asked him to help her leave her husband, Julian. She talked of suffocating control but it was not a story Rowan recognized as abuse because she insisted there was no physical violence. Rowan failed to understand the danger his sister was in and later told her husband that she had come to him for help.
>
> It is the biggest regret of his life.
>
> After Jennifer disappeared in 1960, Rowan learned that Julian had been married once before, to Gertie De Luca, who went missing in 1956. Gertie's family later explained to Rowan the pattern of escalating control she had reported in the months leading up to her escape from his house. She was able to hide with her parents for some weeks, but the abuse had only escalated from there, as Julian stalked and harassed her entire family. Gertie disappeared in the night while her parents slept in the next room, and her remains were finally identified in 1994.
>
> Only in hindsight could Rowan recognize the same patterns in his sister's marriage and the same determined efforts by Julian to isolate her from Rowan, her only surviving family member.
>
> After graduating from law school in 1967, Rowan worked as a prosecutor and served as a district attorney for the State of California from 1980–1995. Along with his wife, Sadie, a social worker, he founded Jennifer's Voice in 1997.
>
> The organization was initially established to educate the community about coercive control through school-based

> programs and awareness-raising campaigns. In 2001, Jennifer's Voice opened the first in what is now a nationwide series of high-security shelters for survivors of domestic abuse. Since 2004, Jennifer's Voice been working to lobby for a nationwide law to outlaw coercive control, which is still not an offence in most states.

"You're scaring me, Fiona," Mum says, and I realize I'm crying again. I push the phone across the table and watch her face as she reads. First there's surprise, then disbelief and then my stoic mother starts to weep again.

There's nothing for me to do except stand and throw my arms around her and hold her close while she reads every page of the Jennifer's Voice website several times. Then we click on a few more Google links and find photos of Rowan testifying before Congress, speaking at conferences and colleges and, in the final photo—which we locate on his Facebook page—posing outside of a large, plush home with his wife, three adult children, eight grandchildren and four golden retrievers.

"What is this it talks about—*coercive control*? I don't know that term. What does it mean?" she asks.

"It's a form of domestic abuse, Mum. It's exactly what Julian did to you. Controlling every aspect of a partner's life. Making them both terrified and dependent."

"I didn't know what to call it," she says, then she touches her fingertips to her lips. "Sometimes I thought it was just me. He made me think I was crazy. That I was weak."

"He tried to break you. He tried to *kill* you. But you found a way to survive. You were always strong."

She gets up to fetch herself some tissues and to wash her face, and then comes back to the breakfast bar and takes my phone in her hand again. She's staring down at the photo of Rowan on the screen, silent tears pouring down her face.

"Rowan and I were so close until I pushed him away."

"You didn't push him away, Mum."

"But he told Julian—"

"Julian *lied*. That's what I'm trying to tell you, and even Rowan says it right here, see? Julian manipulated you and he manipulated Rowan too, isolating you both and making you each think it was your own fault."

"I wish I could tell him I'm okay," Mum blurts, her voice breaking. She looks up at me, her eyes panicked. "Look at this page, Fiona. He's been worried for me this whole time. All of these years—these decades! How can I let him know that I'm okay?"

"We could call him."

"What? How would we—"

"It says here he works out of the charity's San Francisco office. I'm pretty sure it's still daytime there." I quickly check on the clock on my phone and confirm it. It's early afternoon for him, just past 8:30 a.m. for us.

"But what would I even say? It's not like he's going to answer the phone himself. How would we even reach him?" She seems equal parts hopeful and terrified. I'm feeling much the same.

"I'll call. I'll tell them it's in relation to his sister. I'm sure I can get him on the phone."

"What if he doesn't believe us?"

"He probably won't at first! But it won't be hard to prove it to him. I'm sure there's all sorts of things from his childhood that only you would know."

"Well, yes. That's true, but he'll ask about Julian—"

"You can simply tell him that Tad helped you escape and you made a happy life here and that was the end of it," I say. "He doesn't know Julian came after you and he doesn't need the whole story."

"I need to think about this."

"Okay," I say, and what an anticlimax! But it has to be her choice, so I add, "That's totally fine, Mum. We can do it another day—"

"Another *day*?" she repeats, aghast. "Fiona, for *fifty years* my baby brother has believed he's the only surviving member of our family. I need to take a minute or two to clear my thoughts but I'm not waiting another *day*."

"Right," I say, smiling weakly. It looks like we're doing this. "I'll drink my coffee and you tell me when you're ready."

Mum disappears into the bathroom again and I take a minute just to breathe. To reflect on this last shocking week, and everything I have learned about my own family and myself.

I've always known that there is power in uncovering and honoring and sharing the truth about the past. In exposing history, even history that is difficult and ugly, we can learn to walk a better path in the future. I built my entire career on that principle, and I know I'll be seeing it in action in my relationship with Mum over the coming years.

Jennifer Webster walks back into her kitchen, eyes red rimmed but dry, shoulders straight and chin proudly raised and hope sparkling in her eyes, and I *know* that things between us will never be the same.

"Ready?" I ask her, and she smiles—brave and beautiful.

I pick up the phone and dial.

★ ★ ★ ★ ★

Dear Reader,

When I was younger, I spent a few years working at a heritage consultancy a little like the one Fiona founded in this book. I've always loved old houses, but that job gave me a whole new appreciation for them. There's something about the way it feels to inhabit a space many others have also called home over the centuries—like a house itself has lived many lives. A few years ago, I was speaking with a friend who grew up in a quirky historic mansion and I all but interrogated her, completely enthralled with her anecdotes about living in such an environment. That's really where the seed of the idea behind this book started. I wanted to write a story in which the setting itself was fascinating enough that it might be a reader's favorite character. Wurimbirra is not real, but it draws from aspects of many grand old homes in the Central West of New South Wales, including Carrawobitty and Anglesey House in Forbes; Endsleigh House, Duntryleague, and Croagh Patrick in Orange; Abercrombie House in Bathurst; and Harper's Mansion in Berrima.

I'd also been tinkering with an "eccentric writer" character for a while, trying to find the right plot to wrap around him. I don't have much in common with Tad except that like most writers, we both find it hard to pay sufficient attention to real life when we're engrossed in a book. We each peer back at our lives from our work, trying to make sense of it all. And even though we have made careers out of crafting (hopefully convincing!) characters, people often remain a mystery to us! Tad is the answer to the question, What if I took generic writer traits and dialed them all the way up to the maximum? This brilliant and kind and ultimately hapless fellow is one of my favorite characters I've written, perhaps because I wrote traits in him I see in so many of my writer friends.

That brings us to Ginny, Tad's "sister," co-conspirator, and in some ways, co-parent. I wrote about domestic violence ten years ago when I was working on the draft of what would eventually become my book *A Mother's Confession*. At the time I felt so sure increasing conversations about the topic would trigger rapid change, and I didn't expect I'd ever revisit the subject in a future book. But here we are ten years later, and far too many women and children are still in unsafe homes and relationships all around the world. I live in Australia, a country with a relatively small population of only 26.6 million people, and it is also a country where a woman is killed by a current or former partner almost every week. Studies suggest as many as 27 percent of Australian women over the age of 15 have experienced violence, emotional abuse, or economic abuse by a cohabitating partner.

I wrote Ginny's relationship as one where she felt isolated and unsafe long before the first incident of physical violence, long before she understood the term *coercive control*. I wanted to write about the way these toxic dynamics in a relationship can creep up on a victim-survivor, such that she does not fully understand the danger of her situation until it feels like there's no way for her to escape.

Even as I was writing this book, Forbes hit the headlines after the murder of twenty-eight-year-old local Molly Ticehurst, allegedly at the hands of a former partner who was on bail for domestic violence charges at the time. Molly should be here today, smiling her brilliant smile as she raises her son, spending time with her family and friends, caring for the little people of Forbes at the childcare center where she was so loved and adored. The conversation around domestic violence is as urgent as it ever was, and we cannot shy away from it—for Molly and her family and community, and for every other woman in danger in an unsafe situation.

In this story, Fiona visits a readers' group hosted by a local bookstore. I wanted such a reading community to be key to her character journey because I've seen the magic of these groups myself. There is a real bookstore on Templar Street, Forbes, owned and managed by Debbie Prior, who does indeed host regular book clubs. That real-life bookstore is called the Book Dispensary, and I only wish it had existed when I was a teenager growing up in that town! Some of my favorite book events in recent years have been at Forbes, with familiar faces from my childhood and plenty of new friends, all sharing a bond with one another because of the connections they've formed over the books they've read together. But the bookstore in this book is named Turn the Page after another of my favorite book club bookstores, this one based in Westfield, Indiana. I have Skyped or Zoomed into a Turn the Page book club every year for the past few years to talk about my books, and even when the subject matter is heavy, I always leave that group with a huge smile on my face because the joy of those friendships is palpable, even from the other side of the globe.

As sometimes happens, lots of the pieces of the story were percolating in my mind for a long time before the detail of the plot became entirely clear. It was my sister-in-law who gave me the idea of hiding a fictional body in an existing grave, and once I could see that was the end point of Tad and Ginny's story, the rest of the plot came to me.

I've taken some liberties with the location and the details, but I first heard stories about the strychnine poisoning of First Nations groups around Forbes when I was a teenager. I was reminded of these terrible events when I read the History Book Committee of Forbes's 1997 publication *The History of Forbes, New South Wales, Australia.*

So, a huge thank-you to Gina for telling me about your childhood home, and thanks to my father, Mal, for sharing spooky small-town policing stories with me. Thanks to the team at GML for letting me work with you all of those years ago and deepening my appreciation for history and historic buildings—I am certain my interest in historical fiction began with that job, and to this day I'm thankful for that. Thank you to my sister-in-law Diana. I am so very grateful to you for allowing me to use your (diabolical) body-hiding idea in this book!

Thanks to Our Watch and Birds in the Bush for your advocacy and education efforts, and thanks to Kate Amber's End Coercive Control USA for brilliant training resources. The analogy of coercive control as "quicksand" was initially from Kate's training course.

Thanks as always to booksellers everywhere—now that I've joined your ranks with my own store, I have a new understanding of how difficult and wonderful your job is. Thank you for everything you do in connecting readers to my books. To libraries and book clubs and reading groups and bloggers and reviewers—thanks for sharing my stories.

Thanks to my wonderful agent, Amy Tannenbaum, and the entire team at the Jane Rotrosen Agency, and to Susan Swinwood and the team at Graydon House, Rebecca Saunders and the team at Hachette Australia, and Anna Boatman and team at Piatkus UK.

Thank you to *you*, dear reader. Thank you for journeying through this story with me. If you'd like to get in touch, you can also find my contact details on my website at kellyrimmer.com.

Finally—and most importantly—if you or someone you know is in an unsafe relationship or situation, or if this book has raised unsettling emotions or thoughts for you, please reach out to those in your local community who can assist you. You deserve to be safe and you deserve to be happy. Truly.

Kelly

DISCUSSION GUIDE QUESTIONS

1. Fiona and Ginny's relationship has grown increasingly distant over the years, particularly since Tad died. Did this feel plausible to you? Why do you think that dynamic developed?
2. We meet Marie as a woman who feels utterly trapped in a hopeless situation. Did you understand why she felt that way? What do you think would have happened to her and her child had she not escaped with Silas?
3. Why do you think Silas intervened to help Marie escape when so many others in her community were aware of her situation but could not or would not help? Did you understand why her own brother refused to help her when she did try to reach out?
4. Fiona's visit to the readers' club marks a turning point in her thoughts about reconnecting with others in Forbes. Have you ever been to a reading group like the one Fiona visits? If you're a member of any kind of book club or reading group, why do you attend, and what do you get out of it?
5. This story structure features a book within a book. Did you like the use of such a device, and do you think the author made good use of it?
6. Did you believe Wurimbirra was haunted? At what point did you start to suspect otherwise?

7. Which characters in this book did you like best? Which did you like least? Why?
8. Which scene in *The Story Keeper* affected you the most, and why? What emotions did that scene elicit?
9. Were you satisfied with the ending? What do you think happened next for Fiona and Ginny?
10. What will you remember most about *The Story Keeper*?
11. Who would you recommend this book to?
12. Was this your first Kelly Rimmer book? If you've read any of her other titles, do you have a favorite?